THE SPIDER COVENANT

BRIAN KLEIN

THE SPIDER COVENANT

CONSTABLE

CONSTABLE

First published in Great Britain in 2025 by Constable

1 3 5 7 9 10 8 6 4 2

A CIP catalogue record for this book
is available from the British Library.

ISBN: 978-1-40872-104-9 (hardback)
ISBN: 978-1-40872-105-6 (trade paperback)

Typeset in Crimson Text by Hewer Text UK Ltd, Edinburgh
Printed and bound in Great Britain by Clays Ltd, Elcograf S.p.A.

Papers used by Constable are from well-managed
forests and other responsible sources.

Constable
An imprint of
Little, Brown Book Group
Carmelite House
50 Victoria Embankment
London EC4Y 0DZ

The authorised representative
in the EEA is
Hachette Ireland
8 Castlecourt Centre, Dublin 15,
D15 XTP3, Ireland
(email: info@hbgi.ie)

An Hachette UK Company
www.hachette.co.uk

www.littlebrown.co.uk

To Charmy, Bubs and Georgie,
the three inspirations in my life.

Prologue

Munich, Germany

5 August 1922

The five-cylinder, blood-red Megola motorcycle carved an erratic path through the narrow cobbled streets in Munich's old town, weaving through the early evening traffic as though it were standing still, heading directly for the Hofbräuhaus beer hall on Platzl 9. The young student on board was in a hurry and for most of the journey kept the hand throttle fully depressed, maintaining the machine's top speed of fifty-three miles per hour. Thirty minutes earlier he'd received news from his technical college that he'd successfully graduated, achieving an honours degree in agriculture, and he was eager to celebrate with his friends.

The infamous drinking establishment was a magnet for right-wing students and members of the National Socialist German Workers Party, commonly known as Nazis. Although he hadn't yet signed up, the twenty-one-year-old student shared many of the controversial views of the party's charismatic leader, Adolf Hitler, especially those on antisemitism, and was seriously contemplating joining the fascist organisation.

As soon as he reached his destination he parked up and ran inside, forcing his way through large clusters of drunken revellers spilling out on to the street. He made his way upstairs, navigating the rear congested staircase which led to an alcove on the first floor, where he knew a small group of his college friends would already be drinking copious amounts of beer. He wasn't used to alcohol and, four hours later, found himself lying on a filthy threadbare mattress on the floor of a dingy basement studio flat, wrapped firmly in the arms of a young blonde girl, whose naked limbs entwined him like a ravenous anaconda. As he stared into her liquid blue eyes, he'd no recollection of their meeting and his instincts screamed at him to get the hell out. Those feelings of extreme anxiety melted away as soon as she leaned forward to gently caress him on the lips, before lightly pulling away to whisper in his ear. Her voice was like a purr and the silky tone made his entire body tingle.

'You were a virgin, I can tell. How was it for you?'

A deep wave of embarrassment engulfed him, and he closed his eyes, desperately trying to recall anything of the previous few hours. He glanced around the room looking for clues but none were forthcoming.

'I don't know. I can't remember. What's your name? How did I get here?'

Her lips parted slightly to reveal an intoxicating smile.

'My darling, you only had to stumble down a few steps. We're in the bowels of the Hofbräuhaus. I'm a waitress here and this cesspit comes with the job. My name is Franka. What's yours?'

He peered at her through his rimless pince-nez glasses, remarkably still in place, which he mused was something of a miracle. The entire episode was entirely out of character, and he cursed his friends who'd persuaded him to switch from beer to Schnapps. At twenty-one, he'd no intention of getting involved in a romantic relationship. He was a young man with serious political ambitions who had far bigger fish to fry. He managed a fake half-smile as he replied to her question.

'My name is Heinrich . . .'

Franka burst into a sudden bout of teasing laughter.

'My God, were you named after a prince?'

His smile morphed into a frown.

'Actually, I was. Prince Heinrich of Bavaria to be precise. My father was a schoolteacher and tutored him when he was a boy.'

He spoke so earnestly the young waitress had no doubt he was telling the truth.

Forty weeks later to the day, Franka gave birth to a healthy girl but, being only twenty-four, unmarried and only just surviving on a waitress's income, she'd little choice but to hand her over to a protestant orphanage on the outskirts of the city.

Heinrich hadn't seen or spoken to Franka since that first night but had heard about the pregnancy through the grape-vine and tracked his baby girl's progress all the way to the orphanage. He kept the birth a secret from his family and friends but vowed that as soon as he achieved wealth and political power, he'd make up for his unconscionable behaviour and his little princess would grow up to be proud of her father.

Chapter One

Buenos Aires, Argentina

October 2024

It was just after three in the morning when the second prisoner broke his vow of silence. The man known as Manuel made the decision to talk after being shown a short video of the mutilated body of his brother, who'd embraced torture and certain death rather than give up any information. Manuel knew he'd no stomach to match his sibling's bravery, so compliance was his only option.

The interrogator shot a look at the CCTV camera mounted on the low ceiling and gave an almost imperceptible nod. In a small shadowy area directly outside the makeshift cell his employer caught the gesture on a twenty-inch black and white monitor. He rose from his stool and moved towards an arch-shaped solid oak door, grabbing hold of the end of the giant iron bolt which secured it. He heaved it sideways through its rusty mechanism and fully applied his bodyweight to the door, which slowly creaked open.

Moments later, the stocky bull of a man entered the dimly lit cell and surveyed the scene. He allowed a malevolent smile to break out on his lips as he glared at the pathetic figure slumped in the far corner of the room, his hands tied by black leather restraints to the back of a steel chair, cemented to the floor. His head was bowed in a gesture of submission and the beads of sweat dripping from his forehead were those of unbridled fear, rather than heat.

The man running the interrogation bent down over the dejected figure and grabbed a fistful of oily hair in his right hand, yanking the prisoner's head upwards until the two men's eyes were barely inches apart. When he spoke, his voice was a sinister whisper.

'Manuel, I've only two questions for you and I'm sure you know exactly what they are. But just in case you've memory failure, I'll ask you once again. Who did you pass the USB drive over to and where is it now?'

Chapter Two

Buenos Aires, Argentina

Twenty-four hours earlier

Chief Inspector Nicolas Vargas of the Buenos Aires police department was enjoying a beer in El Alamo, the only sports bar in the city centre showing the live US basketball game his old friend, Troy Hembury, was desperate to watch. The former LAPD police lieutenant, who'd flown in on the red-eye from Washington, was a huge fan of the LA Clippers who were playing a top-of-the-table grudge match against the Boston Celtics. Hembury had travelled to Buenos Aires for a two-week break and was staying as Vargas's house guest at his apartment in the fashionable Recoleta neighbourhood, in the north of the sprawling city.

The two men were huddled together in a small red leather circular booth, waiting for the live transmission to start. In many ways they were far closer than brothers, having forged an unbreakable relationship working on several heart-stopping cases that had generated headlines across the world.

They'd also created a remarkable alliance with senior figures inside Mossad and the FBI, helping their respective governments' intelligence agencies combat two international terrorist attacks in the Middle East.

The news-making history they'd been part of generating wasn't important to either of them, especially Hembury. He was living on borrowed time, thanks to the grade 3 tumour buried deep inside his brain. It was being kept at bay by a drug currently undergoing clinical trials on patients like him: people who had a death sentence hanging over them and nothing to lose. But, despite all that, the former police lieutenant was a dedicated fitness freak who worked out seven days a week, making him a difficult man to age. His unlined square-shaped face, sharp jawline and six-one muscular frame looked as though they'd been built from a set of ebony Lego bricks.

Vargas was also deeply troubled but for completely different reasons. Although he was in his early fifties, he'd been a widower for almost fifteen years and had never come to terms with the tragic loss of his wife at the age of just thirty-three. However, unlike Hembury, the drug that kept him alive wasn't synthetic; it was an unrelenting barrage of work, which filled his every waking moment and helped preserve his sanity.

Despite his mental scarring, Vargas remained a striking-looking man whose olive-skinned chiselled features were crowned by a thick mop of chestnut brown hair, slightly frosted at the sides, and his deep-set caramel eyes sat above a classic Roman nose, framed by a set of high-angled cheekbones.

Hembury was the first African American to be appointed Director of Internal Security at the White House and reported directly to the president. At sixty-three, he was ten years older than his friend and just eighteen months away from retirement. He relished the prospect, if only his body could somehow see off the brain tumour.

'Less than two years to go, Nic. If the drugs hold up, then it's just me, my tropical fish, and twenty-four hours a day of ESPN sports.'

Vargas's response was laden with scepticism.

'I'll give you three months with your feet up and, as soon as your beloved team starts losing, you'll be itching to come back.'

Hembury smiled and was about to reply when two servers, laden with trays, approached their corner booth, just as the game was about to start. The enormous food platters covered almost every inch of the round wooden table and heaved with a banquet of ribs, chicken wings, corn, pickles and fries. Vargas burst into laughter as his friend dived into the ribs.

'Christ, Troy, we could feed the entire Clippers team with this feast. What happened to your healthy eating regime?'

Hembury demolished some pork ribs and wiped the barbeque sauce off his lips with a napkin.

'Don't worry, I'm still on it, but basketball brings out my primitive urges and . . .'

Hembury never got to finish his sentence as his attention was grabbed by a young man bursting into the bar like a tornado and coming to a sudden stop, his eyes darting around like a pair of manic pinballs, until they settled on Vargas. After a moment of recognition, he headed towards the detective whose right hand instinctively dropped to the Glock 17 holstered across his chest.

The stranger was in his late twenties, dark-skinned with liquorice black hair, which was badly overgrown and formed a seamless join with his dark beard that was slightly better groomed. His hazel brown eyes were panicked with fear and his body was vibrating like a cheap washing machine as he slowly peeled open his left hand, revealing a small blue USB drive.

'Chief Inspector, you're the Nazi hunter, right? The policeman who exposed Hitler's grandson?'

Vargas grimaced as the stranger made the questions sound like an accolade.

'What do you want with me?'

'Take this drive and share it with your colleagues, it has the names . . . the names of *Die Spinne*.'

Before Vargas could respond, the man grabbed his hand, thrusting the USB drive into it, and made to leave.

'Who are you?'

The stranger stopped for a beat and half-turned to face the chief inspector.

'I'm known as Manuel . . .'

Chapter Three

Buenos Aires, Argentina

The platters of food remained untouched. Vargas and Hembury only lasted until the first timeout of the basketball game before curiosity got the better of them. The chief inspector glanced down at the USB drive clenched in his fist. The potential secrets it contained proved an unbearable distraction to the pair who quickly lost interest in the outcome of the match. As Vargas touched his Mastercard to the wireless terminal offered by the server, Hembury looked up from his cell and took a final glance at the giant wall-mounted LED screen just as the Clippers' captain landed a neat three-pointer. He angled his cell towards Vargas, so he could see the screen. It displayed a literal translation of the two German words spoken by the stranger. The Argentine detective's brow knitted.

'I've always hated spiders.'

* * *

The pair hardly exchanged a word on the short Uber ride back to Vargas's apartment. As soon as they entered, Hembury grabbed a couple of Peronis from the fridge, while his friend fired up his MacBook and cleared the breakfast bar to create a makeshift workstation in the open-plan kitchen. They sat next to each other on wooden stools as Vargas inserted the mysterious drive into his laptop and, moments later, clicked on a desktop folder which revealed five files. Four were named by continent – Australia, Europe, North and South America, while the fifth was identified by the letters HH, which were capitalised.

Both men studied the screen before the Argentine glanced across at his friend, whose face wore a quizzical smile.

'Might as well start on home turf?'

Vargas double-clicked on the file entitled South America, hoping it would open and it duly obliged, revealing a word document. Another click and two short lines of text appeared. Each one displayed two sets of symbols with a space in between. For a moment Vargas assumed they were names as Manuel had claimed but, on closer inspection, nothing made sense. The heavily encrypted text included a mix of random keyboard characters alongside several unrecognisable icons.

Hembury edged closer to the screen, focusing in on the top line.

'This reads more like a mathematical equation than a name.'

Vargas checked through the other three files named as continents with similar results: each contained two lines of incomprehensible text.

'They could be absolutely anything, but I'd hazard a guess we've got ourselves eight names that have been heavily encrypted in case the drive falls into the wrong hands.'

Hembury took a swig from his green beer bottle and nodded in agreement.

'Well, guess what? Someone's worst nightmare is about to come true. Let's send this baby to our friend in Washington.'

* * *

The stellar cast of the Metropolitan Opera Company at the Lincoln Center on the Upper West Side of Manhattan were performing to a sold-out black-tie audience attending a charity event in aid of the Nelson Mandela Children's Fund. The concert featured *Tannhäuser*, Wagner's 1845 three-act classic and, sitting high up in the gods in the cheap seats, was the deputy director of the FBI. Mike Berrettini was a second-generation Italian who kept his passion for opera well under wraps from most of his friends and colleagues. It was undoubtedly the most innocent secret he kept logged away in his computer-like brain and, as the seventy-four-strong choir, along with the principals on stage, boomed out the final aria, he concluded the three hundred dollars he'd paid to a dodgy website for his ticket had been well worth the gamble.

Berrettini wasn't an imposing-looking man in the physical sense and was therefore easy to underestimate. His short portly frame carried over two stone in excess weight and his swarthy rotund face carried at least two chins, camouflaged by an unkempt black beard peppered with grey intruders. However, the FBI deputy director was a mental giant, a brilliant strategist with one of the sharpest intellects in the Bureau.

He'd left his cell on silent throughout the concert but felt the familiar vibration of a WhatsApp land. He tried to ignore it, but curiosity got the better of him and rather than wait until the curtain call, he slid the cell out of his jacket pocket. The brief message from Vargas was intriguing.

Mike, a USB drive containing encrypted files has come my way. Might be nothing but can you give me a safe log-in at the Bureau to upload to. Call when free and I'll give you some context.

Berrettini cursed his own work ethic as he punched in a reply, much to the annoyance of the audience members sitting either side of him.

Give me five and I'll call you back.

As the cast bellowed out the final refrain he rose from his seat and made a swift exit, just beating the standing ovation which he knew was seconds away. Less than a minute later he was striding down Ninth Avenue, heading south, with his cell jammed to his ear.

'Okay, Nic, fill me in . . .'

Five thousand miles away, Vargas switched his mobile to speaker and placed it between himself and Hembury. During the next ten minutes he brought the FBI man up to speed on the events of the previous few hours. Berrettini used the time to head over towards Moynihan Train Hall where he was due to catch the overnighter back to Washington.

'Guys, as you said, this could be something or nothing. Use the log-in I'll send you and let's catch up sometime tomorrow after my tech guys have looked at the files.'

As he crossed West 33rd Street, heading for the station entrance, he glanced down at his watch.

'Right now, I'm in New York and I've got to run to grab the night train to D.C.'

Hembury couldn't resist jumping in with a jibe.

'Christ, Mike, that's a hell of a long way to go for a date . . .'

Berrettini pursed his lips, his spare hand fishing for the return train ticket buried somewhere in his jacket pocket.

'No such luck. Business, guys, just boring business.'

The FBI deputy director ended the call and dashed inside the station hub, having successfully protected another precious secret.

Chapter Four

Washington D.C., United States

The following morning, Berrettini was back behind his desk inside the J. Edgar Hoover building at 935 Pennsylvania Avenue in Washington D.C. His small subterranean office occupied a tiny footprint within the 2,800,000-square-foot labyrinth of safe rooms, corridors and data areas which formed the nucleus of the Federal Bureau of Investigation. From the street, the structure appeared to be just eight storeys tall, but there were another three hidden below ground, which was where Berrettini liked to be: unseen and undetectable by the outside world.

He was totally absorbed in the three-page report his senior analysts had prepared for him, following the partial decoding of the files Vargas had emailed over the previous night. As he flicked though the papers, he held the black folder containing them as though it were a stick of dynamite and once he'd digested the contents, reached for his cell to punch in a WhatsApp message to Vargas.

Nic, you're booked on the Copa Airlines flight this afternoon to

D.C. I'll clear some leave with your chief. Plenty to discuss regarding our eight-legged friend.

Buenos Aires was only an hour ahead of Washington and the local time was just after nine in the morning when Vargas received the message. He was enjoying a continental breakfast with Hembury in a local coffee house and immediately shared the WhatsApp with his friend. Hembury's mouth broke into an amused grin as he read it.

'So much for my holiday break. Turns out you're going to be staying with me instead.'

Vargas demolished the remains of a warm croissant and nodded towards one of the servers to request the bill.

'Yep, can't wait to get reacquainted with your tropical fish collection – hope the boys are okay?'

Hembury gulped down his latte as both men stood to leave.

'All fit and well. Plus a few newbies since you last visited.'

Vargas let out a fake groan.

'Let's get back and sort ourselves out and then head to the airport'.

* * *

It took the pair less than five minutes to walk back to the chief inspector's apartment block and, as they headed up the stairs, Vargas stopped dead in his tracks. His front door was slightly ajar. Closer inspection showed the lock had been forced and the mechanism was clearly damaged which explained why it wouldn't close. He gestured silently towards Hembury, who instantly picked up on the cue and nodded his understanding. Vargas stealthily opened his jacket to indicate to Hembury his chest holster was empty. His Glock 17 pistol was locked away in his desk drawer.

The men moved in lockstep towards the front door and Vargas gently edged it open, glancing through the gap he'd created. Two bedroom doors off the small interior hallway were wide open and he could see through to the open-plan kitchen, which looked as though it had been hit by a small hurricane. For a second, he couldn't hear anything untoward from inside but then, as he eased the door open further, it created a tiny grinding noise.

Moments later a shadowy figure leapt out of the main bedroom at speed and turned left, instantly making eye contact with Vargas, who was now totally exposed standing in the open doorway. The intruder was a young, slim Asian woman, dressed from head to toe in black. Her face was milk-white, and her coal-black hair was cut short, creating a slightly masculine appearance. She had a cruel mouth, if there was such a thing and, as her dark brown eyes focused in on Vargas, he could sense they showed no sign of fear, just raw hatred and excitement.

She knifed him with a glare before snatching the real thing from her rear pocket: a mother-of-pearl-handled switch blade which she wielded with the confidence of an orchestra conductor waving a baton. Vargas moved forward and stepped to his left, allowing Hembury to instantly fill the void. The intruder held her ground for a moment, taking on board the new odds. Unfazed by the turn of events she sprang forward with the prowess of a king cobra, her knife slashing through the air like a venomous tongue. Her rapid movements took both men by surprise and although they were wary of the knife, they both made a grab for her. Remarkably she slithered between them and seconds later exited the front door of the building at warp speed.

The confrontation lasted less than three seconds and it was only after the assailant had gone Vargas realised he'd been hurt. Her knife had sliced a three-inch cut on the inside of his left arm, which was leaking blood on to the white oak floorboards in the hallway. Initially the adrenaline had masked the pain, but now it stung like an attack from a hundred-strong army of angry hornets, and he wasted no time sourcing a small towel to wrap around the open wound, while Hembury called 107.

In the ten minutes it took for the ambulance to arrive, Vargas established the USB drive, which had been locked away in his gun drawer had disappeared, although the Glock and two packs of 9mm rounds were still in place.

Chapter Five

Washington D.C., United States

Twenty-four hours and eighteen stitches later, Vargas and Hembury arrived in the US capital, where they immediately met up with Berrettini in a secure meeting room, deep inside FBI headquarters. After a quick debrief with an in-house agent, who took down a detailed facial description of 'knife girl', the deputy director took control of the meeting, beginning with a strange question:

'After the fall of Nazi Germany in April '45, do you know how American intelligence agents managed to identify SS officers who ran the deathcamps?'

Both men looked slightly bemused, wondering what on earth the Second World War had to do with whatever was on the USB drive, and shook their heads, prompting Berrettini to continue.

'Well, one of Adolf Hitler's most despicable sidekicks, Heinrich Himmler, held the grand title of Reichsführer of the Schutzstaffel, meaning he controlled the notorious SS and during the war he ordered his men to have tattoos of their blood group inked on the inside of their left arm, in case they were injured and needed a transfusion. Of course, it hadn't occurred to him Germany might lose, and that these markings would be something of a giveaway when the Allies came searching for war criminals but, when the penny eventually dropped, he ordered those same tattoos be removed—'

Vargas cut in, even though Berrettini was in full flow.

'Mike, where the hell is this history lesson heading?'

'Nic, stay with me a bit longer. These SS officers were monsters, responsible for the most heinous crimes in history which they knew would earn them the death penalty, but removing the tattoos wasn't the answer because they were then left with scars which could still easily identify them. So, that's where the ODESSA came in—'

This time it was Hembury's turn to interrupt the FBI chief.

'I remember the movie. Jon Voight was in it. Wasn't it about high-ranking Nazis escaping to South America?'

Berrettini nodded before glancing down at the papers on the table in front of him.

'Exactly. ODESSA is the acronym for *Organisation der ehemaligen SS-Angehörigen*, which translates as *Organisation of Former SS Members*. It was formed on 10 August 1944 at a covert meeting in Strasbourg, where a small group of leading German industrialists and politicians met to plot the aftermath of the war. They could see the writing was on the wall. The Nazis were only months away from total defeat and business leaders wanted a refuge for their money, while SS officers needed passage out of Germany to a bolt-hole. ODESSA supplied false papers for them and safe houses along routes that became known as ratlines. At the same time, massive funds were transferred out of Germany to South America and Europe as leading industrialists emptied their bank accounts.'

Berrettini paused for a moment to pick up a loose sheet of paper containing a list of names.

'This is where the information contained on your USB drive comes into play. Himmler personally established and ran a clandestine subgroup of ODESSA, known as *Die Spinne* or the "Spider Network". This organisation focused on a long-term strategy to help perhaps as many as two thousand elite Nazis escape and then reinvent themselves outside of Germany as prominent figures in the worlds of banking, industry and politics.'

The FBI deputy director paused one last time and breathed deeply before unveiling the denouement.

'Gentlemen, there's credible intelligence to suggest that almost eight decades after its creation, *Die Spinne* still exists today in one form or another. Its reason for being is to protect the true heritage of high-ranking politicians, media magnates and business leaders who are hiding in plain sight and who still harbour ambitions for a new world order based on Nazi philosophy.'

The two men took a moment to digest Berrettini's story until eventually Vargas glanced down at the paper in the deputy director's hand.

'I'm guessing from what you've said, some of the names listed on that drive are alarming?'

Berrettini's expression changed to that of a man who, despite having seen and experienced a great deal in his life, was now truly perplexed.

'They are, but there was something else we found on the USB that was far more disturbing.'

Chapter Six

Berlin, Germany

December 1943

Heinrich Himmler was leading a complex triple life, and it was proving expensive. In 1928, the SS chief had married Margarete – a blonde, blue-eyed nurse who perfectly suited his ideals of an Aryan stereotype. A year later she gave birth to a daughter, Gudrun, and, for a while, all was well in the Himmler household. But, as the SS machine became more powerful and he grew closer to Hitler, he spent precious little time at home and, ten years after his marriage, began a serious affair with his secretary, Hedwig Potthast, leading to the birth of their first child, Helge, in 1942.

In addition to supporting his two families, Himmler also made substantial monthly contributions to his illegitimate daughter, Emelia, who was studying mathematics at Munich University and living in an apartment in the city which he'd found for her. It was far superior to regular student accommodation, but the SS chief wanted her to enjoy the trappings of success and wealth. Her existence was still a closely guarded secret, especially from his wife and mistress, and, as Emelia had grown older, Himmler had become totally smitten with her. She'd inherited the natural beauty of her mother and yet there was something about her eyes – the way they sparkled with life – which meant whenever they were together, the physical likeness between biological father and daughter was clear for all to see.

Emelia had been adopted shortly after her birth, in 1923, by a childless, middle-class protestant couple, who lived in the prosperous suburb of Bogenhausen on the outskirts of Munich. Her adoptive father, Albrecht Müller, was a branch manager at one of Germany's oldest banks, Berenburg, and his wife, Birgit, worked alongside him as a head teller. They were both in their forties and, after a disastrous series of miscarriages, had turned to adoption as a last hope. They'd longed for a child and, from the moment she entered their lives, Emelia was brought up in a loving household, where she thrived both socially and academically. For as long as she could remember, she knew she'd been adopted and that her birth parents' identities were buried somewhere deep in the orphanage records, destined never to be revealed.

That all changed the day after her fifteenth birthday. It was May 1938 and a restless Germany, under the leadership of Adolf Hitler, was gearing up for war. Two months earlier, the Führer had carried out the Anschluss, the unopposed annexation of Austria into the German Reich, and now had his eyes firmly set on taking control of the Sudetenland, a narrow strip of land on Germany's eastern border, which then formed part of Czechoslovakia.

At that point, Himmler held two senior positions in the Nazi regime. As well as being head of the SS, he was also chief of the German police. He was a fêted star of the Third Reich and, as he'd hoped, political success had brought him fame, status and wealth. Even though Emelia was the result of a drunken one-night stand, he'd always felt guilty about abdicating all responsibility for her but at that time he was a penniless student with no assets. Fifteen years on, things were very different; Heinrich Himmler was the second most powerful figure in Nazi Germany and he resolved now was the moment for Emelia to discover her true heritage.

He wrote to her in his role as a government minister inviting her for a meeting at his office in the Reichstag on the pretext of needing a part-time researcher, claiming he'd learned of her exceptional academic achievements through the headmistress of her school. Emelia was stunned and thrilled by the invitation which would give her the opportunity of meeting one of the most famous politicians in the country and so, the day before, her mother took her shopping to buy a new dress especially for this once-in-a-lifetime occasion.

The appointment was scheduled to last just thirty minutes but overran by three hours as, within moments of her arrival, Himmler had told her the true reason he'd called her in and given her details of their blood relationship. Emelia was stunned to suddenly meet her real father in such strange circumstances and at first was totally overwhelmed by the revelation. But then, as he recounted the full story of how he'd met her birth mother and how he'd followed her life from a safe distance, she began to relax and embrace this extraordinary development. He ended the meeting by explaining it was imperative their relationship remain a precious secret, owned by just the two of them. Even her adoptive parents could never know the celebrated head of the SS was her biological father.

From that day forward they met regularly, sometimes two or three times a month at various discreet locations in Munich, behaving as though they were a pair of lovers enjoying a secret affair. They adored each other and during the following years, as war raged across Europe, Emelia fell further and further under the spell of her father, who smoothly indoctrinated her with the fascist values and beliefs of the Nazi movement. In December 1943, with his assistance, she left university and proudly joined a clerical unit of the SS, working out of a small office in Berlin.

Five days after she took up the post, she received a letter from her father which she read word-for-word three times, before carefully cutting out the last paragraph and sticking it to the front door of her Siemens refrigerator. Every morning, she read the note with pride, before donning her uniform and heading off for work.

My Darling Emelia, The sheer joy that comes from the knowledge you are now fully part of our beloved movement is beyond description. As you know I fathered two other children, but you are the one who has captured my heart. You are my passion and the future of this great nation. Your loving father, Heinrich.

Chapter Seven

Paris, France

Leopold Legrand drew down deeply on his Gepetto vape as he paced the fourth-floor balcony of his Parisian mansion apartment, surveying the manicured gardens of the Champ de Mars below that framed an enviable view of the iconic Eiffel Tower. The man who was chairman and CEO of France's largest media corporation had plenty on his mind as he turned away and strode back through the floor-to-ceiling glass doors into the spectacular reception room which ran the length of the apartment. He moved with the elegance and arrogance that came with inherited wealth and his aristocratic, six-foot frame was clothed in a handmade, two-piece Savile Row linen suit, accompanied by a Hermès white cotton shirt, unbuttoned at the neck. He was in his late sixties and his perfectly coiffured ash blond hair, complemented by a subtle glint of silver, added extra gravitas to his aquiline nose and steely blue eyes.

Legrand enjoyed the luxurious trappings of wealth, having inherited a billion-euro fortune from his mother, the owner of one of the country's largest private banks. The legacy included the duplex apartment on the Avenue Joseph Bouvard, Paris's most exclusive address, which had been in the family since 1947. The 7,000-square-foot residence with its intricately hand-painted ceilings, Baccarat crystal chandeliers and Versailles-style parquet flooring was valued at a staggering fifty million euros, positioning it amongst the most expensive properties in the city.

Remarkably, one of France's richest and most powerful men had started life as an orphan. On 10 July 1956, when just a few days old, his late mother had adopted him from a slum orphanage run by a disreputable priest, in the back streets of Montmartre. At the grand age of thirty-three she'd decided no man alive was fit to fill the shoes of her beloved father, Heinrich Himmler. If she were to fulfil his wishes and produce a male heir, she knew she'd no choice but to adopt and she vowed to mould the little boy in the image of the man who'd once been proclaimed the second most powerful figure in the Third Reich.

The controversial business mogul, whom many French citizens adored because of the right-wing advocacy of many of his media outlets, wafted through the hallway of the apartment and headed for his office where he sat down behind his Louis XVI cylinder-top mahogany desk, believed to have once been owned by Napoleon. The former emperor had used it when he lived in the Château de Saint-Cloud in Hauts-de-Seine, three miles west of Paris. Legrand, who positioned himself as a man of the people, had bought the unique eighteenth-century desk in a black-market auction a few months earlier. He always felt a surge of pride when seated behind it, knowing it had previously belonged to one of his all-time heroes.

Legrand turned his attention to the only modern item in the room, a black MacBook Pro, which sprang into life as soon as he flipped it open. When the security bar popped up, Legrand typed in a six-digit access code and the screen began to conform. He checked the time in the top right-hand corner which displayed a digital readout confirming it was 18.00.

A Zoom invite pinged to grab his attention and moments later a familiar face filled the sixteen-inch screen. As usual Legrand's features remained anonymous, hidden behind a simple black background, with the letters HH centred in red. The murky image that stared back at him belonged to a like-minded right-wing collaborator, based seven thousand miles away in Buenos Aires. Carlos Salazar's head resembled a floating beach ball perched on a muscular bulldog neck, with a close-shaven scalp and puffed-out red cheeks. His thin pale lips created an ugly slit across the bottom half of his face, which hardly widened when he talked. As usual the Argentine spoke in English, a second language for both men. His rasping voice sounded as though it were coming through a cheese grater.

'Sir, we've moved fast since the security breach took place.'

'Go on.'

'We caught the two men involved. They were brothers. It's clear they'd no way of breaking down the codes on the USB drive.'

Legrand's left eyebrow formed a quizzical arch.

'How can you be so sure?'

'I supervised their interrogation personally. That's how I know.'

'And the drive is now back in your possession?'

Almost on cue, Salazar, who was sitting on a wooden stool

in a dimly lit cellar, raised his right hand to reveal a blue USB drive, which he held close to the camera. Legrand exhaled a deep breath before replying.

'One last thing, is there any chance they might have shown it to anybody else before you caught them?'

The Argentine had anticipated the question and answered a touch too eagerly.

'Impossible, they would have told me during the interrogation, and besides they had it in their possession when we captured them.'

Salazar double blinked as he told the lie, a clear tell he prayed his boss had missed due to the lack of light on his face. Legrand said nothing before hitting the red leave button on the screen, ending the Zoom. Salazar licked his parched lips as he wondered whether the chief inspector and his black friend had managed to break the codes on the USB drive before his Asian assassin had retrieved it from Vargas's Recoleta apartment.

Legrand eased back into the softness of his heavily padded antique chair and slowly closed his eyes. Salazar had just lied to him. However, that was not necessarily a problem, as the USB drive had been quickly and safely recovered. But two persistent questions began gnawing away at his brain. Why would his subordinate lie to him? What was he hiding?

Chapter Eight

Strasbourg, France

The Sikorsky S-92 helicopter gobbled up the miles as it cruised at two thousand feet, kissing the Parisian rooftops and heading directly east towards Strasbourg, the capital city of the Grand Est region of eastern France, formerly Alsace, and home to the European Parliament. The luxurious thirty-two-million-dollar aircraft needed less than two hours to complete the three-hundred-mile journey and, other than the two pilots, the only person on board was Legrand, who'd left his apartment just minutes after the conclusion of his Zoom call. He spent most of the journey fire-fighting emails from senior management figures inside his huge corporation, none of whom had any idea of their enigmatic boss's destination.

The Sikorsky dropped down at speed through the leaden grey skies and landed in the gardens of an eighteenth-century château located in a remote woodland in the north-east of the small French city. The interior of the large property was completely out of keeping with the classical elegance and beauty of the exterior of the two-hundred-and-fifty-year-old structure. It was a massive open-plan, state-of-the-art hub, where highly skilled software analysts and top line editors were glued to their terminals, linked to banks of throbbing computers, spewing out the very latest technological data. The content being created by artificial intelligence was pure cutting edge and Legrand knew his team of coders were at least two years ahead of any commercial competitors in the marketplace. Even the Chinese, whom the US government believed were covertly leading the way in AI development, were miles off producing the level of output Legrand's team were delivering.

He entered the château through the traditional French oak front doors, inset with pine panels, and immediately jumped three centuries, as he was greeted by a second set of eighteen-inch-thick reinforced steel doors that guarded the real entrance to the building's interior. Two armed security guards stood either side of a small glass panel operated by an iris-scanning entry system. The biometric technology was a step ahead of retinal scanning and focused on the thin ring of colour around the pupil of each eye, which, like fingerprints, was totally unique to every individual. It was a system Legrand had championed despite its three-million-euro price tag, as for the media magnate, security inside the château was paramount.

Waiting to greet him inside was his head of operations, Sabine Moreau, who led him along a central aisle which threaded a route through the ground-floor complex, leading to an office tucked away in the far corner. Legrand stopped every few seconds to glance at the visual content being created on various screens, buoyed by what he was seeing. As soon as they entered Moreau's office, he slid into a black leather chair positioned in front of a giant white screen and spoke for the first time since arriving.

'Sabine, how are my babies coming along?'

Moreau picked up a remote from a nearby desk and fired it at a 6K projector fixed to the ceiling directly above her.

'Monsieur Legrand, they've come a long way since your last visit. I've prepared a taster video and I don't think you'll be disappointed.'

Chapter Nine

Strasbourg, France

August 1944

The grandiose, curved red-brick façade of the iconic five-star Hôtel Maison Rouge stood majestically in the Place Kléber, the main square in the old centre of the German-occupied city of Strasbourg. On the evening of 10 August 1944 a small banqueting room on the lower ground floor played host to one of the most significant meetings of the Second World War; a clandestine summit that shaped events, post 1945, just as much as the celebrated peace conferences held at Potsdam and Yalta.

Unlike those historic meetings where world leaders met in public to carve up the map of post-war Europe, the handful of participants who met in secret at the eminent hotel in Strasbourg shared the same nationality – they were all German. There were six in total. Three were leading industrialists who between them owned every significant manufacturing and production plant inside Germany. They were joined by two banking barons: mega-rich financiers whose fortunes were intrinsically linked to the success or failure of the three businessmen sitting alongside them. They were all pragmatists who shared a common goal – the protection of their accumulated wealth that was being threatened by Germany's inevitable defeat, which they knew was now just months away.

The ringmaster who'd summoned them to the private meeting was neither a businessman nor a banker and, despite their immense affluence and privilege, they were all cowed by the legend of the man who was without doubt the most intimidating figure in the Third Reich. He'd kept them waiting for almost an hour and, when he finally entered the private dining room, the illustrious cartel leapt out of their chairs like exuberant salmon, swimming upstream to ensure the future of their species. They proclaimed 'Heil Hitler' as they performed the Nazi salute in unison.

Heinrich Himmler acknowledged the greeting and swept across the burgundy carpet, taking his place at the head of the oval mahogany dining table. He removed his familiar pince-nez glasses and waved them in the air with his right hand, clutching them between his stubby figures. His pale grey piggy eyes glanced furtively around the room at his assembled guests who'd taken their places around the table, creating a horseshoe formation. The man who was universally credited with masterminding the Holocaust loved the threatening power of silence and often weaponised it as a tool for unnerving underlings. He assumed it would work just as well with some of Germany's most powerful men as they knew he could have any of them arrested on a whim. Eventually he spoke and, as ever, his words were minimal and intimidating.

'Gentlemen, you all know why you're here. I assume everyone's in agreement regarding the transfer of funds I requested?'

Otto Schultz, the owner of Berlin's largest private bank, was seated directly to Himmler's left and was the nominated spokesman for the group. The only one brave enough to raise a concern shared by them all.

'Reichsführer, we have the bank codes and are ready to make the international transfers, but we do have a question. It concerns the proposed divisions of the monies: eighty-twenty seems a little high when you consider . . .'

The nervy banker failed to complete his sentence as Himmler let fly with a barrage of abuse, his eyes blazing like a pair of Bunsen burners.

'You contemptible worm! You dare to question my orders?'

The SS gangster switched his gaze to the other four men who'd lowered their heads, eyes glued to the tabletop, and wishing, at that precise moment, they could be anywhere else in the world.

'So, Schultz, you represent this pathetic bunch. Who amongst you wants to back him up?'

No one spoke, leaving the terrified banker hanging out to dry. Schultz tried to rescue the situation by asking a fresh question but as the words left his lips, he realised he'd made an even bigger mistake.

'The Führer has always been very fair with us when it comes to funding the Reich. We only pay a fifty per cent tax to the government. Does he know anything about these new donations and percentages?'

Himmler rocked back in his chair and broke into a high-pitched laugh that could easily have come from a deranged hyena. His reply was laced with a mixture of irony and contempt.

'My dear friend, our beloved Führer still labours under the mistaken belief our soldiers are going to produce a heroic victory on behalf of the Fatherland. Unfortunately, no one has passed that message on to the Russians in the East nor the Americans in the West.'

His voice now calmed to a monotone and was even more menacing.

'The money is needed to fund a special project close to my heart – *Die Spinne.* You should be grateful I'm allowing you to keep twenty per cent for yourselves. By my calculation that still leaves you with a pot of well over two hundred million dollars to share out for your personal use.'

Himmler paused and turned back towards Schultz.

'Perhaps I'm being far too generous. I know full well you've already squirrelled away millions of dollars from your personal funds to Swiss banks. So, as we're discussing corporate money, I think we should move to a ninety-ten split. After all, I know how keen you are to help your fellow Germans disappear and begin new lives in faraway continents. Believe me, that doesn't come cheap.'

Himmler knew his verbal onslaught had crushed the hint of revolt and he smiled to himself at the recognition that the failed rebellion had cost the pathetic businessmen millions of dollars. His final words were designed to assure them there was no going back on the deal. As ever he favoured the carrot and stick approach.

'Remember, we must look at protecting your immediate future and that of generations to come – your children and grandchildren – which means planning for a Fourth Reich. The more senior Nazis we can set up under new identities in positions of influence and power around the world, the quicker that day will come.'

He paused for a moment for maximum impact before issuing a thinly veiled threat.

'One last thing. My people have eyes and ears everywhere. Should any of you renege on our deal or attempt to discuss this arrangement directly with the Führer, you can be assured you'll receive an intimate visit from senior officers of the Gestapo. Now, can one of you reprobates do something useful, like find the maître d'? All this talk of money has fuelled my appetite.'

Chapter Ten

Washington D.C., United States

Vargas and Hembury watched on as Berrettini mirrored the feed from his laptop on to a giant wall-mounted TV screen and immediately two head shots appeared side by side with their names written underneath.

'So, the files on the USB drive are proving particularly challenging for our analysts to crack. We believe they contain a list of eight names in total. Six have been encoded by a superior level of AI we've never come across before. We don't think they're impenetrable but it's going to take some time for our team to break them open. However, we've had a break with the other two.'

He paused for a moment to study the faces staring back at him. One belonged to a middle-aged man whose rugged features were dominated by a three-inch zigzag scar carved deep into the centre of his broad forehead. The other image featured a black-haired, olive-skinned woman in her early forties, whose green eyes appeared to sparkle, even though they formed part of a still image. Her heart-shaped lips gave way to the hint of an enigmatic smile which added a touch of mystery to her features.

'Strangely, the names of these two politicians were encoded by a completely different AI operating system. It's also state of the art but at least it's one we've some knowledge of. So, two out of eight isn't a bad start. The hairy one on the left is Jack Cook, treasurer for the Australian government and the other is Alessia Carrozza, the Italian minister of the interior. Both frontline players in their respective parties, tipped for great things. So why the hell are their names secretly embedded on a stolen drive?'

Vargas's forehead creased up as he frowned.

'Why indeed? And why did "knife girl" break into my flat to steal it?'

'Another good question. Right now, my team are doing deep dives into their backgrounds, but early signs are they're both kosher.'

Vargas downed his black coffee before asking a question that was also troubling Hembury.

'Mike, earlier on you said you discovered something else on the drive?'

Berrettini took the cue.

'Yep, and I think the best thing I can do is show it to you rather than talk about it.'

He clicked on his laptop mouse and moved the cursor on to a QuickTime movie identified on his desktop by the letters HH.

The photos of the two politicians disappeared and were replaced by a colour thumbnail image, which instantly animated. The video showed a man dressed in military

36

uniform, sitting behind a large antique mahogany desk topped with a red leather inset, talking directly to camera. He was speaking in fluent German and English subtitles ran in sync across the bottom third of the picture.

Behind him was a plain white-plastered wall broken up by two Nazi flags, with the notorious black swastika against a blood-red background, which framed him perfectly. He was wearing a charcoal black, open-collared service tunic, decorated with white oak leaf wreaths, along with a red swastika armlet set just above above his left elbow. Underneath he wore a plain white shirt buttoned to the neck, accompanied by a thin black silk tie.

His high-pitched voice was monotonic with an edge of hysteria. Hembury and Vargas were genuinely unsettled by the content of the film show Berrettini had laid on, but ultimately it was the distinctive features on the face of the man in the video that startled them. He was soft-chinned and thin-lipped with a flimsy gossamer iron-grey moustache. His eyes were partially hidden behind a set of rimless pince-nez glasses, sitting below a prominent forehead, which blended into a thinning black hairline. It was a face from the history books, the face of a monster who'd died almost eighty years ago.

Berrettini could sense the discomfort in the room as it was apparent both men had recognised the former leader of the notorious Waffen-SS. He paused the video before closing his laptop.

'Heinrich Himmler, the self-proclaimed architect of the Holocaust and the second most powerful man in the Nazi regime.'

Vargas nodded as he turned away from the screen.

'Mike, I recognised him straight away. What threw me was the quality of the footage. I've only seen him in black and white before. Why would someone go to the trouble of colourising an old speech?'

'That's the problem, Nic, they didn't. Only a handful of Himmler's speeches were ever filmed and, believe me, the clip we've just been looking at wasn't taken from any of them.'

The FBI deputy director paused for a few seconds to allow the shocking impact of his words to fully register before continuing.

'The video runs for about eighteen minutes and here's the thing. After the brief introduction which you've just seen, he focuses on contemporary geopolitics and references several political leaders, including Putin and Kim Jong Un. He even manages a dig at Trump. He references *Die Spinne* on two occasions and most of the content is about the strategic political influence of the Reich on international events: the Fourth Reich.'

Chapter Eleven

Washington D.C., United States

W hile Vargas and Hembury were occupied viewing the eighteen-minute clip in its entirety, two visitors entered the meeting room and were warmly greeted by Berrettini who ushered them to a pair of empty seats alongside him at the end of the table. Neither worked directly for the FBI but the deputy director had contacted them once he'd seen the contents of the USB drive.

Himmler's speech had concluded with a reference to an upcoming UN climate conference, known as COP, where members from around the world would be gathering to negotiate the reduction of greenhouse gas emissions. He hailed it as a 'golden opportunity to cement the emerging economic and political landscape the new Reich has worked so hard to achieve'.

Before Vargas or Hembury had time to catch their breath and react to the content of the astonishing video, Berrettini cut straight in with introductions.

'Troy, Nic, I'd like you to meet two specialists in the field of deepfakes who can hopefully shed some light on the footage you've just seen. Spencer Devane heads up our National Counterintelligence and Security Center, while Barbara Starling runs SOCOM, a Special Operations Command unit, responsible for deep undercover operations, including internet deception campaigns. Although it's not common knowledge, since July 2022 both organisations have kept small elite teams on site here at the Bureau working closely with some of our intelligence agents, specifically tasked with assessing online threats, particularly deepfakes.'

Starling was first out of the blocks.

'Gentlemen, what you've just witnessed is a superb deepfake video of a man who committed suicide on 23 May 1945. I'd say without question it's the best I've seen, and that fact alone is a matter of grave concern for the US government – especially for my department. Until a few hours ago, I believed our synthetic media technology was cutting edge, right up there with the Russians and close to the Chinese but, sadly, I've just been proven wrong.'

Starling was an imposing-looking woman – late forties, athletic build, oval-faced and brown-eyed with dead straight hair that was predominantly grey, a fact she didn't bother to disguise with help from a bottle. Her notable family was dripping in military history. Her late father had been a four-star general in the Marine Corps and his only child, Barbara, was carrying on a tradition that scaled five generations. As head of a Special Ops unit, she wasn't required to wear military uniform and was conservatively dressed in a sober navy two-piece cotton suit, with a white open-necked blouse beneath the jacket. She'd evidently no fondness for small talk and Vargas and Hembury hung on every word she uttered.

'Ever since the emergence of the infamous deepfake Obama video back in April 2019, our department has spent hundreds of millions of dollars developing this controversial tech so we can apply it ourselves as an offensive weapon, should the need arise. Can you imagine the fallout we could cause if a video surfaced of Putin talking openly about the billions of roubles he's stolen from the state. We in the West know it's true but if the Russian people were to hear it directly from the horse's mouth, it would seriously threaten his credibility, if not his entire regime.'

She paused for a moment to glance down at her iPhone to check on a WhatsApp alert and Hembury filled in the void.

'What about the ethics? Surely, people have the right—'

Starling's voice moved up an octave, as she shut him down.

'Mr Hembury, there are no ethics in war and let's be clear on this – as technology advances at a frightening pace, it'll inevitably be used for harm as well as good. AI and the creation of believable deepfakes by our enemies is possibly the biggest live and current threat our country faces. We need the ability to fight fire with fire. A few years ago, one of our research scientists, a tech wizard, Ian J. Goodfellow, invented a deep-learning system called GAN, which stands for Generative Adversarial Network. It was revolutionary at the time as it combined two neural networks working together to create a synthetic copy of an image, which in this instance was a human face. A "generator" network created the fake and then a "discriminator" network attempted to detect if the image was real or not. This process was then repeated numerous times and, on each iteration, the two systems used the feedback to create a highly lifelike simulacrum of a human face – a deepfake.'

Starling could see by the three blank expressions staring back at her she'd totally lost her audience, so she decided to dumb down her analysis.

'In layman's terms, Goodfellow had created a new kind of software that, with the help of AI, generated human faces that were damned near perfect. At first there were subtle giveaways – a lack of regular blinking and wrongly angled shadows but, in recent times, most of those wrinkles have been ironed out and I'd say we are currently capable of creating a deepfake that is ninety-eight per cent believable. But, critically, it still has inherent flaws that tech experts who know what to look for can easily spot and therefore expose. For example, there are numerous tiny muscles around the lips that come into play when we speak and, to date, we've struggled to perfectly simulate how they work – so, often with a deepfake, the mouth is a giveaway.'

She paused for a second time, as she gathered her thoughts.

'Getting back to the Himmler video, my senior tech analysts believe it's the first example of a truly flawless deepfake. One that is one hundred per cent perfect – a Frankenstein's monster that could fool the entire world. Imagine the potential threat of this technology being weaponised by one of our enemies if it were utilised on present-day politicians.'

Vargas and Hembury exchanged looks as Berrettini gestured to Devane to begin his briefing. His demeanour was far more relaxed than Starling's, having honed his impressive people skills during the previous three years presenting intelligence reports directly to the President and his Cabinet. Devane's perfectly tanned, child-like features made him difficult to age. His sandy blond hair spilled over his forehead, below which lay a penetrating set of cobalt blue eyes.

Vargas speculated to himself that if Devane hadn't made it in national security, he could easily have cracked it as a Hollywood heartthrob. When he spoke, his Midwest Fargo-ish accent was unexpected but the intelligence chief who hailed from Minnesota was a smooth talker who, unlike his counterpart, didn't get bogged down in technical data.

'Guys, think of this episode as being a bit like the space race back in the sixties – only this time, based on what you've just seen, it appears we've lost. Right now, the scary thing is we haven't a clue as to the identity of the people who've won and, what's more, we've no idea what they're planning to do next.'

Chapter Twelve

Washington D.C., United States

L ess than an hour after the briefing finished, two game-changing phone calls took place on different floors inside the massive Bureau building at 935 Pennsylvania Avenue. One was incoming, the other outgoing. The first involved Vargas, whose assistant in Buenos Aires, Juan Torres, was informing him of a double murder.

Two bodies had been discovered, partially buried, in the outskirts of the Pinar del Norte forest, located about two hundred and fifty miles south-east of the capital. The murderers had been interrupted by a large group of hikers who were on a night forage when they witnessed the burial taking place in a small woodland clearing, about fifty yards away from the main trail. The description of one of the bodies was harrowing as the victim, only just recognisable as a man, had evidently been tortured and his mutilated remains made an ID almost impossible. The second body, also male, had been shot twice through the heart, but his facial features were untouched. Before Torres had even completed the description, Vargas knew the corpse belonged to the man he'd met two nights earlier in the sports bar. The man he knew as Manuel.

The second call was made from an encrypted burner cell and the person making it was crouched inside the end cubicle of a basement washroom, while the recipient was four thousand miles away, sitting behind an antique desk in his Parisian mansion apartment. Legrand hung on every word as his informant clinically brought him up to speed.

* * *

Carlos Salazar was a bag of nerves. Less than an hour earlier, he'd been sitting at an intimate banquette at one of Buenos Aires' finest eateries, accompanied by his favourite whore, working his way through an extortionately priced tasting menu. Then he received a WhatsApp message summoning him to an unexpected Zoom call, which meant an early return to his apartment. He cursed under his breath that he'd read the message as he knew the sender would have received two blue ticks confirming the fact, so he had no choice but to leave the delicious food and his stunning companion whom he'd booked for a five-hour session. Between the restaurant and the courtesan, he'd blown almost five thousand dollars, and the night was now a total write-off.

The fact his handler had demanded a Zoom call at midnight meant something was off as they'd only spoken recently, when he'd lied through his teeth about recovering the USB drive before anyone could lay their hands on it. He was sure at the time he'd got away with it. But had he?

The taxi dropped Salazar off in the pull-up area directly outside the front of his luxury apartment block in the trendily named Palermo Hollywood district. It was four minutes before midnight, and he couldn't afford to be late. He flung a wad of ten-dollar bills at the bemused cab driver and sprinted up the concrete steps, bursting through the glass entrance doors, heading straight for the bank of lifts located behind the concierge desk. For once he cursed the fact he lived in an apartment on the twenty-third floor, as time was of the essence.

The elevator silently moved upwards without stopping and seconds later the doors slid open on to an exclusive hallway which led to two penthouses, one of which was his. A final dash to his front door meant he was sitting at his desk, laptop running, with one minute in hand. His breathing was heavy, and his heart was going like a jackhammer but at least he was on time. Finally, he used his club of a hand to swipe away some of the sweat beads that were forming rivulets down his forehead, before clicking the join icon on the Zoom invite.

Moments later Salazar was online and, as soon as he registered the face of the man staring back at him, he felt an instant wave of nausea and feared for his life. Something was very wrong. All bets were off, and he wondered how long it would take to empty his safe and get the hell out of the apartment. He speculated probably five minutes at best, but did he have that time?

For the previous two years, all Zoom calls with his handler had followed the same pattern. He would only see a black screen with the capitalised letters HH centred in red. An anonymous voice would issue instructions which he'd follow to the letter in return for a generous retainer, regularly topped up by a healthy bonus. But now, for the first time, he was looking at a face – and it was the face of a man he recognised. Why had his handler suddenly decided to reveal his identity? Unless . . .

When Legrand spoke for the first time, Salazar felt a shiver run down his spine as it confirmed the voice he'd heard so many times belonged to one of the richest and most powerful businessmen in the world.

'My friend, it appears you were far from truthful the last time we spoke. In fact, I'd go so far as to say, every single word you uttered was a lie. Have I not been a generous employer?'

Salazar's eyeline had moved away from the computer screen to a large, framed Picasso print on the wall opposite, behind which his safe was hidden. His mouth was as dry as the Sahara but somehow he managed to spit out a reply.

'No, sir, I would never lie to you. In fact—'

Legrand's eyes narrowed and his face distorted as he snarled back.

'Don't take me for a fool, Salazar. I know all about Vargas and his black friend, Hembury. Right now, both are in Washington, sharing the contents of the USB drive with the deputy director of the FBI. They've already identified two of the names.'

Salazar figured his only hope was to beg for forgiveness; buy a little time and then get the hell out of Dodge. The safe, which was only a few tantalising yards away, contained enough cash to cover a flight to his beloved Thailand, where he knew he could live the high life for at least five years. That would give him the chance to reinvent himself. But before he could speak, the image on the screen changed and the fresh one displayed an 18.9 ratio, typical of a video filmed from a cell phone. It showed four figures moving at speed down a hallway. The two men in the centre appeared to be carrying the limp body of a woman between them. She was clearly unconscious, and her bare feet dragged along the carpet creating a macabre blood trail. Two other men were striding forward, slightly ahead and to one side, lugging what appeared to be some kind of battering ram.

Salazar did a double take at the footage and his bowels gave way as he realised what he was he was staring at. He'd just charged through that same hallway. The men were heading directly for his apartment.

The ear-shattering thud created by the 35-pound Enforcer as it smashed through the heavy wooden door echoed around the spacious corridor. Moments later, two of Legrand's men grabbed the petrified Argentine, ripped him from his chair and forced his arms behind his back, holding him so tight, he stood on the spot as rigid as an upturned ironing board.

When Legrand next spoke, Salazar couldn't see the computer screen, but he could hear well enough. Somehow, it was even more terrifying just hearing the disembodied voice.

'As you can see, I've decided to reunite you with your Asian friend, Seiko, who retrieved the USB drive from Vargas's apartment. Unfortunately for both of you, that was after he'd downloaded its content and emailed it to the FBI. She's heavily drugged but not dead . . . yet.'

Salazar's eyes were almost popping out of his head as they darted around the room looking for some kind of deliverance. He'd a gun hidden in a secret drawer in a compartment of his desk just a few feet away, but what were the chances?

'Please, sir, I believe I can still be of use to you and your cause. I just need—'

48

Legrand replied with a question, his voice charged with malice.

'Señor Salazar, do you understand the laws of gravity?'

He paused, relishing the absolute power of the moment. He found it intoxicating but he'd no intention of waiting for an answer from the man who'd betrayed him. Salazar was trying to process the question as Legrand cut back in.

'When my men throw you, your friend Seiko, and your laptop from the balcony of your twenty-third-floor penthouse, which of you do you think will hit the ground first?'

That line was the cue for Legrand's gorillas to begin moving, frogmarching Salazar towards the open windows, while the other two followed closely behind, dragging the girl and grabbing the laptop. Salazar begged for forgiveness, pleading hysterically for his life as he was forcibly carried towards two ornate metal doors that opened on to a wraparound balcony.

The screaming continued right up until the moment he was hurled over the top of the curved smoked-glass barrier from where he plunged downwards to his death, accompanied by Seiko and his MacBook.

As soon as the signal on his own laptop disappeared, Legrand reached across his desk for a fresh vape, took a deep drag, and clicked off the Zoom.

Chapter Thirteen

The Black Forest, Germany

December 1944

By the beginning of December 1944, it was apparent to every sane German general the war in Europe was lost, but Hitler ploughed on, refusing to listen to his senior military officers whom he routinely accused of being doom-mongers and traitors. As the Allied invasion grew in momentum, the Führer felt increasingly isolated and turned to his dwindling group of loyal aides for support. He appointed Himmler military commander of the Army Group Upper Rhine, tasking him with retaking the border town of Strasbourg which had recently fallen to the French. It was an appointment ridiculed by the generals as Himmler had zero military experience, but the SS leader was unfazed by their opposition and willingly accepted the post. His self-belief still burned as strongly as ever.

He set up headquarters inside eight refurbished carriages of a specially modified train, parked deep inside an old tunnel in the heart of the Black Forest. The train was invisible; concealed from prying eyes both from the air and the ground, making it the perfect hideaway.

On the morning of 14 December, Himmler sent a telegram to Emelia urgently requesting a face-to-face meeting. Later that evening she was collected from her apartment on the outskirts of Berlin by his chauffeur and driven through the night on a non-stop journey, reaching the hidden location just before eight the following morning. When the black Mercedes-Benz 770 eased to a halt just outside the entrance to the tunnel, Emelia thought something must be wrong, as the destination made no sense. That feeling changed moments later when the driver led her cautiously inside the dimly lit tunnel and headed straight for carriage four, the secret lair of her father.

Himmler hadn't seen his daughter for months and the pair hugged for almost a minute, tears flowing down their cheeks. When they eventually broke off the embrace, Emelia glanced around the opulently furnished carriage and her eyes quickly settled on a massive mahogany desk. The inlaid red leather surface was mostly obscured by dozens of maps, packages and loose papers. Pride of place was given to an antique silver picture frame, precariously perched on a raised section at the very edge. It contained a black and white photo of her she knew was her father's favourite. He'd taken it on her eighteenth birthday, when they'd dined together in a private suite at the celebrated Hotel Adlon in the centre of Berlin. She'd been standing on a balcony, offering up a beaming smile with the iconic Brandenburg Gate framed perfectly behind her. She wiped away a fresh tear before hitting her father with a barrage of questions.

'Papa, what's happening? I heard you've been made a military commander, is that true? This train in the middle of nowhere . . . what's going on?'

Himmler gestured for her to take a seat on a black leather club chair which faced a more conventional high-backed dining-room chair, which he opted for. As he sat down, his left hand shot out with a flourish, pressing a green button which formed part of a small switchboard.

'My darling girl, so many questions, all of which will be answered in good time. But first, you must be starving after such a long journey. We have a small oven on board and my chef bakes the most wonderful croissants. As I knew you were coming, I ensured we stocked up with your favourite peach preserve.'

Emelia was no longer crying. Her face was glowing with happiness.

'Papa, it's so wonderful to see you but why the secretive last-minute invitation?'

'First let's eat and then we'll talk. I've so much to tell you, my darling. Your life is about to change forever.'

Emelia devoured her breakfast of warm croissants, fresh fruit and jam, while Himmler hardly touched any food but gained immense pleasure watching his daughter consume everything in sight. He took a swig of sweet, steaming-hot black coffee before beginning his well-rehearsed tale.

'My darling, I'm afraid to say the German people are being fed a pack of fairy stories – a tissue of lies, drip-fed by Goebbels and his disgusting Propaganda Ministry. The war is pretty much lost and whilst I and those still loyal to the Führer will fight until the bitter end, it's an end that is inevitable and, sadly, not too far away.'

Emelia was clearly deeply shocked by her father's revelation, as, like millions of German citizens, she believed the daily news bulletins that reported a relentless succession of dynamic victories for a German army and air force that appeared invincible. Her forehead creased up with concern and she was poised to interrupt but as she stared into her father's eyes, she could see he was speaking the truth and clearly had plenty more to say, so for now she kept her counsel and nodded for him to continue.

'Believe me, Emelia, when the war ends, the Allied forces will be looking for revenge. They'll seek scapegoats, and honest politicians like me who served the Nazi regime with passion and loyalty will be accused of unspeakable war crimes and my reputation will be ruined. I'll face total humiliation . . . and the rope.'

He paused for a moment of reflection before reaching forward and cupping his daughter's hands inside his own.

'You know how I've personally handled the Jewish question during the last few years – exterminating millions across Europe for the betterment of mankind. My creation of gas chambers in the concentration camps spared thousands of our brave soldiers from mental torment, which most certainly would have been the case had they been forced to pull the trigger and kill the rats one by one.'

Himmler had been consumed with antisemitism for well over two decades and Emilia was at one with his obsession to rid the world of the Jewish race, having been indoctrinated by him on the merits of the Holocaust from the day they first met. When she spoke, her words were chilling.

'Papa, in my opinion you deserve a medal for every single Jew you sent to their death.'

Himmler's slit of a mouth gave way to the hint of a smile, and he tightened his grip on his daughter's hands.

'Thank you, my darling, those words truly touch my heart. But now we must talk about the future, yours and mine.'

He released her hands, stood up and moved towards his desk, picking up a thick brown padded envelope which he handed to her. Her eyebrows formed a quizzical expression as she took it. He sat back down to face her, his poker face giving nothing away of what was to come.

'Emelia, a few months ago I formed a secret organisation tasked with the single aim of helping SS officers escape Germany and start a new life with a fresh identity in a different country. I've raised huge funds from leading financiers and industrialists and have opened bank accounts across Europe and South America, dedicated to this single purpose.'

'Papa, where do you plan to go? Wherever it is, I'll come with you.'

'No, my darling, I'll stay here as long as possible and then I plan to head to Argentina or Bolivia, where I can hopefully spend my remaining years. But you . . . you, my darling, have your whole life ahead of you and, as my daughter, you also have a destiny to fulfil. The Third Reich may well be in its death throes, but I believe a new one can, before too long, rise from the ashes. Emelia, your future will be outside of Germany, but in Europe where you'll have the financial platform to achieve great things and work together with like-minded collaborators.'

Emelia was totally stunned and when she spoke she surprised herself, as her voice became a pleading scream.

'Papa, I beg you . . . Come with me.'

Himmler sternly cut her dead.

'My features are too well known to ever be safe in Europe. The matter is closed.'

Then he softened his tone and glanced down towards the package in her hand.

'Now, my darling, take a look at your new life. You'll have more money than you've ever dreamed of. As of now, you're a Swiss heiress and the major shareholder of a small private bank in Paris.'

'What on earth? Papa, have you lost your mind?'

'Not at all, Emelia, you're a brilliant mathematician, your adoptive father worked in a bank, so why not run one of your own.'

She laughed hysterically as she picked up the envelope and tilted it downwards, spilling its contents on to the small side table next to her. A number of documents appeared but the first thing that caught her eye was a light brown Swiss passport, embossed with black lettering. Her right hand was drawn to it like a magnet and moments later, as she flicked through it, she landed on the home page which revealed a black and white photo of herself. For a moment she was dumbstruck as she couldn't recall posing for it but then, when she saw the name beneath it, she let out a small gasp. Himmler watched her every move and when he spoke his voice was a reassuring whisper.

'Yes, my darling, from this moment forward, Emelia Müller ceases to exist. You're now a Swiss national and you'll be known as Amelie Legrand.'

Chapter Fourteen

Berlin, Germany

February 1945

Ten weeks after her clandestine meeting with her father, Amelie received an unexpected visit. It was just before ten at night when the silence inside her spacious apartment was shattered by a thunderous triple knock on her front door. She'd been preparing for bed and froze on the spot, paralysed with fear, as she wondered who on earth could be outside. For a few seconds she remained stock-still and then she heard a familiar voice call out her new name.

'Amelie! Amelie! Your father sent me.'

The male voice coming from the communal hallway was muffled but her spirit soared as she recognised its owner. She flung her toothbrush into the tiny stone sink in front of her and bolted towards the door, as the voice called out again.

'Amelie, it's Werner, your father's aide-de-camp.'

Amelie opened the door and threw herself into the arms of the man she knew rarely left her father's side. Werner

Grothmann had been a mid-ranking SS commander who was injured in action during the Western Campaign in June 1940, after which he was seconded to work in Himmler's office. Two years later, in July 1942, he was appointed personal assistant to the Reichsführer of the SS, becoming Heinrich Himmler's aide-de-camp.

The pair broke off their warm embrace and Amelie led Grothmann inside her apartment where they sat down next to each other on her small brown leather couch. She could hardly contain her excitement, as she knew his appearance signalled something important must be happening with her father. Amelie suspected she was about to be transported on another secret visit to see him and was bursting with questions.

'Werner, it's so lovely to see you. How's my father? Are you about to take me to see him?'

Grothmann resembled a shop window mannequin, immaculately turned out in his grey-green SS garb. His perfectly coiffed slicked-back brown hair crowned a skull-shaped face, boasting a pair of piercing hazel eyes.

His forehead creased up to form a set of tram lines, as he shook his head.

'Amelie, these are difficult times. Your father wants you to know the war is lost. The Fatherland is two, maybe three months at best, away from capitulation. I know on your last visit the Reichsführer told you about *Die Spinne* and its web of ratlines across Europe. The time has come for you to leave Germany using the network as a safe escape route.'

Amelie was rocked by twin emotions of disappointment and shock and took a moment to absorb what she was being told.

'When do I need to be ready?'

'By tomorrow.'

She remained silent as it was apparent Grothmann hadn't finished delivering her father's message.

'At midday you've a meeting scheduled at the Café Zelter on Kurfürstendamm. It's with the man your father has appointed to run the Berlin side of the operation. There will be a reserved table set for two in the rear section just to the right of the kitchen door. Take a seat there and wait.'

Grothmann had one last task before he finished. He reached inside his tunic pocket to retrieve a small notebook, no bigger than a pocket diary.

'Your father gave me this to pass on to you. It contains the names of hundreds of Nazis who've left the country during the last four months and settled in other parts of Europe and South America under new identities. Everything is written in his own hand. In years to come he hopes you'll contact some of them and build a network of your own.'

Himmler's aide handed the book over and Amelie grasped it, instinctively hugging it close to her chest as though it were a precious gift. Grothmann summoned a glimmer of a smile as he rose to his feet.

'Good luck, Amelie. I hope you prosper in your new life.'

* * *

The Café Zelter was bustling with activity, with some diners finishing off a late breakfast, while others tucked into an early lunch. Amelie arrived forty minutes early for her appointment, settled at the nominated table and patiently waited for her mystery host to arrive. When the waitress took her order for a black coffee, she enquired as to the name of the table reserva-tion and was informed it had been booked the previous day by a Herr Mayer.

She sipped her drink slowly for over half an hour and precisely at midday, her eyes locked on to an SS captain enter-ing the café and making straight for her table. Immediately she spotted something odd about his physical appearance that made him stand out from the crowd. His olive skin tone, deep-set brown eyes and mop of black hair were the complete antithesis of the Aryan stereotype coveted by the SS. He was short and stocky but navigated a smooth path through the bunched-up tables with the elegance of a ballroom dancer. As he approached, Amelie stood to greet him and extended her hand which he shook warmly. He instantly read her eyes as though he were clairvoyant.

'Amelie, I can see what you're thinking. My complexion is easily explained. I was born in South America, in the beautiful city of Córdoba in Argentina, but when I was three years old, my family emigrated here. My name is Carlos Mayer, and I have the honour of being the leader of the Berlin section of *Die Spinne*, an appointment instigated by your esteemed father.'

His left hand instinctively moved up and brushed the insig-nia on his collar.

'Please don't be fooled by my appearance; I wear this uniform with pride. I'm an SS captain, a Nazi to my very soul and would give every drop of blood to protect the Reichsführer or his beautiful daughter.'

Amelie was instantly captivated by the rugged young man and lowered her eyes in embarrassment as she felt her skin burn. Her throat was suddenly as dry as parchment and she could sense the adrenaline racing through her veins as she struggled to think of a single thing to say. After a few seconds of painful silence, she finally managed to come up with something.

'How is this going to work, Captain?'

'Be ready to leave your apartment at nine tonight when I'll personally collect you. Pack only one case; everything else must stay behind. I understand your father gave you fresh documentation along with a Swiss passport?'

Mayer paused for a moment while Amelie nodded to confirm.

'Good. So, we'll have a ten-hour drive through the night, crossing into Switzerland, heading for Fribourg. We'll overnight there at a Franciscan monastery on the outskirts of the old city. The following morning we'll continue south-west to Geneva, where your short journey will end. Under your new name, you recently purchased a nineteenth-century château by the famous lake, where your father intends you live for at least two years, before you begin your new life in Paris.'

Amelie's thoughts scrambled as she struggled to process the prospect of the future in a foreign country her father had mapped out for her.

'Anything else I need to know?'

Mayer switched his eyeline, glancing down at his watch and his genial mood vanished in an instant.

'Amelie, I've a second meeting scheduled shortly, so I need to leave now.'

'Is it with another fugitive?'

Mayer's reply was curt.

'No more questions. I'll collect you tonight at nine.'

'But we'll be travelling on our own, just the two of us?'

The SS captain rose to his feet, signalling their meeting was over.

'No, Amelie, there'll be three of us.'

'Does my father know of this?'

'Yes, I'm following his orders to the letter.'

Before she could come up with a reply, Mayer turned away and strode out of the café, leaving Amelie to puzzle over the identity of her fellow escapee. Whoever they were, they clearly weren't comfortable being seen in a public place and the prospect of the meeting had sent the SS captain scuttling on his way like a scalded cat.

Chapter Fifteen

Berlin, Germany

February 1945

Amongst the hierarchy of the SS, it was common knowledge the intelligence services of the invading Allied powers had a list of proscribed war criminals – Nazis who'd committed abhorrent crimes against humanity – and the BBC regularly broadcast inside Germany the names of senior SS officers earmarked for arrest. The shadowy figure sitting in the back seat of the black Mercedes-Benz 170 V that pulled up outside Amelie's apartment, with Carlos Mayer at the wheel, was high up on the notorious inventory.

Karl Fritzsch had no intention of waiting around to face the hangman's noose. His sole priority was to save his own skin. The former deputy commandant at Auschwitz was heralded by Hitler as the man who came up with the plan of using the poisonous gas Zyklon B as a tool of mass murder in the death-camps inside Poland. He was a career SS officer who'd served his apprenticeship at Dachau before moving on to the most notorious deathcamp masterminded by the Nazis. His chilling address to the camp's initial seven hundred and fifty-eight inmates was legendary. 'For all of us you are not human but a pile of dung. For such enemies of the Third Reich as you, the Germans will have no favour and no mercy. We are delighted to drive you all through the grates of the crematorium furnaces.'

When Amelie joined Mayer in the front of the Mercedes, she only managed a brief glimpse of the mysterious passenger sitting in the back. He was soberly dressed in a dark grey gaberdine suit, his facial features partially masked by a black-felt Fedora. Mayer had placed Amelie's suitcase in the trunk of the car and escorted her to the passenger seat. No words were spoken as the 1.7 litre, rear-wheel-drive sedan pulled smoothly away in the dimly lit street and began its marathon six-hundred-mile journey south to Fribourg.

A few minutes into the trip Mayer broke the wall of uncomfortable silence as he glanced at Amelie.

'I spoke with your father a few hours ago. He's relieved to know you're on your way to safety and wants to hear from us as soon as we reach Geneva. I've seen photos of your new residence – it's truly magnificent. Perfect for a Swiss heiress who owns a private bank in Paris.'

The tension inside the Mercedes that had hung in the air like a murky fog instantly evaporated as Amelie laughed for the first time in weeks. She was infatuated with the SS captain whose good looks and easy charm had enthralled her from the moment she'd set eyes on him. Amelie knew he was teasing her and was enjoying it.

'Captain, who knows, maybe in years to come you'll choose to live in Paris and open an account at the Legrand bank.'

'It's a tempting thought. Who knows what the future holds for either of us?'

For the next hour the pair chatted incessantly, oblivious to the third person in the car. Although Amelie was twenty-two, her love life, or lack of it, meant she was incredibly inexperienced when it came to relationships. She'd had little time for men but there was something about the young SS captain sitting inches away from her that had stirred up feelings she'd never had before. On two occasions when Mayer changed gear his hand brushed against hers and each time it felt as though a bolt of electricity had shot through her body. Amelie wondered if he liked her but was racked with self-doubt, so couldn't be sure if he was just being kind, carrying out her father's orders.

As the Mercedes approached the Swiss border crossing, Fritzsch spoke for the first time. His rasping voice spat out a command, dripping with arrogance.

'Remember, Mayer, not a word out of place. At this point my safety is paramount. When the guards check our papers, keep to the story, and hold your nerve.'

Mayer glanced in his rear-view mirror and locked eyes with the former Auschwitz deputy commandant.

'Fritzsch, I'm not one of your former inmates, so if I were you, I'd respect the fact your life is in my hands. I take my orders directly from the Reichsführer and be under no illusion, as far as he's concerned, the most precious cargo inside this car is sitting up front next to me.'

Fritzsch bared his teeth like an irate Rottweiler and, for a moment, Mayer was grateful his rear passenger couldn't see the giant grin that had just broken out across Amelie's face. In reality, he knew passing through the soft border into

Switzerland was little more than a formality, having crossed it over a dozen times in the previous three months, while transporting other prominent SS officers on forged papers.

There were good reasons for his confidence. Utilising illicit funds provided by *Die Spinne,* Mayer had set up a bureau in Berne which generated false paperwork for SS escapees, rubber stamped by senior members of the Swiss police department who were Nazi sympathisers and partial to massive bribes. The funnel for the payments was the deputy chief of police, who was a devout antisemite and enjoyed a personal relationship with Himmler. In September 1944 two V3000S military trucks laden with Reichsbank-stamped, one-kilo gold bars had passed safely through the border crossing, ending up in a warehouse in Zurich, thereby cementing a working relationship between the Swiss authorities and *Die Spinne.*

As expected, the two border guards showed little interest in the three people inside the Mercedes and spent less than two minutes examining the fake papers and forged passports, before sending them on their way. For the next eight hours Mayer drove solidly through the night, only stopping twice to refuel, feeding petrol directly into the tank from two large plastic containers stored in the trunk.

It was just after nine in the morning when Amelie spotted the first signs for Fribourg, but the Mercedes never actually entered the medieval city nestled on a large rock promontory, as the location of the Franciscan monastery lay on the outskirts. The Sacred Cross, a magnificent Baroque-style abbey was one of the oldest in Switzerland, dating back to the ninth century and had been reconstructed several times after numerous fires. The main white-plastered façade was flanked by two ornate towers, crowned with a stunning red-tiled roof, while the interior, which was covered in giant frescoes and stucco, reflected the exterior grandeur.

It was Mayer's fifth visit, and he followed the same routine as before; parking up in a converted stable block to the side of the main building, ensuring the Mercedes instantly disappeared from sight. He led his two fugitives around the back of the abbey and through a large vegetable garden, from where they entered an unimposing black wooden door, which filled a small arch. Inside, they entered a large flagstone-floored kitchen, with an oblong dark-oak refectory table positioned in the centre. It was laid with place settings for three people and wooden platters of home-made bread along with an impressive selection of cheeses, cold hams and fruits. Silver goblets containing fresh water and red wine were placed at each setting. Sitting at one end was a Franciscan abbot, dressed in a traditional dark brown woollen habit with a string of thin rope tied around his midriff. As soon as he saw the new arrivals enter the kitchen, he lifted his hood, rose from his chair and approached the small party.

Abbot Josef Holzherr was an imposing-looking man. He stood six-two in his open sandals, weighed one hundred and eighty pounds and, although he was in his mid-sixties, moved with the gait of a man twenty years younger. His short silver grey hair, surrounding his tonsure, framed a heavily marked olive-skinned face which was dominated by a probing set of sapphire blue eyes. He stopped about three feet in front of them and placed his hands palm to palm in front of his heart before bowing and then issuing a warm greeting.

'*Pax et Bonum.*'

Mayer reciprocated by bowing and then introduced his companions. The abbot was immediately intrigued by Amelie, as previously Mayer had only appeared with male fugitives.

'Why are you here, my dear?'

Bursting with pride and excitement, Amelie was more than happy to reveal her identity to the priest.

'My father is the Reichsführer of the Schutzstaffel and . . .'

Mayer frowned at Amelie as he cut her dead.

'Father, we've driven non-stop through the night from Berlin and we're hungry and tired.'

In the following hour the famished guests tucked into the mini banquet laid on by the abbot and conversation quickly turned to the war and the impending defeat of Germany. Amelie had filled up on numerous portions of goats cheese and bread and was drinking red wine for only the second time in her life, and it was starting to make her feel light-headed.

'Father, I must be honest with you. There's never been a natural coalition between the Nazi party and the Church. Indeed, despite being born a Catholic, the Führer loathes religion, a fact I'm sure you're aware of.'

The abbot placed a large handful of bread down on the table and leaned forward, raising a quizzical eyebrow, encouraging Amelie to continue.

'So, why are you helping *Die Spinne?*'

'It's a question of self-preservation, Amelie. The Church has endured many threats over the centuries to its very existence, but its survival instinct has ensured its longevity. Pope Pius and his advisers at the Vatican have two grave concerns about the aftermath of the war: Communism and Jewish capitalism. For the last decade Stalin has attempted to stamp out religion inside the Soviet Union and, as the Red Menace spreads across the globe, this new ideology threatens the very fabric of religion. Fascism can be our shield against this evil disease. And then we have the Jewish problem.'

It was Amelie's turn to lean forward.

'A problem the Nazi movement and my father in particular have tried to eradicate.'

'Which, my dear, gives you the answer to your earlier question.'

Chapter Sixteen

Fribourg, Switzerland

February 1945

It was only ten in the morning but all three of the diners were exhausted. Fritzsch had barely spoken a word throughout the meal, constantly refilling his goblet with the abbot's home-made wine, while Amelie had long given up on her private game of trying to count how many top-ups the former Auschwitz deputy commandant had got through. It was crazy they were drinking, but their body clocks were all over the place, having driven through the night with no sleep.

Mayer and Holzherr did most of the talking, with Amelie hanging on every word the SS captain uttered. She was truly captivated by the man charged by her father with the task of safely transporting her to a new life and every time he threw a casual smile her way, she felt her stomach churn.

Holzherr called time on the gathering, reached deep inside the pocket of his habit and produced three large antique iron keys, which he held in the palm of one hand.

'Captain Mayer, you know where our guest rooms are. I suggest you all get some much-needed sleep. I assume you'll wait for the cover of darkness before you move on?'

Mayer was already on his feet and reaching for the keys.

'Yes, we'll be on our way by eight. We face a much shorter journey this time – it's less than a hundred miles or so to Geneva.'

The abbot's expression changed to one of surprise.

'You're not travelling to Rome, as usual?'

Mayer shrugged and bit down hard on his lip, immediately regretting the loose comment. The abbot knew the Church ratline involved a direct route to Rome and then on to Genoa, where a boat would be waiting, ready to set sail for South America. There was no point in him knowing about Amelie's château in Geneva and Mayer kicked himself for making the slip. Too much red wine had made him careless and although Holzherr was a man of the cloth, Mayer knew that was no assurance he was trustworthy.

The three bedrooms were spread out down a long gloomy corridor. Amelie's and Mayer's were diagonally opposite each other, while Fritzsch's was three doors away from both. Amelie's room was enormous, with high vaulted painted ceilings and three huge arched leaded windows offering spectacular views over the beautifully manicured rear gardens. She felt restless as she lay, fully clothed, on top of a rock-hard single bed, which looked lost in such a massive space.

Later that night she was due to arrive at her new home: a seven-bedroom, nineteenth-century château overlooking Lake Geneva but for now the raw excitement coursing through every inch of her body was focused on a single room situated no more than fifteen feet away.

Another hour passed as Amelie lay in a half-sleep, drifting in and out of consciousness, fantasising on what might happen should she conjure up the courage to knock on Mayer's door.

When she heard a gentle knock on her own door, she wasn't quite sure if she was dreaming. It was unlocked and moments later it pushed inwards, just as she opened her eyes to see the unmistakeable silhouette of SS Captain Carlos Mayer appear in the dimly lit doorway.

* * *

Amelie was cocooned in Mayer's arms, the side of her face buried in his chest, her legs knotted with his, as they lay as one, fully entwined on top of the tiny bed. She could feel her heart racing as well as her mind. She'd always considered herself to be tough but as she lay in the dark, thinking about the intimacy she'd shared with the man she'd only just met, she discovered a softness within she hadn't known existed, so she was pleased she couldn't see his reaction when she spoke. Had she been able to, she'd have witnessed a glowing smile break out across her new lover's face.

'You know, it was my first time.'

'So, what did you think?'

She wrapped herself around him even tighter, as though she were trying to squeeze every breath out of his body.

'I think I need to try it again, just to be sure I liked it.'

The pair of them broke into spontaneous laughter, as a prelude to a second round.

* * *

71

After a few hours' sleep, Amelie declared she was famished so they quickly threw on some clothes and crept downstairs to the kitchen where they began to demolish the remainder of the feast. Mayer had a mouthful of goats cheese when Amelie began bombarding him with questions.

'Where are you taking Fritzsch? What's the route? What will you do after that?'

He gulped down his food and wrapped his arm around her shoulder, pulling her close.

'So many questions, Amelie. All you need to know is that tonight I'm taking you to Geneva and moving on with Fritzsch.'

Amelie was like a dog with a bone and completely ignored his response.

'I need to know. Tell me about the journey you face.'

Mayer studied the wilful look on Amelie's face and knew he was beaten.

'Okay, okay, I give in. The ratline runs from here across the border into Italy, through Milan and Florence and on to Rome where we will stay with a prominent bishop. Fritzsch will be given a change of identity and new papers there and then we'll travel north-west along the coast until we reach Genoa. From there he'll board a cargo ship heading for South America.'

'Carlos, you almost pass Genoa before you get to Rome, that doesn't make any sense.'

'I promise you it does if you knew the fresh identity Fritzsch will receive from the bishop based there. With big fish like him, *Die Spinne* takes no chances. It's part of the escape plan personally approved by your father.'

Amelie was now firmly on the hook, desperate to learn more.

'Go on, you've got to tell me what my father has lined up for Fritzsch after that tease.'

Mayer sighed and then switched his gaze towards the opposite wall where over a dozen brown woollen habits were neatly hung in a line on individual hooks. Amelie did a double take as he nodded towards them.

'What the hell—?'

Chapter Seventeen

Fribourg, Switzerland

February 1945

'C arlos, I'm coming with you to Genoa and that's the end of it. Once you put our pain in the ass "priest" on the boat, you can escort me back to Geneva.'

Mayer eased back in the wooden dining chair, frowning as he shook his head.

'I have strict instructions from your father. Should I deviate from them it would no doubt cost me my life, so the answer must be no. Also, he's expecting to hear from us once you arrive safely at your new home in Geneva and besides, we'll face all kinds of danger once we enter Italy. The Allied invasion has been going strong for months and their forces are scattered all over the country.'

Amelie was used to getting her own way and continued to bulldoze through Mayer's concerns.'

'The entire trip will only add a few days, and I promise you, right now, my father has far bigger concerns on his mind – like keeping himself and thousands of his men alive. So, he really doesn't need to hear from me. But if you're worried, we can call him from Rome. Right now, I don't feel safe being dumped at some huge château in Switzerland and left on my own.'

'Listen, your new home has a staff of five, as you'd expect at a Lake Geneva mansion belonging to an heiress, so you'll hardly be on your own. In fact, you'll be drowning in company.'

Amelie was busy concocting a rough sandwich from the debris of the bratwurst and Gruyère and, just before she set about devouring it, decided to play her trump card.

'I wonder if my father would be interested in hearing how his favourite daughter lost her virginity to a dashing SS captain.'

Amelie's mischievous grin disappeared as she took an enormous bite from her freshly made snack, while Mayer's face crumpled with a look of disbelief. He hadn't lost many battles in his life but knew full well this was one he had to concede.

* * *

With fresh canisters of fuel loaded in the trunk, courtesy of the abbot, the Mercedes set about tackling the six-hundred-mile trip to Rome. Like the first journey from Berlin, they drove through the night, heading south-east, crossing the Swiss-Italian border just before midnight. Once again, the guards at the crossing only made a cursory check of their forged papers and it was just approaching sunrise when they reached the outskirts of the Eternal City.

When they'd embarked on their journey, Fritzsch had enquired of Mayer why Amelie was still travelling with them and had been firmly placed back in his box by a brutal put-down from the SS captain.

'Just worry about your own skin. My job is to deliver you safely on to a boat in Genoa but that doesn't mean I need to keep you happy in the meantime.'

It was just after eight in the morning when the Mercedes pulled up outside the Santa Maria church on Via di Santa Maria dell'Anima, in the heart of Rome. Mayer cut the engine and glanced through the front windscreen at the elegant three-storey rectangular façade of the sixteenth-century structure.

'Welcome to the hub of the German Catholic community in Rome. And more relevant for us, its rector is the only Nazi bishop in the city.'

Alois Karl Hudal was a controversial Austrian bishop who'd left his home country in 1933 to take up a prominent post in Rome. He was an ardent anti-communist, a zealous German nationalist and one of the most significant figures in the *Die Spinne* network. Himmler first identified the bishop as a key ally in autumn 1944 after hearing one of his antisemitic rants on the radio, which confirmed Hudal as a passionate Nazi, right down to his holy soul.

Hudal's role was twofold. He arranged for safe locations – a mixture of churches and private properties to form a web of ratlines across Italy, where fleeing Nazis could harbour while on the run. In addition, and most importantly, he worked hand in hand with the International Red Cross in Rome, an organisation empowered to issue new passports to genuine refugees. His personal relationship with one of the senior administrators meant that any applications he put forward were never queried, enabling hundreds of Nazi war criminals to receive new passports under fake identities, without scrutiny.

Mayer led them inside the church through the porched entrance that opened directly on to the rich interior, which followed the classic architectural model of a Gothic German church, with two aisles, flanked by eight chapels which rose up into the vaulted ceilings. Hudal was standing in front of the spectacular high altar, dominated by Romano's much-admired painting, *The Holy Family and Saints*. The church contained many antique treasures and Mayer speculated the value of the altar alone was worth far more than everything he'd earned from the SS since joining straight from college fifteen years earlier.

Dressed in full regalia, Hudal looked the part, and he played it to perfection. His ego was as massive as the altar behind him. His piggish face was dominated by a pair of circular steel-rimmed glasses perched on his nose, in front of a set of ruthless brown eyes. As his baritone voice boomed around the vast space, it immediately became clear he was infatuated with the Auschwitz deputy commandant and his horrific reputation as a sadistic killer.

After a quick introduction Hudal led them through to his private quarters, which were almost as ostentatious as the church itself. The four of them sat down around a marble-topped table, which could comfortably have seated another six guests. It was bare except for a large brown envelope positioned directly in front of the bishop. Hudal was clearly puzzled by Amelie's presence but completely ignored her, focusing solely on Fritzsch.

'Commandant, I've read many accounts of your time at Auschwitz. Some of your speeches have been truly inspiring to me. Unlike many of the men who've passed through my hands inside this holy place, you're a genuine hero of the National Socialist movement and it's an honour to assist you on your journey to a new life in Argentina.'

Having felt thoroughly disrespected during the previous forty-eight hours, Fritzsch lapped up the adulation coming his way, while Mayer and Amelie watched on with contempt. The bishop leaned forward, picking up the package in front of him and passing it across the table to the infamous deathcamp luminary.

'This contains your paperwork and new passport which will allow you to travel freely across Italy and also protect you on the boat crossing to South America.'

Fritzsch grabbed the package and weighed it in the palm of his hand.

'What's my new alias?'

Hudal exhibited his teeth like a hungry shark, exposing an evil smile.

'You're now a priest of the Catholic Church: Father Angelo Lugari.'

* * *

Hudal escorted the three of them to a giant villa on the historic Via dei Coronari, less than a five-minute walk away. It was a safe house owned by the church where Hudal placed Nazi escapees while their new papers were being processed. In this instance that was unnecessary, but Mayer wanted somewhere to rest and recuperate ahead of the final leg of the journey to Genoa, some three hundred miles away.

A few minutes after they arrived the bishop disappeared upstairs with Fritzsch, leaving Amelie and Mayer alone in the vast lounge, spanning the front of the villa. The ornate furnishings and artworks that adorned it were an eclectic blend of Baroque, Rococo and Neoclassical styles. Amelie was perched on the edge of a Louis XVI tapestry settee, with a carved frame, gilded with gold leaf.

'This place feels like a museum. No wonder my father detests the Church, look at this vulgar display of wealth. While the masses live in poverty, the Catholic elite live like kings. If Stalin's got one thing right, it's his utter contempt for religion.'

Mayer was leaning against a giant Rococo-inspired Carrara marble chimneypiece. On the central cartouche of the mantelpiece was a coat of arms belonging to Pope Clement XI, who'd ruled Italy for twenty-one years from 1700.

'Amelie, I despise their hypocrisy as much as you do but right now, we need their help and thankfully, they're more scared of communism than fascism. I think—'

Mayer stopped dead, as he was interrupted by the bizarre sight of the bishop re-entering the lounge alongside Fritzsch, now dressed in a black woollen priest's cassock, with a purple trim, under which he wore a black cotton shirt with the stiff white collar of the clergy. Mayer glanced across and caught Amelie's eye and a moment later they both burst out laughing. The SS captain couldn't resist an easy jibe.

'Fritzsch, how fitting for a former deputy commandant of Auschwitz to convert to becoming a man of God.'

* * *

They left Rome just before six in the evening and headed north, hugging the epic coastal road on a six-hour drive, until they reached the port city of Genoa, the capital of the Italian region of Liguria. As well as being one of the most important ports sited along the Mediterranean coastline, it was the busiest in Italy and the historic old town was one of the most densely populated areas in Europe. The medieval streets and narrow alleyways, known as the Caruggi district, created a claustrophobic warren, a perfect landscape for fugitives to hide away in while waiting for a ship to arrive to transport them to a distant land and a new life.

In the past, Mayer had sometimes spent weeks hiding out in small back-street boarding houses with groups of Nazis, awaiting the arrival of a ship that had made the seven-thousand-mile sea crossing from Buenos Aires. On this occasion the cargo ship, *The Libertad*, which had been commissioned by *Die Spinne*, was already docked in the harbour and in the previous three days had loaded up with fresh containers for the return journey, one of which accommodated a stack of gold bars earmarked for the private bank vault of the Argentine vice president, Juan Peron.

On this occasion, Mayer had booked three rooms in a flea pit which didn't appear to have a name, situated less than a ten-minute walk from the dockside. As soon as Fritzsch disappeared into his room, Mayer appeared in Amelie's. She flung herself into his arms, the door still wide open, but before they could kiss, Mayer broke off the embrace.

'My darling, I must visit the cathedral which is only a few minutes away. I need to make some calls and the priest there is a friend – part of our network. I promise I won't be more than an hour.'

They hugged again and then Mayer departed the hovel, heading for the Cathedral di San Lorenzo, a Gothic structure, consecrated in 1118, while Amelie wondered how many cockroaches she could count scurrying between the ancient wooden floorboards before his return.

It was nearly three hours later when Mayer returned to Amelie's room. She was fast asleep, fully dressed, lying in a foetal position on top of a filthy bug-ridden single mattress. Her plans for a night of passionate lovemaking had long evaporated as her body had given way to a tidal wave of complete exhaustion and her mind had drifted off into a deep sleep. Mayer breathed a heavy sigh of relief. It made what he had to do next so much easier.

* * *

The continuous knocking on Amelie's door finally did the trick, startling her from a deep slumber which had lasted for almost ten hours. Her first instinct as she awoke was to feel around in the half-dark for Mayer but then as consciousness kicked in, she realised it must be him at the door. As she rose to her feet, she was slightly mystified as she was certain she hadn't locked it when he'd left for the cathedral.

When she opened the door, she was horrified to find that the man standing on the landing facing her was a stranger. Unlike Mayer, he was the Aryan archetype: a tall, strapping body, with chiselled facial features, sparkling blue eyes, butter blond hair and a demeanour that projected a natural air of superiority. He registered the complete look of shock on her face and measured his tone accordingly.

'Fräulein, I am Captain Mayer's deputy. He has arranged for me to escort you to your home in Geneva. I have a car ready to leave and will wait outside while you pack.'

The Nazi android lifted his left hand and glanced down at his watch.

'The time now is 10.23. I suggest we leave at 10.45.'

Any drowsiness Amelie was feeling vanished as she came to her senses and let rip.

'Where's Carl? Where's Captain Mayer?'

'Fräulein, he asked me to give you this.'

He fished inside his leather jacket pocket, retrieved a white envelope and handed it over. Amelie was too stunned to reply and retreated into the sanctuary of her room before slamming the door shut. She moved across to her bed in a daze and without thinking sat down on the corner of the mattress and glared at the letter clasped in the palm of her right hand, which was now shaking with terror.

She visualised it as a hand grenade, waiting for someone to extract the pin and for a few minutes she refused to open it. When she did, the handwritten message inside was just as explosive.

My darling Amelie,

The fact you're reading this means you've met my deputy, Matthias Krüger. He is a good man, and you will be in safe hands as he escorts you to your new home. He will value your life ahead of his own.

I am now at sea with Fritzsch, on my way to Buenos Aires. It's not what I planned or what I hoped for but after I left you last night, I spoke with your father, and he insisted I personally

escort Fritzsch to Argentina. I wish I could tell you I will be able
to visit you on my return but I fear that may not be possible.
    He knows.
    You will forever be in my heart.
    Carl

Amelie read the letter three times before curling into a tight ball and weeping like a baby. Sixty miles off the coastline, on board *The Libertad*, Mayer slipped the latch on his tiny cabin, locking himself in. As he lay on his bunk and stared up at the ceiling, he wondered who else was onboard and, knowing Himmler's ruthless reputation, had serious doubts he'd survive the twenty-four-day crossing.

Chapter Eighteen

Washington D.C., United States

Berrettini had set Vargas and Hembury up in a small windowless office in the subterranean labyrinth, deep in the heart of the J. Edgar Hoover building. The two men were sitting on one side of a circular wooden table staring up at a giant whiteboard, which was pretty much obscured by black marker handwritten notes, courtesy of the Argentine detective. Vargas was nursing a polystyrene cup of black coffee which had long gone cold. Without thinking he took a swig, which he immediately regretted and shook his head before parking it on the table.

'Troy, I think it's worth having a quick history lesson on Heinrich Himmler, as whoever's deploying him as a deepfake must be pulling the strings in this organisation and if they share his same philosophy, it means we're dealing with a political zealot.'

'Yep, they're obviously a big fan of the Nazi poster boy.'

Hembury gestured towards the board which contained several bullet points about the former SS leader.

'Talk me through this.'

Vargas looked down and opened a word doc on his laptop.

'Okay, here are the headlines. In 1929 Himmler was appointed head of the SS by Hitler. At that time, it was little more than a group of thugs – a tiny rabble of a few hundred men who did Hitler's bidding. Just ten years later, by the time war broke out in Europe, Himmler had increased its size a hundred-fold and membership was a staggering two hundred and forty thousand. When it came to organisation, the man was a machine. Like his boss, he was consumed with antisem-itism and the creation of an Aryan race and in the mid-thirties he brought in a decree stating you could only join the SS if you had a clear bloodline tracing back to the end of the Thirty Years' War in 1648. He was obsessed with racial purity so any sign of Jewish blood in your ancestry within the previous three hundred years meant you were excluded from membership of his beloved organisation.'

Vargas paused for a moment to bring up a fresh page on his laptop.

'I've been checking out a few of his quotes – some of them are spine-chilling. Try this one. "The best political weapon is the weapon of terror. Cruelty demands respect. Men may hate us, but we don't ask for their love; just their fear."'

Hembury rose from his chair and walked across to the whiteboard, where he stared for a moment at the phrase, 'Architect of the Holocaust', scrawled on the board.

'Was he really the force behind it?'

'Totally. Himmler supervised the building of the first concentration camp at Dachau in 1933, which was a prison for Hitler's political enemies, and then during the war he used that model as a template to build the deathcamps for the millions of Jews and other "undesirables" rounded up by the Nazis across Europe. But his greatest claim to fame was the creation of the infamous term, *The Final Solution*. Himmler personally took the credit for the installation of the gas chambers that enabled mass genocide to become a real possibility.'

Vargas paused again as he flicked through the word document.

'Hang on, there's another monstrous quote you need to hear. "Antisemitism is exactly the same as delousing. Getting rid of lice is not a question of ideology, it's a matter of cleanliness."'

'So, the guy was a monster which begs the question: why would anyone in their right mind want to use him as a front?'

Vargas looked up from his laptop, went to grab his coffee and had second thoughts.

'Troy, we know from what Mike told us, Himmler was the mastermind behind the creation of *Die Spinne,* so whoever is running it today must see him as some kind of hero – a Nazi legend. The more I learn about him the worse the story goes. If Hitler was the king, Himmler had his own kingdom in the shape of the SS and his senior officers ran the extermination camps on his behalf. God knows who we're dealing with right now.'

Hembury retook his seat at the table and glanced down at his iPad Pro to check on his own notes.

'The deepfake video of Himmler was not only perfect but technically it was like a Netflix release, embedded with sub-titles in ten languages. Its audience may be a small select group, but they're obviously based across the world in different conti-nents. I guess our starting point must be the two names Mike's

86

tech boys managed to break open: our politicians in Italy and Australia. We've got to assume they're members of this covert organisation – whatever it is.'

Vargas nodded thoughtfully as his mind searched for a name.

'Troy, have you heard of the Bilderberg Group? They're a bunch of former political leaders, financiers and media moguls who supposedly meet every year in a secret location – a different one each time. The story goes that Bilderberg seeks to control financial markets and world events to shape a New World Order that suits their own agenda. Supposedly bank rates, inflation, elections, even wars are manipulated by them.'

Hembury arched an eyebrow, curious to see where Vargas was heading, and the chief inspector ploughed on with his thought process.

'No one knows for sure if Bilderberg really exists but thanks to the content we've uncovered on the USB, it appears the Spider Network is real, very live and potentially far more dangerous.'

Vargas closed his laptop and rose from the table.

'Yep, people have already started dying because of it. Let's check in with Mike and decide where we're heading first – Rome or Sydney.'

Chapter Nineteen

Rome, Italy

T he Gulfstream G550 knifed into Washington's onyx black sky at three in the morning and made light work of the four-and-a-half-thousand-mile Atlantic crossing, smoothly transporting Vargas and Hembury to the Italian capital known as the 'Eternal City'. Berrettini had requisitioned the FBI's counterterrorism jet for the unscheduled trip and after touching down at Leonardo da Vinci airport, the pair jumped into one of hundreds of white taxis parked outside Terminal 3 and headed for the city centre.

After a brief pitstop at their hotel they made their way to a rendezvous with Franco Mancini, the head of L'Agenzia Informazioni e Sicurezza Interna, the government security division inside Italy, more commonly known as AISI. Mancini was an old friend of Berrettini's, and their shared Italian heritage ensured a close working relationship between the two agencies. He was waiting for them at a strategically placed table on the massive rooftop terrace of Rome's foremost restaurant, the Aroma, which boasted unrivalled panoramic views of the city, dominated by the Colosseum which appeared to be within touching distance.

The three men had worked together briefly a year earlier when they'd collaborated on an international terrorism case and that episode ensured a warm reception from the Italian spy chief when they met up. Mancini was wearing one of his trademark carbon-grey Canali suits, with perfectly matched accessories. After a traditional Italian double-kiss greeting they joined him at his table where they were promptly served with a round of ice-cold Peronis, along with several plates of mixed nuts, pecorino cheese and black olives. Hembury had visited Rome before but for Vargas it was his first time, and he was utterly mesmerised by the jaw-dropping views created by the ancient architecture. He gestured with his green beer bottle towards the world-famous amphitheatre which domi-nated the skyline.

'Franco, seeing the Colosseum for real is something else. I must have watched *Gladiator* twenty times – it's one of my favourite movies – and right now I'm expecting Russell Crowe to march through the restaurant in nothing but a loincloth.'

Mancini smiled and rested his arm on Vargas's shoulder.

'My friend, your imagination is not too far off the mark. Look over there.'

Vargas twisted around and immediately spotted a large framed and signed headshot of the Australian actor on the wall behind the bar, alongside several other famous celebrities who'd frequented the Aroma. Hembury burst into laughter and took a large gulp from his beer bottle before changing the subject.

'Franco, I believe Mike filled you in as to why we're here.'

Mancini's expression gave way to a slight grimace as he nodded.

'Yes, of course, but it seems you guys have very little to go on about this Spider Network?'

Vargas picked up on the cue.

'That's right, which is why we're keen to talk with Carrozza, as she's one of two politicians we believe might be linked to it. We're on a fishing trip. What can you tell us about her?'

'Well, she's a very bright, powerful, well-connected woman with strong right-wing views, who's risen to a high government position and is heavily tipped as a future prime minister. In my role as the head of AISI, I report directly to her once a week, which is very fortunate for you guys as it means I've been able to secure you a face-to-face meeting, which trust me, is no easy matter.'

Hembury eased forward in his chair.

'When are we seeing her?'

'Tomorrow morning at nine in her office at the Palazzo Montecitorio. You've got ten minutes, which is often more than I get – so don't be late. I'll be present as well. I'll text you the address but it's no more than a five-minute walk from your hotel. I've told Carrozza you're working for Berrettini at the Bureau and that you need to discuss a possible imminent terrorist threat.'

Vargas glanced across at Hembury, knowing his colleague shared the same thought as him.

'Christ, Franco, that's a bit strong as a reason for—'

Mancini cut in.

'Trust me, anything less and you'd have stood no chance of getting to see her. I've done my bit as a favour to Mike, the rest is up to you guys. But I am curious to know what the hell you're going to ask her?'

Neither man replied for a moment and then Hembury broke the silence.

'We might just enquire if she has a love of spiders.'

Mancini rose from his seat indicating their meeting was over. His almost permanent frown had given way to the hint of a smile.

'I've ordered you both the tasting menu – the Taglioni in sheep sauce is a real highlight. Plus, they keep over six hundred different labels of champagne in their cellar, so I've ordered you a bottle of 2016 Pol Roger, which is my favourite.'

Mancini registered the slightly incredulous expressions on both men's faces.

'Don't act so surprised. Mike asked me to look after you both, so have a good night and I'll see you in the minister's office in the morning.'

The Italian nodded a final goodbye and then departed at speed, weaving an elegant path through an assault course of small tables packed with tourists as he headed towards the exit. Hembury reached for his Peroni bottle and drained the contents. As a lover of Italian food, he could hardly believe his luck. Just before he spoke, he looked across at Vargas who had a beaming smile plastered across his face.

'What the hell. When in Rome . . .'

* * *

The Pasticceria Caleffi situated in the heart of the Eternal City offered everything you could possibly ask for from a family-run Italian café: old-world charm, first-rate coffee, friendly service, and delicious home-made chocolate-filled croissants. All those factors combined to make it a regular haunt for Alessia Carrozza, Italy's minister of the interior, but its main attraction for her was its location. It was less than a three-minute walk away from the Piazza di Monte Citorio where the Palazzo Montecitorio was situated, one of Italy's two parliament buildings.

At forty-four, Carrozza was a rising star in Italian politics, a conservative-leaning populist and nationalist branded by her political opponents as a dangerous right-wing fascist. She described herself as a Christian and proudly declared she sought power to defend three pillars: God, family and the fatherland. She vigorously opposed same-sex marriage and LGBTQ+ parenting, claiming nuclear families could only work with male-female pairings.

Carrozza's first foray into mainstream politics had taken place sixteen years earlier in 2008, when she'd been appointed Minister for Business in the fourth Berlusconi government, a role she'd held for eighteen months.

She was a classic Italian beauty, having inherited her looks from her mother who'd been a *Vogue* model back in the day, before retiring at twenty-three after marrying into one of the wealthiest families in Rome. Carrozza's sparkling green eyes, high cheekbones, full lips and perfect olive skin made her a head-turner.

Three mornings a week, her government ride, a chauffeur-driven Maserati Quattroporte, dropped her off at the Pasticceria, where she'd enjoy a freshly baked chocolate crois-sant, along with copious amounts of black tea, courtesy of a classic Spode Blue Italian teapot. The café's owner, Enzo Conti, was always there to serve his VIP guest in person and to ensure her single table, tucked discreetly away in the back corner and dressed with a white tablecloth and single fresh pink rose, was always available.

It was just after eight thirty in the morning when Carrozza double-kissed Conti before taking her seat. She immediately dived into her copy of the *Corriere della Sera*, Italy's foremost national newspaper and five minutes later washed down her first bite of chocolate croissant with a cup of black tea, which Enzo dutifully poured for her. She didn't live long enough for him to pour a second.

* * *

The previous day, Arsène Boucher, one of Legrand's most trusted freelance operatives, had taken the TGV from Paris to Milan and then travelled on to Rome where he'd arrived just before midnight. Boucher was a gun for hire, a hitman with twenty years' experience of working for the mob out of Sicily, as well as a select group of high-net-worth employers who paid well for his unique skills and never questioned his fees.

Boucher was in his early fifties, a plain man who looked at least five years older than he really was, which suited his purpose. His wiry brown hair was combed over a growing bald patch, and heavy skin pouches under his deep-set brown eyes, along with a bulbous nose and thin lips completed the nondescript look.

His willowy six-foot frame was clothed in a dark blue cheap high-street suit, a white cotton shirt and matching plain blue tie. Over the top he wore a full-length single-breasted black polyester raincoat that was almost as old as he was. Like its owner it had seen better times. He was the sort of man you'd never pick out in an identity parade as he blended in with the crowd, which was just the way he liked it.

It was just after midnight when Boucher exited Roma Termini station and headed straight for a nearby McDonald's he knew stayed open until 2am. He'd no accommodation booked as he wasn't planning to stay for more than a few hours and no luggage to speak of, just a black rucksack, firmly strapped to his back. It contained materials provided by Legrand – everything he required for the job. He selected a quiet table in the huge downstairs section which was deserted except for a couple of late-night stragglers who were hanging around for the warmth and shelter on offer, having long finished their food. He double-checked he was out of sight of the three CCTV cameras positioned around the dining area before opening the backpack and spreading its contents over the white Formica-topped table.

Boucher allowed himself a wry smile as he glanced down at the meagre contents that had been stashed inside the bag when he'd left Paris, and which were now about to earn him a six-figure payday. There were only four items: a transparent plastic folder containing three 6 x 4 inch colour photos, a small cardboard box the size of an aftershave container, a keyring holder with a set of two keys and a pair of laminated Norfoil gloves, especially manufactured for the handling of toxic and corrosive chemical products. When Legrand had offered him this last-minute assignment, he'd jumped at the chance to earn some easy money but knew the job didn't come without risk.

He laid out the three photos in a neat line and spent a few seconds studying them, even though he'd previously viewed them on his twelve-hour train journey. The first one showed the exterior of the Pasticceria Caleffi, the second was a shot of the back entrance situated in a small dark alleyway and the third was a picture of an ornate blue teapot. Once he was happy, he shuffled them together and placed them back inside the folder. Next, he collected the keyring and put it inside his jacket, then he grabbed the gloves, stuffing one into each of his raincoat pockets. Finally, he warily picked up the small cardboard box which he placed back inside the backpack, along with the folder.

He exited the fast-food diner and typed the address of the café into the Google Maps app on his cell. It informed him it would take thirty-five minutes to cover the two and a quarter mile walk that lay ahead. None of this came as a surprise and after a quick look at his watch, he estimated he'd reach the café at about one thirty in the morning. Once he arrived, he'd still have a thirty-minute wait before he could act as the night cleaners weren't due to finish much before two o'clock.

Boucher took his time on the walk and finally arrived outside the front of the Pasticceria Caleffi at one thirty-five. A couple of ceiling strip lights were on inside and he could see the silhouettes of two cleaners moving around, one cleaning tabletops, while the other appeared to be mopping the floor.

He crossed the road and about fifty yards along found a perfect hiding place in a recessed shop doorway of a double-fronted leather handbag shop. Now it was just a case of waiting. He retrieved a pair of earbuds from a jacket pocket and within moments his brain was flooded with the sound of his favourite aria – the Toreador Song from Act 2 of *Carmen*. The unpretentious hitman always found opera to be the perfect prelude to a high-risk assignment.

Despite the music, his eyes never left the café and at one forty-five, two elderly women appeared in the doorway, one locking up while the other carried some equipment across the sidewalk to a small white van parked up directly outside. In less than a minute they'd pulled away and Boucher smiled to himself as he figured they'd short-changed their employers by fifteen minutes, but he wasn't about to report them and was grateful for the extra time.

He casually exited the doorway, crossed the street and made his way around the back of the café to a small murky alleyway. As he peered through the gloom, he could make out a couple of giant black wheelie bins at the far end, parked up alongside a single wooden door. He grabbed the keyring from inside his jacket pocket and moved stealthily towards the rear entrance of the café. The mortice and Yale keys provided by Legrand sweetly opened the locks and the entire operation took less than fifteen seconds.

The back door opened on to a narrow hallway which in turn revealed an unlocked internal door, leading directly into a large kitchen area. It was pitch-black inside, so Boucher switched on the torch light on his cell. It illuminated a long run of four wall-mounted cupboards, a double aluminium sink and two free-standing wooden-topped workstations, where food was prepped every day.

Nothing was on display, so he figured the crockery and, most importantly, the blue Spode teapot was stashed away somewhere inside one of the cupboards. After a quick search he found it but moments later his wry smile morphed into a scowl. The cell torch perfectly illuminated the blue teapot resting on a lower shelf but alongside it was the outline of a similar object and as he slowly panned the light source to the right, his heart skipped a beat as he realised there were two teapots – and they were identical.

Legrand's planning had been close to perfection, seemingly factoring in every permutation but it hadn't allowed for this scenario. For a moment he considered calling his employer for guidance but then his instincts shut down that thought, and a fresh one entered his mind. He rested his backpack on one of the workstations, pulled on the Norfoil gloves and retrieved the small cardboard box, carefully opening the top section.

The silver gloves were so bulky they made delicate actions tricky but he'd plenty of time and if he were to survive the night, he had to be careful as he knew he was handling some kind of poison. Inside the box was a tiny 15ml glass vial, 2.5 inches high, containing a colourless liquid. He appeared to move in slow motion, cautiously removing the black plastic cap as though he were disabling a small, fully armed bomb.

Boucher turned his attention to one of the teapots, gently removing its lid and placing it on the wooden surface of the free-standing unit. He took a deep breath before picking up the bottle between his two fingers and moved his hand forward until it was hovering directly above the open teapot. He recalled Legrand's strict instructions to use only two drops, but the amount of liquid released appeared so tiny he decided to double the amount. Had he known the identity of the poison, he'd never have improvised.

Polonium-210, a highly radioactive isotope, is regarded as the most toxic poison on the planet when swallowed or inhaled.

It's a rare natural element, found in uranium ore, and the only country known to actively produce it is Russia. In liquid form it's colourless and tasteless, making it the perfect killing machine. Back in 2006, former FSB agent Alexander Litvinenko was murdered in London by two Russian intelligence agents who had allegedly transported the radioactive poison from Russia to the United Kingdom.

It was one of the most sensational assassinations of recent times which is why it intrigued and excited Legrand and, as the tentacles of *Die Spinne* reached far and wide across the globe, he'd been able to secure the lethal dose from a black-market source who worked at the Mayak nuclear facility in Ozyorsk, near the city of Chelyabinsk in the Urals, where most of Russia's polonium-210 was produced.

Boucher replaced the teapot before reaching for the one next to it. In the following two minutes he carried out an identical procedure, adding four drops of the liquid poison to the inside. His random decision to double the amount of polonium-210 meant whoever drank tea poured from the pot would be swallowing many times the amount consumed by Litvinenko.

As he left the café through the same door he'd entered minutes earlier, he mused about the unlucky customer who wasn't his target but who would undoubtedly suffer a painful and ugly death purely due to their love of black tea. An unfortunate casualty but once the hitman had discovered a second teapot, he couldn't chance fifty-fifty odds. With Legrand as his employer, failure wasn't an option.

* * *

CHAPTER NINETEEN

Later that morning Carrozza arrived at the Pasticceria Caleffi at her usual time and took up residence at her regular table. A few minutes later she'd demolished her croissant and hadn't quite finished her cup of black tea, when a scorching pain began in the pit of her stomach that had suddenly transformed into a blast furnace. The back of her throat felt as though it was being invaded by an avalanche of razor blades and seconds later she slumped forwards, smashing her head against the table before tumbling to the floor. Two teenage girls seated nearby witnessed the entire event and screamed in horror but by the time the café's owner reached her, she was dead.

At that precise moment, Boucher was sleeping soundly on a high-speed train heading to Milano Centrale station, from where he planned to transfer to the TGV that would take him safely back to Paris. The backpack resting in the rack above his seat still contained the glass vial as Legrand had insisted he return it after completing the job. Its contents were far too valuable to waste on one assignment and the media mogul already had plans to use it again in the near future.

* * *

Less than a hundred yards away from the café, Vargas and Hembury were soaking up the magnificent architectural sights as they strode across the Piazza di Monte Citorio, heading for the Italian parliament building and their meeting with Alessia Carrozza. Hembury was the first to spot the commotion as he heard frantic screams moments ahead of seeing dozens of people stream into the square from a small side street where the Caleffi was situated.

99

Thirty years of instinct as a police lieutenant kicked in and he was drawn like a magnet towards the source of the chaos. Vargas followed suit and the two men sprinted towards the cause of the mayhem as everyone else fled in the opposite direction. Moments later they burst into the café, which was now deserted except for the distraught owner who was kneeling over the lifeless body of the woman they'd flown four and a half thousand miles to meet. Her dead eyes were bulging and beginning to turn bloodshot and her lips, covered in froth, were slightly parted.

Vargas studied Carrozza's death mask.

'Troy, it looks like some kind of poisoning.'

Hembury shook his head in disbelief at the tragic sight in front of them.

'Christ, whoever's behind this network is wasting no time in cleaning house.'

Chapter Twenty

Sydney, Australia

Jack Cook was an unusual politician. The forty-eight-year-old federal treasurer of the Australian government was viewed by many right-leaning politicians inside parliament as an untrustworthy turncoat. For many years he'd been the pin-up for the right-wing nationalists when they were in power as part of a centre-right coalition with the Liberal Party. But in 2021, twelve months before the socialists won by a landslide, he'd switched allegiances and signed up with the Labour Party. His cautious conservative principles made him the perfect fit to run the treasury for the new left-wing government as he could help counter the obvious accusation from the right that the new socialist government would be obsessed with excessive spending.

The public lapped up his born-again stance but those who knew him best were sceptical, refusing to accept he'd genuinely ditched his political ideology, suspecting instead his change of heart was just a cynical ploy to grab power.

Cook was certainly untrustworthy when it came to his personal life, particularly in his marriage. He was a serial womaniser and Cathy, his wife of twenty years, finally called time after she discovered he'd been keeping two mistresses on the go for over eighteen months. One of them, a casino croupier, was based in an apartment he funded in Canberra, just a few miles from Parliament House, while the other, a local radio reporter, lived in Hunter Valley, a two-hour drive away from his Sydney home. The double humiliation was the final straw for his wife, who kicked him out of the opulent penthouse apartment in Double Bay which he shared with her and their two teenage daughters.

For the last three weeks he'd taken a suite at the Park Hyatt hotel which was situated on the edge of Sydney Harbour and boasted a spectacular view of the world-famous Opera House. It was a three-hour drive from his day job in parliament, but he planned to stay there for the foreseeable future in the hope that, once the sensational headlines wafted away, his wife's red-hot temper might cool, along with her threat of divorce proceedings. For now, he'd take his medicine and ask for forgiveness, expressing extreme contrition and remorse for his behaviour.

He was a stunning-looking man, and he knew it. His sculpted jawline was accentuated by a neatly trimmed light beard, while his deep-set hazel eyes and perfectly groomed thick brown hair combined to striking effect. A Harry Potter-esque scar on his forehead, the result of a knife attack he'd received as a student when he'd worked as a temporary nightclub bouncer, simply added to his attraction. Although he was only five foot nine, just like his hero, Tom Cruise, he wore elevator shoes which boosted his height to six feet.

CHAPTER TWENTY

Cook was working late in his office, taking one-to-one meetings with government ministers who were pleading their case for above-inflation increases for their respective departments ahead of an upcoming financial review. A hundred and eighty miles away, back in Sydney, a woman he'd never met and never would, was making careful preparations for his untimely death.

* * *

Ava Kelly was her fake name; nobody knew her real one. She was a freelance operator who worked for two of the main criminal gangs based in Sydney. One was run by a Middle Eastern syndicate; the other was homegrown. There were over a dozen crime gangs in the city, all of which distributed class A drugs and most of Kelly's work involved taking down over-eager members of the smaller ones when they threatened to tread on the toes of the big boys.

When things turned quiet, she dabbled in the dark web for anonymous clients who paid astonishingly well and always in Bitcoin. This latest one really intrigued her as the job didn't require her to kill anyone in person. She simply needed to collect a package and transport its contents to a hotel room in the city. The whole procedure would take less than two hours, for which she would receive the equivalent of fifty thousand dollars. As she strode across the giant concourse in Sydney Central Station heading towards the section housing over two hundred lockers, she smiled inwardly, wishing all jobs could be as easy as this one. In her left hand, she gripped the handles of an empty green leather holdall and in her right, a tiny key with

103

a white circular tag numbered 137, which she'd just collected from a designated rubbish bin in Hyde Park.

It only took Kelly a few seconds to locate the correct locker and the key did the rest. Inside, as expected, was a sealed white envelope and a small rectangular Tupperware box, containing four live arachnids. Sydney funnel-web spiders are native to the eastern coast and regarded as the deadliest spider in the world and, unlike some venomous spiders which don't necessarily inject venom when they bite, funnel-webs invariably do. The male of the species is by far the most dangerous as its giant fangs are capable of biting through fingernails and leather shoes and, right now, Kelly was staring at four of them, crammed inside the plastic container. She stuffed the envelope into the inside pocket of her puffer jacket and carefully slid the box into her holdall, secured the zipper and made her way to the taxi rank.

Fifteen minutes later she entered the opulent white-pillared lobby of the Park Hyatt and headed directly for the bank of lifts located behind the reception desks. The prestigious hotel only had four floors, with one hundred and fifty-five guest rooms. Kelly was only interested in one of them – a harbour suite situated on the fourth floor – room 430. Her instructions had been very precise. She was to arrive in the corridor outside the suite at exactly seven thirty in the evening when the maid working that floor would be doing the turndown service.

Kelly exited the lift, checked the room number signs, and turned left, following the directions stamped on the wall. As she walked along the corridor she glanced down at her digital watch. She was two minutes early and once she reached the room, she turned and checked back over her shoulder as she'd reached a dead-end, but the long, straight corridor was empty.

Then she heard a door opening and, as she spun around, she came face to face with a chambermaid emerging from room 430. The young Asian girl stood frozen in the doorway, using her foot as a temporary doorstop. There was an air of panic about her as she looked around, scanning the hallway behind Kelly for any other sign of life. The two women locked eyes and for a moment neither spoke, then the chambermaid offered up her hand.

'Have you got my money?'

Her strong New South Wales accent suggested she was at least second-generation Chinese Australian. Kelly reached inside her jacket and took out the white envelope and handed it over. The transaction took less than five seconds, after which the young chambermaid shot off down the corridor leaving Kelly to enter the suite alone. As the spring-loaded door closed behind her, the first thing she saw was the breathtaking view of the Opera House which seemed so close, she felt she could almost touch it. The iconic structure was perfectly framed by the floor-to-ceiling glass windows which ran the entire length of the wall. It was her first time inside such a magnificent hotel room, and she took a moment to savour the splendour of the giant open-plan suite.

As Kelly looked around the room, she noted the wall-mounted Bose digital music system, the giant LED flatscreen and the four private balconies which wrapped around the 145-square-metre suite. Finally, her eyes landed on the prize: a huge, king-size bed, fully turned down, with two Swiss chocolates laid out perfectly symmetrically on the pillows. She made her way across the room and gently placed the holdall on the blue carpet by the side of the bed. She carefully peeled back the white duvet and matching sheet underneath, revealing another one that covered the mattress. As she leaned over the bed, her hands appreciated the natural softness of the finest Egyptian cotton sheets money could buy, which were about to become a temporary home for four of the deadliest creatures on earth.

Kelly stood upright and stared down at the bag. In the previous twenty-four hours she'd simulated the next move dozens of times at home, using four small bars of soap inside a plastic box as substitutes. She'd perfected a technique which allowed her to tip the funnel-webs on to the mattress and then cover them with a sheet and duvet in one fluid movement. As she unzipped the bag and retrieved the plastic box, she realised her hands were slightly shaky. Four bars of soap were no substitute for the real thing. As she stared at the contents it appeared as though the spiders had gathered as one and there was no sign of movement. For a second, she wondered if they were dead.

She prised open the lid but kept it firmly in position as she moved the container on to the bed, placing it upside down. The four black blobs inside separated as they slid forward and were now resting on the lid. It was as though the sudden movement had woken them from a deep sleep. She took one last deep breath and then, in a flash, slid the lid across and tilted the Tupperware box, emptying the spiders on to the mattress. With consummate skill she pulled the sheet and duvet on top of them before they had a chance to move. She sprang back and glared down at the bed that was now a potential death chamber. She knew the spiders would enjoy the warmth and darkness provided but had no idea how long they'd remain in place, so she grabbed her things and ran out of the suite.

As Kelly exited the front entrance of the hotel carrying the now empty holdall, she couldn't help but wonder who the suite belonged to. Maybe the occupant was a drug baron from out of town or a high-roller with too many debts. Either way, they were a dead man walking. Had she known his identity and how risky taking on the might of the Australian government could be, she'd have either declined the job or charged ten times more for it.

Chapter Twenty-One

Sydney, Australia

I t was just before midnight when Jack Cook returned to the Park Hyatt following the long drive from Parliament House with his protection officer. The treasurer was exhausted having faced down six angry socialist ministers, rejecting their arguments for extra departmental funding with ease. He despised them all as they were evidently too stupid to realise he had a completely different agenda.

Cook craved a hot shower to wash the idiots out of his thoughts but then a massive wave of tiredness swept over him, and he thought better of it. It took just a few seconds for him to undress, flinging his two-piece linen suit, shirt and tie on to a tub armchair by the giant window. He ripped back the duvet and top sheet and flopped on to the bed where he lay perfectly still for a few moments before reaching across to switch off the sidelight, plunging the room into total darkness.

Before long, he was in a deep sleep and it was fifty minutes later, just before one in the morning, when an excruciating, indescribable pain jolted him awake. It felt as though the soft, fleshy skin on the inside of his right thigh had been stabbed by two red-hot pokers. He yelled out as he writhed around the bed in agony – the searing sensation engulfing every part of his body. His right hand instinctively shot downwards to the source of the pain, swiping at the spider, which had released its fangs from the bite but was still clinging to him. The funnel-web was swept away and at the same time, Cook rolled to his left until he fell over the side of the bed, crashing down on to the floor.

Despite the agonising pain, he had the presence of mind to turn on the sidelight and grab his cell from the bedside table. He'd realised what had happened and knew what he needed to do next. He punched in the 000 emergency number and within seconds he'd informed the paramedic service of his where-abouts and the need for a dose of antivenom to be waiting for him at the hospital as soon as an ambulance could get him there.

Having lived in Sydney all his life he'd seen dozens of TV shows explaining what actions to take in the event of being bitten by a funnel-web and, although he hadn't seen it, he'd no doubt the lethal spider was the cause of the two giant puncture marks on his thigh. His next move was to create a pressure bandage, which he improvised with the help of a wet hand towel from the bathroom which he tied tightly around his leg. The pain was savage, but he had one more call to make.

He reached again for his cell and after two rings his protection officer picked up.

'John, I've been bitten on my leg by a bastard funnel-web – can you believe it? An ambulance is on its way. Can you make the appropriate calls and I'll either see you here or at the hospital.'

John Patterson, Cook's personal protection officer, had leapt out of bed and was already dragging on his trousers.

'Sir, I'm just around the corner. I'll be there in less than five minutes.'

The red and white chequered ambulance screeched to a halt directly outside the main entrance of the hotel and, moments later, two paramedics dashed through the lobby wheeling a stainless-steel gurney, aiming for the lifts. The lead paramedic shouted at the night porter to join them as they needed a key to Cook's suite. When they entered, they found the government minister lying on the carpet, curled in a tight ball, clutching his right leg with both hands. His face was ruby red, dripping with sweat and his eyes were bulging as if they were trying to escape from his head, but he was still conscious.

He relaxed his body as the first responders carefully lifted him up on to the gurney. They were strapping him into place when he did a double take. Although his vision was blurred, he was sure he saw two large funnel-webs scurrying along the skirting board between the door and the windows.

'Christ, this place . . . It's riddled with them.'

The paramedics ignored his ramblings and wheeled the gurney along the corridor at speed. As they reached the lifts one of them noticed the towel strapped to Cook's right leg.

'Nice work, sir. We'll improve on that as soon as we get you into the ambulance.'

Cook was in far too much pain to reply but nodded his appreciation. He could feel himself drifting in and out of consciousness and the next thing he knew he was being hauled inside the back of the ambulance when a familiar voice cut through the murky fog in his brain.

'Sir, how are you feeling?'

John Patterson jumped into the back of the vehicle, much to the annoyance of the paramedics, who were just about to shut the rear doors. The senior one was clearly furious.

'Can you get out? There's no room for you here. This man needs treatment right now, so—'

'I'm not going anywhere, my job is to protect the minister, so you guys are just going to have to work around me.'

The paramedic grunted as he slammed the doors shut. The ambulance sped off and Patterson crouched low alongside the gurney, his head next to the government minster's, who'd lost consciousness once again.

'What hospital?'

Both paramedics ignored the question. The one closest to the gurney was busy filling a syringe and didn't even bother to look up. Patterson upped the ante.

'I said: what hospital are we taking the second highest government minister in the land to?'

Syringe man glanced up but avoided eye contact with the protection officer and seemed to take an eternity before answering.

'Royal Prince Albert, the antivenom serum is being prepared for our arrival.'

'That makes no sense. It's five miles away. St Vincent's is less than half that distance. What the hell are you—'

Patterson never finished his sentence. The paramedic closest to him leapt upwards like a Jack-in-the-box, launching himself towards the officer with the precision of a guided missile. His right hand had a vice-like grip on the hypodermic syringe, now filled to the brim with the anaesthetic, Propofol, which he plunged deep into the side of Patterson's neck as if it were a knife. The protection officer's body folded inwards like a cheap deckchair before collapsing on to the floor of the ambulance, with his assailant lying on top of him. Cook, who was still drifting in and out of consciousness, was oblivious to the whole event.

The paramedic withdrew the syringe and clambered over the prone body of the protection officer, to reach the comms unit. He nodded to his colleague and then pushed the button to speak to the driver.

'Danny, things are going to turn tasty in the next few minutes when the real ambulance turns up. Keep to the B roads as much as you can and, hopefully, we'll avoid any problems.'

The fake paramedic refilled the same syringe and injected a similar quantity of the anaesthetic into a vein on the inside of Cook's left arm. His colleague was busy searching Patterson's body. It didn't take him long to find what he was looking for. He triumphantly held a cell phone up in the air and waved it at his colleague.

'For all we know matey boy's phone may be trackable by someone at ASIO, best get rid.'

ASIO was the acronym for the Australian Security Intelligence Organisation, based in Canberra, and the kidnapper wasn't wrong. Since notifying them he was about to board an ambulance with the minister, Patterson had ignored six texts from a colleague which had triggered an alert as right now no one in the security services had any idea where he or the treasury minister were. The only thing they did know was that both men were currently in the back of an ambulance that had nothing to do with the emergency services.

Thirty seconds later the ambulance pulled to a halt in a quiet side street and the back doors swung open for a few seconds, allowing one of the kidnappers enough to time to leap out and dart across to a black rubbish bin in the front garden of a suburban bungalow. He'd already disassembled the cell and removed the SIM card so it only took a moment for him to drop the parts inside.

After that short stop, the ambulance travelled directly south for two hours before reaching its destination; a remote pig farm situated inside Morton National Park, close to Fitzroy Falls. The thirty-acre spread was home to over three hundred saddlebacks and run by a small farming family who'd been delighted to be offered a five-thousand-dollar cash payment twenty-four hours earlier, to let the property out for two days to a man claiming to be an animal photographer, who wanted the place to himself. Even though the black and white breed was quite rare, it was still a very odd request, but the money was welcome, and the pig farmer and his wife simply travelled eight miles across the National Park to stay with his in-laws, who ran a smallholding.

The man who used the alias, Peter Howard, had no interest whatsoever in the saddlebacks but was very excited about a piece of machinery located in a small section of heavy wood-land towards the rear of the farm. The machine in question was a Morbark Eeger Beever 1415 – a state-of-the-art mobile wood-chipper and, by the time the ambulance arrived and parked up by a copse of trees, Howard had learned how to operate it, having spent the previous four hours shredding a selection of tree stumps and large branches. As the ferocious machine demolished the incoming wood, thousands of tiny chippings shot out of the end of a giant funnel and landed in a large steel skip positioned underneath it.

Howard watched as the two bogus paramedics and the driver, still dressed in their phoney uniforms, offloaded Cook and Patterson's bodies from the back of the ambulance. He'd never met the kidnappers before but straight away spotted an obvious problem. As far as he was concerned, he was being paid to dispose of one body and these clowns had turned up with two. He couldn't tell if the bodies were drugged or dead and he didn't really care; he just wanted to double his fee. As the kidnappers approached him, struggling to carry Cook's body between them, he let rip.

'Is this some kind of joke? Are you guys trying to take the piss out of me? My deal was to shred one dead body.'

The kidnappers let Cook fall to the ground as though he were a sack of potatoes. The senior of the three men reached inside his trouser pocket and produced a syringe.

'Listen, mate, unless you fancy a dose of what these guys have just had, I suggest you keep your mouth shut and help me and my friends here load these bastards into the chipper. If you've got any issues, take them up with whoever employed you. The quicker we do this, the better.'

Howard grimaced, cursing under his breath, as he decided he didn't fancy the odds of three against one. But he didn't want to totally cave.

'Anyway, I was supposed to be dealing with a dead body not a drugged one.'

'Don't you worry about that. The triple dose these guys have had would knock out an elephant.'

The kidnapper half-turned and gestured back towards the other body lying by the back of the ambulance.

114

CHAPTER TWENTY-ONE

'Fancy giving us a hand with the other one?'

In the following hour the gruesome killings of Cook and Patterson were harrowing to watch, even for experienced murderers. The only consolation for the two victims was they were completely unaware of their appalling fate, being so heavily anaesthetised. The Eeger Beever, now transformed into a macabre slaughtering machine, produced an ear-piercing grinding noise as it turned human bone and cartilage into tiny blood-splattered pieces. The shredded human remains created a grisly red and white blanket on top of the dark brown wood fragments inside the skip, so for another hour, the three men combined forces to shred dozens of branches, creating a fresh duvet of chippings that completely covered any evidence of what lay underneath.

As the four men went to go their separate ways, Howard, who was still simmering about being ripped off by his anonymous employer, fired off a parting shot.

'By the way, who were those guys?'

Syringe man winked at his colleagues before replying.

'Just a couple of no-marks who didn't pay their gambling debts.'

Chapter Twenty-Two

Geneva, Switzerland

May 1945

E melia Müller, alias Amelie Legrand, had been ensconced in her new home for just over two months. The seven-bedroom nineteenth-century château set in twelve acres of parkland, purchased with *Die Spinne* funds, was truly spectacular. Himmler had ensured Amelie's recently assumed position in life as the mysterious heiress of a moneyed banking family would be played out in the splendid grandeur of a Swiss mansion befitting her improved status.

The château stood on a vast travertine stone terrace in the middle of manicured gardens with breathtaking panoramic views of the lake in the foreground, with Mont Blanc and the French Alps beyond. The main rectangular-shaped white tuffeau stone façade was flanked by cemeterial turrets lined with burgundy-tiled roofs which stood proud of the central building, creating a castle-like appearance. The gardens running down to the lake were divided into three sections by tree-lined alleys. One contained a rose garden dotted with sculptures of mythological figures including Dionysus the god of wine, while another housed a grass tennis court and the third, a heated outdoor pool alongside a free-standing pavilion.

Since the day she'd arrived, Amelie had never ventured out from her luxurious lakeside property and despite numerous attempts to contact Mayer, she never heard a word from the SS captain. She'd no idea if he were dead or alive and on the two occasions she'd mentioned his name to her father, he'd told her in no uncertain terms it was a no-go area. While one side of her brain grieved his loss, the other clung to the slight hope he might still be alive, and that small flicker of belief kept her going.

Her reclusive lifestyle was interrupted twice a day at precisely nine in the morning and three in the afternoon when two local French tutors came to the château to give her lessons. Amelie's schoolgirl French was pretty good, but she was determined to be fluent by the time she migrated to Paris, which according to her father was still eighteen months away. She could understand the language far better than speak it and to supplement her home tutoring, she tuned in every weekday at noon to a French radio station to hear the latest news on the aftermath of the war. It was during one of those transmissions, on Thursday 24 May, that her life changed forever.

* * *

Bremervörde, Germany

21 May 1945, three days earlier

Following Germany's formal surrender on 7 May, and with Hitler declared dead, the Allied forces turned their attention to tracking down prominent Nazis who were desperately trying to flee the country. Top of their list were Martin Bormann and Heinrich Himmler.

Ironically, despite arranging for his daughter and hundreds of SS colleagues to escape through the web of ratlines provided by *Die Spinne,* Himmler had made no plans for his own disappearance as he'd expected to form part of the new provisional German government headed by Admiral Karl Dönitz, the new Head of State, following Hitler's suicide. But the former chief of the German Navy High Command loathed Himmler and refused his overtures for a post as deputy leader.

Overnight, the man who'd been the second most powerful figure in Nazi Germany was on his own and on the run. As well as donning civilian clothes and changing his name, Himmler made several superficial changes to his appearance. He shaved off his toothbrush moustache, replaced his trademark rimless spectacles with a pair of thick horn-rimmed glasses and beneath them wore a black patch over his right eye.

The Reichsführer of the SS had been on the loose for ten days along with his two assistants, Werner Grothman and Heinz Macher, heading north towards the soft border with Denmark. The three men took new identities as discharged regular soldiers, with Himmler utilising a forged army paybook in the name of Sergeant Heinrich Hizinger. Despite the knowledge that capture by the Allies meant certain death, his huge ego demanded he cling on to his Christian name. The group of men had made it as far as Bremervörde, a small town in the Lower Saxony district of Rotenberg, when they were spotted by Allied troops. The soldiers, who belonged to the British 51st Highland Division, were on the lookout for SS soldiers who were categorised as 'automatic arrests', if captured.

Himmler and his assistants were crossing a sandstone bridge running over a narrow stream when they were approached by a two-man patrol carrying out routine paperwork checks. The former SS chief panicked at the prospect of being searched and stealthily reached inside his jacket pocket for a thick brown envelope containing over five thousand dollars in US currency and the same again in Reichsmarks. The soldiers were still about twenty feet away, so he angled his body to try and hide his hand movement as he threw the packet into a small clump of bushes, on the other side of the water, mentally marking the spot where it had landed.

One of the two soldiers spotted the furtive move and lifted his short-magazine Lee-Enfield rifle into a firing pose, shouting a warning, using the tiny amount of German he'd been taught.

'*Stoppen . . . Sie die hände in der Luft.*'

Grothmann, who was slightly ahead of the other two, was unaware of his leader's reckless action and froze on the spot, lifting his arms high in the air. Macher and Himmler followed suit, and all three men held their breath as the soldiers drew closer. The one who'd shouted the command came to a stop about three feet in front of Himmler. He gestured with his rifle towards the clump of bushes, which had just become a hiding place.

'Go and get the package. Now!'

Himmler, whose grasp of English wasn't great, certainly knew enough to understand the instruction but played dumb. That all changed when the soldier jammed the end of the rifle barrel hard against his forehead and screamed in his face.

'Go, now!'

Grothmann and Macher watched on in horror as Himmler walked past them along the last part of the bridge, turned left and continued for about ten feet before reaching the package that had partially flattened a small bush. A few seconds later, after the contents had been revealed, the lead soldier broke into a huge grin as he waved a thick wad of dollar bills in Himmler's face.

'Looks like you boys were planning a luxury holiday in Denmark. Instead, you're going receive some free accommodation courtesy of the British Forces. The beds are rock hard, the food is crap, and where you're going you won't be needing any of this.'

As the two soldiers handcuffed their fresh captives and marched them back over the bridge towards a parked-up Willys Jeep, neither had any idea they'd captured the one Nazi Churchill had informed British Intelligence he wanted the pleasure of interrogating in person.

Chapter Twenty-Three

Lüneburg, Germany

May 1945

The man known to his captors as Heinrich Hizinger sat alone in a tiny makeshift cell inside British Second Army headquarters, near the medieval town of Lüneburg. He was naked, having been strip-searched earlier by an army medic who was looking for anything incriminating. Himmler's clothes had been taken away to be checked over and, as he refused the offer of a standard British uniform to replace them, he was handed a threadbare brown cotton towel, which he double wrapped around his midriff. His fake papers and passport had been confiscated along with the cash he'd tried to hide earlier. The medic granted his plea to keep a small black and white photograph of a young girl, which was currently lying next to him on the filthy lice-ridden mattress where he sat.

The interior of the cell was icy cold and, despite being exhausted, sleep eluded him as his entire body shivered as though he had a fever. Two hours had passed since his medical examination when the cell door opened and the captain of the unit, Robert Reece-Jones, entered, along with a plain-clothed translator. The captain had already spoken with Grothmann and Macher and had concluded his unit had captured three deserting middle-ranking SS officers. He was curious about the source of the large sums of cash on the man named Hizinger, however, but had no concept of the size of the fish his men had reeled in.

Reece-Jones cut a dashing figure in his military fatigues with his tall muscular frame. His nose which was as straight as a razor blade and his neatly parted rust-brown hair signified a natural aristocratic quality which reflected the fact that, in peacetime, he was part of the landed gentry, having inherited a small estate in East Sussex. When he spoke, the tone of his voice reminded Himmler of a typical BBC radio announcer.

'How's your English, Herr Hizinger?'

Himmler shrugged and dismissively waved his right hand in the air with an arrogance that immediately got under the captain's skin, who gestured towards the man standing to his right-hand side.

'I see. In which case my colleague, Patrick, will do the heavy lifting.'

'Where did the money come from?' the interpreter began in German.

Himmler had spent his life asking questions rather than answering them and his natural self-importance informed his response. He ignored Patrick and addressed Reece-Jones.

'What is your exact rank in the British Army? I demand to speak with a field marshal or at least a general.'

The English captain hit back hard.

'It would be foolish of you to mistake my tone for weakness. I believe you and your friends are SS filth, hiding in plain sight as regular soldiers. I suspect you stole the money from incarcerated Jews in Berlin or maybe from your own superiors. But, be in no doubt, if you refuse to respond to my questions, you'll be imprisoned in one of our camps along with hundreds of your fellow Nazis. Then in due course, once we establish your identity, you'll be charged with war crimes, and I suspect you'll face the gallows.'

Remarkably, Himmler was unmoved by the verbal assault and doubled down on his demands.

'I insist on meeting with Field Marshal Montgomery or General Eisenhower to discuss my position. It's imperative the Western powers join forces with Germany to combat the threat of world communism emanating from the Soviet Union. This is an urgent priority, and I refuse to negotiate my position with a low-ranking soldier.'

'My God, man. I suggest you watch your tongue. Who the hell do you think you are?'

Himmler rose from the mattress and stood directly in front of Reece-Jones. His diminutive five-foot-seven frame was dwarfed by the captain's huge physical stature, but he wasn't deterred from making his demands.

'I'm Heinrich Himmler and I hold the title of Reichsführer of the Schutzstaffel. I am the chief of the SS.'

* * *

Reece-Jones was far from convinced by the outrageous claims made by the man currently sitting nearly naked in one of his cells and who carried papers in the name of Hizinger. But the captain was a process man who played things by the book and so, following the confrontation, he contacted a friend who worked for MI5 in London to ask for advice. The first thing he was told was to instigate a medical inspection of the prisoner's teeth, in case they concealed suicide pills referred to by the MI5 man as 'cough drops'. If the detainee was indeed a high-ranking Nazi, he'd almost definitely have one on his person. Then, head shots of the prisoner should be taken with the eyepatch and glasses removed and telexed over to the intelligence department for scrutiny.

Fifteen minutes after his long-distance call to London, Reece-Jones re-entered Himmler's cell along with the translator and two medics, one of whom had body searched the prisoner earlier. Himmler's mood had significantly darkened since the previous meeting. He was engulfed by a wave of despair as he sensed his options narrowing. He reissued his demands, although this time his voice sounded weaker and carried a wisp of desperation.

'Captain, I demand to be seen by Montgomery or Eisenhower and won't tolerate further delays. I also—'

Reece-Jones had heard enough. He gave a furtive eye signal to the medics before lunging forward and savagely grabbing Himmler's torso with both arms, jerking him into the air and violently rotating his body by a hundred and eighty degrees, so the back of the German's head was tightly wedged against his chest.

One of the medics took his cue and wrenched Himmler's jaw open using both hands, while the other mounted an attack from the other side, inserting his right index finger deep into his mouth, feeling around his molars.

Himmler summoned every ounce of strength in his being and bit down hard. The medic screamed in pain as he extricated his bloodied finger, while a moment later, the SS chief used his tongue to release a cyanide capsule secreted in a gap between his back left-side lower molar and his cheek. Ironically, the glass ampoule had been manufactured in Sachsenhausen concentration camp, under the supervision of Hitler's private physician, Dr Ludwig Stumpfegger. Himmler crunched down for a second time smashing the glass and releasing the lethal contents. In the mayhem that followed, Himmler wriggled free from the captain's grip and fell forwards, bouncing off the mattress and plummeting down on to the wooden floor.

The deadly chemical agent began working almost instantly as Himmler writhed on his back like a tormented eel. The senior medic leapt down and grabbed his head, prising his lower jaw downwards, while his colleague delved into a small black Gladstone bag and retrieved a long thin needle and thread. Reece-Jones watched the grotesque spectacle in horror, as the medics stitched the thread through the tip of Himmler's tongue and began stretching it outwards, allowing one of them to thrust a hand deep into his throat, in a desperate search for any remnants of the poison. The frantic actions were too late. Himmler's body performed a terrifying death rattle before the infamous Nazi gasped his final breath. Clutched tightly in his right hand was a crumpled photo of the only person he genuinely loved.

* * *

Four hours later, having studied dozens of headshots telexed over to London from Lüneburg, Sir David Petrie, the director general of MI5, met with Winston Churchill in the cabinet war room hidden beneath the streets of Westminster. The intelligence chief laid out a selection of grainy images in front of the Prime Minister, who was sitting at the end of a huge oval walnut desk.

'Sir, there's no doubt the man our forces apprehended in north Germany, using the alias Heinrich Hizinger, was in fact Himmler. Unfortunately, our people on the ground were ill-prepared and failed to identify him. He took his own life before our medics had a chance to locate the cyanide capsule.'

Churchill shook his head as he sucked down heavily on one of his favourite Cuban cigars. Moments later he exhaled a vast plume of grey smoke as he carefully rested the Romeo y Julieta in the designated groove on a circular glass ashtray.

'The perils and chaos of war, I'm afraid.'

The Prime Minister glanced down at a thin blue file resting on the table which contained a single-page report on Himmler's death.

'So, apart from the money which I assume was probably his own, the only other intriguing reference in the brief was the unexplained photograph of the young girl.'

'Yes, it's a puzzler. We've plenty of images of Himmler's wife, his mistress and his daughter and none of them are a match for this girl. Her identity is a mystery.'

Churchill eyed his cigar which was slowly burning down. He reached for it, craving another drag.

'David, I hate mysteries, so I suggest you find out who this young lady is, because as of now, she is a figure of great interest to the British government.'

* * *

The following day, twelve hundred miles away in Geneva, Amelie was sitting at her kitchen table tuning the radio to the midday news service. The lead story was sensational and turned out to be the only item on the thirty-minute bulletin. After hearing the headline, everything that followed became a distorted blur. The French journalist who hosted the lunch-time news began the broadcast with an announcement that left her devastated.

'The British government has just announced the death of Heinrich Himmler. The SS chief was the number one target on the Nazi most wanted list. Himmler was captured by a British patrol three days ago, trying to flee Germany. He was travelling under false papers with two German soldiers. Yesterday he committed suicide by swallowing a suicide pill during an initial interrogation.'

Amelie's sense of shock was palpable. She felt as though all her bodily functions were shutting down. It was as though a mystery force had suddenly clicked an 'off' button inside her brain. There'd been no communication from her father in weeks, but she'd assumed he'd made good use of the same *Die Spinne* escape route she'd experienced a few months earlier. Having heard nothing from Mayer since his letter in Genoa, she feared the worst when it came to his fate and now, hearing of the death of her father, she felt truly alone. The two men she regarded as the mainstays in her life were gone and she felt abandoned.

Strangely, Amelie didn't cry and wasn't quite sure why not but, somehow, she knew what she needed to do next. After being rooted to the spot for almost an hour, she stood and walked, zombie-like, upstairs to her bedroom. She headed straight for her safe which she'd only opened once before, when she'd first moved into the château. It was cleverly hidden behind a false back wall in one of her giant wardrobes and as she punched in the eight-figure combination – *07101900* – she felt as though she'd been kicked in the stomach, as the code was her father's birthdate.

She retrieved the small notebook her father's aide-de-camp, Werner Grothmann, had given her when he'd visited her apartment in Berlin the night before she left. She knew it contained details of the new identities taken by senior SS officers who'd used the *Die Spinne* ratlines. It had been her father's intention for her to develop and maintain close links with some of these people so that, in time, *Die Spinne* could develop a life of its own, with like-minded fascists collaborating across the world in key areas such as finance and politics.

As Amelie began to study the contents of the notebook, she became totally absorbed by the level of detail it contained. Each listing gave the original name and level of seniority of the SS officer, along with his alias and, crucially, his new location. The diaspora of Nazis spread across the globe was truly impressive and Amelie vowed to learn the contents of the notebook by heart, primarily in honour of her father but also in case she ever needed to destroy it.

Around the same time she was immersing herself in the contents of her father's handwritten notebook, his burial was taking place in a forest deep in the heart of Lüneburg Heath, in the north-eastern part of Lower Saxony. Coincidentally it was where, three weeks earlier, the German military had formally surrendered to Field Marshal Montgomery. It was a vast, heavily wooded swamp area, away from prying eyes, which made it perfect for an unmarked grave. Churchill had decreed Himmler should never be allowed to become a martyr in death, so only the four British soldiers who buried his corpse knew the exact location of the grave and none of them gave a shit about it.

Chapter Twenty-Four

Washington D.C., United States

Twenty-four hours after the murder of Alessia Carrozza and the disappearance of Jack Cook, Berrettini held a 'war cabinet' in a secure room of the J. Edgar Hoover building, with Vargas, Hembury, Starling and Devane in attendance. The five participants were clustered together around one side of a large circular table, while Vargas and Hembury updated them on their visit to Rome. Facing them was a white drop-down screen showing a still image of Carrozza's body, lying spreadeagled on the floor inside the Italian café. The FBI deputy director's eyes were red and puffy as communications with his counterparts in Italy and Australia necessitated nighttime calls, so he'd had virtually no sleep for two days. He swigged the last dregs of his black coffee and gestured towards the screen, before starting the briefing.

'We obviously need to discuss the killings in Rome and Sydney, but before we do, we have our own shit to clean up and it's right here on our doorstep. Other than the five of us in this room, how many people knew about Carrozza and Cook's names being identified from the USB? Because one thing's for sure, those names got leaked and I'm damn sure it didn't come from anyone sitting around this table.'

Berrettini paused to look directly at Starling and Devane who were seated next to each other.

'It had to come from somebody on one of your teams.'

Hembury was the first to break the silence that hung in the air like a bad smell.

'Mike's right. We know there are eight names encoded on the drive and the two we managed to break so far were burned before we got a chance to speak to them. Whoever's running this organisation we've stumbled across is covering their tracks. They must have an informer inside the Bureau.'

Barbara Starling, who ran the Special Operations Command unit, cleared her throat before joining the conversation. Her intuitive brown eyes locked on to Berrettini's like a nuclear-powered magnet. As usual, her words were economical and devoid of sentiment.

'Of course, there can be no other logical explanation. I suggest Spencer and I immediately set up internal security checks on all our people who've been involved in the decoding so far. In my case, there are three potential suspects. Spencer?'

The head of the National Counterintelligence and Security Centre didn't take the bait.

'Barbara, hang on a second. I'm not prepared to throw my guys under the bus as easily as that. I've a tight team of five working on this, all handpicked by me, and I trust each of them implicitly. Remember, it was one of my team that broke the codes in the first place.'

The physical gap between Devane and Starling noticeably widened and the mood in the meeting room turned frosty. Berrettini swiftly took back control.

'Spencer, drop the personal shtick, we've no time for it. People are dying as a direct result of our decoding those names. No one's making direct allegations, but the facts are undeniable. If it wasn't one of us, it must be one of the eight analysts working for you guys.'

Devane's slight nod was understood by everyone in the room as consent, so the FBI deputy director took it as a cue to move on. He leaned forward across the table and picked up the remote that operated the projector.

'Okay, so Alessia Carrozza, Italy's minister of the interior, was poisoned in a café situated just three minutes away from the Italian parliament – a location she frequented three times a week – and this was the murder weapon.'

The image on the screen cut to reveal an extreme close-up of a blue Spode teapot.

'Initial tests carried out on the poisoned black tea Carrozza drank and the teapot itself indicate huge traces of polonium-210 and that normally—'

Vargas cut in and completed the sentence.

'—comes from Russia. And as far as I know, only Putin and his thugs in the FSB have access to it, as they produce it themselves.'

'You're right, so we must factor in that maybe Putin is involved in all this. But somehow, it just doesn't add up. The man who died giving you the USB drive referred to *Die Spinne* which was formed by senior Nazis eighty years ago and they were no friends of the Russians.'

Devane rose from his chair and began pacing around the room, as if searching for an answer.

'Look, we already know from what's on that USB, this organisation has a network spread across the world, on several continents. I've come across at least two instances in the last ten years where gangsters in Moscow have been offering significant quantities of polonium for sale on the dark web to the highest bidder. So, anything's possible.'

Berrettini clicked the remote and the image changed again. This time it showed a large glass Kilner jar containing four spiders resting on what appeared to be a duvet cover.

'This picture was taken inside Jack Cook's suite in the Park Hyatt in Sydney. Four funnel-webs were found there, and we know at least one of them bit him. Whoever planted them wasn't taking any chances – a single spider would have been more than enough to kill him. They knew that, immediately after he was bitten, he'd place a call to the emergency services, which would trigger his kidnap. Having said that, based on what happened to Carrozza, we must assume Australia's treasury minister is also now dead.'

Devane retook his seat at the table, as Hembury asked the question on everybody's lips.

'Mike, what's our main takeaway from all this?'

'In both instances, it would have been impossible for whoever's behind these killings to have set up such elaborate scenarios from scratch with such a short lead time. These attacks must have already been planned, perfectly thought out, so if any time these politicians needed to be taken out, the operation to make it happen was already in place. It simply needed sanctioning. In Cook's case, when AISO ripped his hotel room apart, as well as finding the funnel-webs they discovered a tiny high-range microphone hidden behind the headboard. That meant whether Cook used his cell or the hotel landline to contact the emergency services, the call would be heard straight away. We've CCTV showing the fake ambulance parking up in position just behind the hotel, minutes after the minister arrived back from a late night in parliament. They knew when he'd got there because his car was bugged too. Our friends in AISE in Italy have discovered a similar device hidden inside Carrozza's government car – the one that dropped her off at the café.'

Starling was the first to join up the dots.

'So, that means in theory the other six names on the list must also have their own death plans allocated and are in imminent danger – whether we break their codes or not.'

Berrettini nodded.

'Yes, I suspect we're going to see a spate of killings amongst international politicians in the next few days, as the clean-up from above continues. Which leads me to ask, how close are we on the other names?'

Starling glanced at Devane who indicated she should reply on behalf of them both.

'Nowhere near right now. As you know, the encoding has been created by a superior version of AI we've never come across before and yet, for some reason, Carrozza and Cook's names had been coded on a far simpler system, one we were familiar with.'

She paused to gather her thoughts and Devane jumped in to fill the dead air.

'Who the hell is behind all this and why have strategies in place to wipe out your own people?'

CHAPTER TWENTY-FOUR

Vargas was staring at the projected image of the Kilner jar on the screen.

'Whoever it is has a macabre sense of humour. Those funnel-webs may have been a killing machine for Cook but I suspect they were also an ironic warning message to other members of the organisation that calls itself the Spider Network.'

Devane nodded and stood for a second time before beginning his now familiar pacing routine.

'There's someone I think you should all meet. She's not one of my core team of five who've been working on this, so is above suspicion, but I think her brainpower could be a real asset right now. She's a bit of a loner and reports directly to me doing some pretty dark stuff – working out of a department that doesn't really exist.'

Berrettini cut in.

'Jesus, Spencer, who the hell is she?'

Devane stopped pacing and a wry smile broke out on his face.

'She happens to be the best darn computer hacker I've ever come across.'

Chapter Twenty-Five

Washington D.C., United States

Three hours later the meeting resumed in the same location, with an extra chair set in around the conference table. Devane and his mysterious colleague were the last to arrive and sat alongside Berrettini and the others. The young hacker was still processing the minute details of an intense debrief she'd received from her boss but remarkably, by the time they took their seats, was pretty much up to speed on all areas of the case.

Anna Kovalenka was a twenty-nine-year-old Ukrainian national Devane had recruited to his team three years earlier, following her arrest in New York. In fact, she wasn't doing any illegal hacking at the time but was on vacation with her mother; the first time either of them had left their mother country. She was busy racking up an obscene shopping bill in Bloomingdale's when a team of federal agents working for Devane took her into custody. Kovalenka had been on his radar for some time and for good reason.

Five years earlier, having graduated from Kyiv University with a first-class honours degree in applied mathematics and computer science, she joined a tight team of highly skilled hackers working out of Ukraine's capital city, as part of one of many criminal gangs which were based there at the time. They specifically targeted financial and business institutions in the US and UK and, after a brief apprenticeship learning her trade, she moved three hundred miles south of Kyiv to the coastal city of Odesa, where she joined the infamous 'Ukrainian Mafia'. Between 2019 and 2021 she became one of their prized assets as she masterminded an audacious spree of cyber-attacks on prime US financial targets such as Western Union, Mastercard and American Express and, just for the hell of it, hacked the US Senate website.

Kovalenka first met Devane while incarcerated in a safe house, stashed away in a rundown cul-de-sac in Queens, where he gave her a no-brainer choice: multiple jail sentences which added up to over one hundred and fifty years, or a defection to join the so-called 'Good Guys'. Not a tough decision to make for a bright, ambitious woman with a strong survival instinct and an IQ of 175.

As part of the switch, she was given a new identity. Overnight, Anna Kovalenka became Liliya Soletska. Three years on, she'd more than proved her worth, having success-fully hacked into sensitive government websites in both Iran and Russia, with sensational results. Her unique expertise lay in uncovering 'back doors' into what appeared at face value to be impenetrable computer systems, and her unique skillset also included extensive knowledge of the latest AI models, plus she had a fascination with the creation of deepfakes.

Her physical attributes were just as impressive. As Soletska took her place at the table and glanced around at the big hitters already in place, she resembled a famished lioness stalking her prey. Her electric blue eyes were startling and had a penetrating alertness behind them, which made her stare somewhat disconcerting, if you happened to be the recipient of it. The rest of her facial features followed through with classic Eastern European characteristics, a round face, high cheekbones, straight nose and full lips. Her olive skin was makeup free, and her shoulder-length blonde hair was pulled back into a tight bun. Soletska's petite size four frame was simply dressed in a tight-fitting plain black T-shirt tucked into stonewashed 501s, along with a pair of black Converse trainers.

After a brief introduction from Devane, she opened with her thoughts on the case and when she spoke, far from being intimidated by her elite audience, she commanded the room. She'd brought a laptop with her which was closed and had no notes to work from, as her computer-like brain was well-versed in storing, assessing and processing information at lightning speed.

'Guys, I've set up a safe online portal which the six of us will have access to and a few minutes ago I uploaded two videos we've just received from AISO and AISI. They're both about five minutes long and were found on Carrozza and Cook's laptops. My initial assessment is they were made specifically by the victims themselves to provide footage for the creation of their own deepfakes.'

She paused for a moment to reach for a small bottle of Evian which she poured into the glass tumbler in front of her. Berrettini, who was still reeling from being referred to as 'guys', glanced across at Vargas and Hembury. He could tell by their expressions they were both impressed by the newcomer and were hanging on her every word. The young Ukrainian hacker who'd suddenly joined the party wasn't one for small talk and they'd clearly need to be on their 'A' game to keep up with her. She took a couple of large gulps of water and picked up where she'd left off.

'In both cases, the footage contains two different set-ups. A stand-up piece to camera framed in a mid-shot and then a second where they're standing behind a podium with a green screen background, again talking straight down the camera lens. It appears the first set-up was filmed in their own home but the second was clearly recorded in a studio.'

Her boss was probably the only one in the room brave enough to interrupt her mid-flow.

'Liliya, what makes you think these videos were filmed specifically to help create a deepfake?'

'Because, sir, although my Italian's not brilliant, I'm pretty sure in both instances Cook and Carrozza are using exactly the same words – or should I say reading the same words.'

Berrettini cut in.

'What the hell? How can that be?'

Soletska ploughed on, ignoring the FBI deputy director.

'They're clearly both reading from a teleprompter, and I think the script has been carefully prepared to include a specific vocabulary that AI machines require to produce a synthetic audio library, needed to create a perfect-sounding deepfake. When I listened to Cook's video, the content and language used is totally random, which is why I believe he was reading a script created by an AI machine, using Diffusion techniques.'

She stopped talking for a moment as she was hit by a wall of blank expressions.

'I believe General Starling briefed you all on GANs – Generative Adversarial Networks: computer systems that employ two AI machines, which then combine resources to create a deepfake, using thousands of images of video and stills as source material. Diffusion is a more sophisticated AI tool that needs far less raw material to work with and the result is an almost perfect deepfake. Their faces were filmed perfectly head on and five minutes of footage would be more than enough to provide the source material for what's needed. We think the Chinese are currently the leaders in this field but whoever produced the Himmler video has taken the process to a new level. There's an internal department at the Pentagon, called DARPA, that's spent millions of dollars on media forensics to produce AI machines capable of identifying deepfakes, however good they may appear to the naked eye.'

Soletska paused and turned to Devane.

'Sir, I'd like DARPA to take a look the Himmler video and see what they think.'

Devane nodded his approval.

'I'll sort that. Any other thoughts for now?'

'Just one. The super intelligence produced by AI on show here could be capable of producing content far more sinister than a simple deepfake video.'

Vargas shuffled in his chair and spoke for the first time since Soletska had entered the room.

'Where are you going with this, Liliya?'

The Ukrainian hacker hardly paused for breath as she opened her laptop. Her fingers flew across the keyboard at a mesmerising speed and seconds later she stood and angled the monitor on her MacBook towards the other five people in the room. Vargas shook his head in disbelief.

'Liliya, do you ever come up for air?'

For a moment the Argentine chief inspector thought he detected the slightest hint of a smile on Soletska's face, but he couldn't be sure. The fact she totally ignored his comment answered his own question.

'On the screen is an image of the renowned surrealist artist Salvador Dalí, who died in January 1989. Thirty years after his death in May 2019, the Dalí Museum in Florida created a life-size deepfake of him that greets people when they first enter. The tech guys at the museum who produced it added a functioning AI brain encoded with 190,000 possible answers to questions likely to be posed by museum visitors. So, the deepfake engages in what appears to be a live conversation, if it recognises the question. I've seen it myself and it's a mind-blowing experience. Of course, I managed to fool it by asking a question it couldn't possibly have been pre-programmed for.'

Hembury was first out the blocks.

'Which was?'

'I asked Dalí to the name his mistress with whom he fathered a daughter. I knew he was terrified of his partner, Gala, and right up until his death he denied the affair ever happened, so guess what? The deepfake defaulted to a standard reply, "I'm afraid I can't help you with that." The Dalí experiment was trialled four years ago. Imagine the implications of a modern-day deepfake of a prominent politician with an AI brain programmed with over a billion answers to every conceivable question.'

There was a stunned silence in the room as Soletska closed the laptop and leaned back in her chair indicating she was finished. Berrettini wondered if he should start a short round of applause but instead remained poker-faced.

'Liliya, have you any questions for us?'

As had been the case throughout her briefing, Soletska didn't appear to need any thinking time before replying to the FBI deputy director.

'Just one for now. How do you intend to catch the bastards who are developing this incredible tech?'

Chapter Twenty-Six

Washington D.C., United States

When Soletska left the room, Devane bathed in the afterglow.

'What did I tell you? That girl's a one-off. Great at what she does, although not so good when it comes to following orders.'

Starling, who'd remained quiet during the briefing, didn't seem totally convinced.

'Indeed, she's a remarkable find, Spencer.'

She turned her attention to the FBI deputy director who was busy checking messages on his cell.

'So, Mike, next steps?'

Berrettini rested his phone on the table and glanced across at Starling.

'We need to crack those other names on the USB and get to those people before they're taken out, and that makes it imperative we find our mole, so we're not undermined again.'

Vargas had just finished reading a fresh email on his laptop and was the first to stand.

'There are some interesting leads coming to light in Buenos Aires relating to our dead friend Manuel, who started this whole thing off. It seems he and his brother were murdered shortly after he gave me the USB. His girl-friend wants to see me in person. Not surprisingly she's frightened for her life and from what she's let slip already, my deputy, Torres, thinks she has an interesting tale to tell. Hopefully, she can shed some light on how Manuel got his hands on the drive.'

Hembury was up on his feet, standing next to his friend.

'Nic, do you want me to come with?'

'No, hopefully it'll be a quick in and out, although things seem to be hotting up over there. A second double killing took place twenty-four hours ago. Two people were literally thrown to their death from a penthouse in Palermo.'

'And their connection to this case is?'

Vargas smiled at his friend like the cat that got the cream.

'Even though their bodies were battered by the fall, it sounds from the preliminary ID as though one of the fatalities was another recent acquaintance of ours.'

Vargas continued to grin at Hembury, teasing him to take a guess, but his friend was stumped.

'Put me out of my misery, Nic.'

'Knife girl.'

* * *

The public morgue in the fashionable neighbourhood of Chacarita in Buenos Aires was conveniently situated less than half a mile away from the cemetery of the same name, the largest

144

in Argentina. The iron-grey, sixties-built two-storey structure could hold over fifty cadavers, toe-tagged and stored in refrigerated human-sized drawers. Vargas, who'd travelled there straight from the airport, was only interested in visiting four of them. As soon as the cab dropped him off, he was escorted by a mortician to the main storage room where his long-time collaborator, Detective Juan Torres, was waiting to greet him. The pair, who'd worked together for almost fourteen years, had an almost telepathic relationship and a verbal shorthand that could cut straight to the heart of a complex case.

After a quick catch-up with his boss, Torres moved straight into a debrief. There were four trolleys lined up in the room – clearly separated into two groups. He indicated to the mortician to pull back the white sheets covering the top half of the two bodies closest to them, revealing the faces of Manuel and his brother. Manuel's face was untouched, and Vargas recognised him instantly, while the other looked horrendous, even in death. The man's forehead, cheeks and chin had been badly carved up and resembled a macabre roadmap while his left eye was missing, having been gouged out. Even though Vargas had seen many gruesome sights, he couldn't help wincing as he stared at what remained of the dead man's face. Torres registered Vargas's reaction and leaned forward to pull the cover back in place.

'His name is Thiago Romero, and I think you recognise his brother, Manuel.'

Vargas nodded and switched his gaze to the face of the man he'd met earlier that week, whose motive for passing over the USB was as yet unknown but whatever it had been, it had cost him his life and set off a chain reaction of killings.

'Sir, Thiago's entire body is pretty much mutilated all over. The man was clearly tortured before he was killed. Whoever did it must be some kind of sadist.'

Torres paused briefly to take a fresh look at Manuel's face.

'Strangely, Manuel's body is as clean as a whistle. He died instantly following a direct shot to the heart from a 9mm round – possibly from a Glock.'

'Juan, I think it's fair to say the brothers were interrogated by someone who wanted the USB back and by the look of things, only Thiago held out, leaving Manuel to spill the beans. After that, I guess they sent knife girl over to my apartment to retrieve it. Speaking of which . . .'

Vargas nodded towards the other two gurneys and as he and Torres moved across to them, the mortician pulled back their sheets. Once again Vargas only recognised one of the victims. Considering the distance of the fall, knife girl's face was still relatively untouched as her body had taken most of the impact.

'Yep, no question she was the assailant in my apartment who took the USB, but who was she and what was her connection with the Romero brothers and who's her buddy?'

'No ID on the girl yet I'm afraid but we know plenty about the other victim. Carlos Salazar was a gangster and drug baron with plenty of friends in high places, which is why he had a clean police record, even though he was up to his neck in high-end organised crime. I think the girl, whoever she was, was probably working for him. Something obviously went badly wrong after she recovered the USB, and someone gave the order to wipe them both out. Bearing in mind Salazar's status in the underworld, whoever authorised their double hit must be a heavyweight.'

'Jesus, there are so many unanswered questions.'

Torres frowned as he rested his hand on his boss's shoulder. 'Let's get back to the station. You need to meet Manuel's girlfriend, Julieta. I think she might be the key that unlocks all this.'

* * *

Hembury was an early riser, and it was just before six thirty in the morning when he entered the small makeshift office Berrettini had sorted for him and Vargas inside the J. Edgar Hoover building. To his surprise, it wasn't empty. Sitting in the Argentine's seat with her head down, furiously typing away on one of three laptops that were all open in front of her, was Liliya Soletska. She didn't react to his entrance and then he spotted the white airpods in her ears and smiled to himself as he wondered what type of music the young Ukrainian hacker listened to as a backing track while she worked her way through invisible 'back doors' into what were supposedly impenetrable computer systems.

Scattered across the table in front of her was a short trail of six empty Red Bull cans, mixed in with a couple of screwed-up crisp packets and chocolate wrappers. Although she didn't hear him enter, Soletska sensed his presence and greeted him with a beaming smile as he sat down opposite her, resting his own computer on the table. With a dramatic flourish she closed her laptops, removed the earbuds and placed them neatly back inside their small white plastic container.

'Morning, Troy. Thought big-shot White House office guys like you were more nine-to-five. Sorry about the mess but I pulled an all-nighter, so needed some fuel to keep going.'

147

'I'm more of a six-to-six guy and not a great fan of all-nighters. I'm a bit old for those these days and the truth is I really like my own bed.'

As he was speaking, Hembury caught sight of a half-opened bulging backpack resting on the floor just behind Soletska's chair.

'Planning to move in full-time?'

Soletska rocked back in her chair as her welcoming smile morphed into a throaty laugh.

'Don't worry, I get a bit obsessed sometimes when Devane sets me a challenge he thinks I can't handle, and this one is right on my sweet spot. Other than the two names on that USB that were coded using systems we've seen before; the rest have been individually built by AI machines operating on a superior level to anything I've ever come across. So far neither Starling's nor Devane's teams have been able to crack them open. I'm determined to break the coding, but it can only be done on an individual basis as they've all been created by a different AI system. If I can manage one, Devane wants the name kept between the six of us to avoid any more tipoffs.'

'Makes sense. What are the chances?'

'Well, I'm currently hooked up with AI machines operated by the FSB in the Kremlin and the Chinese Ministry of State Security, hoping one of them has the brainpower I need.'

'Jesus Christ, is there any system out there you can't hack?'

Soletska arched a cynical eyebrow.

'Not unless you know of one. Every computer network, however secure, always has a way in – you just need to know where to look.'

Hembury flipped open his Mac and hit the power button.

'Bet you'd struggle to work out my password on this baby.'

'Don't need it, Troy. I could bypass it in less than sixty seconds. But don't worry, your secrets are safe with me.'

Once again, he was charmed by her infectious laugh. As Devane had so lucidly put it, 'this girl was something else'. Hembury leaned across and picked up a discarded chocolate wrapper.

'How about some proper fuel? I'm heading to the canteen for croissants and coffee. Fancy some?'

Soletska stood and dipped her right hand deep into the front pocket of her jeans and dug around until she retrieved a hand-ful of dollar coins.

'No thanks but on the way there you'll pass the vending machine. A couple of Red Bulls would be very welcome.'

Hembury gave the wry smile of a beaten man.

'Okay, you got it. By the way, what music were you listening to as you were breaking and entering Putin's supercomputer? Let me guess, The Killers?'

Hembury was a betting man at heart and secretly speculated on Swift, Beyoncé or Sheeran but once again Soletska was full of surprises.

'*Sticky Fingers* by the Stones. When I was twelve, I had a poster of Jagger on my bedroom wall.'

'Christ, even back then he was old enough to have been your grandfather.'

Soletska's mouth broke into a mischievous smile.

'Yes, well maybe I just like older men.'

Hembury's pained expression confirmed he felt truly defeated by the wonder girl from Ukraine. He grabbed the coins from her open palm and quietly exited the room, heading straight for the vending machine.

Chapter Twenty-Seven

Buenos Aires, Argentina

J ulieta Toledo had been sitting alone in a police interview room for over five hours when Vargas and Torres finally entered, armed with a blue folder, three black coffees, a cheese and ham sandwich and a pack of Marlboro Red. The young woman who'd been Manuel's girlfriend was tired, hungry and scared – a fatal combination Vargas was keen to exploit, as he was desperate to find some answers.

Toledo was barely twenty-five, but the deep black circles engraved under her wide-set amber eyes added at least a decade to her makeup-free face. Her wispy brown hair was severely scraped back, and she was simply dressed in a cheap black track-suit accompanied by a pair of non-branded white trainers. Her hands were noticeably shaking as they grabbed the pack of ciga-rettes and fumbled for a tab. Torres obliged with a plastic lighter and she inhaled deeply before breathing out though her nose, jettisoning two long streams of white smoke. Two more drags followed quickly and then the nicotine hit seemed to do the trick. She placed the cigarette in a small glass ashtray and dived into the sandwich, wolfing it down like it was her last meal. She followed that up with a large gulp of coffee from a white polystyrene cup and then eased back into her chair with an enormous sigh. Vargas watched the scene play out in front of him as he mulled over his tactics for the interview.

'Julieta, I'm so sorry about what happened to Manuel. I intend to catch the people who killed him and his brother and bring them to justice. But I need your help with—'

'I'm scared. The people behind these killings are ruthless and powerful. You've seen what they can do.'

She seemed to shrink in her chair as tears began to stream down her face.

'Julieta, you're safe here. I can offer you formal police protection.'

Her crying was overridden by a hollow ironic laugh.

'Chief inspector, Carlos Salazar was the monster who tortured and killed Thiago and Manuel. He was a gangster who ended up mixing in circles way above his station, which is why he lost his life as well. There's no way you can protect me from them.'

Torres flicked a quick look towards his boss who acknowledged the gesture. The floodgates were opening. Toledo was gushing like an open tap and Vargas let her words flow.

'Go on. Who are these people?'

'They're your bosses. One of them is a senior minister in the government.'

Toledo stopped for a moment and reached for a fresh cigarette as her first one had burned out in the ashtray, leaving a caterpillar of grey ash. Once again Torres did the honours with the lighter.

'What's his name?'

'I don't know, Manuel never told me, but he's got something to do with the COP summit that's taking place in the city next week. That's where the USB came in.'

Vargas leaned forward in his chair, engrossed in the story he was hearing from the young girl who was clearly terrified by recent events and scared for her own life.

'Julieta, take your time and talk us through exactly what happened.'

After another deep drag on her Marlboro Red, she was good to continue.

'Salazar was a mobster who ran a major drug operation in Recoleta, along with several high-class brothels, frequented by judges, soccer players and politicians and, from what Manuel told me, the scumbag even dabbled in people trading. Thiago and Manuel worked for him, doing menial jobs like driving, collecting money and taking photos of celebrities visiting his whores, which he planned to use for blackmail down the line. Anyway, for some reason he took a shine to Manuel and during the last few months, he regularly invited him to his penthouse apartment for late-night drinking sessions. Salazar's idea of a big night in entailed a lethal cocktail of whisky and cocaine when he'd get completely off his face.'

Another pause was caused by yet another long drag on the Marlboro. Vargas stayed quiet and let it play out.

'But then, two weeks ago, everything went to shit. Salazar issued a routine hit on a guy called Valentino Suarez, a middleman who set up deals for him and other drug barons. He was convinced he'd double-crossed him on a deal with a rival and had him taken out by an Asian assassin – a female psycho he kept on a tight leash to do his dirty work.'

Vargas's eyeline momentarily flicked across to Torres, acknowledging the reference to the assailant he'd christened 'knife girl'. Julieta caught the look but continued with her tale.

'The bastard had no idea Valentino was Manuel's uncle, who'd brought him and his brother up as kids, after their mother died in a car crash and their father disappeared shortly after. He'd "fathered" them alongside his own children and they were devastated by his murder. That's when Manuel came up with a plan for revenge. I warned him it was risky, but he wouldn't listen.'

Once again, Toledo came to a dead stop to allow her brain to catch up and process what she was saying. For a moment she feared she'd said too much but then decided she'd already gone too far and had nothing to lose.

'Salazar may have had power, but he was a moron who couldn't keep his mouth shut. He loved to show off and Manuel was a perfect audience. One night he told him about an organisation he was working for who were paying him far more than he could ever earn from dealing drugs. It had a German name, *Die Spinne*. I'm not sure what it is but somehow it had connections to this government minister, who Salazar was dealing with in person.'

Vargas slightly adjusted his position, leaning forward across the table towards the young woman, intrigued to hear what was to come next. Julieta was unravelling in front of him, and she didn't disappoint. She locked eyes with Vargas for a moment before continuing.

'Salazar loved boasting about their relationship and last week he showed Manuel a USB drive he'd been instructed to deliver by hand to the politician in question. After a late-night drinking session, Manuel stole it from Salazar's desk and tracked you down to hand it over, hoping whoever was running Salazar would take him out as a punishment. Turns out he was right, but sadly it didn't happen quickly enough. The maniac got to Manuel and Thiago before whoever he was working for sanctioned his death, along with the psycho Asian bitch who killed their uncle.'

Vargas had heard enough and paused the interview. Minutes later he was on an encrypted line to Berrettini in Washington.

'Mike, I hope you're sitting down – you won't believe the story I've just heard from Manuel's girlfriend.'

'Go on, I'm all ears.'

'We know what happened to the politicians in Italy and Australia and it's clear now that this organisation, whatever it is, has tentacles everywhere. It appears the USB Manuel gave me was intended for a senior government minister here in Argentina. Four people have already brutally lost their lives because of what's on that USB. Mike, we're facing an enemy that will stop at nothing.'

Chapter Twenty-Eight

Geneva, Switzerland

5 March 1946

Amelie checked her diary just to be sure. As she thought, it confirmed it was exactly a year to the day since she'd first arrived at the château. Her father had planned a two-year residency for her in Geneva, before she moved on to Paris to begin her new life, so she registered the fact she was halfway there. Right now, as she reflected on the previous twelve months, she concluded her life was dull and uneventful and couldn't wait to begin a new adventure in France.

Her French was coming on a treat and, in addition, every day she studied complex paperwork from the Legrand Bank, which was telexed over to her by the financial director taking care of business in her absence. Her father had bought a controlling interest in the bank during the last few months of the war, using a holding company registered in Zurich, which funnelled illicit funds out of Germany. The ninety per cent stake was more than enough to justify the name change. So, in December 1944, the Banque privée Auclair and Blanchet, which had been established in 1897, became the Banque Legrand. Its imposing headquarters were discreetly situated on the Rue du Faubourg Saint-Honoré, in the 8th arrondissement of Paris, running parallel with the world-famous Avenue des Champs-Élysées. It was one of the most respected private banks in the city, its exclusive clientele boasting high-ranking politicians, industry leaders and a movie star amongst its high-net-worth clients.

Amelie was upstairs in her bedroom when she heard her housekeeper escorting a visitor through the grand entrance hallway below. She promptly made her way downstairs and was about to enter the enormous ground-floor study where she normally met her guests, when the housekeeper appeared from inside it and met her in the corridor outside. She was red-faced and clearly flustered.

'Mademoiselle, you have an unexpected visitor. The gentle-man doesn't have an appointment but insisted on meeting with you. I said you weren't available, so he asked me to inform you he'd come from Genoa to help you celebrate your first anniver-sary in Geneva and that—'

Amelie almost knocked the bemused woman clean off her feet as she flew past her like a hundred-yard sprinter, who'd just heard the starter gun. She bolted though the open doorway into the heavily panelled study and saw him standing across the room. He had his back to her and was staring out through the open French doors across the perfectly manicured gardens, hypnotised by a run of symmetrically placed giant fountains, whose water jets appeared to be dancing to non-existent music. Then he heard footsteps running across the herringbone parquet floor and spun around just in time to grab Amelie as she flung herself into his arms like a frenzied spinning top.

* * *

For Amelie, the next three hours were a whirlwind. She spent them locked in her bedroom with Mayer, where, in between passionate rounds of lovemaking, the pair talked non-stop, catching up on each other's lives. They both had so much to ask and tell and Amelie lapped up every morsel of news as though she'd been starved of any since the day they parted. He gently spooned her in his arms and stroked her hair as they took another breather. Mayer broke off from nuzzling Amelie's neck and whispered into her ear.

'My darling, I'm so sorry for my silence. But for many reasons I did it to protect you.'

Amelie slowly eased her body around until they were facing each other. She smiled tenderly as she drank in his features which were now covered by a full beard, as black as liquorice. She stroked it softly, allowing her fingers to become entwined in the longer whiskers.

'Tell me about the boat trip. I'd always feared you never made it across to South America.'

'I didn't believe I would. Your father was pumped full of fury when I spoke with him, and I assumed he'd ordered my death. So, every day on the boat I looked around at the crew, wondering who'd been given the job. But it never happened.'

'How did he find out about us?'

'It must have been that cretin, Fritzsch. I confronted him on the journey but of course the coward denied it. Once I reached

Argentina, I figured your father had too much else on his plate to think about sanctioning my execution. Whatever the reason, I was so grateful for my life, I vowed to carry on helping as many of my colleagues escape as possible, and that's what I've continued to do in the last year. There are still hundreds of SS officers hiding out in Germany, desperate for my help. The ratlines across Europe offer their only hope of escape to a new life. My duty is to honour your father's memory and ensure the future success of *Die Spinne*.'

Amelie's body stiffened as she digested the implications of Mayer's words.

'Carlos, how long will you stay?'

'One night, and then I return to Berlin.'

Mayer pulled her closer, cushioning her face on his chest. So close she could hear the steady beat of his heart.

'Will I hear from you? See you?'

'It's not possible. Now Germany is controlled by the Western powers, I'm playing a treacherous game. My only hope of survival is to stay deep under cover. Even my presence here today poses a real danger to you, which I dare not repeat.'

She felt her eyes well up as she pleaded with him.

'What if I need you? You must leave me with some means of contact.'

'Amelie, if you ever feel in real danger, there is a way. Place a small ad in the job section of *Die Zeit*. Simply say: *Lakeside château in Geneva requires a head gardener*. I'll check the page every week.'

She melted back into his arms as his mouth gave way to an adoring smile.

'Now, let's make the most of the time we've got left.'

Chapter Twenty-Nine

Geneva, Switzerland

January 1947

It had been almost ten months since Amelie's brief reunion with Mayer, when the letter arrived. The first time she read it her heart sank to her boots and she was consumed with terror. Then despair morphed into white-hot anger as she digested the contents for a second time. Someone was threatening to destroy her life and she'd no idea who they were. The envelope bore the postmark of the Swiss capital, Bern, the sole clue as to the identity of her blackmailer.

Amelie was sitting at her desk in the ground-floor study and was about to slide the letter into the top drawer when a bout of paranoia set in. The thought of her staff reading the contents filled her with dread, so she headed upstairs, opting instead for the secret wall safe hidden in her bedroom. She was a just about to open it when she decided to read the note one more time, desperately searching for clues. She sat down at her dressing table, removing it from its envelope for a third time, once again scrutinising the contents.

Private and Confidential

Mlle Legrand,

You are not who you purport to be. Your name is fake, as is your entire story. Your father, Heinrich Himmler, was one of the most reviled figures in Europe. I believe he used stolen funds to purchase your home in Geneva and the bank in Paris, which you claim to own. I'd be doing the world a great service if I were to reveal your identity to the Swiss and French authorities, who will no doubt strip you of your assets and put you behind bars, where you deserve to be.

If you wish to avoid this fate, I will offer you a way out. Deviate from my instructions in any way, however, and I assure you, I will expose you. I will write to you again in two weeks to explain exactly what you need to do. In the meantime, withdraw a cash sum of one hundred thousand Swiss Francs in small denominations.

Instructions will follow in the next communication. Do not discuss this matter with anyone or you risk instant exposure.

After locking the letter away in the safe, she lay on her bed weighing up her options. Although the sum of money being demanded was high, she could easily manage it but suspected it would be the first of many which would eventually wipe her out. But then again, she'd no choice. The alternative to not paying was having the world discover her real identity and that prospect filled her with horror. It was Friday morning, and she resolved to spend the weekend searching for a solution. She ploughed the depths of her mind for anything that might help and that's when she decided to place an advert in the following week's job section of *Die Zeit*.

Forty-eight hours after the advert for a head gardener at the château appeared in the Swiss national paper, Mayer phoned.

Amelie took the call in her bedroom and poured her heart out to him. The SS captain insisted she read the letter to him numerous times before offering his thoughts.

'I've an idea who might be behind this but it's nothing more than a hunch. I'll call you every other day at around this time, until you receive the second letter.'

Amelie was finding the stress of the blackmail threat unbearable, and tears flowed down her cheeks.

'Carlos, please come and stay with me, at least until the letter comes.'

'I'm afraid that's impossible, my darling. Trust me, you are no longer alone. I'll find the person behind this and—'

'And what?'

There was a short pause before Mayer replied.

'Eliminate them.'

* * *

The blackmailer was as good as their word and the second letter arrived two weeks after the first. The following day, Mayer called, and Amelie read its contents to him over the phone. He carefully wrote a copy, word for word, and then read it back to her, ensuring he'd made no errors. It was shorter than the original.

Private and Confidential

Mlle Legrand,

I trust you have the funds. Come to the Church of St Peter and Paul on Rathausgasse in Bern at midnight, this Saturday 25 Jan. The main entrance will be unlocked. Deposit the case containing the money in the middle of the fifth row of pews on the right-hand side.

Come alone and then leave immediately. Do as I request, and you will not hear from me again. Deviate from any of these instructions and the consequences that will follow will be of your own making.

There was a pregnant pause while Mayer considered the options.

'Okay, this is what we're going to do.'

* * *

The striking Church of St Peter and Paul sat alongside the Town Hall in Bern's Old City, its layout virtually unchanged since its construction. The nineteenth-century structure designed in Romanesque style was the first Catholic church built in the Swiss capital following the Reformation. Its impressive façade was enhanced by a sixty-foot Gothic bell tower and spire, while the three vaulted ceilings inside were ornately decorated with a colourful blend of giant frescoes and friezes.

Amelie stood on the street, facing the arched front entrance and checked her watch. It was eleven twenty: she was forty minutes early having walked directly from the train station, a mile and a half away. The one-hundred-mile trip from Geneva had taken two and a half hours and she'd opted for a train that would ensure she wasn't late.

The chocolate brown and gold Louis Vuitton Keepall bag which had accompanied her on the journey was stuffed full of cash. As instructed, Amelie had travelled alone and now all she could do was wait. She hovered in the shadows, partially illuminated by the amber glow of a lone streetlamp, as she counted down the minutes to midnight. Her nerves were frayed, and she could feel her right hand tremble as she tightened her grip on the leather handle of the bag.

Every minute seemed to last an eternity but eventually, at one minute to twelve, she approached the entrance, pushed open the front door and entered the historic church. The nave was dimly lit by a scattering of votive candles and the eerie silence that hung in the air like a thick curtain was shattered by the brutal sound of Amelie's footsteps on the stone floor, which echoed around the vast space. As she walked along the centre aisle towards the fifth row of pews, she struggled to breathe and her legs felt as though they were strapped to lead weights.

It didn't take her long to find the row and as she placed the bag in position, she looked around for any sign of life; there wasn't any. Amelie followed the instructions to the letter and immediately departed the church, heading back towards the station. There was one remaining slow train scheduled to Geneva, departing from platform five at twelve thirty. It only had a handful of passengers on board, but Amelie wasn't one of them. As she watched the train disappear, she knew all she could do now was wait and trust in the actions of the man she loved.

* * *

Inside the church, nothing transpired for two hours and then, just after two in the morning, a small wooden door peeled open, and a hooded figure emerged from a back entrance to the side of the high altar. The intruder held his position, masked in the shadow of the doorway as he furtively looked around, ensuring he was alone. Once he was happy, he broke cover and headed directly towards the pew where the bag had been left and, in a matter of seconds, held it firmly in his grasp. He made to return the same way he'd entered but just as he reached the open door, a strong male voice broke the silence.

'Abbot Holzherr, place the bag down and turn around. There's a gun aimed directly at your head.'

The priest froze with terror, rooted to the spot as the command was repeated.

'Turn around, Father. Unless you want your head blown away.'

The abbot released his grip on the bag which fell to the floor and toppled on to its side. He slowly turned to face his accuser. Mayer was standing less than eight feet away, having emerged from his hiding place behind the high altar. He was holding a Luger PO8 semi-automatic pistol in his right hand, aimed directly at the elderly priest. Holzherr's eyes rattled around his head like a pair of spinning plates as he searched for some means of escape. Mayer stealthily moved a couple of steps forward, closing the gap between them.

'Father, I thought it was you, but hoped I was wrong.'

Holzherr's forehead crunched up, creating deep furrows.

'How could you possibly know?'

'Bern is only twenty miles from the abbey in Fribourg, so it would be simple for you to go there and mail the letters so nobody could connect you to them. Also, I recalled your reaction at the abbey when Amelie gave away her identity. Then I slipped up, referencing Geneva as her end destination. At the time I consoled myself our indiscretions would go unpunished as you were a man of the cloth and yet, here we are.'

'Mayer, there's so much you can't possibly understand.'

'I understand you're a blackmailer and imagine this wouldn't have been the last time we'd have heard from you. Avarice is one of the seven deadly sins named in the Bible and no one should know that better than you, Father.'

This time it was the turn of the abbot to step forward. He slowly extended his right arm as though intending to rest it on Mayer's shoulder in a gesture of friendship. It was a deliberate, controlled movement that just kept going and then in a flash its trajectory changed. An extra hem stitched inside the cuff of the abbot's right sleeve concealed a small ivory-handled knife that doubled as a letter opener. With a tiny physical adjustment, it dropped smoothly into the palm of his hand and then at a speed which belied his age, Holzherr leapt forward, plunging the razor-sharp blade deep into the side of Mayer's neck.

Simultaneously, the SS captain fired off a single round that ripped through the wall of the abbot's stomach. The momentum of the frenzied attack threw both men downwards and they instinctively clung to each other as their bodies slammed against the floor, with Mayer's back taking the bulk of the impact. Their faces were jammed hard against each other, their eyes inches apart. The abbot's were burning with terror while Mayer's were calm, reflecting the truth that, as a soldier, he'd achieved his goal in silencing Amelie's blackmailer. As they lay together, locked in a bizarre embrace, both men knew it was only a matter of time before they bled out.

Across the city, Amelie checked her watch for what seemed like the hundredth time. Mayer had travelled to Bern by car and assured her he would pick her up from the station sometime after midnight. He'd insisted she stay put no matter what happened, but something had clearly gone wrong, and she couldn't wait around any longer. Amelie ran the entire way back to the church and, as she darted through the front entrance, was overwhelmed by a sense of foreboding. Somehow it seemed darker than before, and it took her eyes a moment to adjust as they scanned the gloomy interior of the church.

Everything appeared the same, so she decided to check on the holdall and wasn't surprised to find it was gone. She exited the pew back into the aisle and began moving forwards. A few seconds later she saw something strange; a puzzling sight which instinctively prompted her to stop. She could just about discern the outline of what appeared to be an uneven structure on the floor, blocking a side door to the left of the high altar. As she strained her eyes to focus in the darkness, the horrific image became clearer, and her heart felt as though it had just jumped out of her chest. Hardly able to breathe, she edged slowly forward until she confronted the bloodied tableau of Mayer and Holzherr, wrapped in each other's arms in a death embrace.

The sense of shock and pain that flooded Amelie's brain was unbearable. She collapsed in a messy heap just a few feet away from the bodies and wept uncontrollably. She was too weak to stand but somehow managed to crawl across the cold stone floor, until she was in touching distance of Mayer's body. His face was heavily blood splattered and his brooding dark brown eyes were wide open, staring upwards into space, and for a moment she felt as though they were looking directly at her.

An hour later Amelie exited the church: a zombie in a trance. As she headed back towards the station carrying her bag, she knew whatever lay ahead, a huge part of her life was over. She'd never find another man to love and, as time passed, that prophecy came true.

Chapter Thirty

Buckinghamshire, England

Dorneywood House is an eighteenth-century eight-bedroom mansion set in two hundred and fifteen acres in the flourishing village of Burnham, deep in the heart of the English countryside. Historically the illustrious property is best known for being the grace-and-favour home of the United Kingdom's chancellor of the exchequer, a privilege granted by the prime minister of the time to the man who holds the title First Lord of the Treasury. Over the years it's played host to many eminent British politicians such as Sir Winston Churchill, Gordon Brown and John Major. Its most recent occupant, Sir Mark Wedgewood, was a sixty-year-old Tory politician who'd worked his way up the greasy pole of politics to land the plum role of running the country's economy.

The house was intended to be used by the chancellor and his family as a weekend retreat, but Wedgewood tried his best to get down there on a weekday, ideally a Wednesday, at least twice a month and normally on his own. He told his wife and colleagues the sedate countryside environment offered the perfect antidote to his hectic political life in Westminster and inspired him to do much of his best work, especially when it came to financial planning. During those weekday visits, meetings were held on Zoom and by conference call and fellow government ministers got used to the chancellor's slightly eccentric routine.

But the tranquillity offered by Dorneywood House wasn't the true reason Wedgewood loved going down there; it was its location. The mansion was less than seven miles away from a small luxury apartment situated in the historic town of Windsor on the banks of the River Thames. The one-bed flat was home to a twenty-six-year-old political research assistant who, two years earlier, had landed a three-month internship in the Treasury Department. The pair became secret lovers within weeks of meeting and, despite numerous attempts to end their dangerous relationship, it was a drug the older man simply couldn't wean himself off.

Wedgewood was a dazzling academic, having bagged a first-class honours degree at Magdalen College Oxford and an MBA at Harvard, but wasn't so well blessed when it came to the looks department with his reptilian face and hooded eyes that were slightly too close together. An aquiline nose and a pair of pencil-thin lips completed an unfortunate set of facial features, while his greasy greying hair appeared as though it had been cut by a butter knife. His five-eight frame was slightly hunched and carried too much weight, a physicality he tried hard to disguise courtesy of one-thousand-pound-a-piece, hand-made Savile Row suits. The chancellor sometimes questioned what his young lover saw in him but quashed any self-doubt by telling himself what an intoxicating aphrodisiac political power could be for the young.

Wedgewood hadn't slept for three nights and was on the verge of a meltdown. The recent poisoning of the Italian minister of the interior and the mysterious disappearance of Wedgewood's counterpart in the Australian Treasury were playing heavily on his mind. No one in the media or indeed inside his own government had joined up the dots yet but he certainly had. He knew both were prominent members of the clandestine Spider Network, as indeed was he. In recent months they'd shared several Zoom calls, although he didn't share their extreme right-wing views, or in Carrozza's case, her Germanic ancestry. For some reason a purge was taking place and he wondered if his name was on the kill list.

It was just after midday when he upped sticks from his office in Downing Street and made an impromptu trip to Dorneywood, from where, after spending less than hour, he headed off in his government car towards Windsor. Only his driver and protection officer, who rode up front in the armoured Range Rover Sentinel, knew the address he was heading for. Both men had suspected for some time their boss was enjoying an illicit affair as the trips were frequent and normally only lasted for just over an hour. Pathetically, he claimed he was visiting an elderly relative and, as part of the subterfuge, always picked up a bouquet from a riverside florist on his way to the liaison. His WhatsApp message to his research assistant, confirming the unscheduled visit, had been sent three hours earlier and, when he arrived at the apartment, it was business as usual.

As ever, the sex was a fraudulent transaction as, for one of them, the passion displayed was completely fake. It was mechanical and over in a matter of minutes as Wedgewood's lover knew exactly what buttons to press and what toys to use. For the chancellor it was a dream setup. At the age of sixty he'd finally discovered what he was looking for and was enjoying the best sex he'd ever known, and he didn't even have to pay for it. Each time they met, the formula was pretty much identical. The sex would happen almost straight away, followed by a half-hour pillow talk session, where the pair would share a bottle of ice-cold Bollinger and a plate of black olives. After that, Wedgewood would enjoy an assisted shower before quickly dressing and heading off back to Dorneywood. Normally, their post-sex chat revolved around political matters of the day as the chancellor naively believed his besotted lover valued him as a mentor.

As the pair lay spreadeagled on top of the white cotton bed sheets, Wedgewood's mind was in turmoil and impulsively he decided to share his fears his with his young lover – the only person in the world he could possibly trust with the stick of dynamite he was about to reveal.

'Georgie, my darling. Can I trust you; can I really trust you?'

His young lover shifted a little, so their eyes locked, and reached across to gently caress one of his nipples.

'Mark, you fool. Do you even have to ask? Look at us right now. This place is your sanctuary – no one will ever know about it. I would die for you, my love.'

Wedgewood smiled and heaved a huge sigh before beginning his sorry tale, a dark secret he never thought would pass his lips. He began though with a question.

'Have you heard of Little Saint James Island?'

'No, should I have?'

'It's better known by its nickname – Epstein Island.'

Chapter Thirty-One

Buckinghamshire, England

Georgie sprang upwards like a startled cat and stared into Wedgewood's dark brooding eyes which were full of sheer terror. For the first time in their two-year relationship the young political researcher wasn't acting, being genuinely interested in what the chancellor had just said, and the result was an avalanche of questions.

'What the hell? You knew Epstein? What was he like? Did you ever go on his plane? What was it called? Lolita?'

Wedgewood erupted like an oil gusher, desperate to unburden himself of the guilt and self-loathing he'd carried around like excess baggage inside his brain for the last twelve years.

'His friends nicknamed it The Lolita Express and I flew on it twice to visit the island. The first time was in 2012. I was a junior minister in the Foreign Office, a rising star, when I first got sucked into Epstein's perverted world. I met him at a dinner party in Washington while I was there on a government trip and extended my stay into the weekend. I'd never been to the Virgin Islands before and suddenly I find myself the house

171

guest of one of the richest men in the world. It was mesmerising stuff. His mansion was incredible; he must have had over a hundred staff running around doing his bidding and the place was dripping with young girls who were flown in with one task in mind: keep Epstein's guests happy.'

Georgie binged on Wedgewood's memories.

'I saw a doco on him. What was the plane like?'

'From the outside it looked like a regular Boeing 727 but inside it had been customised with black padded floors and I remember there was a giant bed right at the back where seats had been removed. Soon after we took off the flight turned into one long orgy, which continued when we landed at Little Saint James.'

'I think the locals called it "paedophile island". Mark, I've got to know, was Clinton there or Prince Andrew?'

'If they were, I never saw them but, to be honest, I spent most of the weekend completely out of my head as coke and girls were constantly on tap and yes, Epstein obviously liked them young and to be honest no one asked any questions, including me. And now I'm paying the price.'

Wedgewood's voice tailed off as he ruefully reflected on his predicament.

'About eighteen months ago, three years after Epstein died, I was in Paris at a three-day economic summit when an envelope was slipped under my hotel room door.'

He paused for a moment as if the memory he was dredging up was too painful to reveal.

'That's when the blackmail started. The package contained dozens of compromising photos and sworn testimonies from three underage girls who claimed I'd raped them multiple times. There was also a memory stick with over five hours of video footage taken from three different angles, filmed inside my bedroom. Turns out the sick pervert had cameras everywhere on that bastard island.'

Georgie cut in with an obvious question.

'But how could Epstein threaten you from beyond the grave?'

'Ironically, in many ways, I wish it was him. My blackmailer is a secret political organisation which goes by the name of the Spider Network. Somehow, they got their hands on those pictures and videos after Epstein died, knowing full well if they leak them to the media, my career and marriage are toast. It's a powerful outfit with major politicians in their pocket, many of whom hold high-ranking government posts across the world and it's run by a fanatic; a neo-Nazi who speaks of establishing a political Fourth Reich.'

Georgie was now all ears.

'Who is he?'

'I've no idea but when we meet on Zoom, he hides his identity behind a full screen HH logo which are the initials of one of the greatest war criminals of all time – Heinrich Himmler.'

'What does he ask you to do?'

'Political shit you're better off not knowing about. Not all the members are coerced like me, some are zealots, who believe in their cause. They're a dangerous organisation and recent events make me think my life may be in danger. In the last few days, two politicians, who I know were active members of the network have been brutally taken out and—'

'You think you might be next on the list?'

Wedgewood nodded as he let out a huge sigh.

'I'm thinking of going to see Leo Hamilton at MI5. He's an old friend from Eton. Maybe, if I come clean with him, he might help me escape their clutches and expose their twisted organisation.'

'Yes, but what if they release the Epstein stuff – you'll be destroyed. Everything to do with that man is toxic.'

'Georgie, right now I feel like a dead man walking, so I've not got much to lose.'

Wedgewood leaned across and reached for his iPhone resting on the bedside table. He punched in the code and as he glanced at the time he let out a cry which seemed to wash away everything that had gone before.

'Christ, I only planned to stay half an hour. I've got a Zoom with the PM at four. I'll grab a quick shower, then I'm out of here.'

As soon as Wedgewood disappeared inside the bathroom, Georgie rolled across to the other side of the bed to fire off a short WhatsApp message to a contact named Will.

Listen to the last five minutes and come back asap.

By the time the reply landed, Wedgewood was standing with his back to the bathroom door, towelling himself down and didn't stop when he heard Georgie enter for what he imagined was a farewell hug. He smiled and allowed the towel to slide to the floor as the familiar embrace of his lover's arms encircled him from behind. He felt himself go hard and for a moment the notion of rushing off to his country home vanished from his mind, as he figured he'd time for a 'quickie'. That was the last coherent thought Wedgewood ever formed, as moments later his neck was sliced open from ear to ear, courtesy of a black walnut-handled Swiss army knife that slashed through both carotid arteries, meaning he'd bleed out in a matter of seconds. His body jerked backwards, and Georgie instinctively stepped aside, allowing it to slump on to the tiled floor, then turned away, not bothering to glance down at the startled look of betrayal on the chancellor's face.

Five minutes later, George Loveridge, known affectionately to his friends as 'Georgie', exited the front entrance of the apartment block, helmeted up and dressed from head to toe in classic black bike leathers. As he crossed the pavement and headed for his blue Yamaha R1, he sauntered past the olive-green Range Rover with Wedgewood's driver and protection officer inside, neither of whom gave him a second glance. He straddled the motorbike and, just before he pocketed his cell, took a quick glance down at the screen and smiled as he registered the kitchen knife emoji.

Loveridge's gloved hand gunned the throttle which burst into life with a throaty roar and moments later he sped off, heading directly for Terminal 5 at Heathrow, just ten miles away. His mind flicked back to his recruitment in France and the briefing file he'd been shown informing him Wedgewood had displayed gay tendencies for many years but had never succumbed to his urges. That resistance ended the night the man who held the grand title, Chancellor of the Exchequer, was seduced in his own office by an irresistible young intern. For two years George played the role of Wedgewood's infatuated gay lover, a part which sickened him, although the pay compensated for the unsavoury twice-a-month encounter. Now, he was on his way to Paris to collect a handsome bonus and, as he navigated his Japanese superbike through the early evening traffic on the M4, he wondered what his next assignment from the Spider Network would entail.

Chapter Thirty-Two

Washington D.C., United States

The BBC online news platform was in chaos, as was every other media outlet in the United Kingdom, as the Tory government was rocked to its core by the biggest political sex scandal to break in decades. Berrettini had linked his laptop to a projector screen in his office, where he was joined by Hembury, Vargas and Soletska who were all following the breaking story on the UK website. The headline was compelling: *Chancellor Murdered by Gay Lover*. The salacious details of Wedgewood's gruesome killing made for remarkable reading as information emerged of his naked blood-soaked body being discovered in the bathroom of a one-bedroom flat in Windsor. The name of the young man who rented the apartment had also broken but the police admitted they'd no idea as to the whereabouts of George Loveridge.

The FBI deputy director turned away from the screen and picked up his cell.

'I learned about the killing just over eight hours ago from my colleague, Christopher Denton, at GCHQ in the UK, well before it went public. The police pretty much know the exact time Wedgewood was murdered; his protection officer was on the scene within minutes of it happening.'

Vargas tried to put the pieces together.

'So, even though we don't know whether the chancellor's connected, we must assume whoever's running the Spider Network has decided to blow away some of their key assets and Wedgewood may well be one of the names on the USB. They're no doubt thinking it's only a matter of time before we crack the encoded names who, it appears, have now become part of an active kill list. I know from what I learned on my recent trip that one of them is a senior figure in the Argentine government, which leaves four more on the drive to identify.'

'Any idea who they might be?'

'It's a long shot, but Manuel's girlfriend thought it was someone involved in setting up the COP summit in Buenos Aires, so I guess we should take a look at the environment minister for starters.'

'That's a great lead, Nic. I'll authorise a full background check on them.'

Berrettini glanced down at an incoming email.

'Listen to this, guys. A few minutes ago, I sent Denton a file containing the videos we found on Carrozza's and Cook's laptops and, guess what?'

Soletska couldn't contain herself.

'I bet a month's salary they've discovered identical versions filmed by Wedgewood and, in one of them, he's standing behind a podium in front of a green screen.'

'Yes, precisely. MI5 found them on his computer and Denton is sending them over.'

Hembury's face broke into a knowing smile.

'This confirms everything we've been thinking. All these politicians are having deepfakes made of themselves, which throws up three obvious questions. Why are they being created, who's behind it and what do they intend to do with them?'

* * *

A few hours later, and four thousand miles away from Berrettini's office, another covert meeting was taking place in a building in Strasbourg, where two participants also analysed the UK media's coverage of Wedgewood's murder. Legrand had instigated the breakfast summit with his head of operations, Sabine Moreau, to run through several items, as well as the slaying of the UK chancellor. The pair were sitting together at a circular black wrought-iron table, set on a large private terrace in the grounds of the eighteenth-century château which housed some of the world's most advanced AI systems. They were enjoying a delicious serving of eggs Florentine along with sides of sliced avocado and lightly toasted brioche. The food was accompanied by crystal tumblers of fresh orange juice and porcelain cups containing Jamaica Blue Mountain coffee, the brand Legrand considered to be the best in the world.

Moreau employed a Michelin-starred chef full time at the facility for occasions exactly like this, because there was no way of knowing when her capricious boss would turn up for a meeting, as he rarely gave advance warning of his visits. Moreau figured that compared to the rest of the extortionate running costs incurred by the state-of-the-art facility, the chef's fees for himself and his small team were a drop in the ocean.

Legrand pushed his plate to one side and savoured a large mouthful of coffee before clearing his throat as a signal he was ready to run through specific items on his agenda. He reached inside his jacket to retrieve a burgundy leather-bound notebook, which he opened and carefully rested on the table. Moreau maintained a smile but held her breath as, whenever Legrand produced it, she knew a barrage of unreasonable demands would be coming her way. She'd privately christened it *Lucifer's Diary*, as long ago she'd sold her soul to the devil. This time, however, she knew she was sitting on an ace in the hole.

Legrand was far too vain to wear glasses and loathed contact lenses, so was forced to lean forward to read his own handwritten notes.

'Sabine, I've several matters to discuss. Let's start with the demise of Wedgewood. Obviously, we can cease work on his deepfake and destroy all evidence of it ever existing. I'm waiting to hear from my contact in Washington, but I believe most people will take the killing at face value; a crime of passion committed by a young man who could no longer tolerate being abused by a powerful politician who was over twice his age. He'll be contacting you shortly and when he does, process a payment to him of five hundred thousand euros from the Belize account and set him up in an apartment in the city on a six-month rental. He's an industrious young man and may be of use to me in the future.'

Moreau used her Samsung cell as a notebook and punched in the details. That request was easy enough to fulfil but she knew there would be more challenging ones to come. Legrand continued issuing his orders.

'Next, I want all delivery deadlines brought forward by two weeks, regardless of their current state of play and that of course includes all versions of my own deepfake.'

'Sir, I've good news on that front. Thomas has been working flat out since we last discussed it, with some remarkable results.'

Moreau flipped open her laptop and pulled up an MP4 file containing a sixty-second video. She stood up and angled the screen towards Legrand and then walked around the table so she could lean over his shoulder as he viewed the clip. She clicked on play and Legrand's eyes widened as he saw a perfect manifestation of himself sitting behind his beloved Napoleonic desk, dressed in his favourite Prince of Wales check suit. He was talking to camera about the upcoming COP conference in Buenos Aires and everything was perfect. The face, the voice, the mannerisms and the delivery were remarkable, considering the deepfake was speaking sentences Legrand himself had never uttered. Moreau could hardly contain her excitement as she knew what was about to happen.

'Sir, watch carefully now. See what happens at 00.44.00.'

She was referring to the burnt-in timecode that was running across the bottom of the screen that was currently at 00.32.00 – twelve seconds before her reference point. Then, as the video reached the exact time, Legrand cried out in disbelief.

'Jesus, rewind, rewind and show me that again.'

During the following two minutes Legrand watched the same clip four times, marvelling at the technological breakthrough he was witnessing. At forty-four seconds into the video, his deepfake moved his right hand up to his face to

180

slightly adjust his hair, a movement that appeared to be a normal human tic but that was the whole point of the demo file. Moreau revelled in her moment of success.

'As you can see, your deepfake's hand moved right across the front of its face seamlessly, without causing any hint of disturbance to the machine-generated image of your facial features. No AI-generated deepfakes have ever been able to achieve that feat before and it's always been an obvious flaw. Nothing physical ever appears in front of an artificial face but now—'

Legrand, whose real face was energised by an arrogant smirk, cut straight across her.

'Now, we are nearing perfection. Thomas is a genius and deserves to be rewarded. Give him a substantial bonus.'

Moreau was hugely relieved the meeting had gone as well as she'd hoped but despite his obvious elation, Legrand wasn't quite finished with her.

'One last thing. We need to talk about my jewel in the crown.'

Chapter Thirty-Three

Paris, France

May 1947

Joffe and Laroche was one of the oldest and most esteemed law firms in France, employing over five hundred lawyers at offices spread across the country in twenty major cities. Its prestigious headquarters were located at 50 Avenue Marceau, close to the iconic Arc de Triomphe. The illustrious building occupied five floors of a historic nineteenth-century structure, formerly the second biggest library in the city.

Paul Laroche was a senior partner and grandson of one of the founders and his client list was spectacular. His stunning office, which was larger than most Parisian apartments, was where he held court to senior politicians, sports heroes and film stars. To make a personal appointment with Paul Laroche you had to be an 'A' lister. At the grand age of sixty, he thought he'd seen it all but even he was astounded by the twenty-four-year-old heiress, whose personal wealth placed her comfortably in France's top ten rich list. As far as he could tell the origin of her money was Swiss, but he was far too shrewd to ask invasive questions of someone who was about to buy the most expensive apartment in the city. When she spoke, her impeccable French gave no clue as to her German origins and her demeanour and self-confidence created the impression of a privileged upbringing, which the eminent lawyer fully bought into.

'Monsieur Laroche, are we there on the paperwork for the new apartment? I'm keen to take possession as soon as possible.'

A three-time divorcee, Laroche was a man who appreciated the finer things in life and that included clothes, jewellery, property and women. The young lady sitting opposite him ticked all his boxes. She was wearing a one-off Dior creation, while the Cartier diamond-encrusted Bezel watch adorning her left wrist was dazzling, as was its rarity and price. Laroche drank in her wealth and her mysterious story.

'Mademoiselle Legrand, the funds required for completion arrived from your Zurich account overnight and I'm delighted to tell you that, as of three hours ago, the magnificent property on the Avenue Joseph-Bouvard is now yours.'

He leaned forward and reached into his leather in-tray for a set of three keys, bound together by a thin piece of string. He rose from his chair, rounded his desk and handed them over.

'Apologies for the lack of a suitable key ring but I'm sure you'll rectify that very shortly. I look forward to an invitation in the future.'

He laughed at his presumptuous quip, but Amelie's deadpan expression informed him his joke hadn't landed. He cleared his throat in embarrassment and remained silent as she popped the keys inside her black Chanel handbag and rose from her seat. Laroche escorted her across his office, stepping on to an enormous blue and gold oriental floor rug, which caught Amelie's eye. If she were to play the heiress convincingly, she'd have to get used to the part.

'Monsieur Laroche, can I enquire as to where you purchased this exquisite rug?'

The lawyer was delighted to be back in her good books and was quick to reply.

'It's Chinese of course. Late seventeenth-century, woven from the finest silk. I'll ask the vendor to contact you directly at your apartment.'

She nodded her appreciation as the pair approached the office door, where Laroche offered a more conventional parting shot.

'Enjoy your new home, Mademoiselle Legrand.'

For the first time since she'd entered his office, Amelie conjured up a smile.

'I fully intend to.'

* * *

On 26 May 1947, just days after moving into her new apartment, Amelie chaired her first board meeting at Banque Legrand. There were eight members present, curious to meet the bank's new owner for the first time. They were all survivors of the previous incarnation, Auclair and Blanchet, but as they now only owned ten per cent of the shares between them, they knew they were nothing more than bit players. Nonetheless, they were highly sceptical about the young woman sitting at the head of the boardroom table who owned the other ninety per cent and were secretly wishing she'd fail. Four of them had already begun to plot against Amelie in the hope that shares in the bank would plummet, allowing them to force her out and buy their way back in, on the cheap.

Back in August 1944 they'd all been happy to sell most of their shares to a mysterious Swiss heiress living in Geneva. None of them had heard of the Legrand family but with a valuation almost doubling the recognised share price, no one asked any questions.

In the two and a half years since the acquisition took place Amelie had immersed herself in the minutiae of the day-to-day dealings of the bank, receiving weekly reports by telex from the financial director who was now sitting alongside her. Even though they'd never met in person, she and Patrice Delon had spoken several times by phone and Amelie felt he was a potential ally in a room full of vipers.

Although there was no way Amelie could know it, at twenty-four, she was the same age as her mother when she'd given birth to her. Through a twist of fate and the intervention of one man, their lives couldn't have looked more different. Franka had been a waitress in a Munich bar, forced to give her baby up for adoption, while Amelie was the owner of a private bank in Paris and one of the wealthiest women in France. Heinrich Himmler had touched both their lives but with starkly different consequences.

When Amelie spoke for the first time, no one in the room was prepared for the tirade coming their way. What's more, they couldn't have suspected she'd rehearsed the speech word for word for months in front of her bedroom mirror. She was the only female in the room but that didn't trouble her in the slightest. Her voice had a maturity that belied her age and a natural gravitas that took everyone by surprise.

'Gentlemen, for many years this bank has been run like a private men's club, where personal relationships have trumped good business acumen. I must tell you, that cosy behaviour is coming to an end right now. As are the ridiculously high dividends you've been paying yourselves twice a year since the end of the war.'

Amelie deliberately paused to study the panicked faces of the disgruntled shareholders sitting around the table who clearly hadn't seen any of this coming. None of them had the guts to challenge her, yet she'd barely scratched the surface.

'To date, we have seventy-four customers whose accounts are constantly falling into the red, in some cases by thousands of francs yet we fail to charge any interest on their overdrafts. Why is that?'

She left another pause before answering her own question and posing some more.

'Could it be because many of them are your friends and family?'

As she glanced around the table, eyelines were looking down, avoiding her gaze.

'I see nearly half these accounts are held by Jews. Maybe they prefer using our credit instead of their own? Well, no more. Where an account is overdrawn, the bank will charge interest on a daily basis and if customers don't like it, they can take their business elsewhere.'

Amelie switched her attention to the oldest and most respected man in the room. He'd sat on the board for over thirty years and was a direct descendant of one of the bank's founders.

'Monsieur Blanchet, I see buried deep in our records an outstanding debt of over thirty thousand francs tied up in a dubious pre-war loan issued to your cousin, Bernard Dubois, which you personally underwrote. The debt has remained on our books for over nine years and yet he doesn't appear to have refunded a single franc during that time. I calculate Dubois owes the bank over ten thousand in interest and, from what I can tell, doesn't have the means to repay us. Monsieur, knowing you're a man of substance and integrity, I insist you personally repay the bank a total of forty thousand francs in the next twenty-four hours, or I'll instigate a repossession order on Dubois's house and notify the police of a dubious loan that took place under the previous ownership.'

Blanchet's deeply furrowed ancient face reddened with a mix of embarrassment and rage but, despite the mutterings of discontent around him, the old man remained silent as Amelie continued.

'Finally, I wish to address the strategy of the bank going forward. I have plans for expansion which will see thirty new branches open across the country in the next five years and eventually I intend us to become the largest private banking group in the country.'

Louis Rousseau, another long-term shareholder, finally erupted, having heard enough.

'We've always been a unique, boutique bank, based in Paris with an exclusive clientele. That's our history and—'

Amelie cut him dead.

'Monsieur Rousseau, that's all in the past. Those of you around this table who choose to support this strategy will see their small shareholdings grow into large fortunes. Those who don't, can either resign now and sell their shares to me or be dropped off along the way.'

She rose from her chair to signal her first board meeting was over and, as she exited the room, those remaining had little doubt the young heiress from Switzerland meant every word she said and would ultimately achieve her goals. Had her late father witnessed such a ruthless performance, he would no doubt have been extremely proud of his favourite child.

Amelie departed the bank on Rue du Faubourg Saint-Honoré and took a brisk ten-minute walk back to her apartment on Avenue Joseph-Bouvard, crossing the Seine on the way. Once inside she headed straight for her study, which hadn't yet been decorated to her taste but for now she was making use of an old safe that came with the property, which contained several precious items, including the *Die Spinne* notebook, compiled by Himmler himself and passed on to her by his aide-de-camp.

In truth, she knew most of the hand-written contents by heart but found great comfort reading the names of like-minded Germans who were also beginning new lives around the world, thanks to the forward planning of her father and the Spider Network. She felt it was her destiny to bring these people together under a cloak of secrecy to keep the Nazi dream alive. Now she was settled with a new identity, it was time to begin the work, and her only question was: who amongst the many names should she reach out to first? She mulled over the problem for a while and, after narrowing the choice down to two, made a decision.

Hermann Koch had served as a commandant at the notorious Buchenwald Camp, near the city of Weimar in Germany, and had been personally involved in some of the worst atrocities of the war, including issuing death warrants on rabbis, who were taken outside the camp gates and buried alive. He was living under a new identity in Madrid, where he was the owner of a massive industrial plant, manufacturing agricultural machinery for Spanish farmers.

It took Amelie a while to find a number for him but eventually she tracked one down and then it took another hour for her to summon up the courage to call. When Koch answered the phone in Spanish, the first thing she noticed was, unlike her, he'd failed to shed his German accent, but she prayed he was fluent enough to understand her schoolgirl Spanish.

'Señor Castillo, my name is Amelie Legrand. I'm the owner of the Banque Legrand in Paris. I believe we share something in common.'

Koch was wary and hesitated for a moment before replying.

'And what might that be?'

'We share a love of spiders.'

Chapter Thirty-Four

Washington D.C., United States

'I find this report very disturbing and, frankly, hard to believe. I sat on this girl's recruitment board and have known her personally for over three years.'

Barbara Starling held the confidential document in her hand and everyone else in the room had a copy of it on the table in front of them and had spent the previous fifteen minutes perusing it. After a brief pause to gather her thoughts, she pressed on.

'But the facts are compelling. I'm horrified the leak came from someone on my team.'

Berrettini had just finished appraising the bullet-pointed conclusions on the final page for a second time.

'I understand how difficult this is for you, Barbara, but remember, I brought in an independent investigator and, as you say, the evidence is crystal clear. On paper she appears exemplary, so you've no reason to beat yourself up. From my experience, informants or even fully fledged spies are often the hardest to spot.'

Another silence followed and Soletska, who was genuinely surprised to have been asked to attend the gathering, took the opportunity to voice her thoughts.

'We're similar ages and I've had lunch with her a couple of times in the last few months in the staff canteen. We weren't exactly friends, but we got on okay. She just doesn't strike me as the type to get involved in something like this.'

Berrettini took back control of the meeting.

'Thanks for that, Liliya. If anything relevant comes to mind when you think back on those conversations you had, anything you think might be useful, let me know.'

The FBI deputy director then glanced back towards Starling.

'Where is she right now?'

'She's in a room on the third floor, under supervision. After I saw the report late last night, I blocked her pass so when she tried to sign in this morning an alert told security she'd arrived. That was about two hours ago, so right now she's no idea what's going down, although I guess she's probably worked out we're on to her.'

'Okay, for the moment we'll keep this whole matter off the radar so no calls to friends, family or lawyers. As far as the rest of your team is concerned, she called in sick. Barbara, you're too close to her to sit in on an interview. I'll see her with Nic and Troy and hopefully she won't prove a hard nut to crack.'

Hembury and Vargas nodded as Berrettini stood, picked up the five-page document and waved it in the air.

'When she sees what's in here, I'm pretty sure she'll decide to co-operate.'

Devane, who'd remained silent the entire time, couldn't resist chipping in before the meeting ended.

'Betrayal is one trait I can't abide – if it were me, I'd lock her up and throw away the key.'

Three hours earlier

Jissika Murkowski was running late for work. The twenty-six-year-old data analyst had overslept and was nursing a monster of a hangover, the result of an unusually late night spent with her two best friends, during which far too many beers and vodkas had been consumed. The threesome had checked out the opening night of a new club in the U Street Corridor in Northwest D.C., which was offering half-price drinks after midnight. She cursed as she failed dismally in her battle to squeeze a useable blob of toothpaste from its tube and opted instead to pop a peppermint gum into her mouth, hoping it would have a similar effect of disguising the smell of alcohol she could still taste on her tongue. Murkowski grabbed the first clean clothes she could lay her hands on and flew down the stairs from her fifth-floor apartment, heading for Cleveland Park metro station, which thankfully was less than a two-minute sprint away.

Murkowski lived and worked in Washington but was born and raised three and a half thousand miles away in Alaska's capital city of Juneau, named after a prospector who led the famous Gold Rush of 1880. With a tiny population of thirty-two thousand, it was unique in being the only US capital on mainland North America not to have a connecting road to any other state. In every possible way, the barren landscape of the Alaskan capital was a stark contrast to the metropolitan city of Washington, which housed a thriving population, some two hundred and forty times larger.

She was proud of her Aleut heritage. Her facial features were a clone of her mother, her grandmother, and many generations before. A broad, open face, crowned by jet black straight hair. Jissika was the eldest of five children, remarkably all girls, brought up single-handedly by her mother who worked by day as a seamstress in a fur factory and by night as an office cleaner. Her father, who fished king crab for a living, disappeared one day when she was only eight years old which left the family in financial difficulties but, fortunately, Jissika was exceptionally bright, so her mother hoped she'd be able to earn well and support them as she got older.

Murkowski's astonishing mathematical prowess earned her a prized scholarship at Fairbanks University, Alaska's finest academic institution. She spent five years there, studying for a combined BA masters in computer science and, during the final weeks of her last term, an impromptu meeting with a visiting professor from Washington changed the course of her life.

Peter Richardson, the man who ran the mathematics department at Georgetown University, had a second string to his bow. He travelled the country recruiting students whose academic results placed them in the top one per cent in their field. If he felt they were the right fit, he earmarked them as potential candidates to join the government's Special Operations Command unit, better known as SOCOM. Although accepting a job there meant leaving Alaska and living with the oppressive secrecy that came with working for a sensitive government agency, the salary on offer was almost ten times what she could ever hope to earn in Juneau. She figured that would allow her to send most of that money back home to her mother, who still had her other four daughters to bring up. So, despite her six-figure income, after paying her rent, which she sometimes failed to hit on time, Murkowski struggled to survive on what was left.

As she dashed through the huge reception area at FBI head-quarters on Pennsylvania Avenue, she congratulated herself on being only sixteen minutes late, rather than the hour she'd feared. Her sense of moderate success evaporated seconds later when her pass failed to work and two security guards, who normally greeted her with a warm smile and some friendly chat, escorted her upstairs to a third-floor meeting room without uttering a word. When they insisted she hand over her laptop and cell, Jissika realised being late was the least of her worries.

Chapter Thirty-Five

Washington D.C., United States

It was just over two hours later when a security guard entered the meeting room and placed three chairs in a line, directly facing Murkowski across the oblong metal table. The anticipation of what was about to happen next made her stomach churn. She didn't have to wait long for an answer as, a few seconds after he left, three men entered, one after the other. Although they'd never met, she instantly recognised the face of the FBI's deputy director, but had no idea who his two associates were. Suddenly, as the gravity of her situation hit home, her eyes welled up and the pain in her stomach became almost unbearable. She bit down hard on her lower lip. Whatever was coming her way, she'd have to remain strong. There were five lives in the tiny Alaskan city of Juneau that depended on her.

As Berrettini took a seat, flanked by Vargas and Hembury, Murkowski felt as though the air had just been sucked out of the room and she gasped for breath. The deputy director placed a slim grey file on the table and issued a brief smile before introducing himself and his colleagues. He was anticipating a short and easy interrogation. The evidence for treason was overwhelming and the petrified young lady sitting opposite him was no hardened terrorist.

'I imagine you've had time to work out the reason you're being detained and why I need to talk to you.'

There was no immediate reply, just a hesitant shake of the head. Berrettini studied her eyes searching for a giveaway sign of deceit but all he saw was naked fear. He reached down for the file and retrieved a document which he studied in silence for the next couple of minutes, acting as though he were reading it for the first time; classic textbook behaviour, a ploy to further unsettle the suspect.

'Jissika, less than a dozen people outside the three of us knew about the decoding of Cook and Carrozza's names from the USB drive, yet somehow they were leaked from inside this building. This, unfortunately, led to both being compromised and taken out. I've no doubt whatsoever you were the source of the leak. I need to know why and who you passed the information on to. Bearing in mind how close some Aleuts are to the motherland, was it the Russians?'

'No, no, no! This is total bullshit. I've no idea what this is but I swear I know nothing about it.'

For some reason her gaze switched to Vargas; her eyes desperately pleading for support. He speculated she was either a great actress or something was off. At this point he couldn't tell which. Berrettini picked up on the exchange with Vargas but ploughed on.

'Okay, so you want to talk about bullshit. We've uncovered a covert bank account in your name, based in Juneau, which in the last year has received regular payments of twenty thousand dollars, always made on the last day of the month. The funds originate from a bank in Panama, which makes the source of the money almost undetectable.'

He paused to glance back down at the document, double-checking what was coming next.

'Three days ago, shortly after the removal of the two politicians, a one-off payment of two hundred and fifty thousand hit. A nice bonus for a job well done.'

'I swear I know nothing of this money . . . I only have one account and that's—'

Berrettini saw an opportunity and dived in.

'That's permanently in overdraft, isn't it? Even though you're a high earner, you live in constant debt and your landlord is threatening to evict you. Isn't that correct?'

Despite her plan to stay strong, it was all unravelling, and she could feel hot tears streaming down her cheeks.

'Yes . . . that's true . . . but the rest . . .'

'Let's talk about the rest, Jissika.'

His right hand settled on a single sheet of paper inside the file, which he slid across the table, placing it in front of her.

'We found this unsent email this morning on your laptop. It's a letter of resignation – undated, but ready to go. It's clear to me what's going down. You know it's too dangerous to touch any of that black money while you're working here. I think you've been asked to wait by whoever's paying you, until the rest of the names are decoded and then you plan to resign and head back to Alaska, where you'll be free to access the money.'

The young Aleut woman slumped forward in her chair, defeated, her head on her folded arms as the tear lines became rivers.

'Jissika, I know how tough debt can be. It appears you send home almost all your income to your family which is admirable but none of that justifies a betrayal on this scale.'

He suspected she was about to crack like a freshly farmed egg but, when she looked up, he was astonished to see a glare of defiance.

'I told you already . . . this is all crap. You're setting me up . . . I've no idea why . . . I want a lawyer . . . I'm not saying another word.'

Berrettini had heard enough and moved up a gear.

'Okay, enough of the games. Remember where you are, Jissika. Right now, you're sitting in an interrogation room inside FBI headquarters. This interview is part of an international investigation which involves several brutal killings, so forget about lawyers. You're in deep with some very bad people and you need to start opening up quickly. If you co-operate, there might just be a way out for you.'

This time she remained silent, so Berrettini decided to play his final card. He reached inside his jacket and pulled out a polythene evidence bag containing a cheap burner cell phone which he held in front of her face.

'After you left for work this morning, two operatives searched your apartment and found this taped to the inside of the toilet cistern in your bathroom. It's preloaded with one number and, as I'm sure you're aware, when you call it, it diverts straight to voicemail. Not great for conversation but perfect for leaving messages. I've no doubt that's how you passed over the names.'

'I know my rights . . . I want . . . I need to see a lawyer.'

Her voice was little more than a whisper and Berrettini read the weakness and tone of it as a sign of defeat, although evidently, she hadn't yet broken.

'Let's leave it there for now. I suggest you take some time to come to your senses before it's too late. Right now, you're heading for a holding cell in the basement.'

With that, he rose from his chair and headed for the door, followed by Vargas and Hembury. Just before they exited, she called out, her voice suddenly back to full strength.

'You've all set me up. I demand a lawyer.'

Berrettini shook his head in frustration before leading his two colleagues out of the interview room. As he slammed the door behind him, he wondered how long she'd need on her own in a cell before she confessed.

Chapter Thirty-Six

Strasbourg, France

L egrand had spent the entire day at his beloved 'facility', working through his latest plans with Moreau, setting unrealistic timetables for the upcoming weeks which promised to be hectic. It was just before midnight and the pair were sitting together in his office, sharing a Zoom call via a giant LED screen with a senior member of the Spider Network.

Javier Galvez headed the Ministry for Environment and Sustainable Development in the Argentine government and was one of Legrand's closest allies. Galvez was one of only three politicans embedded in the upper echelons of the secret organisation who knew Legrand's identity, which meant there was no need for the media mogul to hide behind his red HH screen logo. The closeness of their relationship transcended politics and linked back to their respective heritages – both their grandfathers were Nazis, although in Legrand's case, it was through adoption rather than bloodline.

It was no coincidence the enormous château Legrand had purchased and converted into a state-of-the-art computer complex was situated less than ten miles away from the iconic Hôtel Maison Rouge, one of Strasbourg's oldest buildings, where his grandfather, Heinrich Himmler, had formed *Die Spinne* in August 1944. Originally, it exclusively served the interests of Nazis but eighty years on, members of the covert organisation fell into three categories. A handful, like Galvez, were direct descendants of senior SS officers who'd fled Germany at the tail-end of the Second World War, utilising the web of escape routes provided by the Network. Others were right-wing, neo-fascist politicians who shared the same ideals and principles of the original Nazis and were enthusiastic recruits to the covert organisation. Finally, a handful were prominent figures in governments around the world, who, like the recently deceased UK chancellor, had been coerced, mainly through blackmail, to work against their will for Legrand's operation.

Galvez's grandfather, Heinz Scholz, had the blood on his hands of over two hundred thousand Jews. He'd been a senior government official who worked as a link man between the Foreign Office and the SS and was responsible for rounding up and exterminating German and foreign Jews. By the beginning of 1945 Scholz was terrified at the prospect of falling into the hands of the Allies, so he turned to *Die Spinne* for help. They enabled his escape using a route that took him across the border into Austria then south into Italy, first to Rome and then on to Genoa where he boarded a container ship that transported him to Argentina. Between January and April 1945, the Spider Network masterminded the escape of hundreds of SS officers using this same route.

Once he arrived in Argentina's Patagonia region, he was sent significant funds facilitating the purchase of a substantial home in the city of Bariloche, along with a thriving car repair business. Finally, a new identity courtesy of an Argentine passport saw the demise of Heinz Scholz and the birth of Hector Galvez. The Spider Network had done its job and, two generations on, his grandson, Javier, was a fêted government minister, proud of his secret ancestry. However, despite being a committed member of the covert organisation, he was clearly unnerved by the recent events in Buenos Aires and across the globe in Italy and Australia.

'Leopold, what went down with Salazar and his lackey? I assume you authorised their killings. And what about Carrozza's poisoning and Cook's disappearance?'

Legrand arrogantly flicked his right hand in the air as a gesture of dismissal and eloquently responded with a tissue of lies. He'd no intention of referencing the stolen USB and the trail of death it had set in motion.

'They were both extremely careless in protecting their association with our network and risked exposure. With so much at stake, they had to be taken out. Javier, it's just a blip – nothing for you to worry about. We're still firmly on course to hit our deadlines. As for Salazar, that scumbag tried to betray me and paid the price. Now, let's talk about the all-important votes at COP. I've secured some key allies inside the African Union and of course we have senior people in place in four of the member states.'

Galvez wasn't happy with Legrand's dismissive reply but knew not to question it. For the following forty minutes the two men discussed the upcoming conference in Buenos Aires and two pivotal votes they knew would be on the agenda. They spoke in English for the entire conversation but signed off with the classic German phrase: '*Auf Wiedersehen, mein Freund.*'

Legrand switched his attention to his head of operations who'd stayed silent throughout the lengthy exchange, sitting well out of shot of the Zoom camera. Bearing in mind the sensitive nature of some of the content discussed, she was somewhat surprised he'd allowed her to remain present as an observer. Initially, he'd recruited Moreau to run the technical side of the facility, having headhunted her from the global communications giant, Tavas. She'd been running their European digital division, which had an impressive AI development arm, bang at the forefront of deepfake technology, so he'd made her an offer she couldn't refuse. In fact, she figured two more years at that rate and she'd be able to retire; not bad for a thirty-five-year-old.

In recent months she'd inevitably learned a great deal about Legrand's political ambitions and witnessed first-hand his devious machinations but couldn't nail down the big picture. Unbeknown to her that was about to change.

'Sabine, if you check your bank account, you'll see you've just received a bonus payment of five million dollars and, if all goes well in the next six months, you can expect to receive another similar payment.'

Moreau felt as though a massive bolt of electricity had just surged through her veins and fought hard against the instinctive temptation to check the bank statement on her cell, just to confirm the reality of the seven-figure transaction. She knew this inevitably meant she'd have to pay a heavy price but figured Legrand already owned her soul and now, with the news of these unexpected bonuses, she'd be out of there in less than a year, eighteen months earlier than expected. So, whatever avalanche of shit was heading her way, she knew she could handle it as her escape route was now in touching distance.

'Thank you, sir. I'm not sure I've earned it but it's much appreciated. Life-changing.'

'Good. Now, my dear, it's time for a history lesson.'

Chapter Thirty-Seven

Strasbourg, France

Legrand inhaled deeply from his vape and settled back in his chair, relishing the opportunity to share some of his darkest secrets. Moreau nodded earnestly, still reeling from the news she was now five million dollars richer than she'd been a few minutes earlier.

'In order for you to fully grasp what's at stake in the upcoming weeks and months, I need to bring you further into my confidence. I believe you're resilient enough to take on board everything I'm about to tell you and bright enough to understand that once you hear it, there's no going back.'

Legrand left his last statement hanging in the air and Moreau wasn't quite sure if it was intended as a question. So, she took no chances.

'Absolutely, sir, I fully understand.'

'Excellent. Let's start by talking about the origins of the Spider Network, some eighty years ago now. Even though it was abundantly clear by August 1944 the war was lost, many prominent Nazis believed that, sometime in the future, a

Fourth Reich could be resurrected from the ashes of Hitler's old regime. They were of course delusional.'

He paused momentarily to take a long drag from his vape and carefully studied Moreau's eyes, double-checking he'd made the right call. She appeared transfixed by his tale, so he felt happy to press on.

'Heinrich Himmler, the genius behind *Die Spinne* was a true visionary and created a new concept for a Fourth Reich. He realised that, with elite Nazis being spread across the world, the existing plan for a new Reich was physically impossible. Instead, he foresaw an all-powerful political entity with no conventional physical borders, driven by an ideology where the strong survive, the weak perish and the racially pure triumph. That ideal meant no single leader would ever be accountable to an electorate. Instead, a select group of like-minded individuals, whose identities could be hidden from the masses, would be the true decision makers who would therefore control world events.'

Moreau was genuinely intrigued by Legrand's words and suddenly everything she'd helped put together in the previous months began to make total sense.

'Sir, that's exactly what we're witnessing right now and you're at the very heart of it.'

His words were more chilling than ever.

'Indeed, we both are. For many years I dreamed of being in this position and then two events, neither of which I antici-pated, accelerated the process, which means we're in touching distance of fulfilling Himmler's vision.'

Legrand watched as Moreau's forehead formed a puzzled frown and a Machiavellian smile broke out on his face.

'Let me explain. Firstly, no one, including me, could have predicted the Covid-19 pandemic. The disastrous consequences for the world economy have of course been huge, but for us politically it's provided an irresistible opportunity, especially when combined with the also unexpected and breathtaking emergence of AI technology. Since Covid, it's now commonplace, in fact even expected, for politicans to either release important statements by video message or to be interviewed by a TV journalist on a live link from either their office or their home. The idea of a "face-to-face sit-down interview" in a television studio is largely redundant and the beauty of all this for us is that the masses believe what they see with their own eyes.'

Another short break for a vape drag was accompanied by an ugly smirk.

'Senior members of our Network will deploy their deepfakes as much as possible, knowing the AI brain operating them will always give the right answer – the best answer – however tricky the question. They'll say exactly what the public wants to hear and can never be tripped up by difficult questions. Then when they appear in the flesh, they'll bathe in the afterglow of the performances of their deepfakes and reinforce the message. Rival politicians won't stand a chance against them and voters will love them. During the next thirty years, when many natural resources we depend on such as oil and water become scarce, world climate conferences like COP will no longer pander to the demands of the poor, underdeveloped nations because our people will be in control. Those pathetic countries who try and lever emotional blackmail as a tool to receive billions from the most powerful economies in the world will be abandoned and the richest states will be run either by members of our Network or like-minded sympathisers; right-wing nationalists who'll protect their country's self-interest at all costs, which in truth is what people really want from their politicians.'

A fresh idea gate-crashed Legrand's thoughts and he glanced down at his laptop resting on the smoked-glass coffee table. He flipped it open and worked through some encrypted files until he found the document he was searching for.

'Sabine, take a look at this.'

Curious, she leaned forward and picked up the black MacBook Pro and began reading a medical record containing multiple test results. Lines of numbers were meaningless to her, although she recognised the references to Parkinson's disease and colorectal cancer.

'Whoever this belongs to, it makes for grim reading.'

'Go to page eight and read the prognosis at the bottom.'

There was a brief silence as she clicked her way through the document.

'Christ, this poor bastard only has nine to twelve months to live.'

Legrand's waspish reply was laced with an arrogance Moreau was well used to.

'Wrong. Go back to the front page and check the date.'

Moments later her eyes landed on the date of the report.

'Eighteenth of July. So, now they only have six to nine months left. Their date of birth is seventh of October 1952 which makes them seventy-two, not that old. Put me out of my misery. Whose medical record is this?'

Legrand's devilish eyes widened and his voice hissed like a startled viper.

'Vladimir Vladimirovich Putin.'

Chapter Thirty-Eight

Strasbourg, France

Moreau looked up from the laptop and her eyes locked with Legrand's.

'We've all heard the rumours but are you sure it's genuine?'

'Absolutely, Putin's personal physician, Alexey Lebedev, who wrote this prognosis is dead and he didn't die of natural causes.'

'The wrath of a dictator being given news he didn't want to hear and then blaming the messenger?'

'Exactly. In recent months Putin's illness has forced him to deploy his double to stand in for him at dozens of public events and the irony is, like his idol Stalin, he utilises a human decoy rather than a deepfake. His doppelganger is a fourth-rate carpenter from Belarus called Yevgeny Vasilyevich, who initially was employed to fill in for the President on the odd occasion but now he's wheeled out on a regular basis.'

'How many people around him know of the prognosis?'

'I'm not sure, but Putin's demise gives us an opportunity I didn't think would be feasible for at least a decade. Russia has been run by dictators for well over a hundred years, going all the way back to Lenin. Forget about democracy, whoever holds the post of president single-handedly controls the destiny of the Russian state. Look at the Ukraine war: an invasion unilaterally triggered by Putin, without the need to defer to the State Duma. Imagine what we could achieve as a network if we had Russia in our pocket. Their political influence in Europe and the Middle East is immense and as one of the five permanent members of the United Nations Security Council, they sit at the summit of world geopolitics.'

Moreau nodded as she placed the MacBook back down on the table.

'Hence the urgency to complete our deepfake of Boris Morozov – your cherry on the cake.'

'When the battle for succession starts, as the deputy prime minister, he'll be one of three men in the frame, so we need to give him an edge. On paper he'll be the outsider in the race, so going forward, every time he speaks, he needs to appeal to the soul of the Russian people.'

'Don't worry, sir, our programmers know exactly what's needed. Every word his deepfake utters will touch the heart of every Russian voter.'

Legrand's final words were dripping with irony.

'Even though Germanic blood flows through his veins.'

* * *

Boris Morozov's name was known by less than ten per cent of the Russian people, but he knew that was about to change. The chain-smoking, mercurial deputy prime minister was sitting alone inside his massive oak-panelled office inside the Kremlin, mulling over the contents of the encrypted email he'd received from the man who ran the Spider Network.

It seemed incredible that the secret organisation had somehow secured access to the president's personal medical records, but the evidence was right in front of him on his cell and now he questioned whether he could cope with what lay ahead. Was it really his destiny as his late father had pledged, or would he be exposed as a fraud?

He took a deep drag on a Camel which was burnt down to the filter, before stubbing it out in a heavy glass ashtray, overflowing with dozens of discarded tips and the foul debris of light grey tobacco ash. His right hand robotically reached for the soft pack on his desk as he drew out the final cigarette, which burst into life courtesy of his Zippo lighter.

Morozov was not an attractive man, and he knew it. His long narrow jawline, bulging eyes, large front teeth and fleshy loose lips, combined to create a horse-face which meant he was an easy man to underestimate but those unfortunate features masked an astute intellect and quicksilver brain. He held a master's degree in economics and his rise within the Russian government was nothing short of meteoric. Before reaching his current post, he'd worked for three years as an external economic adviser to Putin, who then appointed him director of finance and economic development in the prime minister's office. His next promotion followed shortly after he joined the cabinet led by Medvedev and then, in March 2021, he took on the role of deputy prime minister.

He was a complex man, riddled with secrets, the most significant of which concerned his lineage. His paternal grandmother, Elmira Morozova, was by far the most influential figure in his life, both as a child growing up and as an adult entering the world of politics. She'd died twelve years earlier at the age of ninety-five and took many dark secrets with her to the grave. During her long life she'd only ever shared them with three people, her late husband, Igor, her son and Boris's father, Ivan and Boris himself.

Unlike her husband, who was a fourth-generation Russian, Elmira was German-born and a fanatical Nazi. During the war, aged just twenty-five, she'd joined the elite band of three thousand women who were recruited by the SS and trained in Ravensbrück to become security guards in the concentration camps. Between 1942 and 1945 she was posted to Dachau, the notorious deathcamp situated ten miles north of Munich which had been opened in March 1933 by Heinrich Himmler in person. As a rule, female guards didn't take part in the killings but participated in rounding up victims. But there were exceptions and Elmira excelled in her role and was proud to receive a medal for shooting twenty-five Jewish prisoners in the back of the head.

She loved to parade the perimeter grounds of the camp alongside her SS-trained Alsatian, who savaged thirteen victims of his own. The two of them were an intimidating sight and the inmates named her 'The Dog Witch'. In March 1945, just weeks before US forces liberated the camp, Elmira fled across the Polish border into Russia and settled in the western city of Kaliningrad. Her escape was facilitated by *Die Spinne* which, as usual, provided a fresh identity and substantial funds. Eight months later she met a like-minded Russian businessman, a German sympathiser, who loathed the Stalin communist regime and shared her hopes of a Nazi victory.

Elmira was the matriarch of the Morozov family and, as a young boy, Boris was brought up with spellbinding tales of the Führer and the Nazi dream of racial purity and world domination. Almost fifty years on, the man who was about to challenge for the Russian presidency was a proud member of the secret organisation that eighty years earlier had saved his grandmother's life.

It was a debt she always reminded him of. A debt it was time to settle. He leaned forward and picked up an oval silver picture frame which had pride of place on his desk. It held a grainy black and white photo of his beloved babushka. Boris lifted it to his lips and gently kissed the faded image. After a few seconds he gently placed it back on the desk and reached inside the top drawer of his desk for a fresh pack of Camel Blue.

Chapter Thirty-Nine

Paris, France

May 1956

Nine years after Amelie's scintillating display at her inaugural board meeting, the roll-out of Banque Legrand across France moved at breakneck speed, exceeding even her own expectations. She'd opened thirty-two branches to date, including three in Paris, with another ten in the pipeline. Meanwhile, apart from the financial director, the entire board had been replaced by like-minded fascists, hand-picked by the bank's enigmatic new owner.

One of them, François Gagneux, shared Amelie's German origins, having been spirited out of the Fatherland back in 1948, utilising ratlines secured by *Die Spinne*. Under his real name, Ernst Ziegler, he'd headed up the Hitler Youth movement between 1934 and 1941 and was a close ally of Amelie's father. Now, seven years after fleeing Germany, Gagneux owned a small chain of chemist shops in Paris and had a seat on the board of one of France's fastest growing banks.

Since arriving in Paris, Amelie had meticulously worked her way through the names listed in her father's precious notebook, reaching out to former SS officers and laying the foundations for a secret network with members spread across the world. In some instances, she facilitated loans from the bank, which she personally secured to help oil the wheels of fledgling businesses set up by former Nazis.

At the age of thirty-three, Amelie resolved to create an inheritance for future generations and that required an heir to the twin pillars that consumed her life: Banque Legrand and *Die Spinne.* Finding a suitable husband would be easy as her natural beauty and immense wealth made her an irresistible proposition to most eligible bachelors in Paris but, like many of her previous life choices, Amelie was never one to opt for the obvious or easy option. Besides, nine years on, she still hadn't fully recovered from losing the love of her life, the man who'd died protecting her new identity.

No man she'd met since stood comparison with Carlos Mayer and she doubted anyone ever would. Her love life was non-existent but that was down to her own choosing as she'd plenty else in her life to focus on. There was another issue, a massive obstacle, that killed off any prospect of a potentially successful marriage. She'd far too many secrets that had to be protected at all costs. Her life itself was one big lie, which meant she could never allow anybody to get too close. There had to be another way to secure an heir and she was determined to find it.

Adoption was the obvious solution, after all, she herself had been adopted, but the extensive background checks required by any reputable agency were far too risky. Then Amelie discovered the Place du Tertre home for abandoned orphans located in the back streets of Montmartre, just a stone's throw away from the world-famous Sacré-Coeur. The run-down, twelve-bed hovel that served as an orphanage was run by an immoral Catholic priest, who relied on random donations to fund his depraved champagne lifestyle which revolved around sleazy night clubs, underage male prostitutes and the occasional unsuspecting, unfortunate altar boy.

Father Gustav Brune applied an obscene formula to any charitable funds that came the orphanage's way. He took eighty per cent off the top for himself, while the pitiful amount remaining was spent on providing basic food and clothing for the unfortunate young children trapped inside his dreadful institution. The corrupt priest couldn't believe his luck the night he received a visit from an unnamed woman who made it clear she'd pay any price to acquire a newborn baby boy. And even better, she'd pay in cash and didn't require paperwork.

Before visiting the rat-infested shelter, Amelie created a cover story to ensure the priest could never come after her in the future. She'd previous experience of being blackmailed by the clergy and had no intention of allowing it to happen again. She reverted to her native German language, employing a spattering of poor French to communicate. On the night she met Father Brune, a ferocious storm conjured up biblical weather and when they sat together in his disgusting cesspit of an office, the corrugated roof echoed to a hypnotic drum of rain.

The priest was dressed in a filthy black cassock that looked as though it hadn't been washed since the first day he'd worn it, twenty years earlier. Hanging loose around his baggy neck was a white starched dog collar that over the years had darkened to a mustard yellow, matching the colour of the gappy teeth in his snake-like mouth, which was formed into a permanent scowl. When he spoke, his voice had a guttural, intimidating edge.

'Fräulein, what you ask of me is obviously illegal. I'd be putting myself and my wonderful institution at great risk. Newborns are rare, so their value is high. Plus, you are insisting on a boy.'

Amelie kept her French to a minimum, cloaked in a heavy German accent.

'How much, Father?'

Brune was sensing a financial killing, so upped the ante.

'There's also a massive issue with you taking the baby out of the country to Germany. The authorities will view that as a serious crime. Which city will you go to?'

'How much?'

His toadish eyes narrowed as he seriously chanced his arm.

'I believe we are looking in the region of one hundred thousand francs.'

The priest felt a dryness in his throat as he held his breath.

'Where do you envisage the baby coming from?'

He answered her question with one of his own.

'Are we good on the fee?'

Amelie nodded and his mouth cracked a malicious smile which vanished just as quickly as it appeared. He sensed a huge payday within his grasp.

'From time to time, young schoolgirls who are heavily pregnant come to see me for help and advice and normally I pass on their details to the city's main orphanage, as sadly my small institution is not set up to look after babies.'

'So, it's possible?'

The priest flashed a toothy grin.

'Yes, if you're prepared to be patient. It could be weeks or maybe months before a suitable girl appears and then of course they need to give birth to a boy. When the time comes, how will I contact you?'

'You won't. I'll call you once a week on a Monday morning at nine. Make sure you are always available for my call.'

The priest sensed he was losing control of the transaction and fought back.

'No, Fräulein, I must have a means of contacting you.'

Amelie ignored his protest and opened her handbag to retrieve a huge wad of cash, bound together by a thick rubber band. Immediately Brune's eyes sharpened as they zoomed in on the high-denomination notes.

'Father, I'm deeply moved by the wonderful work you do here and for your help with this matter. I'd like to donate ten thousand francs, which of course is separate to your fee.'

She contemptuously tossed the money across to the priest who snatched it with the same intensity a drowning man would grab hold of a lifebuoy. The next moment she rose and walked towards the door in his office, turning back to face him just before she reached it. He'd already begun counting the money.

'Father, I will call you next Monday.'

The priest didn't even look up as he replied.

'I look forward to hearing from you, Fräulein.'

Chapter Forty

Paris, France

July 1956

For the next two months, Amelie kept to her word and called Father Brune every week at the same time. The brief conversation between them was always the same and lasted no more than five seconds.

'Father, any news?'

'No, Fräulein. Nothing yet.'

She was beginning to lose faith in the crooked priest and was considering ending their arrangement when a quirk of fate changed her life forever. On the Saturday night before her next Monday morning call, a baby was left abandoned less than seventy-two hours after its birth, on the steps of a tiny medieval church in the celebrated artists' district of Montmartre. The infant, who'd been placed inside a small cardboard box, wrapped in a trio of cotton tea towels, was discovered by the night cleaner of Saint-Jean de Montmartre, as she arrived for work. The towels were soiled with stale urine and faeces but, as a mother of four herself, the cleaner was unfazed and knew exactly what to do.

It was almost midnight, and the interior of the small church was cold, empty and dark, but the woman was familiar with the place, even in the murky gloom. She headed for the priest's private bathroom located off a small corridor at the back of the prayer hall. She stripped the baby and carefully held it above the grubby stone sink, bathing it in lukewarm water.

As she unwrapped the final tea towel, a small object slipped out and fell into the rock-hard sink. It was the slight chinking sound that alerted the cleaner who peered down-wards to see what seemed to be part of a tiny locket. She picked it up and stuffed it inside her jacket while she contin-ued to wash the baby. Once she was satisfied, she wrapped the newborn in one of the priest's hand towels and headed out into the night. She decided to take the baby directly to the local police station less than a five-minute walk away as she believed they would offer the best chance of locating the baby's mother.

Clutching the tiny bundle to her chest, she walked back down the stone steps and headed off towards the station. By chance, as she turned the first corner she came face to face with Father Brune, who'd just emerged from a seedy basement flat, following a torrid encounter with a young rent boy.

Although he was in his trademark cassock, the priest looked even more bedraggled than usual and was clearly extremely embarrassed to bump into the middle-aged woman who cleaned his orphanage twice a week, in such a sleazy part of the city. But to his good fortune she'd far weightier matters on her mind than worrying about his dubious nocturnal activities.

'Father, it's a miracle you're here. I found this tiny baby abandoned on the steps of Saint-Jean. It can't be more than a few days old.'

In the gloomy light the canny priest spotted the outline of the small package she was holding close to her chest. His sordid mind concluded it was indeed a miracle and it had just landed in his lap.

'Béatrice, do you know the baby's sex?'

'It's a boy, Father.'

The priest glanced upwards towards the pitch-black sky dotted with thousands of glimmering stars. Maybe there was a God up there after all, as right now it appeared a superior force was looking down on him, guiding his actions. He reached deep inside one of his cassock pockets and retrieved a bundle of bank notes.

'Béatrice, I believe God has a plan for this poor infant. Take him directly home and look after him for the next few days. But swear to me, you will not mention the baby's existence to anybody.'

'Of course, Father. You have my word.'

He relaxed slightly and gestured towards the cash gripped tightly in his right hand.

'There's almost a hundred francs here. Take this money and buy whatever you need. There will be a similar amount due when you hand the baby over to the orphanage next week. Béatrice, God has chosen you for this special labour.'

The bemused cleaner took the money with her free hand and nodded her understanding. She wasn't quite sure if she was doing the right thing but ultimately was happy to place her faith in a man of the cloth. Plus, she was about to earn a month's money for a few days' work. God must be shining down on her.

* * *

When the usual call came precisely at nine on the Monday morning, the priest picked up after the first ring. He'd been nervously waiting by the phone for almost two hours, rehearsing his script and calculating how much extra money he could extort from the mysterious German lady, who appeared to have endless funds.

'Father, any news?'

'Yes, Fräulein, I have extraordinary news. God has intervened on your behalf and with my aid you will soon have the son you long for.'

Amelie felt as though her heart were about to leap out of her mouth but somehow contained her excitement and continued with her cover story.

'You have a pregnant girl?'

The priest could hardly contain himself a moment longer.

'No, Fräulein. There is no girl. I have acquired a baby, no more than three days old, who is fit and well and ready for you to collect.'

'But how? How can this be?'

'The baby was found last night by my cleaner on the steps of a tiny church, the Saint-Jean de Montmartre, just a few streets away from my institution. I have persuaded the woman, at great cost, to hand the infant over to me.'

He paused before playing his ace card.

'It's a healthy boy, just as you requested.'

He couldn't miss hearing the huge gasp that echoed down the phoneline.

'Unfortunately, there will be an additional price of fifty thousand francs required to pay the woman to ensure her co-operation and future silence.'

'That's fine. When can I collect the boy?'

'As soon as you can get here, Fräulein. I assume you need some time to arrange your transport from Germany?'

Amelie hesitated as, instead of being in Germany, she was sitting in her apartment, less than five miles away from the orphanage and was desperate to collect her baby boy. She managed to calm her voice.

'I will leave later today and be with you by five tomorrow afternoon.'

'Just to be clear, Fräulein, you'll bring the money in cash. One hundred and fifty thousand francs?'

'Don't worry on that score. But, Father, let me warn you now. This baby boy must be everything you claim, or I will make it my mission to expose you and your disgusting institution.'

* * *

As instructed, the following day Béatrice brought the baby to Father Brune's orphanage at three thirty and the handover took less than five minutes. He was sleeping inside a small wicker basket wearing a fresh nappy underneath a pale blue woollen outfit and matching hat that had served two of her own boys as newborns. They had clearly seen better days but, nevertheless, fitted him perfectly. She also provided a brown

223

paper bag containing several more nappies and two cans of the evaporated milk she'd been feeding him with.

The cleaner could sense the priest was on edge and it was apparent he couldn't wait to be rid of her. As he escorted her out of the decrepit building, he stuffed a pile of ten-franc notes into her hand, while virtually pushing her out through the open street door. Just before he closed it, she reached inside her jacket and produced the tiny locket she'd found whilst washing the baby.

'Father, I almost forgot. I found this wrapped in the rags the poor boy was wearing when I found him. Perhaps it's a clue as to his mother's identity.'

Brune snatched it from her outstretched hand and slammed the door shut behind her in one flowing movement. Now all he needed to do was wait.

* * *

Amelie arrived exactly on time, brushing past the priest as he opened the street door, moving like a hurricane directly into his office. The wicker basket was resting on a small wooden desk and when she first set eyes on the baby her heart melted and, without realising it, tears began to pour down her cheeks. His head and face were partially hidden by a blue woollen hat which covered a shock of blond hair, and a pair of huge grey eyes that Amelie knew were destined to turn blue. She was besotted by the boy from the very first moment she clasped him tightly against her chest, while Father Brune circled her like a hungry jackal, asking for his money.

Amelie couldn't bear to lay the baby back down in his basket but had no choice as the money was inside a small attaché case she'd brought with her that the priest's eyes had been glued to since the moment she'd arrived. She reached for it and using both hands flicked open the twin catches, allowing the top to spring open. Inside were three layers of thick wads of bank notes, all neatly wrapped in rubber bands.

Father Brune bent forwards and leered at the contents of the case, salivating at the sight of more money than he'd ever seen before in his life. Amelie slammed the case shut and placed it back on the floor.

'Don't concern yourself, Father. It's all there. Each pile of notes contains ten thousand francs and there are fifteen in total.'

Although Brune never trusted anyone, he'd no doubt the remarkable woman standing in front of him was telling the truth, besides which he was far too scared to challenge her. For her part, Amelie was desperate to leave but had a couple of crucial questions only the priest could answer.

'Father, were these the clothes he was found in? Was anything else left with the boy – anything at all that might identify him?'

'When my cleaner found the baby, he was dressed in rags, but I insisted she buy him new clothes, which of course I paid for.'

He hesitated for a moment wondering whether he should mention the locket. Amelie picked up on the pause and let rip.

'What else, Father? I can see in your shifty eyes there's something else. I warned you before not to cross me.'

The priest reached inside his cassock and produced the tiny silver locket.

'Of course, Fräulein, I almost forgot. My cleaner found this item when she first washed him.'

He passed it over and she held it between her thumb and her index finger, close to her eyes, studying the detail. It was tiny and it took a few moments for Amelie to work out exactly what she was looking at. Then she realised it wasn't complete. It was half the shape of a heart and was clearly one part of two needed to form a whole locket. She'd come across one many years earlier in a Berlin jeweller and, if she remembered correctly, it was called a 'couples locket'. It may only have been worth a few francs, but it was now the most precious item Amelie possessed and, as she gently picked up the wicker basket containing her new son and heir, she couldn't help but wonder where the other half of the locket was and who owned it.

As she stepped out of the street door of the orphanage on to the Place du Tertre and breathed in some much-needed fresh air, she vowed never to return to the hateful place or have any future dealings with the despicable man who ran it.

The ninety-minute walk back to her apartment was one of the most wondrous experiences of her life. She must have glanced down at her son's tiny face at least a hundred times and, as soon as they entered her apartment, she made for her bedroom where a beautiful white wooden cot was positioned alongside her bed. As she gently lifted him from the basket and lay him down on the crisp white bedding, he looked up at her and they locked eyes for the first time.

Amelie leaned down and placed one of his tiny hands inside her own and squeezed it softly. After a few minutes she felt the need to take him back into her arms and tenderly stroked his perfect head as she whispered into his right ear. When she spoke her first words to him, she swore she detected the hint of a smile break out around his tiny mouth. As she drank in his features, she knew choosing his name would be easy.

'My angel, you are my Leopold. Just like my father, one day you'll be known throughout the world as one its great leaders. You may not carry his blood, but now you have one of his names.'

Chapter Forty-One

Washington D.C., United States

In a complete break with protocol, Soletska had invited Berrettini, Vargas and Hembury to her tiny one-bed Chinatown apartment for an off-site meet. Two hours earlier, the Ukrainian hacker had informed the FBI deputy director she needed to discuss urgent new findings but was only willing to do so on her own territory and, notably, Starling and Devane weren't on her invite list. Her flat was above a restaurant on the fifth floor of a nineteenth-century monstrosity, whose grey concrete exterior hadn't seen a lick of maintenance in decades. As the three men jumped out of a red cab and stood outside the Shanghai Delight, Berrettini craned his neck upwards, his eyes homing in on a small window at the top of the building.

'What odds on there being a elevator?'

Vargas was already heading for the black entrance door by the side of the restaurant but shouted back over his shoulder.

'Zilch, Mike. So, consider this a workout. Your first of the year.'

Hembury laughed but Berrettini grunted his disapproval as he caught up with Vargas who'd already hit the entry buzzer. A few minutes later the three men were tightly squeezed on to a bright orange linen sofa bed facing Soletska, who was sitting upright in a lotus position on the cheap lino floor, her hands resting on her knees. Berrettini, jammed in between his two colleagues, was red faced and breathless, a fact that wasn't lost on Soletska who was wise enough to avoid any reference. Instead, she leaned forward and picked up a small notebook resting by her right knee and flipped it open. The front page contained a neat list of hand-written bullet points which were her cues.

'Guys, thanks for schlepping to my place. Anyone want something before we start?'

Vargas was busy scanning the room, fascinated by dozens of colour posters featuring rock stars from the sixties and seventies, obscuring any sign of the whitewashed walls underneath.

'Liliya, I love the decor. Feels like we've walked into a time warp.'

He switched his gaze towards Hembury.

'Troy's so old, he actually grew up with some of these guys.'

Soletska responded with a beaming smile.

'I've always said I was born in the wrong era. I'd take Bowie over Bieber any day of the week.'

Berrettini had barely recovered from the five-storey climb but was keen to get down to business.

'Okay, Liliya. What are these new findings and why the secrecy?'

Her smile quickly drifted away as she glanced down at her notes.

'Firstly, I'm not fully buying the story on Jissika Murkowski – something smells off about it and if she's been set up and isn't really the informant—'

Berrettini burst out the traps, not allowing her to complete her thought.

'If you really think either Starling or Devane is untrustworthy you're out of your mind. They both have security clearance at the highest level. For Christ's sake, I've known Barbara for years and Devane's your boss – he recruited you. Besides, Murkowski is currently staying schtum. Refusing to speak to us until she's lawyered up. Hardly the actions of an innocent woman.'

Soletska held her ground despite the barrage.

'Sir, I'm not questioning any of that, but my instincts don't normally let me down, which is why, right now, I'm only comfortable talking with you guys.'

Vargas could sense a lecture coming down the line from Berrettini, so he dived in, gesturing towards the notebook.

'So, what have you got for us, Liliya?'

She was grateful for the reprieve and left no space for Berrettini to come back at her.

'There's a reason why no one on the data teams managed by Devane and Starling have managed to crack the codes on the remaining six names. As I've said, they've been created by AI machines so superior to anything we have, or even know about, the only way to decode them is to have access to the machines that created them or something very similar.'

Hembury spoke for the first time since the three men had arrived.

'Liliya, if that's true, that's pretty depressing – plus we're totally screwed.'

CHAPTER FORTY-ONE

She paused for a moment to gather her thoughts.

'Not necessarily; I think I know where they're located.'

Despite being wedged in between Vargas and Hembury, Berrettini jerked forward on the couch as though he'd been struck by a bolt of electricity.

'What the hell?'

Soletska glanced across at Vargas who'd also leaned in towards her.

'Nic, it's sort of down to you. Remember when you mentioned the upcoming COP conference in Buenos Aires? You were wondering if the minister for the environment might have been Salazar's contact or involved in some way with the USB. I decided to take a deep dive into his background, just in case you were on to something, and I came up with a nugget – a lead Devane would call paydirt. The minister's name is Javier Galvez. He's a rising star in an extreme right-wing regime and with COP on the horizon, his profile is sky-high, so he's barely off the TV right now. Anyway, last night he was doing a live broadcast from his home in Buenos Aires, being interviewed on Televisión Pública, which is Argentina's public service broadcaster. My Spanish isn't great but from the bits I managed to pick up, he was spewing out bile, stoking the fires of climate change scepticism and questioning the principle of making huge payments to underdeveloped countries. He was sitting behind his desk with the national flag of Argentina draped on the wall behind him. Except, he wasn't.'

Berrettini snapped back.

'He wasn't what?'

'He wasn't sitting behind his desk at home. I knew he was due to be on their evening news programme, so about an hour earlier I hacked into the channel's network and once I figured a few things out, I was able to monitor the live stream coming into their newsroom.'

Berrettini's face reddened.

'Liliya, you'd better have something good at the end of this. Hacking a foreign government's national broadcaster is a criminal offence and right now you're seconded to the FBI.'

Soletska slipped out of her lotus position and reached across to a small low wooden table for her laptop. She powered it up and flicked through a few documents before landing on the one she was searching for.

'Galvez's house is in the Palermo district of Buenos Aires which is less than five miles away from the TV studio but the live stream he was appearing on was being sent, via satellite broadband, from a location seven thousand miles away. What I witnessed on live TV was an interview with a perfect deepfake, which I bet Galvez himself was watching from the comfort of his own home, along with millions of viewers, who were no doubt lapping up his bullshit.'

'Other than its source – any visual evidence it was a deepfake?'

'None – it was beyond perfect. It's outrageous – it was answering questions in a live interview without the slightest hesitation. The tech is superior to anything we've ever seen before. We're all used to viewing edited videos online – but, guys, this was live – no delay, not even a nanosecond. The worst thing is, it's so good, it's impossible to call it out as a fake.'

Being based in Buenos Aires, Vargas was the only person in the room with prior knowledge of Galvez. He eased forward on the couch to face Berrettini and Hembury.

'Look, the man's always been controversial – his politics lie on the very far right of extreme conservatism. But he's also made plenty of headline-catching gaffes – mainly when he went too far and was called out by his political opponents as a fascist.'

Vargas turned to Soletska.

'Liliya, what you're telling us is this Spider Network is creating the perfect politician – an undetectable deepfake, saying exactly what its audience wants to hear and word perfect every time.'

'Pretty much, yes. That's exactly what I'm saying.'

Berrettini's forehead crimped up like an old map.

'Liliya, you talked earlier about the stream being thousands of miles away. Can you tell where it's coming from?'

Soletska swivelled the laptop around in her hands and angled the screen to face the three men who were hanging on her every word.

'The source is somewhere within a ten-mile radius of this part of Strasbourg, a French city bang on the border with Germany, meaning the actual location could be in either country.'

The aerial image on the screen displayed a thin red line circling the north-east of the city, stretching across the Rhine, which acted as the border with Germany. The highlighted area was heavily populated with hundreds, if not thousands, of properties. Berrettini's eyes were locked to the image when he asked the obvious question.

'Liliya, how can you be so sure of this?'

A mischievous smile pre-empted her reply.

'I'm totally sure, sir. I mentioned the stream came into the TV studio via a satellite broadband link, so I did a bit more digging.'

Vargas cut straight across her.

'You mean hacking?'

'Yes, well, I broke into the Galileo satellite system, which is owned and operated by the EU and—'

Berrettini nearly burst a blood vessel as he let rip.

'Christ, is no one safe with you around? I'm pretty sure our president doesn't want to piss off the entire EU – all twenty-seven countries. They're meant to be our allies.'

'I promise you, sir, there's no way they'll ever know. Breaking in allowed me to make a direct trace on the satellite feed. Had the broadcast lasted another ten minutes, I could have identified the precise location.'

Vargas and Hembury were loving every minute of Soletska's tale and revelling in the obvious discomfort it was causing Berrettini. Vargas was studying the visual but couldn't resist interrupting her midflow.

'So, right now we're looking for a needle in a haystack. How are we going to narrow it down? We need to find the building that's hosting the tech behind all this.'

Soletska's fingers slid across the remote mouse and then one of them clicked on an icon, summoning a new image to the screen. A colour headshot of the Argentine minister.

'The next time Galvez does a live interview and hides behind his deepfake, I'll be waiting and, trust me, I'll nail it.'

Chapter Forty-Two

Odesa, Ukraine

The notorious 'Odesa Mafia' came to prominence inside Ukraine in 1992, following the collapse of the Soviet Union. The Russians left behind huge stockpiles of arms and munitions in military depots which were appropriated by mobsters who began a lucrative business in illicit international arms trading to West Africa and war-torn Afghanistan. As the decade progressed, gang leaders switched their focus to the trafficking of drugs and people, as well as producing counterfeit currency and cigarettes on a mass scale. By the time the dazzling young hacker, Anna Kovalenka, joined the largest criminal gang in Odesa in 2019, the business had evolved again, and cyber-crime was its prime source of income.

Within two months, she'd personally been responsible for bringing in over seven million dollars to the organisation, with one hack on the multinational corporation, Western Union, bringing in half that amount on its own. The US giant specialised in transferring funds across the world to over two hundred countries and Kovalenka successfully hacked a transaction which resulted in four million dollars mysteriously disappearing on a digital route between Texas and Amsterdam.

It wasn't long before she caught the eye of the gang's leader, Olek Panchak, a forty-year-old former sergeant in Ukraine's infamous 35th Marine Brigade, the country's elite military unit. Panchak was a ruthless leader, a born killer with an astute financial brain: a lethal combination which made him a fearsome adversary. His physical prowess also added to his legend. At six-four, he was seriously stacked, with a massive frame carrying two hundred pounds of almost sheer muscle. His Hulk-like twenty-inch biceps were constantly on show, rippling underneath a tight black T-shirt, always accompanied by Prada brushed leather black boots and slim-fit black jeans that appeared to be painted on to his thighs. His perfectly round, shaved head and penetrating brown eyes completed the intimidating look that made most men and women go weak at the knees.

Panchak was fascinated by his latest recruit, but the attraction wasn't sexual, even though most of his men were obsessed with her natural beauty. The gang leader's psyche was all about making easy money and lots of it and Kovalenka was potentially the best hacker he'd come across, therefore one to cultivate. He had six others working for him but soon realised she was in another league and so, almost against his natural instincts, he put her on a percentage scheme, paying her one per cent of everything she brought in. A secret deal he kept from the rest of his workforce.

It was an arrangement that worked well for two years: Kovalenka became an unstoppable money-making machine for her boss. One of her most lucrative scams involved hacking into business newswires and stealing yet to be published confidential press releases on end-of-year stock results and then using that information to make swift trades on the markets. A ruse that brought in millions of dollars to the organisation. But then, one day, just as suddenly as it had all begun, it ended.

Panchak totally trusted his star hacker and gave special permission for her to visit New York on a long weekend with her mother, to celebrate her birthday. She was due back in Odesa on the Monday night but never returned. Overnight she ceased to exist. Her cell was cut off, email taken down and bank accounts closed. The notion that she appeared to have vanished into thin air, along with her mother, was hard enough to process but that wasn't the worst of it. Kovalenka was sitting on ten million dollars of the organisation's money, which should have been transferred to the mother ship account and the fact she'd disappeared along with the funds was unconscionable.

It was a level of betrayal that could only have one consequence as far as Panchak was concerned. Retribution would involve a slow painful death at his own hands with the money being returned alongside any interest owing. He'd been humiliated by one of his underlings and that couldn't be allowed to stand. The gang leader wasted no time sending two of his best men to New York to begin the quest of tracking the pair down, starting at the Arlo hotel in Soho, where they'd been staying. But the cupboard was bare. Their clothes and toiletries were still in the rooms, along with Anna's laptop and other personal items. There were no clues or a trail as to their whereabouts. It was as though aliens had abducted them in the middle of the night without a hint of warning.

Panchak knew what a brilliant mind Kovalenka had and was convinced he'd been played. He vowed that one day, however long he had to wait, he'd carry out his revenge. He'd no idea the pair now had new identities, courtesy of the FBI, but figured wherever they were, somehow one of them would drop the ball and he'd be there to pounce on it. He had a long time to wait but, in the end, it turned out he was right. It was almost three years to the day when Ivanna, Anna's mother, made the first mistake.

Ivanna had kept her Christian name but had also taken the surname Soletska for her new identity and lived in an apartment block in D.C. less than a mile away from her daughter. Although she'd given her word to Liliya she'd sever all ties to her past in Ukraine, she hadn't been totally truthful. For three years she'd kept in touch by email with her best friend since childhood, Nataliya Babenko, whom she knew she could trust not to reveal her whereabouts. The pair communicated religiously once a month but, for the previous two, Nataliya had failed to respond and, as Ivanna knew her friend had recently been diagnosed with a rare strain of Parkinson's, she feared the worst. Ivanna felt increasingly desperate as there was no answer from Nataliya's cell and no close family to check in with. In the end, despite having promised Liliya she'd never do anything to compromise their new identities, she placed a call to the one man in Ukraine she believed she could trust.

Father Archaki was an Orthodox priest in Kyiv, whose church was situated in the urban district of Obolonskyi, in the north of the city. Ivanna and Nataliya had been members of his congregation for over thirty years and he was one of the most respected figures in the community. Unbeknown to Ivanna, however, Archaki was also on the payroll of one of the biggest gangs in the city which had close links with the Odesa Mafia and, less than an hour after their conversation, he placed a call to Olek Panchak.

'Father, are you absolutely sure the woman you spoke to was Ivanna Kovalenka?'

'Absolutely, there can be no question it was her.'

Panchak felt his pulse quicken.

'Did she mention her daughter, Anna?'

The priest knew about the mother and daughter's vanishing act in the States and Anna's association with the mob, so wasn't surprised by the question.

'No, and I didn't ask directly. I didn't want to arouse her suspicion. She was calling to ask about the wellbeing of another member of the church, an old lady who recently died.'

'Good, very good. So, where is Ivanna living?'

'Washington D.C. but I've no idea of her address.'

Panchak's voice rose an octave, underlining his frustration.

'Father, Washington's a huge city. I need more than this.'

Archaki paused for a moment, as if he were checking in with a higher authority for permission to go further.

'I know how you can find her.'

'Go on.'

'I remembered how much she loved authentic borscht and wondered how she was coping without it and other home-cooked favourites. She couldn't wait to tell me how two or three times a week she visits the only Ukrainian restaurant in the city, which makes the best borscht she's ever tasted, along with chicken Kyiv and potato pancakes.'

Panchak couldn't contain himself.

'The name? What the hell is its name?'

'It's called Ruta, and it's situated on Capitol Hill.'

'Father, you've been incredibly helpful and as a result I'll arrange for a very generous donation to your cause. I understand from my colleague in Kyiv, you keep a bank account in Switzerland. Please WhatsApp me the details on this number and I'll sort the rest.'

Panchak ended the call and savoured the moment. He'd never had any interest in visiting Washington but now he couldn't wait.

Chapter Forty-Three

Washington D.C., United States

By the time Panchak landed in D.C. accompanied by his personal bodyguard, he knew precisely where Liliya and her mother lived. Just before leaving Odesa he emailed a three-year-old photo of the girl he knew as Anna Kovalenka to a freelance operative who'd been recommended by a fellow gang leader in Kyiv.

Luca Rossi was a small-time gangster, a second-generation Italian born in Washington, who'd do pretty much anything for ten thousand dollars, so for him, a simple surveillance job in a restaurant was a gift. Panchak had booked Rossi on that daily rate for up to a week and on his first night, armed with just the printout of Liliya's photo, he took his place at a small corner table inside Ruta, directly facing the entrance. Then he just needed to wait.

Rossi checked his watch. It was six thirty and he planned to stay put until last orders at nine, which meant he'd have to work his way through the menu as slowly as possible to drag things out. He cringed as he studied the detailed descriptions of dozens of Eastern European dishes, most of which he'd never heard of. From what he could tell, virtually all of them featured beetroot as its star ingredient. It was his least favourite vegetable, but he consoled himself by the thought of his fee, which in theory, if he was lucky, could end up hitting seventy thousand dollars, the biggest payday of his life. He was cautiously working his way through the starter, a beetroot and horseradish dish called Tsvikli and dreading the prospect of what was to follow, when his number came up.

It was evident straight away that the two women who entered the restaurant side by side were mother and daughter, as the family likeness was striking. Rossi glanced back down at the image in front of him for final reassurance but there could be no doubt the younger of the two was the reason he'd been sent to the restaurant. His initial excitement in spotting his prey was tempered by the realisation he'd only receive ten thousand of a possible seventy but then again he wondered if his generous employer might come through with a healthy bonus.

Liliya and her mother made their way across the restaurant and were almost within touching distance when they reached their table. The friendly overtures displayed by two of the waiters confirmed they were regulars and within moments of sitting down they were presented with two shot glasses filled to the brim with vodka, along with a bottle of Nemiroff De Luxe, Ukraine's premium brand. Rather than sit around and watch them eat, Rossi settled his bill and exited, continuing surveillance directly across the road from the entrance, which he knew was the only way in or out. He took up residence in the driver's seat of his hire car, a dark grey Ford Focus, the most inconspicuous vehicle he could lay his hands on, which he knew would seamlessly blend in with the traffic.

The wait was just under two hours and when the pair exited the restaurant they hovered outside the front entrance, with Liliya constantly checking her cell. Rossi figured they were waiting for an Uber and, sure enough, three minutes later their ride arrived. A silver Toyota Prius pulled up and moments later they jumped in the back and set off south on the short two-mile journey to Chinatown.

Rossi gunned the Ford and eased into the Uber's slipstream, ensuring there was one vehicle between them. As jobs went, this was the least challenging he could recall, and things continued to go smoothly as, seven minutes later, the cab pulled over to drop Ivanna off first. Rossi used the camera on his Samsung to capture her walk from the car to a small double-storey block. There was no way of telling exactly which apartment she lived in, but for now he was happy enough knowing she was in one of twelve possible residences.

It only took the Uber another three minutes to arrive in the heart of Chinatown and once again Rossi pulled over and took more photographic evidence for his client. This time there was a bonus in store for Rossi, as shortly after Liliya disappeared behind the street door by the side of a restaurant, a small window on the fifth floor burst into life as a light flicked on in the room inside. He leaned out of the driver's window and clicked away on his cell – happy he now knew the exact address of his target which augured well for his breakfast meet with his client, scheduled for eight thirty the following morning.

***

Panchak had rented an Airbnb in the north-east of the city in one of the poorest and most remote places he could find. It was a detached single-storey two-bed property situated in Brentwood, known to locals and tourists alike as the most dangerous neighbourhood in D.C. and pretty much a no-go area after dark. He and his bodyguard, Artem, arrived by taxi shortly before midnight and within minutes of entering what Panchak described as a 'shitty hovel', the Ukrainian gang leader hit the sack. The jetlag from a long-haul flight and a seven-hour time-shift combined to make sleep impossible but that wasn't a problem for Panchak. His brain was racing with a multitude of different techniques for inflicting extreme pain on the girl he'd once known as Anna Kovalenka, plus the antic-ipation of being reunited with his ten million dollars meant pure adrenaline was flowing through his veins.

The breakfast meet took place at a rundown coffee shop less than a five-minute stroll away from the Airbnb. The three criminals huddled around a small table at the rear of the estab-lishment, with their backs literally to the wall. The coffee was lukewarm and disgusting, and the almond croissants were stale, but none of that bothered Panchak, who was laser-focused on his agenda and nothing else registered. Rossi, however, had been looking forward to breakfast and couldn't help but wonder how a bakery could manage to screw up such simple items.

For the first few minutes Rossi did most of the talking, recalling the events of the previous night, backing his account with the pictures on his cell. Panchak hung on his every word and lingered over the images of Liliya exiting the Uber and entering her apartment block. Any doubts he may have had concerning her identity evaporated as he used his fingertips to zoom in on one of the photos, until he was staring at a head-shot. There was no doubt the grainy face on the cell screen belonged to Anna Kovalenka and at that moment Panchak made a mental note to increase his payment to the priest in Kyiv.

The gang leader winced as he downed a large gulp of the oily syrup masquerading as coffee.

'Rossi, you've done a good job so far. I guess you're not averse to earning some extra money?'

'No, of course not. I'd allocated the entire week for this job, just in case the girl didn't turn up straight away, so I'm at your disposal. Can I assume you'll continue to honour my daily rate?'

Panchak gave a knowing smile as he was about to pick up ten million dollars, so a few thousand was chicken feed. He nodded his agreement as he opened his own cell and clicked on his notes icon.

'I'm planning to visit the girl tonight but before then I've a list of items Artem and I need you to secure, starting with a Merc Sprinter van and a pair of Glock19s with 15-round magazines.'

Rossi could smell a huge bonus heading his way.

'No problem with either of those. What else do you need?'

Chapter Forty-Four

Washington D.C., United States

A few miles away on Capitol Hill another meeting was taking place at Uncle Ian's coffee shop on 10th Street, where Hembury had invited Vargas and Soletska to join him for what he promised was the best breakfast in the city. The three sat together in a circular booth, sharing a platter of smoked salmon and cream cheese poppyseed bagels, accompanied by large glass tumblers of fresh orange juice and ceramic mugs of steaming hot black coffee. They'd only been there a few minutes, but Soletska was already well into her second bagel.

'Troy, these are amazing. I think I could easily become an addict.'

Hembury laughed as he reached for his coffee mug.

'I think I already am. I'm in this place three mornings a week. I come straight from the gym and put back on everything I've just lost.'

'Well, you look in great shape to me, Troy. Whatever your regime is, it's working.'

Vargas couldn't resist a dig at his old friend.

'The guy's a fitness freak and what he's not letting on is he works out seven days a week. He's not human.'

Hembury frowned and swiftly changed the topic.

'Liliya, you absolutely knocked it out of the park yesterday and managed to wind up Berrettini at the same time. Quite a feat. But seriously, all that stuff with Galvez was truly impressive and I guess he's our next lead, especially as whoever's behind this can't possibly know we're on to him. Talking of which, I wonder why they've based themselves in Strasbourg?'

'It's been bugging me too, so I took another look at the file Berrettini prepared for us on the history of *Die Spinne* and the answer was there, staring straight back at me. Himmler created the organisation at a meeting with senior SS officers and German industrialists in August 1944 in a banqueting room inside the Maison Rouge hotel in Strasbourg. So, eighty years on, whoever's running the network is clearly sentimental, as well as being a fan of Himmler – hence the fact they hide behind his deepfake.'

Vargas and Hembury briefly made eye contact, acknowledging how impressed they were with their new associate. But Soletska wasn't quite finished.

'Guys, how about me treating you to a meal tonight – have you tried Ukrainian food before?'

Both men shook their heads in unison.

'Right then, I'll be ordering for both of you. We'll start with a bowl of borscht, followed by chicken Kyiv with mashed potato and mushroom sauce, finished off with a classic Ukrainian honey cake – all washed down by the finest vodka. What say you?'

Vargas responded for them both.

'We're in and I guess Troy will need to schedule an extra gym session to work that banquet off. What time?'

'I'll book a table for seven thirty – so pick me up fifteen minutes before.'

Hembury was holding a chunk of bagel, which he swiftly placed on a side plate.

'Liliya, if I'm going to tackle a menu like that, I'd better pace myself today.'

Liliya beamed with delight.

'Guys, I'm so excited. It's going to be one hell of a night.'

* * *

It was just after five in the afternoon when Rossi arrived at the Airbnb in Brentwood. He parked the van rental on an area of hardstanding by the side of the dilapidated house, walked around to the rear and retrieved a bulging black polythene bag from inside the Sprinter, which he carried over his shoulder like Santa's sack. Panchak's bodyguard, Artem, met him at the door and escorted him into the shabby open-plan living room where his boss was waiting, perched on a heavily stained lime green two-seater couch. Rossi walked across the room and placed the bag down on the floor at his feet. During the drive over he'd made the decision to chance his arm with the Ukrainian gangster.

'I managed to get everything on the list, but it cost almost double what I thought. It was such short notice, I got screwed on most of the stuff, especially the "pieces".'

Panchak ignored the obvious lie and gestured to the bag.

CHAPTER FORTY-FOUR

'Show me what you got.'

Rossi reached inside and scrabbled about for a few seconds before producing a small white plastic bag which he carefully lifted out and handed across. Panchak felt the shape of the improvised package and knew instantly the Glocks were inside. He removed one that was wrapped inside a filthy blue check tea cloth that slipped on to the floor as he weighed the weapon in the palm of his right hand. After a cursory examination of the gun, his relaxed demeanour vanished. He rose up from the couch and took one step forward, his giant frame towering above Rossi, who melted on the spot. Panchak's expression twisted into a hideous scowl.

'This is a 12, you moron. This is an ancient piece of shit. I asked for a 19.'

Rossi felt like a naughty schoolboy being reprimanded by his teacher although the tone of the rebuke was far more terrifying than anything he could recall from his childhood.

'It was all I could lay my hands on . . . I'm sorry.'

'Where's the magazine?'

He fumbled back inside the bag and grabbed a magazine loaded with twelve rounds and, as he handed it over, wondered if he was signing his own death warrant. Panchak clicked it into place and pointed the Glock straight at Rossi's head. When the Ukrainian spoke, his voice was as cold as the steel he was gripping in his right hand.

'I won't tolerate incompetence. So, for your sake, I hope the remaining items are precisely as requested.'

Even though Rossi knew that to be the case, he felt so intimidated and petrified, he questioned his own memory. Panchak carefully checked every one of them and thankfully for Rossi there were no more problems. Nevertheless, despite the instant relief, he regretted getting involved with the Eastern European gangster he now considered to be an unstable psychopath. A job that a few hours ago had appeared so easy was now anything but.

It was just after six when Panchak instructed Artem to grab the van keys and prepare to head over to Chinatown. Before departing, he gave Rossi a final briefing, then made for the door.

'Make sure everything's ready for when we return with the girl. I've no idea on timings but we'll message you when we're on our way back.'

Twenty minutes later the black Sprinter parked up about ten yards from the entrance to the Shanghai Delight. Chinatown was buzzing and so was Panchak. He'd waited over three years for this moment and now it was within touching distance. He had a direct line of sight to the street door next to the restaurant and figured they'd either grab Anna coming home, or if she was already in her apartment, on her way out. Either way, it didn't matter. Now, it was just a waiting game.

Chapter Forty-Five

Washington D.C., United States

Hembury drove Vargas from his Georgetown apartment, where the Argentine was staying, to Soletska's flat in Chinatown in his brand-new Tesla Model 3, his previous car having been blown up during a terrorist incident the year before. The midnight silver electric sedan slid silently through the heavy traffic during the fifteen-minute drive and pulled up on the opposite side of the street to the Chinese restaurant she lived above. Vargas was purring over the ride.

'First time ever in one of these. I've got to admit, I love it. If I were pulling a six-figure salary for just sitting behind a desk, I'd order one tomorrow.'

Hembury smiled but ignored the barb as he checked his watch.

'We're five minutes early. I'll let Liliya know we're here.'

He grabbed his cell and texted her.

Two ravenous men parked across the road. I've checked out those Ukrainian dishes online. Can't wait to try the chicken Kyiv. Don't be long. T.

Liliya had just exited the shower and was towel drying her hair when she heard her cell ping. She quickly replied and started on her makeup.

Running ten minutes behind. The longer the wait the better the chicken will taste. Lx

Hembury showed Vargas the message and then glanced across at the restaurant and then up to the fifth-floor window. Neither he nor the chief inspector paid the slightest attention to the black Mercedes van parked opposite, a grave mistake they later deeply regretted.

The lights inside Soletska's apartment had been on since Panchak had arrived, so he figured she must be inside. He'd no idea if she had any plans to go out, so if there was no sign of her by ten, he'd leave and return at six in the morning. His dark chocolate-brown eyes were like a pair of jet burners, locked in position, scorching a hole through the street door.

At precisely 7.23 it opened and the girl he knew as Anna Kovalenka bounced through it. The breathtaking speed in which events then played out was mind-blowing. Artem switched the van ignition on to idle as Panchak flew out of the passenger door in pursuit of his prey.

As far as Soletska was concerned, Panchak appeared from nowhere and was on her in an instant. His massive arms shot out like the forelegs of a praying mantis, grabbing her upper body from behind and pulling her downwards in one fluid movement. Her eyes were like giant saucers, full of disbelief, as her startled brain recognised the identity of her assailant.

Less than two seconds later his claw-like hand opened one of the rear doors of the Merc, while his other arm held her in a vice-like grip. Their bodies were entwined as he bundled her on to the hard plywood floor of the van and as soon as Artem felt the awful thud, he jammed the gear into drive and his right foot crashed down on the throttle.

Vargas had reacted fractionally faster than Hembury and was halfway across the street when the van powered past him as it fishtailed away, its rear tyres howling, producing a massive plume of black oily smoke. One of the back doors was flapping wildly, creating an ear-piercing screech of metal scraping against metal. Hembury had just exited the car with his gun drawn but realised he was way too late, so jumped back into the driver's seat and yelled at Vargas who was already on the half-turn, about to sprint back and leap into the car.

'Jesus, how the hell did we let that happen?'

Vargas's face was puce with rage as he slammed the passenger door.

'The bastard who snatched her must be part of the Spider Network. God knows how they got to her. They must see Liliya as a threat.'

The Tesla whirred into life and pulled away at speed in pursuit of the van that was already a hundred yards ahead. Neither Artem, who'd been totally focused on the road ahead, nor Panchak, who was deep inside the back of the van wrestling with Liliya, had any awareness of Vargas and Hembury trying to catch them up. Inside the back of the Mercedes, Panchak pinned Liliya to the floor and virtually knocked her senseless with a lethal uppercut to the jaw. He rolled off her motionless body and his right arm stretched outwards as though it belonged to Inspector Gadget, snatching at the edge of the open door and flinging it shut.

The Ukrainian gang leader was in his element as he crawled back on top of Liliya and eased forward until his head was hovering just inches above hers. He stared down into her dazed eyes, a loathsome smile carved across his face, his voice dropping to a threatening whisper. She was barely conscious, her body stiff as a board, paralysed with fear, but she heard every word he uttered.

'Anna, trust me, I'm your worst nightmare.'

From somewhere deep inside her being, she found the strength to summon up a feeble reply.

'I'll give you back all the money.'

'Of course you will, that's the easy part. But think about this. You will also die and the pain you'll suffer beforehand will be so intense, you'll be begging me to end it for you. But I won't. Each time you reach the very edge I'll back off and start again. Anna Kovalenka, you'll truly regret the day you crossed me.'

A second punch, this time a left cross, sent her into a black void. Both blows had drawn blood due to the strategically placed sharp-edged rings on his fingers he wore for that precise reason. Panchak rolled off her and glanced down at his watch. In a few minutes they'd be back at the house and then the fun could truly begin.

Inside the Tesla, Hembury's eyes were glued to the back of the van while Vargas was on his cell, having just reached Berrettini. The normally articulate chief inspector was spewing out words like a crazed man on speed.

'Mike, Liliya's been snatched – right outside her front door – right in front of us. She's in the back of a black Mercedes Sprinter – plate GST 913 – heading south-west from Chinatown. Troy's driving – we're right behind it. The goon who grabbed her was a real pro – it must have been called in by someone from the Spider Network.'

Berrettini kept ice-cool, his computer-like brain calculating the live options.

'Okay, keep this line live and follow from a safe distance. We've no way of knowing how many of them are inside the van and you guys only have one gun between you. As soon as they stop, call it in. I'll have a SWAT team on standby. It'll be minutes away.'

Vargas was calming down and regaining his focus.

'She was right all along, Mike. Murkowski wasn't the informant. She's locked in a cell deep in the bowels of our building, with no access to the outside world. Whoever gave Liliya up is right at the heart of the Bureau.'

'That's got to be right but it's for another day. Let's just get Liliya back safely.'

Vargas nodded, as the Sprinter van, about thirty yards in front of him, took a hard left and headed for the neighbourhood of Brentwood.

Chapter Forty-Six

Washington D.C., United States

A rtem swung the Mercedes on to the concrete drive by the side of the Airbnb, cut the engine and jumped out, just as Panchak was opening the rear doors of the van. He ran around the back to help his boss lift Soletska's limp body from the back. For a moment he'd forgotten Panchak regularly bench pressed 250lbs and watched on in awe as the gang leader effortlessly hauled her body off the floor and threw it over his shoulder, her head and arms dangling down his back.

Having seen the van pull up outside the house, Hembury held back and pulled the Tesla over to the side of the street, just in time to see Panchak carry Liliya inside, with Artem following, before closing the door behind them. Vargas was still on the line to Berrettini and called in the address.

'End location is Brentwood, a single-storey on the south side of Bryant Street, dead on the corner with Downing.'

Berrettini was pacing around in circles inside his office, working two open phone lines, both on speaker, one with

Vargas and the other with the commander of a six-man SWAT unit, who clearly heard the address details. He was sitting in the front passenger seat of a Lenco BearCat armoured vehicle, and it only took him seconds to respond.

'Navigation confirms we're eleven minutes from location. On our way.'

Berrettini came back on the line.

'Nic, I'm sure you heard that. Commander Jim Holloway and his team will be there shortly. Hold position till then.'

Vargas glanced across at Hembury, who'd also heard the instruction from the FBI deputy director. The two men understood each other so well, sometimes there was no need for words, as their thoughts were almost telepathic. Hembury's grim expression and slight nod of the head was the only signal he needed. His response to Berrettini was on behalf of both men.

'Mike, I'm not sure Liliya's got that long.'

With that, Vargas ended the call and pocketed his cell, while Hembury reached inside his jacket pocket for his Sig Sauer P220 semi-automatic pistol.

Inside the Airbnb, Panchak had carried Liliya's body across the living room and roughly dumped it on to a wooden kitchen chair. Artem was holding her upright, while Rossi applied black plastic ties to her wrists, lashing them firmly behind her back. The gang leader was in his element when it came to running an interrogation and relished what lay ahead. He barked fresh orders.

'Rossi, fetch the bucket and the knife.'

Rossi nodded and departed to the kitchen and re-emerged a few seconds later, carrying a black plastic bucket in his right hand and holding a wooden-handled hunting knife in his left. He placed the bucket at Panchak's feet and rested the knife on a small plastic table positioned to the side of Liliya. The Ukrainian kneeled and dipped his right hand deep inside the bucket and swirled it around. A cruel smile appeared on his lips, and he nodded his approval to Rossi, who relished the praise coming his way. In one fluid movement the Ukrainian carried out a manoeuvre he'd performed many times before in his homeland, when interrogating rival drug barons who coveted his throne. It was a brutal move as the bucket was packed to the brim with ice and the temperature of the heavily salted water inside was glacial.

Panchak held the bucket directly above Soletska's head and tipped it one hundred and eighty degrees, ruthlessly pouring the contents downwards, drenching her body, bringing her back to consciousness with a vicious jolt. It was a savage revival technique he'd learned from a former Russian FSB agent he'd met five years before on a visit to Moscow.

Soletska's piercing blue eyes flashed open and in an instant were filled with abject terror as she found herself facing her nemesis. Her face was bruising up badly and the intense shooting pain in her right cheekbone suggested a possible break. The freezing salted water bit into her open wounds and she couldn't prevent her teeth chattering from the intense cold that had suddenly enveloped her body, following the harrowing downpour.

Panchak reached for the hunting knife and pressed the tip of the serrated blade against the side of Soletska's forehead. His face distorted with a grotesque smile as he applied a bit more pressure and drew a few droplets of blood.

'Anna, I plan to carve the word "traitor" across your forehead. A picture of you with my hand-made tattoo will serve well as a calling card to anyone in my organisation who fosters thoughts of trying to betray me. Some people see you as a kind of heroine, who disappeared without trace and ripped me off in the process. That's why it was so essential I track you down and serve out a worthy punishment.'

Soletska was shivering from a potent combination of unbridled fear and physical coldness. It was the first time in over three years anyone had called her by her birth name. Even her mother had adjusted to referring to her as Liliya. She could feel her heart pounding like a pneumatic drill as she desperately struggled to think of any way of extending her life chances. Ultimately, she knew the monster in front of her was motivated by greed and money. As ever, her instincts took over.

'Olek, take my cell from my jacket pocket and I'll show you the bank account details. It's a small Swiss bank and all you need are my two passwords. You can transfer the entire funds across to your own account within seconds. The money's never been touched, plus there's a shit load of interest.'

Panchak paused for a moment and then relaxed the pressure he'd been applying to the knife, pulling it away from Soletska's forehead and placing it back down on the table. He spotted the familiar bulge of a cell inside the left pocket of her stonewashed denim jacket and leaned forward to take it. Her screensaver was a photo with her mum, taken on a recent vacation they'd enjoyed together in Vegas. The pair were standing inside the vast foyer of the Caesars Palace hotel, posing in front of hundreds of slot machines, with Liliya holding Rod Stewart tickets close to the camera lens. Panchak saw another opportunity to inflict further mental pain on his prisoner.

'It was your pig of a mother, Ivanna, who betrayed you. Her stupidity exposed your location and led me right to your door, which reminds me, she needs to be punished as well.'

Liliya's head slumped forward on to her chest, as a torrent of tears ran down her bloodied face. She was beaten and she knew it.

Outside the house, Hembury and Vargas had opted to check out the rear of the property, hoping to gain an edge when they entered, as they'd no idea what size force awaited them inside. So far, they'd only seen the two men who'd snatched Liliya right in front of their eyes but assumed there could be more hostiles inside the rundown Airbnb. There was a small concrete yard at the back of the property and a door in the centre of the back wall led directly into it. Vargas leaned hard up against the old wooden door, resting the side of his face to it, in case he could hear something. He could just about make out the sound of a man's voice, but it was far too muffled to comprehend anything being said. Hembury was standing just behind him with his gun drawn.

'This must be our best option. As soon as they hear me shoot the door lock, they'll be on alert, but this place is tiny and we'll be on them in seconds, so hopefully the element of surprise will work in our favour.'

Vargas checked his watch. The SWAT team was still seven minutes away and right now Liliya's life was hanging in the balance, assuming she was still alive. He glanced at the brushed nickel five-lever lock mechanism and pressed down on the handle just in case it was unlocked and, to his astonishment, the door pushed forward under the weight of his pressure.

CHAPTER FORTY-SIX

Fortunately for them, Rossi had thrown some away brown paper wrappings into a trash can a couple of hours earlier and forgotten to re-lock the door. Vargas shook his head in disbelief and Hembury raised his gun as he silently followed his partner through the open door into a small rear hallway. They moved stealthily forward towards a closed interior door that led directly into the living room and suddenly they could clearly hear a Eastern European voice holding court, tormenting Liliya. Hembury switched places with Vargas and mouthed the words.

'In three, two, one . . .'

Chapter Forty-Seven

Washington D.C., United States

Hembury burst through the door with Vargas directly behind. Both men were shocked by the macabre tableau awaiting them inside the shabby living room; the centrepiece of which was Liliya's bloodied and drenched body, slumped forward and bound to an upright kitchen chair in front of the two men who'd carried out the abduction.

Panchak and Artem both dived to the floor, simultaneously reaching for their weapons. The bodyguard was the quicker of the two, which is why Hembury, who remained unfazed by the horror show in front of him, took him out with a single head shot. The 45 ACP round burrowed its way through the Ukrainian's right eye socket, rocking his head backwards. His life force instantly evaporated as he collapsed in an untidy heap on the floor.

In the hiatus, Panchak had also drawn his gun and pulled the trigger at precisely the same moment Hembury adjusted his aim towards the gang leader, who'd barrel-rolled across the floor towards the front door. To the disbelief of the Ukrainian, the firing mechanism of his twenty-year-old Glock 12 jammed at the crucial moment, allowing Hembury to get off a clean shot. The bullet sliced into the right side of his abdomen, and he howled as he released his grip on the useless weapon and instinctively brought both hands towards the entry wound, the source of the excruciating pain.

Unseen by either Vargas or Hembury, Rossi had been lurking in the shadows, crouching behind a free-standing wooden unit directly behind both men. He watched on as Hembury lowered his pistol and in a frenzied attack, leapt forward, grabbing the hunting knife from the table and launching himself through the air towards his stationary target. Rossi's focus was solely on planting the knife as deep as he could into the soft tissue around Hembury's neck.

Vargas caught sight of the assailant at the last moment and screamed a warning which allowed Hembury to alter his body position, just as Rossi ploughed into him. The slight adjustment saved his life. The edge of the hunting knife pierced the top of his left shoulder, rather than the targeted area. Rossi struck with such momentum Hembury lost control of his gun as both men crunched to the floor, with Rossi frantically trying to inflict a fatal second wound. He wrangled himself on top of Hembury, who was seriously winded from the impact of the fall, pinning him down on the hard wooden floor as he raised the knife high in the air in his right hand, about to deliver the killer blow.

A single shot rang out from close range and in a flash the back of Rossi's head disappeared, leaving a bloody pulp of skin and brain in its place. His body stiffened for a moment and then folded like a cheap pack of cards, slumping sideways on to the floor. Hembury glanced to his left and saw Vargas crouched in a classic firing pose holding the Sig Sauer he'd dropped a few seconds earlier. Neither man spoke for a few seconds and Vargas's eyes scanned the living room, ensuring there were no more surprises left.

Unfortunately, there was one and it was big. Incredibly, Panchak's body was nowhere to be seen. During the episode with Rossi, the gang leader had somehow summoned the strength to drag himself across the floor before miraculously standing up and exiting the front door of the house.

Vargas glanced across to Hembury who'd moved off the floor into a kneeling position. Seconds later they both heard the Mercedes firing up outside. Vargas sprinted across the room and flew through the open front door, just in time to see the Sprinter van disappear around the corner heading north.

Soletska had witnessed the rescue operation in a semi-conscious state and wasn't quite sure if she'd imagined the entire scene. That all changed when Vargas carefully cut her hand ties with the hunting knife and hugged her to his chest, trying to impart some much-needed warmth into her water-soaked limp body. Hembury was now up and about and emerged from one of the bedrooms laden with a heavy grey woollen blanket, which he helped Vargas wrap around her. Her blue eyes which had been blank seconds earlier, sparked into life and although she began weeping again, this time they were tears of sheer relief. No one spoke and some-how the silence seemed to comfort her as much as the blanket.

Hembury's shoulder was leaking blood. His white cotton shirt was saturated, having totally changed colour. He saw the concern on Vargas's face but responded with a reassuring smile.

'Nic, it's fine. It didn't go deep. It's just a flesh wound a few stitches will soon take care of.'

Before Vargas could reply, his cell burst into life and although there was no ID on the screen, he had a pretty good idea who the caller was. He clicked the green icon and a rich baritone voice bellowed in his ear.

'This is Commander Jim Holloway. We're parked up outside the location next to the Tesla. Where the hell are you guys?'

Vargas let out a huge breath.

'Commander, we're inside the house. All hostiles are down, and the rescue target is safe. Have you got a paramedic on board?'

'We sure have. We're coming in.'

Vargas quickly brought Holloway up to speed and the first thing the commander did was send out an APB on the van, which he figured couldn't be more than a couple of miles away. The specially trained paramedic who'd travelled with the SWAT team had already examined Soletska and confirmed no major injuries. What Liliya had suspected was a broken cheek-bone was just heavy bruising. The paramedic moved on to cleaning and assessing Hembury's wound and swiftly diag-nosed between sixteen and twenty stiches. Before she began her handiwork, she applied a simple dressing to the wound and refocused her attention on Soletska, helping her walk across the living room to the bathroom, which had a grim-looking shower cubicle installed. She helped her strip down and then carefully assisted her into the shower tray. Despite the fact over half the holes in the shower head nozzle were blocked, the remaining ones provided comforting jets of hot water that allowed Liliya to start feeling human again, and she began to come to terms with what had been a horrifying ordeal.

Thirty minutes later, Hembury's wound had been attended to and a much-revived Soletska was sitting on the couch, wrapped in two blankets and huddled up close to Vargas. Hembury's arm injury meant he couldn't drive, so Berrettini had dispatched a car to collect the three of them from the Airbnb and transport them back to Hembury's apartment, where he planned to meet them for a full debrief.

For the previous fifteen minutes, the SWAT commander had been outside the front of the house, his cell locked to his ear as he paced the drive. Inside, Vargas received a text confirming Berrettini's car had arrived and moments later he led Soletska through the front door with his arm wrapped around her shoulder, gently propping her up, Hembury following just behind. Holloway, who was still on the call, spotted them and raised his free arm gesturing for Vargas to join him. The three walked across together and the SWAT commander lowered the cell from his ear.

'We've just found the van less than three miles away, parked up in a cul-de-sac in Columbia Heights.'

Vargas spat out a reply.

'And the big guy in black?'

The commander shook his head.

'The front seat was soddened with blood but no sign of the bastard.'

Chapter Forty-Eight

Washington D.C., United States

After a quick detour to Soletska's apartment to collect some fresh clothes, Berrettini's car whisked the three of them to Hembury's Georgetown home. An hour later the mood had begun to lighten. Soletska was sitting on a high-backed stool at the breakfast bar alongside Vargas. They were both enjoying their second glass of Malbec, while they watched Hembury perform magic in the kitchen, prepping the ingredients for his favourite meal while only using his right hand. He waved away any help, insisting he was far better off cooking for the three of them on his own. Hembury was busy making an avocado, tomato and rocket side salad, while also keeping an eye on some fresh pasta he'd just dropped into a pan of boiling water.

'Liliya, I know we were meant to be ravaging a chicken Kyiv tonight, but trust me, my homemade spaghetti Bolognese is earth shattering – as Nic will confirm.'

Soletska laughed for the first time since they'd arrived at the apartment and Vargas eagerly backed up his friend's claim.

'It's true. I think it's the only dish that exists in a very limited repertoire but it really is outstanding.'

Despite the heavy bruising and swelling around her cheeks and lips, Soletska's eyes sparkled and she relished the moment, as she knew once Berrettini arrived, she'd be forced to relive her recent nightmare as part of her debrief.

'Bring it on, Troy.'

She lifted her almost empty wine glass and gestured towards Vargas.

'Meantime, can I have another glass of anaesthetic? This Malbec is really helping take away the pain.'

Ten minutes later the group was seated around a small wooden table, digging into the feast Hembury had conjured up. Soletska was famished and worked her way through a huge bowl of Bolognese in record time, prompting Hembury to dole out seconds from the blue Le Creuset saucepan he'd brought to the table. She wrapped her fork around some steaming hot pasta and downed another mouthful.

'Troy, you weren't kidding. This really is the best.'

'Thanks, kid. Now, listen, before Mike gets here it would be good to get an understanding of what Nic and I were part of back there in Brentwood.'

Soletska drained her third glass of Malbec and placed her fork down on the table.

'Guys, I owe you my life, so of course I'll tell you. What happened today has its roots back in Odesa.'

She didn't hold back a thing as she took them through the episode of her life she'd thought she'd left behind. Neither man interrupted, both completely gripped by her tale. Unsurprisingly, the mood was sombre and when she finished, she picked up her empty glass and waved it high in the air.

'More anaesthetic please.'

Vargas opened a fresh bottle and did the honours.

'Liliya, Panchak's a monster. It's hard to believe that even now, with the war going on, he and his like are still able to operate. I'd heard about the "Odesa Mafia" but never expected to come up against it.'

Soletska bit down hard on her lip.

'He's still out there. He'll come for me again, I just know it.'

Hembury tried hard to reassure her, even though he wasn't really convinced by his own words.

'With a stomach wound like that, he'll bleed out quickly. As far as you know he's got no contacts here, so if he checks into a regular hospital, Berrettini's men will hear about it and grab him.'

'Troy, you don't know him like I do. He's got so much money he'll find a way. Creatures like him always do. There's plenty more like that American creep who'll do anything if the price is right.'

Vargas steered the subject away from Panchak.

'Tell me about the money you took from him.'

She smiled ruefully and took a large swig of red wine for courage.

'Okay, so we're looking at the worst mistake I ever made. When Berrettini's men caught up with me in New York, I'd just completed a massive hit on a supposedly impenetrable bank account in Lichtenstein belonging to one of Panchak's biggest rivals in Odesa: an evil bastard who made his money from people trading and drug dealing. It was the biggest single hack I'd pulled off in the two years I worked for Panchak. Anyway, I'd been looking for a way to escape his clutches, but I had every intention of transferring the funds across as usual and then an idea struck me. If I could disappear overnight and reinvent myself with a new identity, why not keep the money? I was sure it would be impossible for my past to ever catch up with me. I would vanish from New York and reappear in Washington, leaving no trail behind, or so I thought.'

Vargas and Hembury shared the same thought, and the Argentine got in first.

'So how did Panchak find you?'

'I'm not sure to be honest. He said it was through my mum but didn't really elaborate. But when I think about the money, I always knew it was a wrong play, which is probably why I've never touched a dime of it. It's still there in a Swiss account gaining interest.'

Soletska paused and picked up her cell from the table and worked her way through a few files until she found what she was looking for.

'Check your cell, Nic, I've just airdropped you the account info, plus if you scroll down, you'll see the two passwords needed to unlock the funds. Pass it on to Berrettini.'

Vargas heard the ping on his cell and checked the new arrival. When he read the account details he did a double take.

'What the hell? Steven Tyler Limited?'

Soletska's mouth did its best to form a smile, despite the swelling around the lips.

'Lead singer of Aerosmith and one of my icons, so why not?'

'Listen, if you help us crack this case, I'm sure Berrettini won't give a damn about the money. He's more interested—'

Almost as if on cue, the doorbell went, heralding the arrival of the FBI deputy director. He was visibly shocked by Liliya's appearance but could sense spirits in the apartment were running high; the Malbec clearly doing a far better job than any medication. Soletska went through a second, more intense debrief, to bring him up to speed, so by the time he laid out his plans, they were all on the same page.

'Liliya, while Panchak is still out there, I'll arrange for you and your mum to be moved to one of our safe houses in Capitol Hill, a stone's throw from the Bureau. An agent will accompany you and her whenever you leave it. There's a good chance the bastard is lying dead in a back street somewhere but until we know for sure, I'm taking no chances. Call your mum and tell her she'll be collected within the hour and that you'll meet her at the safe house.'

Soletska's fragility was clear for everyone to see as she teared up again at the mention of the gang leader's name.

'Yes, for my mum, but I'm fine here. I need to be near my stuff so I can carry on working.'

She glanced across at Vargas and Hembury whose grim expressions made it clear they weren't happy with her decision.

'Besides, I'm sure my two guardian angels will keep a close eye on me.'

Berrettini nodded his approval.

'Okay, if you're sure, but call me if you change your mind.'

As he stood to leave the FBI deputy director had a final thought.

'Liliya, when I heard about your abduction, I assumed it had to be a response from someone inside the Spider Network reacting to the fact you'd uncovered Galvez's connection to them. That would have meant we still had an informer in the camp and, worse than that, we had the wrong person in a cell. Thankfully, that wasn't the case.'

Chapter Forty-Nine

Paris, France

July 1977

Amelie had never been totally sure of Leopold's exact birthdate but had settled on 7 July, which she figured was probably correct. He'd celebrated twenty of them and the party planned for his twenty-first was nothing short of epic.

Leopold had crammed a great deal into his two decades. For the first ten years of his life his mother was incredibly protective and insisted he was home educated by a selection of four hand-picked tutors, as well as herself. Amelie ensured he understood her unique personal take on recent historical events, which meant he was the only schoolboy in France brought up to laud the achievements of the Nazis. By the time he was eleven and ready to attend high school, he'd learned many of his mother's powerful secrets, including the biggest; the identity of her father, who'd been the second most powerful Nazi inside the Third Reich.

Amelie sent Leopold to the prestigious Lycée Henri IV in Paris, where he excelled in both history and languages and, from there, he enrolled at the world-famous Sorbonne, where he majored in Spanish and English. By the time he graduated, he was fluent in both. His aptitude for languages was a natural gift that would play a huge role later in his life.

Although he'd witnessed first-hand the immense power and influence his mother wielded as the owner of one of France's most powerful banks, Leopold was obsessed by a different sort of power – the power of the media. The captivating world of newspapers, radio and television fascinated him and, much to his mother's disappointment, his heart was set on a career in that industry.

His eye-catching looks and effortless charm made him a magnet for girls, as did the knowledge his mother was one of the richest and most powerful women in France. His athletic build, angular face and aquiline nose were complemented by a devastating combination of golden blond hair and striking blue eyes, which created a Scandinavian appearance.

His mother, whom he idolised, was a huge influence in his life and, bearing in mind his upbringing, it was no surprise he identified with her extreme right-wing principles and fascist-based analysis of world events, although both were astute enough to keep those hidden from public view. Their remarkable relationship, which was the envy of their friends, did however have one taboo; a topic Amelie insisted was a no-go area and Leopold knew better than to approach it.

Since the age of four, he'd known he was adopted but Amelie had never given him any details of how it had come about. As he grew older, a nagging part of his brain thirsted for more information, but none was ever forthcoming. In the end he concluded his mother fulfilled all his needs and he buried his natural curiosity in a place so deep, his conscious mind forgot all about it.

It was just a few days before his party and the two of them were enjoying breakfast together on the wrought-iron balcony of their Paris apartment, taking in the views of the Eiffel Tower, when Amelie hijacked his day.

'My darling, forget any plans you might have. We're spending the day in my study; it's time to learn about your birthday presents.'

'Maman, I'm dying to know about them, but really, all day?'

Amelie responded with an enigmatic smile that piqued her son's curiosity.

'Surely, whatever they are, I'm either going to wear them. Or hopefully drive them.'

'Leopold, trust me. One is so precious; it's been in my possession since before you were born.'

* * *

Leopold was bursting with curiosity as he sat down next to his mother on her favourite antique marquetry sofa, inside her vast study. The first thing he noticed were two packages balanced precariously on her lap. One was a thin brown envelope and the other appeared to be some kind of notebook.

'Maman, please don't keep me in suspense.'

Amelie beamed as she passed the envelope across to her son. 'Let's start with this.'

She could barely cope with the anticipation of his reaction, as she watched him withdraw two documents from inside the envelope. The top one was a one-page share certificate and, as she hoped, he was stunned by the details.

'What the hell? When did this happen?'

'Our board has been working on it for the last four months. I wanted the deal completed before your birthday. As of two days ago, Banque Legrand owns *Les Nouvelles*.'

Les Nouvelles was one of France's oldest newspapers, having been founded in 1842. The right-wing publication was one of the 'Big Three' dailies, which included *Le Monde* and *Libération*.

Amelie had an even bigger surprise tucked up her sleeve.

'Take a look at the other document. It's a contract granting you full ownership of the paper. You just need to sign it to become CEO.'

Leopold rocked with laughter, which wasn't exactly the reaction his mother was expecting.

'Maman, is this some kind of joke?'

'Leopold, listen to me carefully. You're not much younger than I was when my father made me owner of the bank. Unlike you, who live and breathe everything to do with the media, I knew absolutely nothing about banking but, in time, I learned. For now, you're the new owner of the paper, but to begin with, you won't be operational. The managing editor, Laurent Barbier, will be your mentor. I've met with him twice and I know you're going to like him – he's a good man who shares many of our values. The *Les Nouvelles* group also owns several smaller publications, which you can cut your teeth on. But, Leopold, if you're the son I think you are, this purchase will prove to be just the first step on your journey towards creating your own media empire.'

Leopold was literally shaking with excitement and leapt across the sofa to embrace his mother. They hugged for a while, tears streaming down both their faces. Eventually they broke apart, but he kept hold of one her hands in his as he tried to find the right words to express how thrilled he was.

'I was hoping for a nice watch or even a car for my twenty-first, but this is beyond my wildest dreams. I always dreaded you'd insist I join you at the bank but now I'll carve my own path and make you truly proud.'

'Leopold, I have no doubt of that. I know very little about the media, but I do recall my father telling me what a genius Goebbels was, when it came to controlling it. He ran the Propaganda Ministry and his favourite quote was, "If you tell a lie big enough and keep repeating it, people will eventually come to believe it."'

'Maman, did you ever meet him?'

'No, but of course my father knew him well. Reading between the lines, I don't think there was much love lost between the two of them. In fact, even though he recognised him as a genius, I'm pretty sure he loathed him.'

Leopold's vibrant blond hair moved with a life of its own as he shook his head.

'Sometimes I find it incredible to grasp the fact of who your father was. From what I've read both he and Goebbels vied for position under Hitler – fighting each other for his stamp of approval.'

'Actually, I think Göring was also in the mix when it came to winning the Führer's affections.'

Amelie reached down for the notebook that had slid off her lap on to the sofa during their embrace. She carefully opened it and peered down at the first page.

'Now, we come to your other present, your true inheritance – your legacy. Its importance for both of us is far greater than any monetary present I could ever give you.'

Leopold was instantly hooked and intrigued to discover what valuable secrets were contained inside the tiny note-book his mother was holding so delicately it could well have been a Ming vase. For the next hour he didn't speak as he hung on every word Amelie spoke, totally mesmerised by her story.

She began by explaining how and why Himmler created *Die Spinne* and moved on to her personal experience of using the ratlines it provided to escape Germany and start her new life in Switzerland. He cuddled up close and leaned over her shoulder to focus on numerous pages full of names, ranks and new aliases; all in his grandfather's neat handwriting.

'Incredibly, I learned all these names off by heart. I spent hours every day while I was in Geneva, memorising them. Once I reached Paris in 1947 and established my new identity, I slowly began contacting every single name listed in this notebook.'

She flicked through a few more pages and suddenly the handwriting changed – Leopold immediately recognised it as his mother's.

'As you can see, these are now my own notes. With each name, I document when the initial contact was made and then any ongoing communications. You'll see in many cases there are now second and third generation family members like us, who've all vowed to carry the Spider Network forward.'

She paused for a moment to gaze into his clear blue eyes that were locked on to her own.

'Leopold, the time has come for you to take over from me. Over the next few months, I want you to study my notes and then when you feel ready, begin to make personal contact.'

A few hours later, Leopold lay on his bed attempting to process the events of the previous few hours. Every single aspect of them was momentous for him. He glanced across at the notebook and share certificate resting on his bedside table and his thoughts turned towards the future, and he wondered how the two new threads in his life might combine one day to serve each other.

Chapter Fifty

Washington D.C., United States

'Galvez has been burned.'
The voice on the cell phone was measured and calm, while Legrand's waspish response was anything but. The media baron was sitting behind his precious eighteenth-century desk in the office of his Paris apartment when the encrypted call came in.

'Jesus, that's impossible. There's no way they could have broken any more of the codes. My machines are impenetrable. Why are you lying to me?'

The voice was unfazed by the ferocious rebuke.

'It's worse than that. They know the deepfakes are coming from a stream somewhere near Strasbourg.'

Legrand's right hand formed a clenched fist which brutally pounded his beloved desk, and his face contorted as he unleashed his fury at the messenger who was imparting the unexpected and destructive news.

'I should never have trusted you. Never have brought you inside the Network.'

'I'm risking everything I have by passing this on to you, as I've done all the way through the course of our relationship. I still believe in the same ideals as you. I promise, I'm not your problem. A Ukrainian hacker working for Berrettini is responsible for all this. Her name is Liliya Soletska. Save your venom for her.'

Legrand began to calm down and focus on what his informant was saying. His voice dropped to a sinister whisper.

'Tell me everything.'

There was a short pause while the person behind the voice gathered their thoughts.

'Vargas went to Buenos Aires and did some digging. He discovered that a gangster called Salazar, whom I assume you know, was dealing with a government minister involved in the upcoming COP. This girl, Soletska, went rogue and hacked into a live interview Galvez was giving to the public broadcaster on a whim – gambling he might have been Salazar's contact. She got lucky and discovered the stream wasn't originating from his house in the capital but from a transmission hub in Strasbourg. That of course confirmed a deepfake had been deployed for the interview, which I'm aware could compromise the entire operation.'

'How precise was the trace?'

'Fortunately, it was only able to identify a ten-mile radius, and the epicentre was in the north-east of the city, so Berrettini isn't sure if the origin of the stream is in France or Germany. What do you want to do now Galvez is compromised?'

Legrand was carefully digesting the implications of every word he was hearing.

'COP starts soon, so for now I'll leave him in place, as I can't see Berrettini acting against him too quickly. Relations between the Argentine and US governments are not great, so let's just monitor the situation. As host, Galvez has a huge role to play in ensuring the main vote goes our way, so we need him in post. Keep me informed if they plan to make a move against him.'

'I will. If I were Berrettini, I'd probably use Vargas as a means of getting to Galvez. Remember, he's a chief inspector in the Buenos Aires police department and I wouldn't underestimate him.'

Legrand had already switched his thoughts to confront the other imminent threat.

'As far as Strasbourg is concerned, there are thousands of buildings in an area that size. The FBI doesn't have the resources in France capable of finding us.'

'You need to know that the hacker is waiting for Galvez's next interview. Berrettini believes if she has enough time working on the live source of the deepfake stream, she'll be able to pinpoint its origin to within a hundred yards.'

'Don't worry, we've many different methods of streaming and won't make the same mistake again.'

Legrand was starting to relax, as he felt back in control. He reached across his desk for a fresh vape and clicked the power button. He inhaled deeply, savouring the sensation of two grey jets of steam exiting his nostrils.

'Tell me, where did you learn all this information?'

'From the horse's mouth. I've known Berrettini for almost twenty years and he's no reason whatsoever not to trust me. We just had lunch and he was happy to fill me in.'

'Excellent. Keep close to the bastard. With so much at stake, if he gets too near to the truth, you may have to take him out.'

* * *

Three hours after Legrand's call with his informant, Sabine Moreau arrived at his Paris apartment, having been summoned from Strasbourg by her boss for an emergency face-to-face meeting. It was her first visit to his spectacular home and his Sikorsky S-92 provided the luxury transport for the three-hundred-mile journey. Although she knew he was the wealthiest man in France and one of the richest men in the world, nothing quite prepared her for the breathtaking interior of his mansion apartment and its position on the Champs de Mars, Paris's most exclusive location.

Legrand greeted her in person and led her along the vast double-height entrance hall which, amongst other treasures, accommodated a custom-made Bösendorfer grand piano. Then they moved through one of three palatially decorated living rooms and into his African blackwood-panelled office, where he took his customary place behind his Napoleonic desk. He ushered Moreau to sit opposite him in a crocodile-hide club chair, a priceless handmade antique, created in 1922 by the hands of the renowned craftsman, Jean-Michel Frank.

Their previous meetings had taken place either in the Strasbourg facility or by Zoom but facing Legrand in his own lair was a far more intimidating experience than anything she could ever have imagined. He was of course aware of the unnerving effect his majestic surroundings had on first-time visitors; indeed, it was entirely intentional, serving to ensure he always kept them off-balance, thereby giving him the upper hand.

Moreau had no idea what Legrand's agenda was but, judging by the pained look on his face, she doubted she was about to receive another bonus. She maintained her exterior composure, although inside her nerves were jangling, terrified she was about to receive a severe reprimand. She'd witnessed first-hand a tongue lashing he'd dished out to a senior Canadian politician who'd dared question his methods and was dreading one coming her way, even though she'd no idea why. His vape was already activated and he played with it between the fingers on his right hand for a few seconds before slowly lifting it to his lips and inhaling deeply, while maintaining eye contact the entire time. Moreau was waiting for him to exhale the smoke but instead he began speaking, which caught her off-guard.

'We've had a security breach. Something you led me to believe was impossible. Or did I imagine that?'

Moreau felt a sudden turbulence in her stomach at the chilling delivery of the unexpected rebuke. Her mouth suddenly went dry but, from somewhere deep inside, she mustered up the inner strength to mount a response.

'Sir, I find this very hard to believe. I promise you I'm totally unaware of any such occurrence. What are you referring to?'

'I'm referring to the recent Galvez interview you simulated from his home. A hacker at the FBI broke into the stream and traced its origin to within ten miles of our facility. Have you any idea how dangerous that is for our entire operation – indeed for our entire Network?'

Moreau's brain went into overdrive as she processed the information, realising she needed to come up with a coherent reply. She was desperate to know how Legrand had discovered the breach but, evidently, he'd chosen not to share that intel with her.

'Sir, even though we'd no idea the stream was being monitored, we took our normal rigorous precautions. The encrypted signal went via the Galileo satellite system, which has thousands of streams going through it at any one time, so it's incredible it was identified. We opted for the satellite broadband to prevent any obvious time delay during the interview.'

Legrand's facial expression was one of sheer disdain.

'A recent unfortunate event has brought our operation to the attention of a small task force, working out of the FBI. At first, I wasn't too concerned but with so much at stake over the next couple of weeks, every move we make must be completely secure. Do you understand?'

This latest revelation was another metaphorical punch to her gut, as the thought of being on the FBI's Most Wanted list filled her with dread.

'Sir, we'll revert to direct broadband streaming from one of our dedicated AI machines, which we know are totally impregnable.'

Legrand stood from his desk and waved his left arm insolently towards the door, indicating their meeting was over.

'I do hope so for your sake. Enjoy your trip back to Strasbourg. I suggest you take the train as my helicopter is no longer available.'

Chapter Fifty-One

Buenos Aires, Argentina

With the COP conference just twenty-four hours away, Javier Galvez, the Argentine environment minister and host of the conference, was the man of the moment and very much in demand. He'd scheduled several 'in person' TV and radio appearances in Buenos Aires but a ten-minute live satellite interview with the BBC, the UK's public broadcaster, seemed the perfect opportunity once again to deploy his deepfake, instead of appearing in the flesh.

Having been scalded by Legrand, Moreau had no intention of screwing up and was taking no chances. The broadband feed, set up by her data analysts, was generated in-house by one of their own machines. Unlike the previous Galvez broadcast, there was no third-party hook-up with an independent satellite and, with the inbuilt protections provided by the AI algorithm, the feed was pretty much impenetrable and therefore untraceable.

Five thousand miles away in Washington D.C., inside one of the FBI's safe rooms, buried deep in the basement of the Bureau headquarters, Vargas and Hembury were huddled around a small metal table watching Liliya perform her magic with two MacBook Pro laptops. Her fingers flitted across the keyboards at a terrifying speed and neither man had a clue what she was up to. She broke off momentarily to check the time on her iPhone.

'Okay, Galvez goes live in two minutes with a broadcast to the UK. It's two in the afternoon in Buenos Aires and six in the evening in London, so he's appearing on the BBC's peak-time early evening news. Looking at his media schedule, this appears to be the only interview he's conducting today down the line; all the rest are in person, so there's every chance he'll be tempted to deploy his deepfake.'

Vargas and Hembury immediately shared the same thought, but the Argentine got in first.

'So, what have you illegally hacked into this time – a government satellite or a public broadcaster, or maybe both?'

Soletska's eyes remained glued to her screen as she responded.

'Do you guys really want to know?'

Vargas didn't let up.

'Yes, we really do.'

'Will you promise not to rat me out to Berrettini?'

Both men laughed and Hembury jumped into the conversation.

'Liliya, if you can pinpoint the exact location of the business premises transmitting the signal, Mike won't give a shit about how you managed it.'

The Ukrainian hacker pointed to one of the laptops which had a box taking up a quarter of the screen.

'Okay, as you can see, I'm currently live inside the BBC news feed in London and I've also hacked into the Astra 28.2E satellite which will receive the incoming feed from Buenos Aires. Except, I suspect we'll find it's coming in from Strasbourg. Hold on, here we go.'

Soletska clicked on a key and the BBC feed went full screen. The female news anchor linked out of a short video item setting up COP and introduced Galvez. The Argentine minister appeared to be sitting behind his desk at home, exactly as per his previous broadcast.

'Yes, we're in business. Hold on to your hats, guys, I've just gained entry to the satellite feed.'

She focused her full attention on the second laptop screen, which was throwing up multiple coloured lines of data, completely incomprehensible to Vargas and Hembury. Neither cared as they watched on in awe, waiting with bated breath to see the result. Soletska was totally focused, energised by the prospect of the imminent discovery of the AI facility's location and then her mood changed, almost as quickly as the flick of a switch. She slammed the laptop shut as though it had betrayed her and slunk back in her chair.

'Shit. They know, for Christ's sake, they know.'

Vargas put his arm around her, which she shrugged off like a petulant child.

'Guys, the people transmitting the signal from somewhere in Strasbourg know they're being monitored. They've changed their MO from the other day and are using a broadband signal generated by one of their in-house AI machines. There's no way they'd choose that option if they didn't have to because the Astra satellite guarantees zero time delay which is what they'd want. Going direct from their own broadband can't guarantee that same level of perfection. Just a few frames per second delay in the audio feed wouldn't necessarily expose the deepfake but, ideally, they wouldn't want to risk anything that might unsettle the AI brain operating it.'

Hembury rose from his chair and took a couple of steps away from the table.

'Liliya, are you totally sure about this? Couldn't they just have opted to try a different method of transmission?'

'No way. They know we're on to them and that means from now on they're not going to take any risks.'

Vargas picked up on the enormous implications of Liliya's analysis.

'It also means we have the wrong person locked in a cell one floor below us and the informer is still out there, somewhere inside this building'.

* * *

The sour look on Berrettini's face said it all. He'd been joined in his office by Vargas, Hembury and Soletska, who'd just completed their debrief on her failed attempt to trace the source of Galvez's fake transmission. He hadn't said a word the entire time but had listened intently to her interpretation of the events that had played out a few minutes earlier. Vargas broached the obvious elephant in the room.

'Mike, how the hell has this leaked? Unlike the USB content, the only people who know about Liliya's breakthrough with Galvez are sitting in this room.'

Berrettini looked as though he'd just seen a ghost, as blood noticeably drained from his face. When he spoke, his strained voice sounded as if it had been dragged up from somewhere deep inside his soul.

'That's not strictly true, Nic. I did tell one other person.'

* * *

Barbara Starling's personal assistant never got the chance to warn her boss Berrettini was about to enter her office for an unscheduled meeting. The FBI deputy director darted past the bemused assistant's desk in the outer office area, flung open Starling's door and slammed it shut in one flowing movement, before she'd even had time to flick the intercom button.

Starling was working on her computer and glanced up as Berrettini glared at her across the desk. His face was ruby red, and two veins were pulsating in his forehead. When she spoke, her voice betrayed a strange calmness, almost a sense of relief.

'Mike, how did you find out?'

For a moment, Berrettini was taken aback by her immediate admission of guilt. He'd expected a heavy-handed denial but there was none on offer.

'Galvez. You were the only person I confided in.'

A knowing look broke out on her face.

'Of course. It was a high-risk move, but you were getting too close: I felt I'd little choice but to make it. I underestimated the hacker – she's a talent.'

'Yes, Soletska is that and a great deal more but none of that explains your actions. We've known each other for years, Barbara, and as far I know, you've no financial worries, so why?'

Starling maintained her composure and conjured up a genuine smile of affection.

'Mike, this has zilch to do with money. For years now, I've sat back and watched our liberal governments, Republican and Democrat, spend billions of our people's hard-earned dollars on helping so-called poor and deprived countries across the world, while neglecting the needs at home. We also contribute billions to NATO to protect European states from the so-called threat of Putin, yet many of them don't contribute a bean. The people behind the Spider Network have values and policies I associate with and genuinely believe in. I've been part of it for over ten years. The irony is, until Vargas got his hands on the USB, you'd no idea the organisation even existed.'

Berrettini exploded with rage.

'These people are Nazis. Fanatics who in recent days have sanctioned brutal murders across the world of anyone who might possibly expose them. They've demonstrated the ruthlessness of psychopathic killers and you've been happy to help them along the way.'

He stared deep into her eyes but saw no sign of remorse.

'I assume you set that poor girl up as the informer. Destroying her life while protecting yours?'

'A casualty of war, Mike.'

For Berrettini, the next few seconds were a blur. Without losing eye contact with him, Starling used her right hand to slide open the top drawer of her desk and retrieve a Glock 19 which she casually raised upwards towards her face. He watched on in horror as she calmly placed the barrel of the gun inside her mouth and despite him throwing himself towards her, without a second thought, she pulled the trigger.

Chapter Fifty-Two

Washington D.C., United States

Berrettini had witnessed more than his fair share of unexpected brutal killings in his career but watching an old friend blow her brains out right in front of him was one of the worst experiences of his life. In the aftermath, he retreated to the sanctuary of his office shower, where he allowed his body to be pummelled by boiling hot jets of water for over fifteen minutes, scrubbing away the blood splatter, desperately trying to cleanse his thoughts of the macabre scene he'd just been present at. Starling's actual moment of death was burned on to the inside of his retinas, and he kept his eyelids slammed shut the entire time.

He'd called a council of war with Vargas, Hembury and Soletska, who were waiting for him in their usual meeting room, deep in the bowels of the Bureau. He was just getting dressed when an overwhelming sense of sadness consumed his thoughts, and he felt compelled to get out of the vicinity of the slaying as soon as possible. He grabbed his cell and punched in a message to Liliya.

Can we all meet at your flat as we did recently?

Her reply was pretty much instant. Two emojis, side by side. *A thumbs up and a red heart.*

Like obedient schoolkids in a classroom, the three men resumed the same positions in Soletska's apartment they'd taken last time they'd met, wedged next to one another on her tiny couch, while she sat cross-legged on the floor, directly facing them. Before the elephant in the room grew too big, Liliya broached the topic.

'So, Starling framed Murkowski to protect herself from exposure?'

Berrettini seemed grateful no one was asking for actual details on the suicide as he jostled the other two, trying to find a comfortable position on the couch.

'The poor girl's been released already and has returned to her flat. I spoke with her by phone on my way here in the car to personally apologise and although the episode only lasted a few days, I intend for her to receive some financial compensation and a hefty chunk of paid leave. She wants to go back to Juneau to see her family for a while and, after the ordeal we've put her through, you can hardly blame her.

Vargas immediately steered the conversation back towards Starling.

'Mike, I know you said her motivation wasn't money but is it still worth checking through all her accounts?'

'Absolutely. Liliya, that task seems right up your street. Trawl through her financial records and see if any unusual payments turn up from a third party. Just in case.

Soletska smiled warmly at the FBI deputy director and nodded to signal her agreement. Berrettini took the cue and continued addressing her.

'That's not all, I'm afraid. Interpol have sent through over two hundred properties within the designated area around the transmission point in Strasbourg that I need you to check out. Look into their ownership in case something jumps out at you. They could all be hokey, but we've got to start somewhere.'

Soletska appeared far more enthusiastic about her second assignment than the first.

'Let me get stuck into that list. I won't rest till I track those bastards down.'

* * *

Moreau had been dreading her upcoming Zoom with Legrand as it was the first time the pair had spoken since her savage mauling. Her spirits sank even lower when she spotted his burgundy notebook open on the desk in front of him with which he seemed deeply absorbed. There was an eerie silence as he effectively ignored her presence on the call and when he eventually looked up to make eye contact, her fake frozen smile evaporated. He greeted her with a face like thunder, patently offering no olive branch of forgiveness. She swallowed hard and tried to hold her nerve.

'Good morning, sir. How are you?'

He ignored her greeting and switched his eyeline back to the notebook.

'We've several matters to discuss and I hope, this time, you won't disappoint me on any of them.'

For a microsecond a bizarre thought entered her mind. If only she were talking to one of his deepfakes, she could tell him what she really thought and then power him down. That delicious idea vanished just as quickly as it arrived as he began working through his agenda.

'Firstly, all content we have relating to the three politicians we've lost must be deleted from all our servers.'

Moreau almost blurted out a response, desperate to turn the tide.

'That task has already been completed, sir.'

Legrand gave the slightest of nods before moving on.

'Galvez is obviously compromised, so we should begin working on his junior minister, Eduardo Flores, who may have to replace him in the coming weeks. Galvez recruited him to our cause two years ago. I believe you have all his information and contacts on file, as well as preliminary video test files.'

Before Moreau could reply, Legrand switched topics again.

'Are we good to go with Morozov? I understand he has an interview coming up with the main government news channel and we need him to start cutting through to the Russian people ahead of an election we know is going to happen sooner than people think.'

'Yes, I believe we're all good. We just need precise details of the planned broadcast.'

Moreau felt the call was going well so tried to ingratiate herself further by playing on his vanity.

'By the way, sir, knowing you have the CNN broadcast soon, Thomas has just signed off on all three of your own videos. They look incredible. Would you like me to send them through?'

Legrand responded by immediately re-establishing his authority.

'Yes, that item is also on my list. I need to choose one of them, ahead of the interview, which Thomas can then give a final polish to.'

For a moment she thought she detected the hint of a slight smirk but couldn't be sure as Legrand still had one more box to tick as he switched topics again.

'Now, as COP begins tomorrow, the time has come to unleash some chaos. Are we ready?'

'Never more so. Just waiting for your green light.'

'Moreau, you've just had it.'

This time around, there was no mistaking the fully formed smirk of satisfaction that broke out across Legrand's face, moments before he abruptly ended the call. He'd decided the time was right to play his first ace and could hardly wait to see how it turned out.

Chapter Fifty-Three

Buenos Aires, Argentina

As often happens when controversial videos go viral, the explosive organic growth that follows within seconds of the original post makes it almost impossible to trace the source. That fact played perfectly into Legrand's hands, especially as the one created by his technicians clicked up over a million views within thirty minutes of going live and quadrupled that number in the following hour, spreading like a contagious virus across multiple sites in dozens of languages. The fact the ninety-five-second clip featured one of the most respected political leaders in the world participating in a drug-fuelled orgy with two hookers, one of each sex, made it simply irresistible.

The video, which consisted of three short clips edited together, appeared to have been filmed through a two-way mirror in an unidentified high-end hotel bedroom. The colour footage had a timecode running in the top right-hand corner, adding a soupçon of authenticity. The pornographic content featured the president of one of the largest independent Caribbean countries, Charles Griffiths, participating in explicit sexual acts with a young black man and an older white woman. His distinct voice, known to millions of his citizens, could be clearly heard on at least four occasions as he jovially issued sexual commands to his two willing companions.

Attentive viewers spotted notable clues that appeared to further confirm the video was authentic. A two-thousand-dollar bottle of Andrés Brugal rum, known to be Griffiths's favourite tipple, was just about distinguishable, strategically positioned on one of the bedside tables, while a six-inch keloid scar, the result of an old knife wound, could be clearly seen on the politician's chest, just above his right nipple. Conspiracy theorists jumped on that visual clue as an absolute clincher while they posted old photographs of Griffiths where the distinctive wound was clearly visible. Regardless of the truth, one thing was apparent; if the video was a fake, as Griffiths claimed, it was a digital masterpiece, eclipsing anything that had gone before. When Legrand first saw it, he christened it his 'Renoir'.

Griffiths first came to prominence on the international stage at COP27, where, in a no-holds-barred passionate speech, he proclaimed a two-degree rise in global climate temperatures would prove to be a 'death sentence' for Caribbean countries such as his own. He argued the world was crying out for moral leadership from leaders of the richest nations in the world in the fight against climate change and technological and economic inequality. Griffiths was due to lead the campaign at the Buenos Aires COP on behalf of the Global Climate Action Partnership, which was seeking guaranteed initial payments of billions of dollars from the Western powers. He also stirred the pot by demanding trillions of dollars in reparations from former slave-trading countries, such as the United States, the UK, France and Spain.

Now, in just a matter of hours, his reputation lay in tatters and even his wife of twenty-five years had not yet publicly backed him, which was proving damning to his chances of surviving the crisis.

By the time Griffiths's eight-hour flight from the Caribbean landed at Ezeiza international airport in Buenos Aires, over twelve million people had viewed the video and snap opinion polls online indicated eight out of ten believed the content to be genuine. Inside his own country and within his own political party, he was haemorrhaging support. The world's press, who'd gathered in the Argentine capital for the upcoming COP, created an unruly media scrum that hounded him and his small entourage as they walked through the arrivals terminal, desperate to reach the sanctuary of their hotel.

An hour after arriving in Buenos Aires, Griffiths found himself holed up inside the royal suite at the Four Seasons hotel, along with his closest adviser, Alvin Walcott, who'd been by his side for almost ten years. The president, who was anxiously pacing around the large lounge area like a caged panther, suddenly looked every one of his sixty-six years. His hazel eyes which normally twinkled had a deadness behind them and his curly salt and pepper hair seemed to have turned completely grey overnight.

Walcott was trying every trick he knew to calm the president down, but nothing was working.

'Charles, we've an entire tech team poring all over the video. Anytime now they'll provide us with proof it's a deep-fake, released by your enemies to discredit you ahead of the COP. Once we can prove that to the world, the crisis will be over.'

Griffiths stopped pacing and looked across at his colleague, who was also his closest friend.

'Alvin, it just looks too real. My voice, the scar. People online are trusting their own eyes and believing this shit. Even Christine isn't sure right now whether to believe me.'

Griffiths gestured to his cell that was held in a vice-like grip in the palm of his right hand.

'I've already had over twenty texts from senators in our own party demanding I resign.'

'Stay strong, my friend. We can ride this one out. Once we have clear evidence it's a fake the clamour will die down. Besides which—'

Walcott was interrupted mid-sentence by the ping of an incoming text on Griffiths's cell. The president picked it up and clicked on the new message. Any remaining blood in his face drained away as he read it.

Stand down within the next two hours or we'll release a second video which is far worse.

He reread it before handing the cell across to Walcott, as though it were a nuclear weapon.

'I'm done.'

Walcott could see the president was crushed by the message and when he saw the contents, he understood why.

'Charles, this is your personal number. Only a handful of us around you have it. Who the hell are the people behind all this?'

The president's face gave way to a rueful smile.

'They're pure evil – and they've won.'

* * *

300

Soletska, working alongside an FBI data analyst, had viewed the Griffiths video dozens of times before she briefed Berrettini, Hembury and Vargas on her initial findings. The small meeting room where they met inside the Bureau headquarters had the benefit of an eighty-inch wall monitor, linked to a 4K digital projector. As the video played through, she provided her own commentary.

'Yet again, we're looking at a deepfake far superior to anything that's gone before. To be honest it's flawless, which is why it's had such a huge impact. There's no question the video has been created by the same AI machines that were behind the Galvez broadcast.'

Berrettini waited for the short video to finish before he picked up.

'Well, it's certainly done its job. I've just heard the president has resigned with immediate effect. He's vowing to clear his name but for now he's stepping down. This all plays right into Galvez's hands – Griffiths was a fearsome politician who was spearheading the charge for huge reparations on behalf of the Global Climate Action Partnership. As COP host, Galvez would have had to deal with Griffiths personally but, by discrediting him, the Spider Network has landed a killer blow.'

The FBI deputy director glanced across to Vargas.

'Nic, I know you've only just come back from Buenos Aires but I think you need to try and get a meeting with Galvez. Confront him with what we know and try to unnerve him. Bearing in mind the huge circus surrounding COP, do you think you could get near him?'

Vargas had been having similar thoughts and was one step ahead.

'I think I can use the Salazar murder inquiry as an initial way in. We've a statement from Manuel's girlfriend suggesting Salazar had held meetings with a senior government minister closely involved with setting up the COP conference so it would only be natural for the Buenos Aires police department to show an interest. Galvez's job as environment minister justifies an interview, if for no other reason than to eliminate him from our investigation. On that basis, as chief inspector, I think I can get to him. And besides I could do with the air miles.'

Berrettini smiled for the first time since Starling's suicide and rose to his feet indicating the meeting was over. But Soletska wasn't quite done.

'Nic, can I come with you? I'll keep digging into Galvez's background and might come up with something we can use to seriously disarm him when you meet him in the flesh.'

Vargas's eyeline flicked across to Berrettini to judge his reaction, a gesture Soletska picked up on.

'Guys, I promise I'll pull my weight over there. I really think I can be useful.'

Berrettini nodded as a sign of approval.

'Liliya, I've no doubt about that whatsoever. Just try to resist the temptation of hacking into the Argentine government's main computer systems while you're there, please.'

Chapter Fifty-Four

Paris, France

August 2003

In a weird twist of fate, Leopold learned of his mother's death through a live radio transmission, just as she herself had done fifty-eight years earlier, with her father's suicide in Germany. Amelie had been travelling on a solo trip across Egypt, sailing down the Nile from Luxor to Aswan on a river boat, as part of her eightieth birthday celebrations. At the last minute she opted to take an excursion by small charter plane to Abu Simbel, a village close to the Sudan border, famous for two of the most spectacular rock-cut temples in the world.

The four-seater Beechcraft Bonanza disappeared off the radar just ten minutes into the flight and went down somewhere in the desert, about fifty miles south of Aswan. Only Amelie and the pilot were onboard. It was about four hours later when the story broke. Amelie Legrand was the owner of the second biggest banking chain in France and her tragic death was the lead story on the midday news.

Leopold, who at forty-seven was well on his way to building the biggest media corporation in France, was riding in the back of his chauffer-driven Mercedes S-Class, on his way across Paris to a contract signing for a chain of radio stations, when he heard the breaking news on the car radio. His instant sense of shock and disbelief was palpable and for a few minutes his brain seemed to shut down as it struggled to process the news.

His driver, Benoit, knew Legrand's mother well and was also shaken by the bombshell he'd just heard and, without asking permission, turned off into a side street and pulled the Mercedes to a stop next to a small park. He glanced in his rear-view mirror just as Leopold let out a blood-curdling primeval-sounding roar, that seemed to come from a place deep inside his soul. Realising the car was stationary, Leopold leapt out and bolted into the park, disappearing from Benoit's view within seconds.

A few minutes later, he found himself sitting alone on a wooden slatted bench by the side of a circular lake, staring aimlessly at the heart-warming sight of a proud duck effort-lessly leading a procession of her newborn ducklings across the water. He found the image strangely comforting as he slowly began to come to terms with the reality he was now an orphan, and a sense of loneliness enveloped his brain.

They'd always spoken every day; she'd even called from Egypt the night before, to tell him all about her upcoming trip to Abu Simbel and how fortunate she'd been to charter a private plane at such short notice. She'd always been there for him and now she was gone – now, he was on his own.

* * *

Five days had passed since Amelie's death and Leopold had spent most of that time dealing with the Egyptian authorities, trying in vain to agree a timeline for his mother's body to be flown back to France for burial. He'd so far avoided visiting her Paris apartment, which was now part of his massive inheritance. Leopold had grown up there, only leaving when he was twenty-two but as he walked around it, he could sense his mother's presence everywhere, except she was gone, and the breathtaking home now belonged to him.

He found himself wandering aimlessly around the vast apartment and eventually entered her spectacular bedroom, which triggered a distant childhood memory. He must have been about eight at the time and he vividly remembered lying on her giant emperor-size bed, watching her place some documents away in the wall safe. She'd caught his gaze and smiled across to him, gently saying, 'My darling boy, this is where I keep all my secrets. One day, when I'm no longer here, they will all be yours and you'll truly understand everything.'

He'd always known the safe's combination – it was Himmler's birthdate – yet had never felt the slightest curiosity about its contents. But now, following her tragic death, it morphed into a giant magnet, drawing him towards it like a moth to a flame – its potential secrets suddenly irresistible. It was hidden behind a large Louis XV antique mirror which he drew back on a hinged lever and a few seconds later he opened the safe door and peered inside.

From what he could see, the contents were arranged in two neat piles. At the back was a stack of jewellery boxes, which resembled a wall of coloured bricks shielding the back wall of the safe. In front was a bundle of documents of varying sizes, many of them in envelopes, others in files, while some were just loose papers. Leopold carefully gathered them up before making his way to the bed where he flopped down and spread them all out across the silk covered eiderdown.

There appeared to be a mix of contracts, account reports and assorted statements but just as he thought he seen them all, his heart skipped a beat. A small white envelope had been sandwiched between two files and he'd missed it on his first pass. On the front, written in his mother's hand, was a single underlined word, *Leopold*. He struggled to breathe as he slowly peeled open the envelope and slid out the letter inside.

Leopold recognised two sheets of his mother's personal note paper which were neatly folded in half. He rolled on to his back, held the letter up in the air and began reading.

My Darling Leopold,

You have brought such joy into my life and wherever I am, you will forever be with me in my heart and soul. I want you to know that from the very first moment I held you in my arms I loved you more than life itself and I'm so proud to have witnessed your journey from childhood to the man you've now become.

We have always been honest with each another, and I've shared so many of my secrets with you, the biggest being the reality of my birthright. But as you know, I've never told you the full story behind your adoption and you've never questioned me about it. I have always felt ashamed of my behaviour, and never wanted you to think badly of me. Every time I decided to tell you, I just couldn't go through with it and so now being a coward to the end, this is the only way I can do it. Whether or not you wish to act on it, you deserve to know the truth.

Leopold placed the letter down on the side of the bed as he considered whether he really wanted to read on. A huge part of him didn't want to learn information that could possibly change his life forever but, in the end, he felt compelled to continue and reached for the letter, as he knew there was no escaping his destiny.

On 10 July 1956 you were left on the steps of the Église Saint-Jean de Montmartre at around midnight. You'd been wrapped in some tea towels and placed inside a small cardboard box. I believe you were no more than three days old, possibly only two. By chance you were discovered by the night cleaner who took you to a small back street orphanage she also worked for, close to the church, which was run by a discredited, loathsome priest.

Father Brune was a hateful man who exploited orphans for his own monetary gain. I'm pretty sure he was an abuser as well. I only dealt with him because I was desperate. Obviously I couldn't go to an authorised orphanage as I knew they would dig deep into my background, which of course I couldn't risk. I'm truly ashamed to say I gave Brune one hundred and fifty thousand francs in return for him handing you over to me, with no questions asked.

None of this helps with identifying your birth mother, as even back then the trail was cold, but should you wish to go down that route these are the only clues I can give you.

I hope you can find it in your heart to forgive me.

Forever yours,

Your loving mother,

Amelie

Unbeknown to Leopold, his late mother hadn't been totally honest. She'd deliberately failed to mention the locket found in the rags he was wearing as a baby. That was the biggest clue as to the identity of his birth mother and even from beyond the grave Amelie couldn't bear the thought of her beloved son ever finding her and possibly sharing his love.

Chapter Fifty-Five

Paris, France

August 2004

A year had passed since his mother's death and Leopold had buried himself in his work, obsessively buying media outlets as though he were at a shopping mall, relentlessly growing his empire. He'd inherited a huge fortune in cash and assets and had moved into his mother's apartment on Champ de Mars, which he'd completely refurbished to his own taste.

For most of the year he'd been able to disregard the startling contents of his mother's letter but since her death he'd felt brittle, like a cracked pane of glass that that could shatter at any moment and with the first anniversary of her death approaching, he finally broke. Two weeks earlier he'd met with a private detective based in Montmartre, whom he'd commissioned with three specific tasks relating to events that had taken place in the famous village forty-eight years earlier. The investigator's usual rate was five hundred euros a day, but Leopold wanted him fully committed to the job, so doubled it to a thousand and added a twenty-thousand kicker for each of the three assignments he managed to pull off. As a further incentive, if he succeeded in all three, he'd receive a fifty-thousand-euro bonus.

The investigator, Paul Chapelle, was somewhat bemused by the job but fully embraced the challenge as the potential rewards were eye-watering. His task was to trace the whereabouts, alive or dead, of three people. A priest called Father Gustav Brune, a nameless church cleaner who worked for the Église Saint-Jean de Montmartre in July 1956 and a woman who gave up her newborn baby boy at that same time, leaving the infant on the church steps.

Having arrived at Legrand's apartment armed with his report, he entered his magnificent study to be met by the intimidating sight of the media mogul sitting behind his Napoleonic desk, head perfectly framed by the French flag on the wall behind.

Chapelle was a French cop who'd gone private three years earlier and had built a decent reputation for being industrious and discreet. He sat opposite Legrand and produced a large white envelope from his tobacco brown briefcase which he placed on the desk between the two of them. He didn't need to read from it, having personally typed up the contents of the two-page report just a couple of hours earlier.

'Monsieur, I'm gratified to say I've had some success in discovering most of the information you seek. I've located the whereabouts of two of the three subjects.'

Legrand's eyes were out on stalks.

'Which two?'

'The priest and the night cleaner, who it transpires, worked for his orphanage as well as the church. Her name is Béatrice Dubois. They're both alive, although in the case of the priest, only just.'

Legrand hid his disappointment and zoned in on what was on offer.

'Tell me everything you've discovered.'

'Dubois lives with one of her sons in a flat in Montmartre. She's in her early eighties but, by all accounts, is in reasonable shape. The priest is a bit of a mystery. No one knows his exact age but if some old church documents I found are accurate, I think he might be ninety-eight. He lives alone in an exclusive apartment block just off the Champs-Elysées, not far from here. I've no idea where his wealth originated as the service charges alone are higher than most people's monthly income.'

Legrand's mind flashed back to his mother's detailed account of the huge sum the hideous priest had demanded for handing him over. He nodded to Chapelle, urging him to continue.

'I spoke to the concierge in the block who's only met him twice in the last five years. The last occasion was a couple of years ago. Apparently, the old man lives like a hermit, hardly ever venturing out from the apartment and has very few visitors. He recalled the priest told him he was suffering from severe emphysema, so he must be close to the end. As requested, I haven't made direct contact with either of them, but their addresses are in the file.'

'You've done good work, Chapelle. You've earned your bonuses.'

The private detective gave a slight smile and stood up, assuming the meeting was over. But Legrand wasn't quite finished. His voiced strained slightly as he tried to disguise the desperation he felt.

'So, nothing on the woman who gave up her baby?'

Chapelle nodded.

'Nothing but a dead end.'

* * *

The following morning Legrand found himself standing by the side of a streetlamp on Rue Paul-Féval, deep in the heart of Montmartre, staring up at the third-floor apartment he knew belonged to Béatrice Dubois's son. He'd spent the previous evening working up a cover story for his visit to the former church cleaner's home and, although he had nagging doubts about what he might discover by digging up the past, he was determined to put it into operation.

The intercom inset into the wall alongside the street door was answered by a strong male voice.

'Who is it?'

'My name is Monsieur Sellier. I wish to speak with Madame Béatrice Dubois.'

Legrand was met with a wall of silence and was just about to speak again when the entry buzzer sounded, releasing the street door. The inside of the building was far shabbier than he'd envisaged from the street exterior, and he made his way up the three flights of narrow stairs until he reached Dubois's apartment level. Waiting on the tiny landing, outside a partially open door, stood a large middle-aged man dressed all in black, the typical garb of a café waiter. His dark brown eyes were filled with suspicion as he weighed up the well-dressed visitor standing before him.

CHAPTER FIFTY-FIVE

'What business do you have with my mother?'

Legrand switched to autopilot having rehearsed his script numerous times.

'I'm an old friend of a man who believes your mother did him a great service in the past. He was born in Montmartre but emigrated to New York over twenty years ago where he now enjoys an extremely successful life. He recently received information which suggests Madame Dubois was helpful in some way with his adoption and, if that transpires to be true, I believe he will find a way of expressing his gratitude.'

Pierre Dubois's puzzled facial expression indicated he was no longer suspicious but intrigued.

'Monsieur, wait here.'

Five minutes later he reappeared and ushered Legrand inside the small apartment. The old woman was sitting upright, supported by a couple of padded cushions in a wing backed armchair Legrand suspected was even older than her. Its original red velvet covering was threadbare and so badly faded it was impossible to assign an accurate name to its dirty brown colour. Her grizzled hair was pulled back in a tight bun while her heavily wrinkled face was dotted with a mix of brown and black liver spots. But her dark brown eyes, framed by a pair of semi-rimmed glasses, were warm and welcoming and it was clear she wore her age as a badge of pride. When she spoke, her voice was strong and clear as a bell.

'Monsieur, welcome to our home. Please take a seat.'

She gestured with her right hand towards a tiny wooden chair that had hastily been moved from the kitchen into the small living room to face her. Her son stood in front of the sole window, watching on as Legrand sat down.

'I understand from my son you wish to talk about events from my distant past. How can I help you?'

'Madame, I'm here on behalf of a dear friend who lives in America. He believes you were responsible for saving his life and then aiding his adoption.'

Dubois's response displayed her confusion.

'Monsieur, I fear you friend is mistaken. I have never been anything more than an honest cleaner.'

Legrand ploughed on, undeterred.

'It was the summer of 1956, a baby boy was left on the steps of the Église Saint-Jean de Montmartre, dressed in some rags inside a cardboard box. He was found by a night cleaner who . . .'

'Yes, yes that was me . . . I found the boy.'

Dubois's eyes were tightly shut as she willed her mind to flashback more than forty years and visualise the distant memory. It was dark . . . she was standing on the church steps . . . clutching the tiny baby to her chest.

When she opened her eyes, tears began to trickle down her cheeks forming rivulets in the deep crevices in her skin.

'I took him inside the church and bathed him in the sink in the priest's bathroom.'

Legrand's gaze never left Béatrice's face. He was mesmerised by the words of the old woman who'd been his saviour all those years before.

'What happened next?'

She shook her head as though she didn't want to carry on but summoned up the courage to continue, even though her words dripped with regret.

'I fully intended to take the infant to the police . . . I really did. But then on my way to the station I met the priest . . . he persuaded me to take the baby home for a few days and then bring him to an orphanage he ran. He gave me money, and I did as he asked.'

Dubois's tears began to dry up as her sadness morphed into anger.

'I knew of his sordid reputation, we all did. But he was a Catholic priest and . . . I needed the money. He promised me he had the perfect home for the boy and I'm ashamed to say I gave him over.'

'Madame, believe me, you've absolutely nothing to reproach yourself for. Had it not been for your actions, the baby may well not have survived the night. Can I ask, do you have any idea as to the identity of the birth mother?'

She paused for a few moments as she dipped back into her memory bank one more time.

'No, other than the locket, there were no clues. Nothing.'

Legrand's body jerked forward in the chair as if he'd been struck by a bolt of lightning.

'Locket? What locket? Tell me about it?'

'It was just a cheap silver-plated couples' heart locket – one of those types that split into two pieces. So, the baby had been left with one half and I guess the other was . . .'

Legrand finished the thought for her.

'With his birth mother.'

After saying his goodbyes, Legrand dashed down the stairs of the old building and proceeded to run most of the four-mile route back to his apartment. Once inside he made straight for his bedroom, where he opened the wall safe and carefully removed all his mother's jewellery cases. Even though, following her death, he'd changed many things inside the apartment, he'd never found the courage to go near her intimate possessions.

He methodically worked his way through millions of euros' worth of jewellery, all perfectly presented inside their branded boxes. There was a spectacular collection of necklaces, brooches, rings and watches, many of which he recalled her wearing. He was nearing the end of the search when he opened a red and gold leather Cartier case that contained a diamond and sapphire encrusted bracelet. He was just about to move on to the next box when he noticed something slightly odd. The red velvet base wasn't quite flat, one end seemed higher than the other and, as soon as he saw the cause of it, he knew it had to be the locket.

He took a deep breath before using his fingers to prise it away from the bottom of the case. Hidden underneath a two-hundred-thousand-euro Cartier bracelet was half of a cheap silver-plated heart locket. For a few seconds he just stared at it, unable to touch it. He felt as though he'd just lit a match and started an inferno. At that precise moment he sensed its power and understood his mother's reasons for keeping its existence secret. Eventually he did reach down to pick it up and, as he held the tiny object in the palm of his right hand, he marvelled at its significance.

Chapter Fifty-Six

Paris, France

August 2004

A few hours after the discovery of the locket, Paul Chapelle was back in Legrand's study, having been brought up to speed by the media mogul as to its relevance.

'Take as many photos as you need. I want you to put a team together to trawl every pawn shop and jeweller in Montmartre to find where it came from. If that draws a blank, extend the search to the whole of Paris.'

Chapelle had already made a cursory examination of the tiny locket and was sceptical about tracing its provenance.

'Monsieur, let me be frank. I'm at your disposal and will continue to follow your instructions but, you must appreciate, this is a very cheap piece of jewellery with no markings whatsoever which makes it almost impossible to trace – especially as we are talking about a sale that took place over forty years ago.'

Legrand's eyes narrowed as he took aim at the investigator, demonstrating a side of his character he'd previously kept in check.

'Chapelle, negativity is no use to me, neither is failure. It appears I overestimated your capabilities. If you're not up to handling this new task, I'll find someone who is.'

The savage reprimand did its job, as the investigator realised he'd crossed the line. Legrand had bared his teeth, exposing a glimpse of his true nature which Chapelle logged in his memory bank for future reference.

'Forgive me for creating any doubt in your mind. I'll pursue this assignment with the same vigour I demonstrated in track-ing down the church cleaner and the priest.'

Legrand didn't bother to acknowledge his small victory.

'We need to discuss Father Brune. Things have changed and I need you to contact him as soon as possible. Inform him you've been contracted by a client in the United States whose brother spent time as a child at his former orphanage in Montmartre. Explain he recently died and left a significant sum of money in his will to the priest who ran the institution. Tell him you're authorised to make the payment, once you're happy you've found the right man and that your colleague needs an in-person visit to check his ID. If I'm right about this man, he won't be able to resist the temptation of easy money.'

Two days later Chapelle was on the line to Legrand with breaking news.

'It took a while for him to agree to speak with me on the phone. But once he did, he took the bait: hook, line and sinker. The concierge who works the reception at his apartment block placed the call and put me through.'

'How did he sound?'

'Old, but canny. He wanted to know how much money was involved and I explained my colleague would fill him in face-to-face once he'd confirmed his identity. He wasn't too happy but, as you expected, greed won over suspicion. So, Monsieur Sellier, you have an appointment with Father Brune scheduled for ten tomorrow morning.'

'Excellent work, Chapelle. Any news on the locket?'

'Not yet; it's early days but I have ten full-time operatives hitting the shops as we speak.'

Legrand ended the call and eased back in his office chair. He sensed he was taking back control of events, rather than being battered by them, and that was the way he liked it.

He was up early the next morning and made a quick pitstop at one of his own bank's branches on the way to the priest's apartment on Rue Marbeuf, a high-end street which connected Avenue George V to the Champs-Élysées. After exiting a cab armed with a black attaché case, he entered the sprawling marbled reception area of the mansion block and mused on how well the corrupt old priest had done for himself. Years of extorting money from desperate adopters had clearly paid off.

Legrand was nursing a feeling of deep foreboding about the upcoming meeting and, knowing he had to check-in with the concierge first, decided to try and conceal his features, even though he knew few people outside the business world would recognise him. He wore a black felt fedora pulled down low over his forehead, which at least hid his distinctive shock of blond hair. As it transpired, he needn't have bothered. When he reached the concierge's desk, the man at reception didn't look up from his paperwork during their brief exchange.

'I'm here to see Father Brune.'

'Five eleven, fifth floor. I'll let him know you're on the way up.'

The door to apartment five hundred and eleven had been left ajar and the rancid smell wafting through the tiny gap almost made Legrand gag. He cautiously pushed the door and immediately found himself standing in a dimly lit open-plan room, where he was greeted by a grotesque sight. Hundreds of tins of canned foods were stacked in huge piles on the wooden floor, randomly arranged around the sparse furniture. Some of the cans had been opened, which accounted for the stomach-churning smell that hung in the air like a dense fog.

Scattered around them were sections of old newspapers and magazines, some of which had begun to turn yellow. Legrand navigated his way past a low pile of cans containing pork meat and peered through the gloom searching for the priest.

'Monsieur Sellier, don't be put off by the smell, it won't harm you.'

Legrand followed the sound of the rasping voice, and his eyes settled on the bizarre sight of the old priest propped up on an uncovered mattress lying on a metal-framed single bed. Brune was wearing a heavily stained black cassock, which hung off his wizened bony frame like an oversized cloak. His face was skeletal, engraved with deep grooves that looked as if they'd been carved out of his skin with a hunting knife. His breathing was hollow and intermittent, yet, despite his physical frailties, his eyes, which were partially camouflaged by thick layers of flabby skin, were alert and disturbingly menacing.

Legrand looked around for somewhere to sit but the only two chairs he could see were covered with tins and magazines, so he remained standing about four feet away from the priest. He removed the fedora and placed it down on a small wooden chest of drawers by the side of the bed that was also covered with newspapers. Legrand wanted Brune to see his facial features in the desperate and vain hope the old man might recognise him as the baby he sold forty-eight years earlier. But of course the priest's eyes didn't show a flicker of recognition, as he spoke for the second time.

'How much money is involved?'

Legrand was so disgusted by the surroundings he answered the question with one of his own.

'How can you live like this, in such squalor?'

'Don't judge me, Monsieur. My emphysema means I can't leave the flat and I've no desire to entertain visitors. I just need basic food to keep myself alive. Every two months, an old lady who I've known for many years brings me supplies, which I pay her handsomely for. She's the only person allowed to see me. As you can no doubt tell she was only here a couple of days ago. Now, how much money do you have for me?'

Legrand planned to torment the priest before confronting him with his past. He lifted the attaché case he'd brought with him on to the mattress, placing it alongside the old man's chest. He flicked open the catches to reveal a layer of one-hundred-euro notes, bound together in thick wads. Brune's head jerked forward, desperate to see the contents and when he did, his eyes lit up like a set of 500-watt lightbulbs. His gravelly voice came to life, invigorated by greed.

'How much is there? What do you require from me before I receive it?'

Legrand began to enjoy himself and continued to taunt the old man.

'One hundred thousand euros but first you need to fully convince me you're the same priest who ran the orphanage in Montmartre in 1956.'

Brune's breathing quickened as he painfully lifted his bony right hand in what looked like slow motion and pointed to the chest of drawers where Legrand had discarded his fedora. His wicked mouth twisted, forming a poisonous grin.

'Over there, on the chest, are my papers. Passport, ID and birth certificate.'

'I'll get to those, but first I have some questions.'

Legrand was astounded Brune hadn't once enquired as to the identity of his mystery benefactor or given any thought to the fact that by all accounts he'd abused his orphan inmates so appallingly, it was highly unlikely any of them would leave him a bean. But the stone-hearted priest was fully distracted by the huge quantity of cash on his bed that was so tantalisingly close.

'I want to talk with you about a newborn baby boy you were involved with in July 1956.'

The priest broke out of his reverie and snapped back.

'I never dealt with newborns; I didn't have the facilities.'

Legrand moved forward and closed the attaché case ahead of lifting it off the mattress.

'In which case you're not the man we are seeking. It must be another priest.'

Brune's sharp mind was tormented between panic and suspicion, but avarice won the day.

'Wait, wait. Tell me more. My memory is not what it was.'

'A baby boy found on the steps of the Église Saint-Jean de Montmartre by a night cleaner was then adopted by—'

Brune's memory miraculously kicked back into life, bathed in a distorted account of events.

'Yes, I remember now. It was a strange matter. A German woman had contacted me, wanting to adopt a baby boy. I thoroughly checked her credentials and rather than hand the infant over to the police, I decided it was in the baby's interest to give him to the woman who was desperate to start a family.'

Legrand noticeably stiffened as the priest recalled the details of his handover to Amelie.

'How much did she pay for the boy?'

The priest shook his head and feigned an expression of disgust.

'Not a single franc, Monsieur. My motives were driven purely by the wellbeing of the poor homeless baby.'

Legrand exploded like a volcano, spitting out boiling hot lava.

'You lie. You're a corrupt, evil abuser. Nothing more than a stain on society.'

What little blood remained in Brune's shrivelled face instantly drained away.

'Monsieur, I swear by everything I hold holy that—'

'You charged her one hundred and fifty thousand francs which probably paid for this disgusting cesspit.'

The priest adjusted his position slightly upwards on the single pillow that was supporting him, allowing his right hand to slip behind it.

'Who are you? What do you want from me?'

Legrand moved towards him and leaned downwards, until his head was less than a couple of feet away from the priest's.

'Take a good look, Father. Take a good look. I'm your worst nightmare.'

Brune squinted as he studied the face directly in front of him. When he spoke next, he caught Legrand completely off guard.

'Wait, I do know you. I know who you are. Your name isn't Sellier. I've seen your photo in one of my magazines.'

His eyes flashed over to the chest of drawers where a copy of the business magazine, *Le Particulier*, was lying on top of a pile of other periodicals. Legrand followed the priest's eyeline and froze when he saw it. The shrewd old priest registered the distraction and seized the opportunity. Concealed in the palm of his right hand was a small snub-nosed revolver, loaded with six rounds. His hand was remarkably steady as he lifted it off the mattress, angling it towards the back of Legrand's head. But his stubborn index finger, riddled with arthritis, wouldn't obey his instruction as he willed it to pull the trigger.

The delay was fatal as Legrand sensed the sudden movement, saw the immediate danger and flung himself on top of the priest, knocking the stuffing out of him. The revolver slipped from his grasp, tumbled off the mattress and hit the floor. Legrand glared into Brune's hate-filled eyes and knew exactly what he needed to do next. He grabbed the pillow from underneath the priest's head and, as the old man fell backwards, he smothered his face with it, pressing down with every ounce of strength he possessed.

It felt as though he was lying on top of a bag of bones, as Brune's resistance was pitiful, and, unbeknown to him, the old man had drawn his last breath within seconds of the attack. Rather than release the pressure, Legrand continued to press down hard, as he found the whole experience strangely exhilarating.

Five minutes later the clean-up was over. Legrand had replaced the pillow behind the priest's head, sitting his body upright again. He closed the old man's eyelids and stared down at the lifeless body of the vile priest who, thanks to his intervention, had gone to meet his maker a little earlier than scheduled.

Legrand figured his corpse wouldn't be discovered for a few weeks, by which time his body would have begun to decompose and, given his age and physical ailments, everyone would assume death by natural causes.

As he sat in the back of a cab riding back to his apartment, he felt empowered by the entire episode. He'd rid the world of a low-life vermin that needed to be wiped out, just as Himmler had done on a grand scale. At precisely the same time he'd been suffocating the priest, a courier had delivered a package to a small apartment in Montmartre. When Béatrice Dubois opened it and saw the huge quantity of cash inside, she broke down in tears and hugged her bemused son, who'd never seen so much money before in his life.

Back in his apartment, Legrand sat in his bedroom, clutching the silver locket between his hands. He closed his eyes and imagined his mother was looking down on him. He'd settled two outstanding debts on her behalf and was sure she'd have been proud of his actions.

Chapter Fifty-Seven

Buenos Aires, Argentina

T he UN Climate Change Conference, better known as COP, the Conference of the Parties, takes place every year and boasts the membership of almost every country in the world.

More than seventy thousand attendees descended on Buenos Aires to attend the latest one. They included politicians, business leaders, journalists, climate scientists and some heads of state. The venue, La Rural, a vast exhibition centre in Palermo, boasted over forty-five thousand square metres of covered space, spread across six pavilions. The first day of the conference had been largely overshadowed by fallout from the Griffiths video scandal, which had rocked the confidence of the Global Climate Action Partnership, now suddenly rudderless.

Day two had seen a much calmer event, with hundreds of meetings taking place throughout the day, with passionate representatives lobbying for their respective causes on behalf of their own countries. As host, Galvez arrived each morning by helicopter, making the brief eight-minute journey from his home across the city to the exhibition centre. The twin-engine Bell 429 Global Ranger conveyed him, along with six of his team, to and from the conference and, as he expected, immediately sparked outrage amongst many delegates who baulked at the demonstrably hypocritical means of transport. The environment minister relished the attention and loved creating controversy, knowing how well it played with his right-wing base.

Galvez had hidden allies amongst a few key member countries, who shared a single goal to overturn the agreement made at the previous COP, obliging designated countries to pay billions of dollars in reparations. Self-interest would rule once again and the status quo, which benefited the rich and powerful states, would be firmly back in place. Galvez was driven by the mantra of the Spider Network; a set of beliefs Legrand had reminded him of in a chilling WhatsApp message the night before the conference had started.

The new Reich is not a country, it's an ideology which believes rich nations survive at the expense of poor ones. In fifty years, water, oil and all other natural resources will be scarce. Only the strong will survive.

* * *

Vargas and Soletska arrived at their hotel in Buenos Aires around seven in the evening and briefly checked into their rooms before meeting for dinner. As he was on home turf, Vargas took control and arranged a table at Mishiguene, the only Jewish restaurant in the city. It was a ten-minute cab ride from their hotel and, when they arrived, Soletska was clearly mystified by his choice of venue. The large wooden mezuzah on the door frame caught her eye on the way in and, as they walked to their table, she scanned the dark brown walls that were adorned with black and white photographs of Jewish immigrants arriving in Buenos Aires in the late 1930s. Posters and photos paid homage to the traditions and peoples that inspired the food on the menu. As they took their seats at a small table positioned near the kitchen, she couldn't wait to tease him.

'What's a nice Argentine Catholic boy like you doing taking a nice Orthodox Ukrainian girl like me to a Jewish restaurant?'

Vargas laughed, which Soletska noted was something of a rarity.

'My wife Sophia was Jewish and although this place opened a few years after she died, I like coming here. Sometimes I bring her parents along as a thank you for the hundreds of Friday night dinners they've cooked for me over the years. It's also a place I come to on my own and, before you think this is all getting a bit maudlin, the food is amazing – if you know what to order.'

Soletska eased back in her chair and beamed a smile directly at him.

'You know how much I love my food. Bring it on.'

Vargas duly ordered and, while they were waiting, Liliya steered the subject back to Sophia.

'Tell me about your wife – only if you feel comfortable.'

For a moment he was taken off guard. He felt himself swallow hard, as if the words he wanted to speak were stuck somewhere deep in his throat. It was an involuntary action that coincided with his caramel brown eyes watering up.

'I still find it tough to even talk about her, say her name. She's left a scar on my heart. It's been fifteen years this month, yet the pain never seems to leave me.'

Liliya was stunned and genuinely moved by his reaction. She'd heard sketchy details of his past from Hembury but had figured the passage of time would have allowed Vargas to have moved on with his life to some extent but clearly that wasn't the case. She regretted having asked the question but could see there was no going back. He clearly had more to say.

'Look, the truth is my personal life is a screw-up and I guess that's why I need to do this stuff. Cases like the one we're working on together mess with my head, which is just the way I like it. Work is the best anaesthetic, I've found.'

Soletska instinctively offered her hand across the table, but he didn't take the cue. Pain was written across his face, and it was upsetting to see.

'Nic, I'm so sorry. I should never have gone there.'

The familiar sound of a WhatsApp message landing on Vargas's cell came to his rescue. He glanced down at the phone's screen and his mood lightened as soon as he read it.

'It's from my assistant, Torres, who never takes no for an answer. Galvez's office has agreed to give me ten minutes with him tomorrow morning at precisely seven twenty in his office at the conference centre. It's a dead stop interview, as he's chairing a meeting with representatives from the G7 countries at seven thirty.'

Liliya was relieved they were back on track and work had taken over again.

'Okay, let's eat and get back to the hotel. I'm going to carry on digging into his past – see what it throws up.'

329

Vargas had ordered a mini banquet of starters that arrived on a giant platter: a selection of gefilte fish, chopped liver, pastrami croquettes, potato latkes, matzo crackers and pickles. They both tucked into the feast with Vargas providing a running commentary on some of the dishes, relaying anecdotes he'd heard over the years from his wife's parents. For the next few minutes Soletska was happy to just listen and let him do the talking. They'd barely finished eating when Vargas beckoned the waiter back over.

'Nic, I'm stuffed already.'

'This final dish is in your honour. It's the speciality of the house. A fusion of Ukrainian and kosher cooking.'

Before she could protest, an enormous bowl of steaming hot borscht arrived and the surprise ingredient was ground-meat dumplings floating on the surface, known as kreplach, classic Ashkenazi cuisine, usually eaten in a chicken broth. Liliya wolfed it down, while Vargas watched on in awe.

Thirty minutes later they were back in their hotel rooms, both exhausted from the long-haul flight; Vargas was drifting off into a fitful sleep, while Soletska, armed with a couple of Red Bulls from the room fridge, was glued to her laptop, staring at an image of Galvez, about to pull another all-nighter.

As agreed, they met for breakfast at six and the first thing Vargas noticed was that Liliya wearing the same clothes as the previous night. The second was the enormous breakfast she was working her way through: scrambled eggs, chorizo, bacon and sauté potatoes, accompanied by a side plate of tostadas and cream cheese. He pulled up a chair to join her at the table and food was the last thing on his mind as he poured himself a cup of black coffee.

CHAPTER FIFTY-SEVEN

'Someone's got an appetite!'

Soletska finished devouring a mouthful of sausage and then an impish smile broke out on her face, that stretched from ear to ear.

'Lack of sleep always makes me hungry.'

Vargas gestured to her plate.

'Looking at that, I'm assuming you didn't get much.'

'None, to be honest.'

Her grin was still in place.

'How did you get on?'

'I hit the jackpot.'

Vargas took a deep breath.

'Go on.'

Chapter Fifty-Eight

Buenos Aires, Argentina

Vargas arrived at the La Rural Exhibition Centre fifteen minutes early for his meeting, where he was greeted by Galvez's PA, who escorted him to the 'Blue Zone', the office space managed by the UN Climate Change Committee which ran the conference. She showed him into a small office the environment minister was using as his temporary base. She moved with the elegance of a catwalk model; her wavy metallic silver hair seeming to have a life of its own as it bounced mischievously around her shoulders. A pair of intriguing pale green eyes and a set of plump lips completed her supermodel appearance. The room was sparse and she ushered him to an upright padded chair facing an unimposing desk.

'Minister Galvez is in the air and is due to land at 7.16, which means he'll be on time for your meeting. Just to remind you, he must leave promptly at 7.30.'

Vargas took a seat and opened his notebook to check through the list of questions he'd put together with Soletska over breakfast. He knew he'd only have ten minutes with the minister so, although there were twelve written down, only three mattered.

Galvez entered the office at precisely 7.20. Vargas rose from his chair to meet him and after a cursory handshake, they took their seats across the desk. The environment minister was a stunning-looking man, whose features reflected his Germanic heritage. He stood at just over six foot, with a muscular physique that boasted wide shoulders tapering to a narrow waist. The shade of his natural blond hair was so startling it could have been bleached and his penetrating blue eyes gleamed with confidence. He was wearing a dark blue, pure-wool two-piece Zegna suit, teamed with a crisp white shirt and navy silk tie. If he were the slightest bit concerned about the content of the interview, he hid it well. The tone of his voice was smooth, like butter in a warm pan.

'I understand you're investigating a murder. How can I assist you, Chief Inspector?'

Vargas knew a denial was coming his way but had to go through the motions before he could land any meaningful blows.

'A gangster called Carlos Salazar was thrown to his death from the balcony of his penthouse apartment, along with one of his associates. A witness we've interviewed believed you had some involvement with him, prior to his death.'

Vargas expected to detect a slight 'tell' in Galvez's eyes but there wasn't a flicker.

'That's incorrect. Up until a moment ago I'd never heard his name, and I'd certainly never met him. I do my best not to hang around with gangsters, Chief Inspector.'

Galvez couldn't prevent a supercilious grin breaking out on his lips. Vargas was aware he'd already wasted two minutes, so went straight for the jugular.

'What do you know about a covert organisation, called *Die Spinne?*'

This time Vargas detected a slight enlargement of the pupils in Galvez's eyes, which weren't shining quite as brightly as before: a classic tell-tale of a lie.

'Nothing, I'm afraid. Who are they?'

'They're an organisation run by direct descendants of senior Nazis who are currently seeking to destabilise world politics through the deployment of deepfakes. I believe in recent days you've allowed them to utilise your own deepfake in a television interview—'

'Chief Inspector, this meeting is over, and you can be assured I'll be taking this matter up with the chief of police, who's an old friend of mine. Meanwhile, should you contemplate going public with any of these absurd claims, I'll bury you.'

Galvez sprang out of his chair and bolted past Vargas, heading for the door. Just before he reached it, Vargas delivered his trump card, which had been handed to him over breakfast by Soletska.

'How do you think the public would react if they discovered your grandfather, Hector Galvez, was really Heinz Scholz, a senior Nazi, who personally rounded up thousands of Jews across Europe for extermination in the deathcamps?'

Galvez froze on the spot like a mannequin. His knees felt like they were about to give way, and his expression changed as though he'd smelled a rotten egg. He had his back to Vargas, who could sense the dramatic mood change and was just about to land another blow when the minister came back to life and almost ripped the door off its hinges as he exited at warp speed.

Less than two minutes later, Galvez placed a call on his cell to Legrand, who was horrified by the details of his confrontation with Vargas. The puppet master could see things were unravelling at speed and he needed to be cautious as so much was at stake. The one thing he couldn't allow to happen was for Galvez to lose his nerve at such a key moment.

'Javier, Vargas was on a fishing expedition. He and his colleagues have some knowledge of our network but have no idea what's really in play. Trust me, once we get through COP, we can close him down and go dark ourselves for a while.'

Galvez was consumed with the fear of exposure and wasn't taking in a word Legrand was saying.

'How the hell did Vargas get his hands on the information about my grandfather? If that goes public I'll be destroyed, humiliated. I'm not sure I can do this anymore.'

* * *

Almost five hours later, shortly after midday, Vargas and Soletska were sitting at a bar in the departure lounge of Terminal A at Ezeiza international airport, killing time before they caught their flight back to Washington. They'd downed a couple of beers and were about to go to their gate when the TV mounted high in the corner of the bar broke a game-changing news story. The volume was off, but Vargas spotted the dramatic footage filling the screen and barked at the barman to turn up the sound.

A helicopter had come down over the city and crashed into the side of a department store in Palermo. Phone footage, clearly shot by a member of the public, was being broadcast on a loop. It showed the last few seconds of the chopper's descent before impact. The Bell 429 twin-engine Global Ranger was a giant fireball as it spiralled downwards through the air before slamming into the side of the building. A caption plastered across the bottom third of the screen read:

Environment minister, Javier Galvez, and three colleagues have died in a helicopter crash.

Vargas and Soletska watched on in horror as the footage changed to show head shots of Galvez and the three junior ministers who'd died alongside him in the crash. Vargas's cell was on silent, but he felt it vibrate inside his jacket pocket. He pulled it out and glanced at the screen to see an incoming call from Berrettini, who he'd recently debriefed on his meeting with Galvez. He swiped the screen to take the call and, before he could speak, the apoplectic voice of the FBI deputy director blasted into his ear.

'Jesus Christ, Nic, have you seen the news? The bastards have just wiped out Galvez. COP is a massive international event and yet they've brazenly taken him out in front of the world's media.'

Vargas switched his cell on to speaker.

'Mike, Liliya and I are in an airport bar watching the story of the crash unfold right now. The guys behind this are either totally insane or have balls of steel. Who the hell are they?'

Chapter Fifty-Nine

Paris, France

A lbert Gagne was agitated and in pain. The eighty-five-year-old was sitting in the corner of a packed dentist's waiting room, hoping to secure an appointment for a toothache he'd been nursing for weeks. He lived on the breadline and couldn't afford dental fees but, one day a month, a private dentist in Montmartre offered a charity service on a first come, first served basis. Although there were sixteen people bunched together in the opulent waiting room, as far as he could tell he was seventh in line, so had a fair chance of being seen at some point. He suspected the offending incisor would have to be removed, leaving a nasty gap in his upper jawline but vanity wasn't an issue as Gagne had long since stopped worrying about his appearance.

The map of wrinkles on his face encroached on to a bald mottled pink scalp. His blood-flecked eyes, partially hidden by saggy wrinkled folds, revealed a surprising alertness that belied his age. They scanned the room, studying the faces of fellow patients: a sad group of losers, who, despite their similarity to him, he viewed with contempt. He winced as a fresh wave of pain engulfed his mouth and, seeking distraction, reached for a magazine from the top of a large pile resting on a coffee table close by.

L'Express was the premier weekly news magazine in France and featured stories from the world of politics, business and the media. The image dominating the front cover was a head-shot of a man whose contented smile exuded a whiff of arrogance and supremacy. Gagne recognised the face of Leopold Legrand, the media mogul many believed was the richest man in the country. The old man muttered under his breath as his gnarled fingers flicked through the pages to find the article.

'Rich bastard.'

It was a four-page spread and, with nothing better to do, Gagne reached inside his jacket for his glasses and began to read. Legrand had given the interview a few days earlier as he wanted it to appear during the opening days of COP. He knew the content would stoke controversy as its main thrust would reflect his opinion that demands from poor Third World countries for reparations were completely unjustified and counterintuitive to the long-term prosperity of the world. It was a lightly coded message which he knew would be read by world leaders who shared his belief that self-interest was key to survival and the strong shouldn't be dragged down by the weak.

Legrand also chose to use the interview as an opportunity to tell the world about his humble origins. He found it cathartic to talk about being abandoned on the steps of a tiny church in Montmartre and how the only clue to his identity, other than some rags and a cardboard box, was one half of a cheap silver heart locket. The fact he'd risen from such a wretched start in life to become the head of the biggest media corporation in the world only added to the glamour of his life story.

He was already viewed by many as an enigma and loved to perpetuate the mystery that surrounded him. On another level, buried somewhere deep in his mind was the thought his birth mother might see or hear about the story, if indeed she was still alive.

Gagne never finished the article. He stuffed the magazine inside his jacket pocket and scuttled out of the waiting room as fast as his malformed arthritic limbs would carry him, heading back to the shabby apartment he shared with his twin brother. His mind was racing and, oddly, the excruciating pain from his tooth that had persisted for so long had vanished.

The interior of the miserable basement flat located on the rue Saint-Denis in one of the poorest districts in Paris hadn't changed in the thirty years the two brothers had rented it. It was ridden with damp and paper was literally peeling off the walls, while the threadbare carpets exposed ancient wooden floorboards which were being eaten by fungal decay.

Gagne slammed the street door shut, shuffled through the tiny sitting room, and burst into his brother's bedroom. His twin, Henri, had been bedridden for the last three years, a victim of vascular Parkinsonism, which had brought on a series of strokes that had left him incapacitated, although mentally he was as sharp as his brother. Despite being twins, they no longer looked alike as Henri's face had collapsed into itself and his features were almost non-existent. The only resemblance with Albert were his eyes, which still had a flickering ember of life left behind them. Gagne thrust the magazine into his lap. It was already folded open on the relevant page.

'Henri, take my glasses and read this and then we must talk. If there really is a God up there, today he's shining down on us.'

* * *

Gagne was up early the following morning. He'd read in the article how Legrand usually arrived at his office desk promptly at six. The impressive building, located at 6 rue du Général-Alain-de-Boissieu was a five-mile cab ride from the old man's apartment and, despite having less than fifty euros for him and his twin to live on for the rest of the month, he figured the twelve-euro fare was a sound investment. He was dropped off at five thirty and for the next thirty minutes waited patiently, positioning himself to one side of the huge glass electronic doors that formed the entrance.

Legrand's chauffeur-driven Maserati pulled up outside the headquarters of the Legrand Media Corporation at precisely six o'clock. The driver elegantly moved around the front of the black Quattroporte and opened the rear passenger door, allowing his boss to exit. Legrand stepped on to the pavement and headed for the entrance of his building. He hadn't noticed Gagne hovering close to the doors but as he approached him, he spotted him in his peripheral vision and quickened his step to avoid any contact with an old man he assumed was a beggar. But Gagne's movement was deceptively fast and in seconds he was standing directly in front of Legrand, who was forced to check his stride.

'Monsieur Legrand, excuse the intrusion but I have valuable information for you.'

Gagne offered up his bony hand which was gripping a small white envelope. Legrand glared at him, a look of contempt on his face and was about to brush him aside when the old man spoke again.

'I know who your real mother was. All the details you need are in this letter.'

Legrand's expression morphed from contempt to shock as for a moment he was caught totally off-guard. He snatched the envelope from Gagne's hand with such strength he almost knocked the old man flying but, somehow, he managed to maintain his balance. Legrand moved forward and headed through one of the glass doors at speed, but he wasn't fast enough to avoid hearing Gagne's final retort.

'I have no phone, but my address is in there. Contact me when you're ready to make a deal.'

* * *

Legrand sat behind his nineteenth-century Chevrié mahogany executive desk which ironically was worth three times the fee the old man had requested for facts he considered priceless. But the letter had been a hard read and its contents had filled Legrand with feelings of disgust and anger. He'd read it twice already but picked it up to read it for a third time, almost as if he needed to experience the searing pain it caused inside his mind once again. The spidery handwriting was almost illegible, but Legrand had managed to decipher it, even though a large part of him wished he hadn't.

Monsieur Legrand

My name is Albert Gagne. As you have seen I'm an old man but, God willing, I still have a little life left in me, which with your help I might be able to live out in some comfort. I read your article in L'Express with great interest. It triggered a distant memory that had been buried for almost seventy years. In October '55 when I was just sixteen, myself and my twin brother, Henri, got involved with a gang of older thugs who pretty much terrorised younger kids in the Montmartre district.

I'm ashamed to say my behaviour was not the best but then I was very young and easily influenced. There was a girl, who I believe was fourteen. She was very beautiful, and her mature looks belied her age. I asked her out countless times, but she rejected me, laughing in my face as she did so. It was as though I wasn't good enough for her even though she too came from a poor background, as we all did.

Neither my brother or I were good with alcohol and one night we got drunk and were walking home through one of the many back alleyways when we came across her, walking along with two other girls. Without going into heavy detail, we grabbed her and pulled her into a doorway. Her friends ran off and once we were alone, we both raped her. Of course, today as I look back, I'm ashamed of our actions but you must remember our age at the time and the fact we were drunk and didn't know what we were doing.

It was the mention of the heart-shaped locket in the article that caught my attention as I remember the girl was wearing one around her neck. It was one of those clever lockets that split into two parts, although it was whole at the time. I vividly remember I thought about stealing it but then as soon as we finished with her, we ran off and I forgot all about it.

Many months later I heard rumours she was pregnant, but the story went around that her mother was so ashamed she kept her hidden away in their house, so no one ever saw her. I think the family then moved away, so if she had a baby, we never heard about it.

I believe there is strong evidence to suggest she did give birth and that you are in fact her son, which means that either I or my brother Henri are your father. We are both happy to take a DNA test and to pass on to you the name of the girl concerned. All I ask for is a small payment of one hundred thousand euros, which to someone of your means is a mere spit in the ocean.

I am sure a man of your esteemed profile would not want such a sordid story about your birth to become public knowledge and for the world to know that one of us is your father.

Our address is Flat E, 117 Rue Saint-Denis.

Albert Gagne

Legrand felt physically sick as he flung the letter down on his desk in front of him as though it were vermin but, despite the torment it had aroused inside his brain, he knew exactly what he needed to do next.

Chapter Sixty

Paris, France

A rsène Boucher had a history of successfully carrying out jobs for Legrand that no one else had the required skill set for or could be trusted to do. He never asked any questions and always delivered. Most recently, he'd travelled to Rome where he'd murdered a senior Italian politician using the chemical agent polonium-210, one of the deadliest poisons known to man. Legrand had now summoned Boucher for an urgent meeting at his Paris apartment, so when he entered the mogul's study, he was expecting another big payday.

As ever with Legrand, no explanations were offered as a motive for what was a double killing, just the raw details of what needed to be done. What was unusual were the contents of a large black holdall Legrand handed him as soon as he arrived.

'Arsène, there's one hundred thousand euros in this bag. Show it to a man named Albert Gagne as soon as you're at his flat. I will provide you with his address. Say I would like him to keep the money regardless of the results of any tests as a gesture of my good faith. In return he'll give you the name of a woman and hopefully an address in Montmartre where she used to live. Take swabs with you and carry out DNA tests on Gagne and his brother and then when you leave take them directly to my physician's clinic. I believe you have his details from our previous dealings.'

'Yes, Monsieur, I have them.'

'Good. Once you're satisfied you have the information on the woman, kill them both. It's important to me they both suffer as much as possible first, so I'm relying on you to come up with one of your more ingenious modes of killing.'

Boucher nodded to confirm his understanding.

'Monsieur Legrand, I've been researching a new method I'm keen to try out. Trust me, they'll suffer an unimaginable death.'

'Excellent. Once they're dead, take the money as your fee. Both are in their eighties, so this will be the easiest hundred thousand you'll ever earn.'

* * *

Later that evening, Boucher visited the Gagne brothers at their dingy flat, armed with the black leather holdall containing a few extra items he'd added. Albert had been expecting the media mogul to turn up in person and his suspicions were immediately aroused when Boucher appeared at his door. But a quick glimpse of the bundles of cash stuffed inside the bag alleviated any initial concerns and he showed the assassin inside, where his twin brother was sitting in an old armchair, just about upright. Albert took up residence in the only other chair in the room, leaving Boucher to stand. He placed the holdall on the floor and glanced down at it.

'Gentlemen, as you've seen, the bag contains one hundred thousand euros. Monsieur Legrand would like you to keep the money regardless of the outcome of the DNA tests. Speaking of which . . .'

Albert flashed a toothy grin and could hardly take his eyes off the holdall. It only took a few seconds for Boucher to carry out the tests and, once he'd sealed the swabs in two small glass containers, he moved on to the other matter in hand.

'I understand you have a name for me. The name of a woman and an address in Montmartre?'

Albert was literally salivating at the thought of getting his grubby hands on the wads of cash inside the holdall and wanted rid of Boucher as soon as possible. He announced the name with a huge element of pride in his voice, like a proclamation, as though he were announcing the winner of a beauty contest.

'Her name was . . . Joséphine Aubert. I never knew her exact address, but I believe she lived very close to the Sacré-Coeur.'

Boucher's eyes narrowed.

'Are you sure you can't recall her address? One hundred thousand euros is a large amount of money.'

'No, I never went to her house, and you must remember this all happened nearly seventy years ago. I swear, Monsieur, I've given you everything I know.'

Boucher switched his eyeline to Henri, who hadn't said a word since he'd entered the flat.

'What about you?'

Henri shook his head and Albert spoke for him.

'My brother's very ill and remembers nothing from that time. As you can see, he is not long for this world.'

Boucher fought off the temptation to smile as he knew that was the case for both brothers, as death was coming far quicker than Albert could ever have imagined. It was time to carry out the double execution and Boucher could hardly contain himself. He leaned down to open the holdall and retrieved a blue 500ml metal can. Albert was slightly bemused and strained his eyes to try and read the writing on the side of it but without the aid of his glasses it was an impossible ask.

'What is that, Monsieur?'

'This is the instrument of your death – no gun, no knife, just the contents of this small aerosol can.'

Gagne let out a nervous laugh, not sure if Legrand's hench-man was just having some fun at his expense. But when Boucher spoke again, the old man lost control of his bowels and his frail body began shaking with fear.

'This aerosol contains a rare formula of quick drying cement. It claims the entire process takes only twelve minutes to go from liquid to solid. To be honest, I'm not sure I believe it but we're about to find out if the manufacturers are liars or telling the truth. So, for the purposes of this experiment, I'm about to pour it down both your throats and then I'll time exactly how long it takes to harden.'

Albert's eyes widened like a pair of poached oysters as he watched Boucher don a pair of yellow rubber gloves and begin to unscrew the lid.

'Now, who's up first?'

* * *

After dropping off the DNA samples, Boucher called Legrand for a full debrief that included graphic details of the gruesome deaths of the Gagne brothers, as well as Joséphine Aubert's name. Legrand was euphoric and promised Boucher a fifty-thousand-euro bonus for his remarkable efforts. He'd written the name in his notebook and for the next few minutes he just stared at it and wondered if it could possibly belong to the woman who'd given birth to him sixty-eight years ago.

The next call he placed was to Paul Chapelle, the private detective he'd employed over twenty years earlier to track down the church cleaner and the corrupt priest who'd both been involved in his adoption. Incredibly the same number still worked and Chapelle, who was now semi-retired, was on the line within seconds.

'It's been a while, Monsieur, but of course I remember our dealings extremely well. How can I be of assistance this time?'

'Finally, I have a name. It's Joséphine Aubert. She lived close to the Sacré-Coeur in Montmartre.'

Chapelle could hear the excitement in Legrand's voice.

'Is she still alive?'

'I've no idea. She was fourteen at the time, so if she is, she'll be eighty-three.'

'I see.'

'I don't care what it costs, I need you to find out what happened to her.'

Chapter Sixty-One

Paris, France

7 July 2016

Leopold Legrand chose to hold his sixtieth birthday party in the Salon d'Eté banqueting suite at the illustrious Ritz hotel in Place Vendôme. The elite guestlist was drawn from luminaries working in the media, with a healthy mix of high-ranking politicians, industrialists and bankers. Legrand was the owner of the world's second-largest media company, some four billion dollars behind Murdoch's Fox Corporation and was determined to overtake his Australian rival before the end of the decade.

Hidden in plain sight amongst the VIPs were two businessmen and a politician who'd flown in respectively from Australia, Spain and Argentina. They were all big hitters in their own fields but, on the surface, none of them had the credentials to attend such an 'A' list event. For Legrand, however, their presence was essential. They were attending as valued guests in another capacity. All three were key members of the inner circle of *Die Spinne.*

After a sumptuous five-course sit-down dinner, guests spilled out on to the terrace and into the landscaped gardens where black wrought-iron tables and chairs were randomly dotted on the main lawn. The lavish party lasted well into the early hours and at about two in the morning, Legrand joined his three 'special' guests for a nightcap. He'd arranged for a waiter to set up the table with a bottle of his favourite cognac along with four classic brandy snifter glasses. The Louis XIII Black Pearl from Remy Martin came in at an eye-watering thirty thousand dollars for a 70cl bottle. Legrand kept twelve of them in the antique liquor-cabinet in his Paris apartment.

He held the hand-blown Baccarat crystal bottle with the delicacy and respect he believed it deserved and carefully poured the liquid gold into the glasses. Javier Galvez, an up-and-coming politician in Buenos Aires, proposed a toast.

'Happy Birthday to Leopold, our leader and inspiration.'

He raised his glass high in the air and everyone followed suit.

'To the future . . . to *Die Spinne*.'

Leopold downed a large gulp of the extraordinarily expensive brandy, experiencing a satisfying burn at the back of his throat and spoke in English, the common language for the four of them.

'Friends, thank you all for making the trip. We've much to discuss but tonight is not the time or the place. Tomorrow morning, we'll meet at my apartment at eight and work through an agenda I've prepared. I need to be away by midday for a trip to Strasbourg, where I'm completing the purchase of a remote château on the outskirts of the city, which could play a huge part in all our futures. While I'm there, I'm meeting

with a data analyst who's at the cutting edge of AI development. He's going to help me set up a state-of-the-art facility.'

Legrand couldn't miss the sceptical glances exchanged
between his three guests.

'Gentlemen, trust me when I tell you this technology is going
to change the world, and I plan for us to be in the vanguard of it.
Let me ask you a question: have you heard of deepfakes?'

Leo Williams, a typically brash Australian, who ran a huge
law firm based in Sydney, downed his second glass of cognac
before answering.

'Never heard of them. What the hell are they?'

'My friends, I believe in time, they'll be total gamechangers
– our route to political power.'

* * *

The dilapidated eighteenth-century château, discreetly located
in woodlands on the border between Strasbourg and La
Wantzenau, had been neglected for over fifty years and needed
a lot of attention. But it ticked all the boxes for Legrand.

As he strolled through the vast overgrown grounds that
circled the property and drank in the façade of the perfectly
symmetrical rectangular structure, he was satisfied he'd found
the ideal base for his new enterprise. Waiting to meet him
inside, standing in the enormous, vaulted hallway, was Thomas
Schneider, a German data analyst, who'd made the short thirty-
five-mile trip from his Baden-Baden home, just the other side
of the Rhine.

Schneider was one of Germany's leading AI software specialists and, fortunately for Legrand, a committed fascist, whose

grandfather had indoctrinated him from childhood in the virtues of the Third Reich. He was in his late twenties and a rising star in the tech world when the media mogul recruited him from his corporate employer, IBM, by quadrupling his salary and tempting him with an unlimited budget to scale up an AI facility of his own. He looked a typical geek, thin as a rake, with unkempt greasy black hair, an easily forgotten milky-white face, and a pair of pebble frame glasses to complete the look.

After meeting up, Legrand led Schneider through to the enormous high-ceilinged drawing room, which, despite its faded glory, still conjured up traces of grandeur. Some large sections of the original ornate coving were still in place as were fragments of two giant ceiling frescoes. There was no furniture and eventually the two men came to a stop in the centre of the huge room. Legrand, who was still buzzing from his party the night before, couldn't wait to reveal his refurb plans.

'Thomas, this will obviously make a great location for your team of analysts to be based. My architect has drawn up plans showing a layout with thirty workstations in here alone. As you'll see, the ground floor has another three giant rooms that will provide additional work areas, plus meeting rooms and offices.'

'Monsieur Legrand, it's a magnificent space. When can we start?'

'The conversion work is going to take eighteen months but, in the interim, I've approved the purchase of all the machinery and equipment on your inventory, and I want you to use the time to recruit the team you need.'

'Perfect, sir. I have a list for them as well.'

'Of course you do, Thomas. I'd expect nothing less of you, which is why I know you're the perfect man to build this facility. Now, tell me more about deepfakes.'

Schneider had prepped for the question and couldn't wait to unload the fruits of his research.

'Okay, they've been in development for well over a year. I'm aware of at least one major website producer which is currently working on several pornographic deepfakes. They plan to feature huge stars performing sex acts in what will be totally convincing videos. The process involves swapping out the faces of unknown actors with those of the celebrities and they do that by using two AI algorithms, an encoder and a decoder, which will source thousands of still images of a well-known celebrity and then create a "face swap" on a video. The AI machines will replace the original image, frame by frame. I've seen an early iteration of one featuring Taylor Swift which'll stir up a hornet's nest.'

Legrand was salivating at the possibilities of this new technology.

'Thomas, given this is brand-new tech, how far could it go?'

'Sir, as AI develops there's no cap to its potential. In the future, we'll be creating perfect deepfakes who won't just look perfect, they'll sound perfect as well.'

'How long?'

'Maybe ten years, sir.'

'Trust me, Thomas, we're going to do it in five.'

Chapter Sixty-Two

Paris, France

L egrand was lost in his own thoughts, questioning how he'd react if he discovered his birth mother was still alive and there was a chance to meet her. He was a man used to controlling events in his life and any hint of self-doubt was alien to him. His focus was interrupted by a WhatsApp landing on his cell, kickstarting his mind back into the here and now. He glanced down at the screen and read the incoming message from Moreau.

One hour ago the chessman went live for the first time. Early reaction extremely positive.

He brought up the keyboard on his cell and punched in a quick reply.

Excellent. Send me a subtitled link as soon as you have one.

Morozov's deepfake had been deployed in a live interview with the news channel, Russia-24. The state broadcaster believed his feed was coming into them directly from his Moscow apartment and had no idea its real source was fifteen hundred miles away in Strasbourg.

The vice president was basking in the afterglow of the positive reaction he was receiving to the interview he'd supposedly just given, which would have been seen by millions of Russians across the country. His cell was in meltdown with texts and WhatsApps coming in from friends and colleagues, congratulating him on his superb performance. Minutes earlier he'd sat in his own living room, watching on in awe as he gave the most polished performance of his career. Any doubts he'd had about the wisdom of trusting Legrand's cutting-edge technology evaporated as he basked in the plaudits coming his way.

His deepfake had expertly navigated tricky questions on the Ukraine war, the economy and international relations with the West, with a confidence and deftness of touch that perfectly caught the mood of the nation, and his demeanour was that of an heir apparent. It was as though he'd appeared from nowhere. A grey politician who'd dared put his head above the parapet in a bid to boost his popularity with the masses, with the aim of building a profile. However, his sensational performance didn't go unnoticed by a certain resident of the Kremlin, who'd missed the live fifteen-minute broadcast but watched a recording of it two hours later, shortly after it had been brought to his attention.

By then, Morozov was on his way out, heading for a celebration dinner with his wife and teenage children at the White Rabbit restaurant in Smolenskaya Square, their favourite eaterie in the city. He was obsessed with the menu and couldn't wait to be reacquainted with his treasured dish: king crab with morrell mushrooms in a bisque sauce, washed down by a bottle of Mamont vodka. He visualised starting with half a dozen Murotsu oysters as an appetiser to the main course and maybe he'd throw in some beluga caviar blinis. His driver texted to confirm he was parked outside the front of the building and Morozov programmed the alarm in his apartment, salivating at the prospect of what lay ahead. When his cell rang, he'd no intention of taking the call but when he saw the number, he felt his gut tighten and his heart started shuddering.

'Mr President, how can I assist you?'

'Boris, tell me about the wonder drug you've discovered that transforms a mouse into a lion. Where can I source it?'

Putin's voice was laden with sarcasm and the tone had a terrifying edge Morozov had never experienced first-hand before. Suddenly, he felt breathless. It was almost as though someone had forced a polythene bag over his head and his access to oxygen had been cut off. Before he could summon up a reasonable response, the Russian president hit him with a barrage of questions.

'Do you believe there's an upcoming vacancy in the Kremlin? Who's been briefing you?'

Finally, Morozov managed to blurt out a response.

'Mr President, if you felt I was in any way out of line in my recent interview then I apologise profusely. It was never my intention to—'

'You may be labouring under the misapprehension that I already have one foot in the grave but let me assure you of one thing. Give any more interviews like the one I've just seen and it will be you heading for an early burial and that is something I can promise.'

Putin paused before completing the threat, as he instinctively felt the need to add a further layer of terror to it.

'And prior to your death, you'll experience a level of pain that is inconceivable, especially to a weak man like you, who has such a poor imagination. Perhaps, being an intellectual, you've a low tolerance level when it comes to that sort of thing, but the FSB would test that theory out, just in case I'm mistaken.'

The president ended the call and turned his attention to a document that had just landed on his desk, detailing latest military fatalities from the front line in the Donbas. He cursed under his breath, as the figures were even higher than expected.

Morozov shrunk into himself like a deflated balloon and unsurprisingly his ravenous appetite had vanished. His cell sprang into life again, this time acknowledging a new WhatsApp message. He glanced down at the screen, expecting the worst – a summons from Alexander Bortnikov, the head of the FSB, which would mean certain death. But the message was from Legrand.

Congratulations on your debut. More appearances to follow in the coming weeks.

The Russian politician sank to his knees in despair as he stared at the message which might as well have been a death sentence. It only took a moment to delete it, although he knew in his soul that action alone wouldn't make it all go away.

* * *

Soletska and Vargas had returned to D.C. and the Ukrainian, who somehow managed to defy the normal rules of sleep, was back in her apartment poring over Starling's string of bank statements on her laptop. The former head of SOCOM had a haul of checking and deposit accounts with various institutions and was clearly an extremely wealthy woman. Also, as Berrettini had pointed out, Starling's motive for treason had not been financial, so perhaps the trawl through her banking history was a complete waste of time. But, just as she was on the verge of giving up, she found it – the needle in the haystack she'd been searching for.

At first it seemed all Starling's accounts were registered in the United States and Soletska had been working through them looking for any suspicious payments from an unlikely source. What she hadn't expected to find was evidence of a covert foreign account held in Starling's name that the FBI had no knowledge of. It would have been easy for anyone less forensic than Soletska to miss as, although the account had been active for over ten years, in that entire period only one outgoing payment had been made from it. It was registered with the Lotus Bank and Trust Limited in the Cayman Islands and, on 23 November 2022, Starling had transferred seventy thousand dollars from it to her Wells Fargo account in the US. Three days later that exact sum was paid out to a New York art gallery for the purchase of a limited-edition Warhol print.

Starling's records showed the purchase of several expensive artworks, sometimes for six figures, so this specific payment didn't stand out. Having discovered the secret account, Soletska now faced the task of cracking it open, but was unfazed, having successfully hacked numerous banks while working with the Ukrainian mafia.

The main factor in Soletska's favour was that, despite Starling's suicide, her account was still live, and the Ukrainian hacker knew she needed to fool the bank's admin system into believing she was the account holder. Essentially the AI computers controlling the account in the Caymans had to be convinced they were dealing with Starling and that meant switching laptops.

Soletska was sitting cross-legged on the floor with her MacBook resting on a low coffee table in front of her. Alongside it was a Dell Precision 5680, Starling's personal laptop, which had been removed from her apartment by the FBI following her suicide. A data analyst had cracked the password which gave Soletska full access to its secrets. Somewhere hidden on the drive would be a link to the Cayman account and, once she found it, she knew the laptop's built-in cookies would be recognised by the bank's admin system as the authentic device that operated the account.

It took less than an hour for her to locate the relevant file that contained the link to the Lotus Bank and Trust Limited but there was still one final obstacle to overcome. Access to the account required a numeric password, which in theory was impossible to crack but an exceptional hacker like Soletska knew better. The code must have been used by Starling on 23 November 2022 to enable the transfer of funds between her Lotus and Wells Fargo accounts and was buried somewhere in the computer's history; she just had to find it. When she did, she was disappointed by the simplicity behind its creation and kicked herself for not having tried it earlier. The eight number password, 11181998, translated as 18 November 1998 – the date Starling joined the armed forces.

The ten-year-old account had been opened on 6 February 2014 and its entire trading history was contained on a single page. It displayed an initial incoming payment on the day of creation of one million dollars and subsequently nine more payments for that identical amount had landed on that same date every year. In total, ten million dollars had been deposited, while the outgoing column confirmed a single transaction of seventy thousand dollars.

Soletska's eyes focused in on the name of the single payee behind the deposit payments and, when she saw it, a burst of adrenaline surged through her body as her mind was deluged by a tsunami of euphoria. She'd never heard of MDD Holdings Limited before but now she'd come across the name twice in a few hours. The first time had been when she'd been checking through the names of registered owners of hundreds of properties in the Strasbourg area supplied by Interpol as possible locations for the facility behind the deepfakes.

She switched back to her MacBook, reopened the Interpol file and began trawling through the list of properties, searching for just one. It didn't take long. The Bastille Research Institute which inhabited a large château on the outskirts of Strasbourg was part of a larger group, whose parent company was MDD Holdings. She pulled up Google and clicked on several images of the isolated building, surrounded by woodland, situated on the border of Strasbourg and La Wantzenau. There was nothing obvious to signal the eighteenth-century château was housing the most advanced AI facility in the world but then Soletska checked it out from the air, courtesy of Google Earth. Hidden away from prying eyes in the gardens behind the main building were three industrial-size satellite dishes, mounted on a raised redbrick platform.

Soletska smelled blood and set about tracking a pathway through a complex smokescreen of shell companies designed to protect the identity of the owners of MDD Holdings. The internet trail led first to Belize and then on to Lichtenstein and the registration of a company called Rouge Media Alliance.

When she saw the name of its principal shareholder, she grabbed her cell, and at the same time realised her hand was shaking. Suddenly, she recognised the scale of the conspiracy they were facing – it was way beyond anything any of them could have imagined.

* * *

At six in the morning Vargas and Hembury arrived at Soletska's flat. Berrettini was already behind his desk at Bureau head-quarters and opted to join them on a Zoom call. Hembury came laden with warm croissants, while Soletska provided black coffee and fresh juices. Once they settled down she shared her laptop screen and took them through the paper trail that started with the discovery of Starling's covert account in the Cayman Islands and led to the discovery of a company regis-tered in Lichtenstein, that appeared to be the owner of the Strasbourg facility producing the deepfakes.

It wasn't the first time Soletska had stunned the small group with her technical brilliance and once again she had them hanging on her every word.

'Now, we get to the best part. Rouge Media Alliance is one hundred per cent owned by Leopold Legrand. It's one of hundreds of companies that form part of his media empire – reportedly the biggest in the world.'

Berrettini nearly burst through the screen as he shook his head in disbelief at the sensational revelation.

'Liliya, you've done incredible work but even if you're right about the company behind this, it's not feasible Legrand personally has his fingerprints on it. He's one of the most powerful men in the world. For Christ's sake, he's a friend of our president and I'm sure he's even received an honorary knighthood from the King of England, even though he's French. Maybe senior figures in his corporation are involved somehow and, if so, we need to nail them and bring this conspiracy to his attention.'

Hembury echoed Berrettini's concerns.

'The guy's even bigger than Murdoch – it's inconceivable.'

Vargas stayed focused on Soletska's face the entire time. It didn't register a flicker of self-doubt, and he could sense she wasn't about to cave. Her voice didn't waver as she pressed on.

'I've spent the last few hours researching Legrand's background. It's reads like something out of a bad B movie – pure fiction and something about it stinks. In 1947, his mother, Amelie Legrand, turns up in Paris having bought a private bank worth millions of dollars. The press coverage at the time describes her as a mystery Swiss heiress – the mystery being no one seemed to know the source of her money and, worse still, no one really cared. What if she was one of the first Nazis to be squirrelled out of Germany with a new identity and a pot of cash?'

Berrettini kicked back again.

'Interesting background stuff but still wild speculation, Liliya. We need more than that.'

While Soletska had been holding court with Berrettini, Vargas had been trawling through Himmler's Wikipedia page on his iPhone. He smiled for the first time since the meeting had begun as he glanced up from his screen at the others.

'Wait till you hear this. Something about Legrand has been niggling me for a while. When I first heard his name it triggered a recent memory in the back of my mind, but I couldn't nail it. It tormented me for a while and then I remembered the connection. After we saw the Himmler deepfake, I did some preliminary research on the SS leader – watched some black and white footage of his speeches and read up on his background. Then a few minutes ago I realised what was bugging me. It was his name . . .'

Soletska interrupted him.

'Heinrich?'

Vargas rose to his feet in triumph.

'None of us believe in coincidences, right?'

He paused before delivering his bombshell.

'The full name of the man who formed *Die Spinne* in August 1944 was Heinrich Luitpold Himmler.'

Chapter Sixty-Three

Washington D.C., United States

'It's certainly compelling and you're right, Nic, none of us believe in coincidences. Sounds as if Amelie Legrand was a fangirl of the SS leader and went as close as she could possibly dare in naming her son.'

Berrettini was now holding court. Soletska's startling revelations, strengthened by Vargas's discovery, had even convinced the FBI deputy director of Legrand's involvement. He was now busy calculating the potential fallout that would undoubtedly follow, should they move against one of the highest profile public figures in the Western world.

'We must still tread very carefully on this one. Legrand has the ear of many world leaders. We can't just waltz into his house and arrest him. If we're going bring him and his Network down, we must be bulletproof, or I promise you, my ass will be fried.'

Hembury was the first to jump in to address Berrettini's concerns.

'Liliya, is there any way you can hack into the servers of

MDD Holdings and access material that will confirm Legrand is up to his neck in this?'

'You won't be surprised to hear I've already had a first pass, and their level of inbuilt security is off the chart, which only strengthens my belief they're the organisation behind all this. It's almost impenetrable.'

Vargas cut in.

'Even for you?'

'I said "almost". However good it is, there's always a back door in – I just need to find it. There's something else you need to know. Legrand rarely gives live TV interviews these days, but he's announced he's giving an exclusive to CNN to talk about COP. When I read that it struck me, he might be planning to deploy a deepfake of his own.'

Berrettini was the only one not physically in the room but had been listening intently.

'Interesting thought – and what if he does?'

Soletska eyeballed the FBI deputy director straight down the camera lens on her laptop.

'I think I know a way to hoist that evil bastard by his own petard.'

* * *

Directly across the street from Soletska's apartment, a BMW 7 Series Limo glided effortlessly to a stop. The one hundred and fifty thousand dollar car was a head-turner; with a custom paint job and blacked out windows. Hidden inside, along with the driver, was a single passenger in the rear.

Finding a doctor prepared to perform life-saving surgery in a private clinic in Washington D.C. was easy if you had unlimited funds and direct contact with the drug barons who ran the underworld in the capital city. Olek Panchak had both, which explained how, despite a potentially fatal stomach wound, he'd managed to cheat death and was presently lying prostrate in the back of the limo plotting a painful end for Liliya Soletska, the girl he knew as Anna Kovalenka.

A five-hour operation had saved his life and, as soon as he came round from the complex surgery, he contacted his faithful lieutenant in Ukraine. Denys Babich was his enforcer. The man he regularly sent out into the field to collect money from small-time criminals and drug dealers who failed to pay their debts on time. He was known as 'The Cutter' – a nickname related to his knife skills, which were considerable. Panchak had been instructed by his surgeon to stay in bed for a minimum of two weeks but his thirst for revenge trumped that order and, although he struggled to stand, let alone walk, a combination of drugs and a burning desire for retribution fuelled his movement.

Inside the apartment, Vargas was panther pacing around the tiny living room, while the group discussed next moves to play against Legrand. For a moment he stood in front of the sole casement window that broke up the exterior wall, staring out at Chinatown just as the BMW parked up. The appearance of the high-end vehicle seemed somewhat incongruous, especially given the time of day but he didn't dwell on it as his mind flicked back to the matter in hand.

Inside the car, Babich caught a brief glimpse of Vargas at the window.

'Boss, there's a man inside her apartment. Given the fact it's so early it's probably a boyfriend.'

Panchak hauled himself up and attempted to peer out of the car window but was too late to catch sight of Vargas.

'Who knows? For now, we wait.'

Soletska was busy preparing a fresh round of coffee when Hembury rose from the couch. His right hand was pressing heavily down on his forehead.

'Guys, I can feel one of my migraines coming on, so I'm heading home before it takes hold. I've got some meds there and I'll rest until it passes. Nic, you stay and finish up with Liliya and we'll catch up later.'

Vargas constantly worried about his friend's headaches as he knew they were brought on by his life-threatening brain tumour.

'No worries. You sure you're good to drive?'

'Yep, I just need some blackout time at home, and I'll be good to go later.'

Hembury exited the main street door to the side of the Shanghai Delight and walked twenty yards or so to his silver Tesla that was parked up almost opposite the BMW. He'd no idea his every step was being monitored by the driver inside it. Babich half-turned his head over his right shoulder.

'That's not the same guy I saw – he was white. Must be someone else who lives in the same block.'

'No problem. We've all the time in the world.'

It was almost another hour before Vargas called an Uber having wrapped up his meeting with Soletska. He checked his cell to see confirmation a Honda Accord had just arrived and its driver, Tony, was waiting to drive him back to FBI headquarters.

He said his goodbyes to Soletska and made his way downstairs. When he exited the main street door, the silver hybrid was in position, parked up right outside. He was just about to acknowledge the driver when he noticed the BMW was still in place, a good two hours after he'd first seen it pull up. Something seemed off but he'd no idea what. His went with his gut and walked straight past the Honda and took the first street opening about thirty yards away which led directly into a narrow alleyway.

Vargas hit the cancel icon on the Uber booking and took up a discreet viewing position peering around the corner of another Chinese restaurant, his body partially hidden with only the side of his head visible. He was just too far away from the Uber to hear the driver curse under his breath as his app informed him he'd lost the job. Seconds later he pulled away just as an incoming ping on his cell signified a replacement pickup just a few hundred yards away.

Inside the BMW the mood was one of feverish anticipation. Babich had monitored every step of Vargas's departure until he disappeared.

'I'd bet my dog's life that was the guy I saw at the window.'

Panchak felt a sharp pain surge through his body, generated by an involuntary laugh.

'I know how much you love that stupid Shepherd. Let's do this.'

Vargas watched on as Babich leapt out of the car and walked smartly around to the rear door which he opened, allowing the chief inspector a first sight of Panchak. The six-four muscular frame of the Ukrainian mafia leader appeared to be moving in slow motion as he gingerly attempted to get out, aided by his driver. Vargas could hardly believe his eyes as he saw the colossus of a man slowly emerge into full view. He hit Liliya's number on his cell, but to his disbelief, it diverted straight to voice mail. He cursed under his breath as he made a second call, this time to Hembury, who answered after just two rings.

'Troy, get your ass back over here at mega speed and be armed. Jesus has risen from the dead in the form of Panchak. He's got a goon with him, and I suspect they're about to pay Liliya an unscheduled visit.'

'Christ, I'm on my way. I'll call Mike in case he can get support there quicker than me.'

Vargas had already ended the call and pocketed his cell. He was consumed with a wave of nausea as he saw Panchak stand tall for the first time, supported by his driver on one side and a wooden cane on the other. The Ukrainian began to hobble slowly across the road propped up by the other man and, as the pair reached the sidewalk, Vargas decided to act.

He darted around the corner and headed straight for the two men who were less than twenty feet away from Soletska's street door. He approached them from an oblique angle and the first they knew of his presence was when he launched himself through the air like an Exocet missile.

The sheer power with which he impacted the side of Babich's body was reminiscent of some of the biggest hits imaginable in American football, made by a defensive back on a wide receiver heading for a touchdown. The Ukrainian enforcer collapsed under the sheer weight of the assault and took his boss with him. Panchak yelled out in agony as Babich smashed against him and the force of the collision split the sixty stiches holding his abdomen together wide open. As he crashed on to the sidewalk, writhing in agony, a massive blood gusher opened in the centre of his stomach, and he grabbed the wound with both hands desperately trying to stem the flow.

Although he was winded, Babich staggered to his feet and, as he steadied himself, grabbed a massive hunting knife from inside his black leather bomber jacket, which had been intended for use on Soletska. It was of Spanish design, known as the Joker Bowie knife and was Babich's favourite instrument of torture. The serrated edge of the ten-inch blade was crafted from stainless steel and the dark brown handle was hand-carved from a stag antler.

Vargas was also gasping for breath as he staggered to his feet to face Panchak's enforcer who'd raised the knife in his right hand, preparing to attack. Vargas had never seen a pair of more intense eyes. They were so dark they appeared to be black. They were the eyes of a man who'd carried out countless kill-ings without a hint of remorse and was intent on adding one more to the list. His body was lean and wiry, but he was clearly as strong as an ox, without the muscle mass. The man was a pro, and his ice-cold eyes were drilling holes through Vargas's head. The Ukrainian moved forward at breakneck speed but Vargas was poised and ready.

As Babich came at him with a downward thrust, Vargas used his forearm to block and deftly grabbed his wrist, ripping his arm behind him, forcing the elbow upwards past its break-ing point, separating it cleanly and painfully in one fluent move. The excruciating pain that shot through the Ukrainian's dislocated arm forced him to drop the weapon and it clattered to the ground. A follow-up knee to the groin forced him back-wards, sprawling on to the sidewalk.

Vargas reached down and grabbed the knife just as Babich produced a second, far smaller one from a concealed leather holster, tied to the back of his left calf. It was an ivory-handled flick-knife which he grabbed with his only useable hand, but the Argentine was far too quick for him. They were less than six feet apart and Vargas hurled the hunting knife towards his target; the blade smacked into Babich's windpipe, ripping his neck apart. The hitman's eyes bulged with disbelief at the realisation he'd been slain by his own beloved weapon but that was the last thought he ever visualised, as moments later his world went black.

A few feet away Panchak was writhing on the ground in agony, clutching his open wound to no avail as the gusher turned into an unstoppable torrent. His bloodshot eyes glared desperately upwards at Vargas begging for help, but none was forthcoming. It would only be a matter of seconds now before Panchak bled out and Vargas didn't give him a second glance as he walked past his strewn body and headed for the sanctuary of Soletska's apartment.

Chapter Sixty-Four

Washington D.C., United States

It was later that morning when they all met up inside the main Bureau building. Although the immediate threat had passed, Soletska was desperate to get as far away as possible from her Chinatown apartment. The last sight she saw as she slid into the back of an FBI G-Wagon were the bodies of Panchak and his enforcer being zipped into heavy-duty black body bags by plain-clothed FBI agents. Shortly afterwards she joined Vargas and Hembury in Berrettini's office, where he sought to reassure her.

'No one will ever know they were here. Their corpses will be burned and their ashes scattered in the Potomac. Liliya, that part of your life is closed forever.'

Everyone in the room was astounded by Soletska's resilience. She smiled towards Berrettini to acknowledge his comforting words before smoothly switching the subject back to Legrand.

'I've been hatching a plan to bring our French billionaire crashing down but we're going to require a hell of a lot of luck to fall our way, plus I need help from Devane.'

'What kind of help?'

'I want to steal one of his data analysts. Someone who's across the minutiae of the latest tech behind AI-generated deepfakes. They must be the best.'

Berrettini nodded.

'Consider it done.'

Soletska gestured towards her laptop which was open.

'As well as an analyst, I'll email across a list of what we're going to need and there's one other ask . . .'

Hembury thought he could see where she was heading.

'Unlimited supplies of Red Bull?'

'That goes without saying but I'm talking about a PJ to take us to Strasbourg.'

Berrettini mouth formed a quizzical expression.

'How does proximity help us?'

'In several ways, sir. I'll outline them all in an email but, trust me, being close to the facility may just give us an edge.'

'Fair enough, I'll sanction a Gulfstream to be prepared to leave straight away. Realistically, if we're going to discredit Legrand and expose his operation, we need it to happen before the COP vote at the end of the conference. Even though Galvez was taken out, his Argentine delegation were all handpicked supporters of his extremist views, so nothing's changed. We know this is part of a bigger conspiracy propagated by the Spider Network, with Legrand pulling the strings, although the overall agenda isn't totally clear. Interpol have given us access to satellite coverage of the château as well as setting up fake roadworks about half a mile away on the main access road to monitor comings and goings.'

Berrettini paused to gauge the reactions of Hembury and Vargas.

'You guys up for the trip?'

Vargas, who'd begun pacing, nodded.

'I'm up for entering the lion's den.'

Liliya couldn't resist jumping in with the final word.

'Except, this den is full of fakes.'

* * *

Legrand was in his study finishing up a long Zoom call with Moreau which had principally been concerned with his upcoming interview with CNN.

'Was Thomas okay with my last-minute tweak?'

'Absolutely, sir, he took care of it personally.'

'Good, I'd like to see it before we go live and—'

Legrand's cell burst into life and when he spotted the identity of the incoming caller he shut Moreau down.

'Okay, let's talk later after I've approved the change.'

He ended the Zoom and took the call from Chapelle.

'I've found her.'

Legrand felt as though the blood flowing through his veins had turned to ice as his entire body froze.

'Tell me everything.'

'To be honest, she wasn't hard to locate. She's eighty-three, still has the same name and is living in a rundown nursing home in the suburbs – in Clichy-sous-Bois. From what I understand she's bedridden but mentally sharp. Do you want me to set up a visit?'

Legrand gathered his thoughts. The timing couldn't be worse.

'No, I've too much on right now. You do an initial check to confirm she's the right woman. I want you to see her as soon as possible. Swing by my apartment on the way and collect the locket. See if she recognises it.'

'Of course, sir. I've already called the home, and I can visit this afternoon.'

'Excellent. I'll expect a full written report tomorrow morning, along with photos. If she's the woman we're looking for, you'll be in for a significant bonus.'

* * *

The Gulfstream soared into the midday sky and effortlessly climbed to a cruise height of forty-five thousand feet. As soon as they were settled, Soletska enthusiastically introduced her recruit to Vargas and Hembury. Jack Chan may have held the mundane title of senior data analyst in the National Counterintelligence and Security unit but, amongst his peers, the twenty-seven-year-old was affectionately known as 'super geek'; the best AI developer on Devane's team and therefore the best in the FBI. Such were his skills, he single-handedly ran a development budget of six million dollars, most of which was utilised in the pursuit of building 'perfect' deepfakes on behalf of his employer, the American government. This technology could be utilised by the FBI in the future to completely discredit foreign leaders, who they perceived as threats. Chan's all-time hero was theoretical physicist, J. Robert Oppenheimer who developed the first nuclear bomb during the Second World War and, like his idol, he believed he could build a devastating new weapon that, if deployed correctly, could have unimaginable consequences for a new world order.

Chan didn't resemble a typical geek. His distinctive features were a gift from his father; an illegal immigrant from Vietnam who'd settled in Minnesota thirty years earlier where he'd met and married a local girl, whose parents were immigrants from Singapore.

Chan could easily have passed as a movie star rather than a computer techie which made him something of an enigma, as did his autism spectrum disorder, which meant his social interactions tended to lack any kind of filter. When he spoke, his word count was economical and devoid of empathy.

'I've studied the deepfakes of Himmler, Griffiths and Galvez. They're truly exceptional examples; AI creations way ahead of anything we've previously seen or managed to create ourselves. If Liliya can find a way to access the machines that built them, I'm confident I can cope with the speed analysis and manipulate the material to fit our own specifications.'

Neither Vargas nor Hembury knew what to make of what they'd just heard but, before they could interrogate Chan, Soletska cut in.

'Guys trust me on this for now. I'm working up a plan with Jack but I'm not quite ready to share it with you.'

The four-thousand-mile journey fell comfortably within the range of the Gulfstream and the direct flight took just over six hours. The FBI jet had a state-of-the-art Wi-Fi system installed, allowing Chan and Soletska to work on board and both were glued to their respective laptops for the entire flight. While the 'hacker' and the 'geek' did their stuff, Vargas and Hembury spent much of the time reading online articles on Leopold Legrand, familiarising themselves with their new foe. The man was without question one of the most powerful and influential figures in the media world and the tentacles of his massive operation spread across business and politics as well.

The private jet landed at Strasbourg international airport just after midnight and a thirty-minute taxi ride took them into the heart of the city where they checked into the iconic Maison Rouge hotel. As they waited for their keys at reception, Hembury explained why he'd chosen it as their base.

'Remember the history lesson we received from Berrettini? This hotel was the place where *Die Spinne* was born. Back in August 1944, Himmler held a covert meeting in a banqueting room with an elite group of bankers and industrialists who provided the initial funding. I'm sure it's no coincidence the facility behind all this tech is located just a few miles away.'

A few minutes later, having briefly checked into their rooms, they met up in a large suite designated as their new hub. Chan and Soletska immediately set up workstations on an oblong mahogany table, oblivious to Vargas and Hembury. Soletska had already raided the fridge for her regular fuel of Red Bull and had ordered some backups via room service. Hembury knew his fatherly advice was about to fall on deaf ears but nevertheless still gave it a go.

'Guys, please don't pull an all-nighter. We really need you to be fresh on this. I don't fancy working with a pair of zombies.'

Neither Chan nor Soletska glanced up from their laptops to acknowledge Hembury's concerns but the latter did respond without breaking eye contact with her fourteen-inch screen.

'Troy, remember what I told you. However good the fire-wall is on any computer network, there's always a back door in – it's just a question of finding it.'

Hembury raised an eyebrow as he and Vargas headed for the suite door.

'Okay, it's just gone one. Let's meet back here at ten for an update and the next time we see you both, please be wearing a fresh set of clothes.'

* * *

When Vargas and Hembury returned nine hours later, they found Chan and Soletska, still both head down at their stations, beavering away on their laptops. Patently, the pair hadn't left the suite for the duration and the only evidence of change in the main living room were two large platters of curled up, half-eaten sandwiches along with a cluster of empty Red Bull and Diet Coke cans spread chaotically across the table.

When Vargas saw Soletska's face he realised something had changed and he sensed it was massive. As soon as she heard them enter the Ukrainian looked up to greet them with a beaming grin plastered across her face.

'A few hours ago, we struck gold.'

Vargas picked up on her unbridled excitement.

'You're in – you guys actually did it?'

'Nic, we're into their system and we've uncovered rich seams of material – some of it is truly mind-blowing. I can't wait to show you both. It's an Aladdin's cave, packed full of priceless deepfakes of political and business heavyweights, speaking in different languages, based in several continents. There's even a

Russian bureaucrat, Boris Morozov, who they're clearly grooming to succeed Putin. Then there are the documents – hundreds of files that give the historical narrative to these guys' identities. Direct links in many cases to their Nazi heritage – it's all there. The jewel in the crown is Legrand himself. The legend of his mother, a Swiss heiress buying a Paris bank after the Second World War was a bullshit smokescreen, created by *Die Spinne.* Her real name was Emelia Müller – a German national living in Berlin, with connections to the SS. The original source of the funds used to create the Legrand Corporation came directly from the Third Reich.'

'Any indication of a direct link to Himmler?'

'Not that I could see. Müller was in her early twenties when she fled Germany – maybe she was his secret lover or perhaps simply infatuated with him; hence the choice of her adopted son's name.'

Hembury, as ever, was the voice of caution.

'Is there any way they can discover you're inside their operating system?'

'No, for now we're invisible. But there's more; we've just downloaded three almost identical deepfakes of Legrand. In each case he's sitting behind an impressive antique desk, in front of the "Tricolore", in what I guess is his home study. The only difference I can spot between the three videos are the different suits he's wearing. I think the versions are there purely as a reflection of his vanity. There's no way of knowing for sure but I reckon he won't be able to resist using one of his deepfakes for his live CNN interview. It's the lead item on their breakfast show tomorrow morning, the slot which gets them their largest worldwide audience but they're based in Atlanta, so it'll be one in the afternoon for Legrand in Paris and us here in Strasbourg, which means we've just over twenty-four hours to prepare for it.'

Vargas began pacing the room.

'Liliya, I think the time's come for us to drill into the detail of your plan and get this show on the road.'

Chapter Sixty-Five

Paris, France

The Paradis Care Home in Clichy-sous-Bois was situated in one of the poorest suburbs in Paris. Although it was less than twenty miles away from Legrand's grand apartment, it was isolated from the city centre, unserved by a railway station or any major roads. The fifties-built, three-storey concrete structure was an eyesore, even amongst some of the most neglected properties in Paris. Its iron-grey façade hadn't seen a lick of paint for decades, which meant huge chunks of render had long since fallen off, exposing cracked brickwork underneath. The simple hip roof was crowned by four warped clay chimney stacks and one shorter stub giving the appearance of a giant deformed hand reaching out into the leaden sky.

As Chapelle pushed open the battered street door to enter the deserted reception, he was immediately hit by the revolting stench of stale urine which hung in the air like a thick cloak. He'd rung ahead and spoken with a clearly harassed nurse who'd informed him visitors were welcome between two and five in the afternoon and that he'd find Madame Aubert in room six on the third floor. The private detective spotted an iron-caged lift lurking in the shadows, then noticed the thin veneer of rust, so thought better of it and opted for the stairs instead.

The vast rectangular room that was home to eighteen elderly women ran the entire length of the structure. Like the rest of the Paradis, it had an air of decay about it and the temperature was arctic. It certainly wasn't how Chapelle had envisioned heaven. Residents' names were handwritten in black marker on thin squares of cardboard, limply hanging off the bottom of cast-iron bedframes. He scanned the room until he found the name he was searching for. Joséphine Aubert was in the bed positioned furthest away from him, alongside a giant casement window partially covered by a set of dark brown wool curtains. As he made his way along the centre aisle, he speculated as to their original colour.

The old lady was sitting upright in her bed, her head buried in that day's edition of *Le Monde*, so was oblivious to his approach. Chapelle walked slowly towards the bed, but still she didn't stir. He didn't want to frighten her so waited a few more seconds, hoping she'd sense his presence, but to no avail. In the end he leaned in until his head was only a few feet away from hers.

'Madame Aubert, I hope I'm not disturbing you. I would greatly appreciate a few moments of your time.'

Her frail bony fingers released their feeble grip on the newspaper, allowing it to slide downwards, creating a messy pile on the bed covers. She plainly wasn't used to receiving visitors. It had been a long time since anyone had been to see her and, as her head tilted upwards, her penetrating brown eyes, slightly concealed by a pair of cheap wire-framed glasses, were full of suspicion.

Chapelle studied her face intently, searching for clues that might link her directly to his employer, but she'd been ravaged by an ageing process that hadn't been kind. Aubert's olive-skinned face wore the roadmap of a hard life.

Her wrinkles were scarred by a combination of pockmarked craters and liver spots, while the loss of muscle tone and saggy skin combined to create a drooping appearance and a loss of facial definition. Her pink scalp was partially covered by cobwebbed grey hair, while her neck was hidden by a blue cotton scarf that offered a slight layer of protection against the freezing conditions.

'What do you want from me, Monsieur?'

Chapelle glanced around at the dismal surroundings before choosing his words carefully.

'Madame, I represent a client who believes they may be a relation of yours. If that proves to the case, it will be to your financial benefit and, who knows, maybe more favourable living conditions.'

Aubert attempted a laugh, but it came out as a spluttering cough.

'Monsieur, surely you joke with me. Take a good look at my face and tell me how long you imagine I have left?'

Chapelle felt suitably chastened as the old lady continued.

'Now, what would you like to know?'

He reached inside his jacket pocket and produced a small red pouch. He delicately pulled the gold drawstring and tipped the cheap locket into his left palm with the same reverence he'd have shown towards a priceless gemstone. For a moment his mind flicked to a classic fairy tale, where a handsome prince roamed his country with a glass slipper, desperately trying to trace its rightful owner. Chapelle concluded this real-life Cinderella story was far more intriguing than the fantasy version. He lowered his hand and moved it towards the old woman, until it was barely inches away from her face.

'Do you recognise this piece of jewellery?'

Aubert strained her eyes as she attempted to focus in on the tiny object. At first there was no reaction and then her eyes seemed to bulge as she began to breathe erratically, gasping for literally every breath. With a mighty effort she heaved the top half of her frail body forwards towards his outstretched hand. Her gnarled arthritic fingers painfully crawled across his palm like a drunken spider, until they settled on the locket. It took three attempts before she managed to secure it between her thumb and index finger which were obstinately disobeying her orders. Chapelle remained silent, slightly in awe of the dramatic scene playing out in front of him. Eventually she lifted the locket into the air and moved her hand directly in front of her face, allowing her eyes to adjust to the proximity of the object. Her breathing slightly slowed, as her long-term memory took her on a journey from almost seventy years before. When she spoke, her voice was little more than a throaty croak.

'Where did you get this?'

Chapelle knew at that moment he was staring into the eyes of Legrand's birth mother.

'From your son, Madame. The boy you were forced to abandon as a baby.'

Aubert's eyes clouded over as, from deep within her soul, she produced a hollow haunting sound, which lay somewhere between an agonising scream and a guttural howl. Her overwhelming emotions were a mix of horrendous guilt tinged with extreme distress and her heavily lined face wore a look of sheer terror as she feared the stranger had come to judge her. She knew she was close to death and convinced herself it was finally time to pay the price for her actions.

It was as though Chapelle read her mind as he searched for the right words to bring her back into the moment. His voice was calm and reassuring.

'Madame, your son is alive and well and has made a great success of his life. Believe me when I say you've nothing to feel guilty for. He knows the circumstances that surrounded his adoption and understands the pain you must have gone through. He's spent many years trying to find you.'

It took a moment for Chapelle's comforting words to permeate Aubert's thoughts. When they did, the floodgates opened, and she began sobbing uncontrollably. Her senses were flooded with an overwhelming feeling of relief as she shed years of pent-up guilt in a few priceless seconds. It was a cathartic, freeing experience and suddenly she knew exactly what she needed to do next. Her eyes pleaded with Chapelle as she asked for his help.

'Monsieur, can you remove my scarf?'

He leaned down and delicately unfolded the blue cotton scarf until it fell loosely to the side revealing her neck, which was even more wrinkled than her face. Chapelle immediately spotted the missing half of the silver heart locket. It was entwined with a long gold necklace, which supported a sculpted pendant. Chapelle recognised its origin and was slightly mystified by it.

'Madame, can you tell me about the provenance of the other necklace?'

Chapter Sixty-Six

Strasbourg, France

11.00am

No one in the hotel suite seemed vaguely interested in breakfast, so the baskets containing warm croissants, French bread and pastries remained untouched. Soletska and Chan were huddled together over a single laptop at one end of the table, while Vargas and Hembury were standing together in front of a large, curved window, peering down at a packed tram passing directly outside the front of the hotel near the pedestrianised area below. Vargas half-turned and switched his gaze to Soletska.

'Are you guys ready?'

'Given the circumstances, I'd say we're in a good place – if things fall our way. Until the broadcast starts at one, we can't be sure how Legrand will play it. From what I know of him, the man's more than capable of holding his own, without any help – so everything depends on what he decides to do. He's so arrogant he may choose to do the interview in person. There's no way of knowing for sure until he goes live. Jack has programmed all three versions of his deepfake into our system, so once the broadcast begins, if he's deployed one of them, we know we can match it. There's one issue however—'

Chan interrupted her mid-flow.

'We can't cut into the facility's outgoing broadband stream, it's too heavily encrypted, so we need to hack into CNN.'

Soletska saw the look of panic in Vargas's eyes and tried to calm the situation.

'What Jack's alluding to is the fact that although I'm deep inside their main AI machines, I can't break into the coded broadband signal they'll transmit directly to the studio in Atlanta and, for our plan to work, I need to. CNN on the other hand is easy to hack – I've already trialled it and it's a piece of cake. I've even seen the list of questions for Legrand's interview, which have been preloaded on to a studio tele-prompter. Should we ask Berrettini if he'll sanction the breach?'

Vargas glanced across at Hembury to read his face.

'No, we can't compromise Mike by asking the FBI for permission to hack the country's most trusted news network.'

Soletska looked crestfallen. She felt like a jockey whose horse had led the Kentucky Derby for the entire race and then been pipped at the post.

'So, what the hell. Where does that leave us?'

Vargas's mouth gave way to a hint of a smile.

'We don't ask. We just do it.'

***

12.30pm

Chapelle had stayed up till the early hours writing his report on his meeting with Joséphine Aubert. He was nothing if not conscientious and figured he'd truly earned his sizeable bonus, although he wondered what Legrand would make of some of the revelations in the three-page report. Once she'd seen the heart locket Aubert had opened like a freshly cooked mussel, digging deep into her memory bank for the first time in over sixty years.

Legrand's maid opened the front door of his apartment but, instead of showing Chapelle through to the study as usual, she held her position in the doorway, blocking any access.

'Monsieur Legrand is busy preparing for a live interview with a US network so he can't be interrupted.'

Chapelle's adrenaline was running high as he'd been relishing the prospect of a face-to-face with his employer when he'd planned to read the report out to him in person before handing it over.

'Madame, Monsieur Legrand instructed me to bring him my report in person, so I must insist—'

'That may well be true, and yes, he's been expecting you. But fifteen minutes ago, he instructed me to take the report from you at the door and leave it on his desk. So . . .'

Her right hand shot out as though it were on a clockwork spring. Chapelle bit down hard on his lip, incensed his moment of glory had been snatched away from him by Legrand's obstinate maid but knew when he was beaten. He reluctantly raised the thin blue folder in his hand towards her. The resolute maid snatched it from his grasp before he had a chance for second thoughts and moments later the door slammed in his face.

12.56pm

Legrand entered his study, immaculately dressed for a live Zoom interview he'd no intention of taking part in. Instead, he'd be watching intently, a fascinated onlooker, joining millions of other viewers across the world. Even so, the adrenaline surging through his body was just as intense as if he were about to cross swords in person with CNN's long-term anchor, Martha Sawyer, who was busy completing her final prep, four and a half thousand miles away in Atlanta.

After settling in behind his desk, he placed a last-minute call to Moreau, who saw his caller ID and picked up on the first ring. Her fake enthusiasm masked growing nerves, a visible tremor in both hands she was grateful Legrand couldn't see.

'Good morning, sir. We're all set to go at this end. Everything is on track. I never heard back from you regarding the final file I sent over, so I assume you were happy with Thomas's tweak?'

'Yes, excellent work. Now, in the event I don't like the way things are going, I'll message you to immediately pull the transmission – you can say the broadband feed went down. Sawyer is a pushy bitch – not to be underestimated, although this time the odds are stacked against her.'

'Absolutely, sir.'

Legrand's concentration lapsed momentarily as he set eyes on the blue file Chapelle had dropped off a few minutes earlier.

He made a mental note to return to it as soon as the CNN interview was wrapped.

'Just don't screw up.'

With that parting shot, Legrand cut the call and aimed the remote at a wall-mounted LED screen, already tuned to CNN, enabling the audio, just in time to hear Martha Sawyer trail her exclusive with the world's most influential media tycoon. He eased back in his chair and reached for a vintage cut-glass tumbler containing his favourite Scotch, a fifty-year-old Macallan malt. Legrand took a large gulp and felt the satisfying heat burn the back of his throat; life was good, and he savoured the feeling of being one of the masters of the universe.

12.59pm

Inside the hotel suite there was an ominous silence as they waited for the ad break to finish. Soletska and Chan were huddled in front of two laptops, one of which was connected to a digital vision mixer desk, which the analyst referred to as his magic black box. Close by, Vargas and Hembury stood in front of a fifty-inch TV set, positioned centrally on a smoked-oak wall unit. The CNN logo reappeared, accompanied by a dynamic three-second music sting and then the visual cut to a mid-shot of Martha Sawyer, sitting in her trademark black leather Herman Miller chair. Her eyes were glued to the tele-prompter as she introduced her guest.

'Joining me live from his home in Paris is a man who's been described by many as the most powerful and influential media owner in the world. He heads up the Legrand Corporation which owns TV and radio stations across five continents, as well as some of the most important national newspapers in the world. Leopold Legrand, thank you for joining me on CNN Live.'

Soletska held her breath as the picture cut and she caught her first glimpse of Legrand.

1.00pm

Inside his Paris apartment Legrand unconsciously leaned forward in his chair, mesmerised by the bizarre sight of his deepfake sitting behind the Napoleonic desk he was currently inhabiting – wearing identical clothes. Sawyer's opening question was what was known in the business as a 'settler'.

'*Forbes Magazine* has recently named the Legrand Corporation as the world's largest media organisation. On a personal front, how satisfying is that for you?'

Legrand's deepfake reacted with a smug grin, worthy of the man himself.

1.02pm

Soletska's voice was fuelled with adrenaline as it shot up a couple of octaves.

'Jack, they've gone for version three – the dark blue blazer. Cue it up.'

Chan was already there.

'I'm on it – ready to go.'

As she scrutinised the deepfake, Soletska sensed something was off and, when she identified what it was, she felt her mouth go dry and her heart pounded so fiercely she was convinced it was about to leap out of her chest.

'Wait ... something's wrong ... shit, the bastards have changed his tie ...'

Legrand's last-minute tweak to one of his deepfakes involved a new blue and gold zigzag patterned tie he'd recently purchased from his Jermyn Street tailor, Turnbull & Asser. It was the star turn in their James Bond collection and he'd insisted it be included in the final build. The deepfake version in the file Soletska hacked hadn't included the update, so the plain blue silk tie it was wearing didn't match.

Her anguished voice shrieked at the image on the screen.

'We're screwed, dead in the water. If we go with our version, it's a complete giveaway.'

Chan's fingers were flying over the keyboard of his laptop at warp speed.

'Liliya, I can fix this, I can do it. I just need a little time.'

Vargas and Hembury both felt helpless as they watched the live drama unfold in front of them. Soletska scrutinised an insert panel on her laptop screen displaying the teleprompter script in the CNN news studio.

'Okay, we planned to cut in on question three, which is coming up, but there are seven more after that. They've allowed thirteen minutes for the slot and we're four in. That leaves you nine – how long do you need?'

Chan didn't answer straight away. His mind was laser focused on digitally 'cutting and pasting' the new tie on to their own deepfake version, even though it was a moving 3D image.

In theory, he possessed the software to do it although he'd never attempted anything like it before and never against the clock. Chan had taken a still grab of Legrand's deepfake and was busy creating a digital border around the tie – isolating it from the light blue shirt it sat on.

'In theory, I can do this but in the end it's going to come down to the rendering time.'

Vargas's natural gambling instinct kicked in.

'Jack, what are the odds?'

Chan's monotone response wasn't helpful.

'Chief inspector, I don't do odds.'

1.06pm

Legrand had started to relax. His deepfake was performing exceptionally well and was in the process of presenting a compelling case against the wisdom of locking down huge loans to Third World countries blighted by climate change. He generously topped up his Scotch and raised the tumbler high in the air, performing an imaginary toast to his incredible tech team in Strasbourg who'd made the seemingly impossible, possible. The perfect deepfakes they'd created with his funding were finally being unleashed and there appeared no limit to their potential.

1.10pm

'Come on, come on.'

Soletska had one eye on Chan's screen and one on the CNN teleprompter displayed on her laptop.

'Two questions left and three minutes, Jack, we need—'

'I'm there. Good to go.'

'Will it work?'

Everyone in the suite turned their gaze towards Chan, waiting for his response.

'I've no idea . . . I can't road-test it. We'll only know when we run it.'

Chapter Sixty-Seven

Strasbourg, France

Soletska's eyes were out on stalks as she monitored the two remaining questions on the teleprompter. Then, as if by magic, one of them disappeared.

'Shit! They must be running out of time. They've just dumped the penultimate question. It's now or never. Jack, wait for my cue – whatever you do, don't go early.'

The index finger on Chan's right hand was hovering a couple of inches above a slim panel consisting of two raised plastic buttons. In the Atlanta studio, Sawyer received an instruction in her hidden earpiece from the show's producer.

'Just over two minutes left, Martha. Move to the wrap-up question.'

Sawyer's eyes flicked to the teleprompter. She waited a few seconds for an appropriate moment to interject and, when it came, effortlessly took it.

'So, to sum up, Monsieur Legrand, what's your final message to world leaders watching this interview, wondering which way to vote at COP?'

Soletska followed Sawyer's read, word by word on her screen.

'Wait, wait . . . Go, go, go, go!'

Chan's finger depressed the button on the first 'go' and the picture instantly cut away from Sawyer back to Legrand. The magic box in front of him had open access to the CNN live transmission and for millions of viewers watching around the world nothing appeared to change. Inside the production gallery at the studio in Atlanta, a junior engineer came over the talkback system to the show's director.

'We just monitored a tiny glitch in the broadband stream from Paris, but all seems okay now. I'll keep a close eye out in case it happens again.'

There was a slightly unnatural pause before Soletska's version of Legrand's deepfake spoke. Back in the hotel suite in Strasbourg, everyone held their breath. When he did speak, much to Sawyer's surprise, his answer had nothing whatsoever to do with her question.

'I've another matter I wish to discuss, which I assure you, won't have been on your agenda.'

Moreau, who was monitoring the interview in her Strasbourg office glanced at her chief analyst, sitting next to her – a startled look on her face. At precisely the same moment, three hundred miles away in his Paris apartment, Legrand reached for his cell. Moreau's stomach tightened as she took his call which lasted less than five seconds. The tone of his voice was menacing, the command crystal clear.

'Whatever the hell this is, shut it down right now.'

Moreau bolted out of her office like a scalded cat. As she exited the door, she almost crashed into one of her senior operators who'd raced down the corridor in the opposite direction, seeking out his boss. Her face was bright red and distorted with torment as she shrieked at him.

'For Christ's sake, Hugo, pull the plug.'

Hugo Badot was one of the most experienced analysts at the facility and had been supervising the Legrand deepfake transmission inside a viewing booth, alongside two colleagues.

'Madame, that's why I've come to see you. We've tried but we can't.'

'That's impossible. We're sending the stream – close it down, right now.'

'That's what I'm trying to tell you. As soon as our deepfake went rogue, I shut it down but it's still there online. Whoever's controlling this version has somehow managed to hack directly into CNN's own feed – we're shut out and they're inside.'

Moreau was ashen faced as her brain was swamped with fear and panic.

'Find a way in somehow – there has to be a way.'

'Madame, I'm an analyst not a hacker.'

'Just do it.'

Moreau spun on the spot and darted back into her office, like a rat scuttling up a drainpipe. In the few seconds that had passed since the switch, she'd missed a damning admission that had sent shockwaves across the globe to millions of viewers who couldn't believe the television event they were witnessing.

'For many years, I've been heading up a worldwide conspiracy; a covert Network designed to control the political and economic levers of power across the globe. COP is a perfect example of how we attempt to wield our influence. The origins of our organisation lie in Nazi Germany, where in August 1944, Adolf Hitler's deputy, Heinrich Himmler, created a secret organisation called *Die Spinne* which, in English, means The Spider. Its objectives were twofold: to aid the escape from Germany of senior SS officers and to provide them with fake identities, along with huge sums of money to start prosperous new lives across the world.'

The deepfake AI-operated brain paused for dramatic effect, as if it knew the best was still to come. The studio director called a camera cut to Sawyer, whose startled expression summed up the feelings of every technician inside the CNN studio.

'My mother was a Nazi. Her real name was Emelia Müller and the money she brought into France came directly from *Die Spinne*. My own name, Leopold, is a homage to the leader of the SS, Heinrich Himmler. Anybody watching should google him right now and see for yourself. I share his middle name.'

Inside the control room of the production gallery, it was bedlam. The show's executive producer, Jim Edwards, was deep in conversation with his network chief, Mike Levine. The scheduled news item had already overrun by two minutes and Edwards had dumped a commercial break, worth hundreds of thousands of dollars to the network.

'Mike, I've no idea what the hell's happening here but whatever it is, it's got to be the biggest TV meltdown since Frost/Nixon – only twenty times bigger. Legrand is committing professional suicide live on CNN.'

Levine was only half-listening; his eyes glued to the on-air monitors strung across the gallery.

'Just let it play out, Jim. This is pure TV gold. If there's any flak down the line from the network about the lost ad revenue,

I'll take the heat. This footage is priceless, and we own every frame of it.'

Legrand was in total meltdown. A network that had taken almost eighty years to build was being dismantled in a matter of seconds, right in front of his own eyes. His unbridled fury was evident as he raged down the phone at a hapless Moreau, who'd totally lost control of events and was already plotting an escape route from his vengeful clutches. Legrand's waspish tongue lashed out like a whip.

'Moreau, you're no more use than a piece of dog shit on the sole of my shoe. Find a way to end this right now or I promise you'll face a painful death, far worse than anything you could possibly envisage.'

Inside the hotel suite at the Maison Rouge, the mood was euphoric. Vargas and Hembury could hardly believe how well the script they'd written for Soletska's deepfake of Legrand was playing out. They were constantly switching their eyelines between the live transmission and a separate screen where they could follow the document they'd created, word for word. The deepfake was dutifully delivering their message to millions of astonished viewers across the world. Soletska was still huddled close to Chan, intensely monitoring every moment as it happened. Without turning away from the laptops, she spoke for the first time since they'd gone live.

'Guys, time for the main confession and then I've one trick up my sleeve I didn't tell you about as I'm not sure it'll work.'

She glanced at the control panel to confirm Chan's finger was now hovering above the second button. Back on air, the deepfake continued its relentless confession.

'In recent weeks, the Spider Network has unleashed a series of AI-generated deepfakes, so perfect they fooled the world. My personal favourite was the pornographic video that destroyed President Griffiths; an event that brought me great personal satisfaction. The four politicians who died in recent days were fully committed members of our Network. Carrozza, Cook, Wedgewood and Galvez all shared one thing in common – a pride and belief in Nazi ideals. None of them died by accident. I personally sanctioned their deaths to protect the security of the organisation.'

Soletska leaned even closer to Chan and whispered in his ear.

'Standby for the live cut. He's almost there.'

Legrand's deepfake was reaching his finale.

'President Putin, if you get to see a translated copy of this recording, I suggest you ask the FSB to check out the true ancestry of your deputy vice president, Boris Morozov. His maternal grandmother was an SS guard in Poland at one of the infamous Nazi deathcamps. The inmates nicknamed her "the Dog Witch of Dachau". Morozov's file, along with those of dozens of prominent politicians and business leaders, all of whom are direct descendants of SS officers and part of our Network are currently being emailed to the editors of *The New York Times* and *The Times* in London – two trustworthy publications, outside the reach and influence of the Legrand Corporation.'

Soletska was following every word verbatim and could hardly contain herself as she knew the final twist was only seconds away.

'Finally, it's time to reveal the location of the facility I set up eight years ago, where state-of-the-art AI machines, programmed by a team of brilliant analysts, build and deploy our deepfakes.'

Soletska's right hand was hovering high in the air and suddenly she dropped it at speed like a death axe, as a visual cue. Chan hit the second button and the deepfake image was instantly replaced by a live low-flying drone shot, circling Legrand's château in Strasbourg.

'It's situated right here on the outskirts of the city of Strasbourg in eastern France and the exact co-ordinates of its location have been sent to senior members of Interpol who are on their way there right now.'

Inside the château, mayhem broke out. Moreau, who'd already hung up on Legrand, led the charge for the car park, unaware the road outside had already been blocked off at both ends by the French police under instruction from their Interpol colleagues.

Soletska lingered on the drone footage long enough to see the main doors of the château burst open as dozens of people poured out, resembling a panicked colony of ants fleeing a disturbed nest.

'Jack, standby to go back to the master stream in three . . . two . . . one . . . go.'

On cue Legrand's deepfake reappeared and, rather than wait to be wrapped by the news anchor, who hadn't spoken for the previous five minutes, it wrapped itself.

'As you've probably surmised, I too am a deepfake. Unlike the ones created by our network for other eminent figures, I speak the truth. In case you have any doubts I'm not real, I'll sign off using my AI-generated voice, speaking the most complex languages known to man.'

In a bizarre final scene, Legrand's deepfake said goodbye perfectly in Chinese, Icelandic, Arabic, Vietnamese, Hindi,

Navajo, Japanese and Mandarin. Then, inexplicably, its on-air image imploded into a million tiny fragments – a perfect visual metaphor for the demise of the Spider Network. Moments later the screen cut to black.

Chapter Sixty-Eight

Paris, France

Legrand sank into his chair and appeared to physically shrink in size. He struggled to process the cataclysmic events that had just taken place in front of him and, for the first time in his life, experienced a sense of absolute despair. He was a man who'd been groomed for success; failure had never been an option and yet his illustrious life had unravelled in a matter of minutes, and the secret network he'd nurtured over decades had been brutally exposed. His eyes flicked around the walls of his study, decorated with framed photos of himself standing alongside esteemed world leaders, beaming warm smiles in his direction. They provided a visual reminder of his towering status amongst the political elite but suddenly they'd been rendered meaningless. His gaze settled on the blue file on his desk which offered a temporary respite from the disastrous fallout of the broadcast he'd just witnessed. He reached for it like a drowning man and ironically, when he began reading the three-page report, he never made it past the third paragraph.

Interview with Madame Joséphine Aubert.

I met with Madame Aubert at the Paradis Care Home where she's been a resident for the last seven years. I can confidently state she is the woman who gave up her newly born son in July 1956. She described in graphic detail the moment she left her baby on the steps of the Église Saint-Jean de Montmartre. It was a heart-rending memory which she recalled vividly, and I've included a detailed account of it on page three of this report. When I presented Aubert with the half of the silver heart locket you supplied, she recognised it as the single item she'd left behind with her baby. The final confirmation of her identity was her possession of the other half of the locket which she wore around her neck. It was hidden beneath a cotton scarf, along with another pendant, which caught my attention.

It was a large, solid gold Star of David, unquestionably the most valuable item she possessed. In my experience people wear this symbol for several reasons. Some believe it brings luck and good health while for others it's a religious symbol, signifying the relationship between man and God. When I questioned her about its significance, she was at first reluctant to discuss it but eventually she opened up. She explained that Aubert wasn't her family's real name, it was Leibovici. Her paternal grandparents were Romanian Jews who escaped to France at the turn of the twentieth century and her father changed his name in 1938, due to rising antisemitism in Europe and the prospect of a German invasion. They went underground with their religion but contin-ued to practise the Jewish faith behind closed doors.

The shame associated with a fourteen-year-old girl getting pregnant, despite the appalling circumstances of the rape, meant the baby had to be given up and she dared not approach a

*synagogue as, publicly, the family wasn't Jewish. In the end, it
made sense to place the baby in the hands of the Catholic Church,
even though, as far as Aubert was concerned, her son was a Jew.*

Legrand reeled back in horror at the startling revelation of
his true ancestry and suddenly felt dirty. He visualised desperately scrubbing his body clean to try and rid himself of the
Jewish virus he now knew was buried deep inside him, as if
that cleansing process would erase the loathsome feeling of
self-hatred he was experiencing. His mother had indoctrinated
him from a young age to despise the Jewish race and now,
through a weird quirk of fate, he'd discovered fifty per cent of
the blood coursing through his veins came from a Jewess of
Eastern European descent.

Legrand's life was caving in on him and he felt as though he
were suffocating. He struggled to catch his breath and craved
fresh air. He raced out of his study and headed for the massive
wrought-iron balcony that ran across the entire width of the
apartment. For a moment the change of environment appeared
to help as he filled his lungs with giant gulps of air. His head
began to clear, although his mind was packed full of imaginary
alarms, warning him he urgently needed to flee the scene to
regroup and salvage something from the wreckage. He reached
for his cell and punched in the number of his helicopter pilot
just as the sound of the imaginary alarms assaulting his brain
blended into real life ones.

The piercing sound was coming from the east and, as
Legrand glanced to his left, he caught sight of a procession of
four Renault police cars powering down the road, heading
directly for his apartment. He shut his eyes in the vain hope the

sound of the approaching sirens would somehow disappear, but they only grew louder, reaching ear-piercing levels as they got closer.

Legrand knew all that lay ahead now was total disgrace. He questioned whether he possessed the inner strength to end it himself and then an invisible fog lifted as he downloaded a distant childhood memory. He was six years old, tucked up in bed, with his mother sitting on top of the blanket, regaling him with exhilarating stories of the mighty Third Reich. On this occasion she spoke to him for the first time about her beloved father, Heinrich Luitpold Himmler. She recalled his magnificent partnership with the Führer and his heroic attempt to wipe out the Jewish race from the face of the earth. Her tale ended with Himmler's betrayal by the German generals, whom she claimed were weak and eager to surrender to the invading Allied forces. Legrand pictured his mother's eyes welling up with tears as she talked of her father's bravery in taking in his own life when faced with exposure and humiliation. She spoke with such fervent pride of her father's extraordinary bravery; Legrand knew it was his duty to emulate that courage.

He kept his eyes firmly shut as he edged slowly forward towards the edge of the balcony. Immediately below he heard the unmistakeable sound of screeching tyres as a line of police cars pulled up outside his apartment. The last thing he heard was the sound of slamming doors and panicked voices screaming up at him, but they faded into the distance as his brain tuned in to the soft tones of his mother's voice.

'My darling Leopold. You have greatness inside you and one day the entire world will get to see it.'

Legrand's eyes remained closed as his hands gripped the top of the balcony rail. He lunged forward and hurled himself over the edge, spiralling downwards through the air before ploughing headfirst into the concrete pavement below, narrowly avoiding an ugly collision with two police officers, who seconds earlier had approached the front entrance of the apartment block.

His head burst like a ripe melon and his prone body lay spreadeagled in a dark pool of blood. Had anyone looked down on the media baron from the balcony he'd leapt from, they'd have witnessed a truly bizarre sight. Leopold Legrand's mangled corpse closely resembled the shape of a human swastika.

Epilogue

Four days later

It seemed apt for them all to meet up in Soletska's apartment one last time for a final debrief. Vargas had his luggage with him and was heading for the airport, via a lift from Hembury, as soon as they were done. Berrettini had been the last to arrive and, after the usual greetings, his first action was to open his brown leather attaché case and retrieve a weathered notebook. Everyone in the small living room was intrigued as the FBI deputy director waved it in the air with his right hand.

'We found this inside Legrand's bedroom safe and it makes for truly fascinating reading. It contains a handwritten list of many of the SS officers spirited out of Nazi Germany by *Die Spinne* at the end of the Second World War. It gives their original names and rank, as well as their new identities, locations and the amount of funds allocated for their future lives.'

Hembury gestured towards Berrettini who took the cue and handed it across for him to flick through.

'It's a pretty remarkable find.'

'More than you could possibly imagine – it's an important piece of history. We've just had confirmation the handwriting is a perfect match with archived documents written by Heinrich Himmler himself. Further proof, if we needed it, that the head of the SS was personally behind the creation of *Die Spinne*.'

Vargas glanced over Hembury's shoulder at the open book, also intrigued by the discovery.

'Mike, how did it end up in Legrand's possession?'

'We think it must have been passed on to his mother as it also contains details of ongoing communications between Amelie Legrand and members of the network that took place in the post-war years. She catalogued specific dates and accounts of phone calls and face-to-face meetings, all in her own handwriting, which was easy to identify. The question is, what was her relationship to Himmler?'

Soletska was convinced she knew the answer, even though she was way off the mark.

'What if she was his secret lover? After all, she named her son after him, so was clearly obsessed. How old was she when she left Germany?'

'In her early twenties and maybe you're right. One thing's for sure, as well as giving her the notebook, the amount of money she received from *Die Spinne* was extraordinary, when compared to other sums received by SS officers – enough to buy herself a château in Geneva and a bank in Paris. Maybe we'll never learn the truth. Legrand took that secret with him to his grave.'

Soletska wasn't ready to give up on her theory.

'What about the AI facility? I just scratched the surface with my hack and focused on the deepfakes. I'm guessing there must be thousands of files on their systems, one of which might reveal the truth. Give me a few days to work through them.'

'Devane's people are all over it. He's like a pig in shit. As well as inheriting the machines, two of the senior analysts who worked at the château have agreed to work for his department inside the Bureau, rather than face jail time.'

Soletska cracked a huge smile.

'I know that shtick so well. He used it on me after my arrest and look at me now.'

Berrettini cut straight back in.

'Speaking of which, whose idea was it to circle around me when it came to granting permission to hack our premier news broadcaster?'

Hembury was happy to fall on his sword.

'I'll take the rap for that one, Mike. How bad has the fallout been?'

Berrettini's dry expression gave way to a glimmer of an ironic smile.

'Last night I took a call from CNN's Worldwide President, Len Braverman. To date they've sold footage of the interview to over two hundred news outlets around the world. He estimates it will generate a global income of more than five hundred million dollars in the coming months, plus a bidding war has broken out amongst the big streamers to license the rights for a TV series.'

Soletska sucked in a huge breath of relief.

'Doesn't sound as though he was too pissed then?'

'What do you think? Short clips from the interview have gone viral, gathering millions of views and CNN is on everyone's lips.'

Berrettini paused for a moment and, when he continued, the tone of his voice noticeably changed, signalling a more serious matter was on his agenda.

'Liliya we've one final matter to discuss.'

Soletska felt her heart skip a beat as she'd no idea where he was heading.

'We still have the small matter of the illicit funds you buried in a secret account whilst working for Panchak.'

Soletska flew out the traps.

'I've already told them – I don't want a cent of it. I've even given Nic the bank details.'

'Hang on, Liliya, hear me out. Bearing in mind your key role in recent events, I decided to have a chat with an old friend who happens to be a senior figure at the IRS. He's more than happy to just apply the top rate of tax on the initial ten million, plus take the high interest yield the account has earned over the last few years and call it quits.'

For once Soletska was lost for words. Berrettini enjoyed the moment and couldn't wait to get to the best bit.

'According to their calculations that leaves you with a tidy sum of just over six million dollars.'

The young Ukrainian hacker, who'd been sitting cross-legged on the floor, leapt up like a coiled spring and jumped into Berrettini's arms, crushing him in vice-like bear hug, which took him totally by surprise. After a few seconds she broke away and bombarded him with questions.

'Oh my God, Mike, is this real? Can I tell my mum?'

Vargas and Hembury enjoyed seeing their friend so clearly out of his comfort zone.

'You certainly can.'

'Wow, I'm going to take her on a huge trip around the Caribbean and park up on a tropical beach, drinking vodka cocktails.'

Berrettini had recovered his composure after Soletska's surprise assault and was enjoying her reaction.

'When you eventually get bored of that life, there'll be a job waiting for you in my department, if you're interested?'

She left Berrettini hanging, as her enigmatic smile didn't really answer that question one way or another. But the FBI deputy director hadn't quite finished.

'Liliya, now you're a bona fide millionaire, promise me one thing. Never hack a US-based company or government institution ever again.'

'Are you kidding? I give you my word, those days are firmly behind me.'

Vargas was the only person in the room with a clear line of sight of Soletska's left hand, which was tucked behind her back. Somehow, he managed to maintain a poker face, even though he could see two fingers were tightly crossed.

Author's Note

I've been fascinated by the controversial nature of deep-fakes since they first burst on to the scene in 2017. When I was searching for an idea for my fourth novel, I wondered if they could provide me with a chilling backdrop for a fresh, contemporary story. With AI progressing at lightning speed, I began to consider how far developers could take them. Could they produce versions capable of operating 'live' in the political arena that could fool the entire world?

As I began to research this murky topic, I discovered intelligence agencies across the globe, in China, Russia and the United States, to mention a few, are currently pouring millions of dollars into this new technology, as they seek to 'weaponise' deepfakes against their foes. Their potential to create radical disinformation on numerous social media platforms is terrifying.

When I learned about the Dalí deepfake that greets visitors at a Florida museum, I began to formulate the germ of an idea. Liliya sites this true example in my fictional story as a means of explaining to Hembury and Vargas how a functioning deep-fake can interact 'live' with humans. In *The Spider Covenant*,

Legrand's Frankenstein's monsters go a lot further, boasting AI-programmed brains that can cope with billions of questions concerning controversial domestic and international topics.

During my research, I was fortunate enough to meet up with a senior global technology figure who proved to be incredibly helpful and supportive. His tech knowledge was awesome, and he confirmed the evolving world of AI is not a million miles away from creating perfect deepfakes that could perform in 'live' situations, as I suggest in the book. A truly scary prospect, as it means eventually we won't be able to believe the authenticity of what we see with our own eyes.

Although I knew deepfakes would provide a fascinating element to a novel, I still needed a hook to hang the whole story together and that's where *Die Spinne* came to my rescue. I was surfing the net looking for inspiration when I stumbled across a small reference to the secret organisation. The more I read of its origins in August 1944 and its operations after the fall of Germany, the more intrigued I became and so *The Spider Covenant* was born!

The fact some people believe direct descendants of prominent Nazis still meet up today through the vehicle of *Die Spinne* inspired me when it came to mapping the plot. Himmler seemed a natural focal point to begin with and, once I came up with the idea of giving him an illegitimate daughter, the story really began to take shape. Amelie's escape across Europe and her time in Paris during the post-war years took on a life of its own and she became a far more significant character in the story than I'd anticipated.

The same can be said about the charismatic Ukrainian hacker, Liliya Soletska who, as the book progressed, became one of my favourite characters to write. If you've read any of my previous three novels you'll be as relieved as I am she survived to the end of the story, as in the past I've been guilty of killing off popular characters many readers had hoped would live to fight another day!

As ever with a new book I can't wait to receive your feedback, so please feel free to contact me on Instagram – *@klein443* – by email at *brian@otbprod.com* or check out my website *brianklein.com* for upcoming news.

I've begun work on a new Vargas/Hembury adventure which should be ready for publication next year. I can't reveal too much yet, except for the fact it's called *The Devil's Estate* and involves Vargas and Hembury, two godsons of Pablo Escobar and a world-famous businessman, with a fistful of secrets, who holds serious political ambitions. I've included the first two chapters to give you a taster of what's to come.

Acknowledgements

As ever I am indebted to many people who helped me bring this book to fruition. What starts as a solitary process always ends in a collaboration with several key people. In the first instance my wife, Charmaine, works tirelessly and extremely creatively on a detailed edit pass which we then work through together in a meticulous fashion. Only after that process is complete do I deliver the manuscript to my publisher where fresh eyes begin a new edit pass. That task was undertaken in forensic fashion by copy editor, Colin Murray.

One of the first people to read an early draft of *The Spider Covenant* was my agent, Jon Smith, whose wise words were constructive and incredibly supportive. Another great help with the story itself was Gregory Roekens, who is a chief technology officer in the marketing, media and entertainment industry, who helped me to understand the basic principles involved in creating a deepfake, which of course is key to the story.

I also want to thank the entire team at Little, Brown, especially my wonderful Publishing Director, Andreas Campomar, along with the awesome Project Editor, Holly Blood, and finally Jessica Perdue and the entire Rights team who have begun selling my books around the world.

NEW IN 2026

Keep reading for a sneak peek at
Brian Klein's next book, *The Devil's Estate* . . .

Prologue

Hacienda Nápoles, Puerto Triunfo, Colombia

7 April 1982

I t was feeding time and the world's most notorious criminal watched on in awe as four ravenous cheetahs stealthily
emerged from a towering forest of forty-metre-high wax
palm trees, fuelled by the scent of fresh blood, heading towards
a grotesque pile of human body parts recently dumped in the
usual place by one of the groundkeepers.

Pablo Emilio Escobar Gaviria lay on the grass verge close by,
basking in the baking sunshine, watching on as his favourite
creatures demolished their exotic lunch. His treasured AK47
lay within reach, just in case, although this macabre scene was
a common spectacle, and he'd never had cause to reach for it in
the past. The three females and solo male formed part of the
world's most bizarre private zoo, which housed an eclectic
ensemble of animals who'd been illegally transported across
the globe at the whim of the world's most infamous drug lord.
The cheetahs shared the compound with herds of wild

elephants, giraffes, zebras, hippos and flocks of exotic birds, which included two rare black macaw parrots, who cost over a hundred thousand dollars a piece. One of them named Chin Hon was personally trained by Escobar to recite the names of the Colombian national soccer team.

Escobar owned over three hundred properties, but Hacienda Nápoles was his favourite hideaway, hidden deep in the Colombian countryside, located ninety miles east of Medellin and a hundred and fifty miles northwest of Bogotá. The single track that led up to its imposing entrance was lined with armed guards, strategically positioned over twenty miles, ensuring any unwelcome visitors were spotted well in advance of their arrival. At the heart of the five-thousand-acre luxurious estate, stood a Spanish style colonial mansion and alongside the zoo, the sprawling grounds contained several swimming pools, a functioning bullring, an F1 style racetrack and a private airstrip, which was kept busy twenty-four hours a day, as cocaine-laden planes came and went by the hour.

The estate resembled a small town with over five hundred staff living on site, alongside two hundred armed guards, who formed a small militia, designed to keep Escobar and his family safe. Although its location was well known to both his enemies and the government, nobody was brave or stupid enough to contemplate an attack on the heavily guarded compound. Escobar's reverie was broken by the unexpected arrival of his chief bodyguard, Diego Santos, who knew exactly where to find his boss at that time of day.

'El Patron, you've a visitor. It's the American you've been expecting.'

Escobar maintained his gaze on the feeding frenzy but

slightly nodded his head before waving his right arm in the air in a dismissive gesture.

'Tell him I'm busy . . . but he needs to wait for me. Take him onto the south terrace and offer him a whiskey – a Jack Daniels. All Americans like that drink, for some reason I've never managed to figure out. Once my babies have finished their lunch, I'll be over.'

Santos watched the solo male crunch down on what he was pretty sure was a severed leg and figured his boss wouldn't be too long. He turned and began to make his way back to the main house but was still close enough to hear Escobar scold the ravenous cheetah.

'Hector, you greedy bastard . . . share your food with your sisters or I'll take your teeth out, one by one.'

* * *

The young American businessman was sitting alone on an enormous sun deck located at the rear of the mansion, nursing a whiskey, totally engrossed in an infamous US magazine which prided itself on unearthing scandalous celebrity gossip. Escobar had arranged for it to be deliberately left out on display on a large marble coffee table. The front cover heralded a head-shot of the world's most notorious and celebrated criminal which unsurprisingly caught the eye of the American visitor. He knew Escobar was a hugely wealthy man but was astonished to discover speculation about his enormous wealth that placed him in the top twenty richest men in the world. He was poring over the article when the head of the Medellín Cartel appeared through an open archway and strolled across the wooden deck to greet his guest who leapt out of his chair like an exuberant salmon. The pair shook hands before Escobar gestured towards the manicured gardens.

'Let's take a walk – as you haven't visited the Hacienda before, I'll show you some of my favourite animals.'

It was the first time they'd met and there was a huge physical discrepancy between the two men, as the blond-haired American was six-three and towered over the five-foot-six frame of Escobar. However, the Colombian's short, stocky muscular build along with his brooding brown eyes, which appeared to be almost black, eroded the air of superiority that height advantage normally provided.

The American was instantly intimidated, as was everyone who met the man known by millions as 'El Pátron'. His reputation for unbridled violence, which he was happy to dish out first-hand, was legendary. The businessman's opening gambit was drenched in sycophancy. 'It's an incredible achievement to be named amongst the world's top twenty richest men, Señor Escobar. You're ranked amongst some of the most influential businessmen in the world. It's a tribute to your—'

Escobar let out a huge roar of laughter as he stopped on the spot and turned to face his guest.

'Listen, the men who write this crap know nothing of my true wealth. I have over a billion dollars in cash hidden in the grounds of this very compound and own hundreds of other properties across the country, which all house huge deposits.'

The American was dumbstruck as Escobar continued his rant.

'I spend two and a half thousand dollars a month on rubber bands, just to keep my money tidy. My brother Roberto, who runs our financial operation, has calculated every year I lose five hundred million dollars of buried cash – eaten by rats. Despite that, I'm still the richest man on the planet.'

Escobar paused for a moment to contemplate his favourite topic.

'The truth is I've no idea of my actual wealth. It changes by the hour.'

His face morphed from a smile to a scowl as he turned and began to walk again and the American followed suit.

'So, the reason you're here is I'm told you can help me with my freight entering Miami. Far too many of my land and boat shipments are being intercepted by those bastards at the DEA and the AWAC planes used by the US Customs are becoming a giant pain in the ass. Their onboard radar is identifying our secret flights, long before they even land. Last month they got their hands on the biggest individual haul yet – three thousand six hundred pounds of pure cocaine on one plane – that's worth over a hundred million dollars to me. If things don't change, the thieving bastards are going bleed my business dry.'

The American was relieved he now had a chance to show his worth and justify the rationale for their first face-to face meeting.

'Señor Escobar, I believe, no, in fact I know, I can be of great assistance to you in these matters, which is why I'm here. I've senior contacts in all these areas but, of course, extreme discretion and caution will need to be displayed and many palms will need to be greased along the way.'

The most famous man in South America nodded and his right eyebrow raised in an almost unnatural quizzical arc.

'If you can improve my stats by just ten over cent, you'll be very happy you're doing business with me. Can you guarantee that?'

His voice was dripping with scepticism.

'Yes, I believe I can achieve that figure for you and maybe more, but I'll need access to a cash-based fund, as it's far too dangerous for me or my contacts to leave a paper trail.'

The American watched on in awe as he witnessed Escobar make some rapid mental calculations.

'How about a million dollars a month to begin?'

The staggering figure was quadruple the amount he'd been hoping for but he maintained a poker face to disguise a surge of excitement.

'Can I ask . . . What about my personal fee?'

Escobar stroked his trademark moustache with his right hand and remained silent, allowing the suspense to build, while the American held his breath. His voice dropped to a menacing whisper.

'Hit my targets and you can expect the same amount again – every month.'

'Señor Escobar, I have small request to ask of you in return, which is of paramount importance to me.'

'Go on . . .'

'It's essential my identity is kept secret from everyone inside your organisation – however senior. That's my only request. I'll need a codename.'

For a moment the most infamous criminal in the world produced what the American sensed was a death stare aimed exclusively in his direction, before breaking the ominous silence with a throaty laugh. At the same time, he lifted his left hand to the side of his temple, tapping it with his forefinger.

'A man such as me keeps many important secrets but be assured, none of them are ever written down. They all stored inside here, where only God can see them.'

Escobar offered his hand, and as they shook the businessman knew he was doing a deal with the devil but at that precise moment he didn't give a damn as he figured that at the tender age of twenty-five, he was on his way to becoming a very rich man.

Chapter One

Cartagena, Colombia, March 2025

Forty-two years later

Established in the middle of the sixteenth century as a major Spanish port, the walled city of Cartagena is known as the Queen of Colombia's northern coastline. Its stunning colonial architecture, fairy-lit stone archways and bright pink balconies combine to make it one of the shining jewels of the Caribbean.

An unofficial deal struck between the Colombian government and the Gulf Clan cartel, allowing the city to thrive as a safe tourist hotspot, protected its unique status within the country. The San Pedro restaurant located in the Plaza in the heart of the old town lay in the shadow of the magnificent church of the same name. It was renowned for serving the best ceviche in the city, while its drinks menu offered twenty-four types of martinis, fused with tropical flavours, such as passion fruit, gooseberry and tree tomato. As usual it was packed to the rafters with wealthy locals and tourists, fortunate enough to get a seat at one of the city's favourite eateries. However, the best table in the house, located on a small cobblestoned terrace, directly in front of the main restaurant entrance, remained conspicuously empty.

* * *

At precisely ten o'clock a black Maybach Pullman wafted into the square and as soon as the restaurant's maître d' set eyes on the familiar two-million-dollar armoured Mercedes, he darted forward like a startled rabbit and took up residence by the side of his most prized table, anxiously awaiting the arrival of his VIP guest.

The middle-aged man in question, dressed in a designer, light blue linen suit, with matching accessories, was indeed a head-turner. He was one of best known and most feared men in the country. Carlos Santacruz was the most powerful drug lord in Colombia and his arrival outside the San Pedro eatery caused a wave of excitement amongst diners, many of whom were seeing the legend known as 'El Patrón' in the flesh for the first time. It was a nickname he'd proudly taken in honour of his beloved godfather, who was without doubt the greatest drug baron of all time, Pablo Escobar.

Santacruz ran a notorious cartel, responsible for supplying eighty per cent of all cocaine consumed in America, grossing over one hundred billion dollars a year. Like his godfather, he ran his operation with a clinical efficiency and a brutal ruthlessness.

He micro-managed his drug empire, constantly on the look-out for signs of deceit and betrayal amongst his men, which made him a fearsome kingpin, who dished out torture and execution on a weekly basis, in many cases in person. He trusted no one on his payroll and his younger brother, Gilberto, worked closely alongside him, as his number two. As far as Santacruz was concerned, blood was thicker than water, another quality he shared with Escobar. His younger brother shared his own taste for power and violence and had personally carried out executions on rival gang members, even though he was still a teenager. The brothers ruled the Colombian drug scene with a tried and tested combination of terror and bribery.

Santacruz took his seat at the allotted table, while his four bodyguards spilled out of the limo and split into two groups, taking up strategic positions at tables either side of their boss. The drug lord soaked in the admiring looks of fellow diners, most of whom knew exactly who he was and the power he wielded, as head of the notorious cartel. He ran his right hand theatrically through his flowing coal-black hair and glanced down at the dial of his five- hundred-thousand-dollar, Vacheron Constantin watch to check the time. His dinner companion was running two minutes late which was disrespectful but tolerable, as he calculated the outcome of the meeting would potentially net him well over fifty million dollars.

The obsequious maître d' was fussily rearranging cutlery on the table while trying to engage his famous customer in some small talk about the staggering rate of inflation. Santacruz totally ignored him as his eyes were cemented on a stunning girl who was walking past the front of the restaurant as though she was patrolling an imaginary catwalk. Her wafer-thin, size-eight frame wore a skimpy black dress that was glued to her body as if it were a hot wax mould. Her features were as sharp as a knife, and she looked capable of cutting a man in many ways.

Just then his guest arrived, and Santacruz broke out of his temporary trance to stand to greet his dining companion, who was now three minutes late. The two men shook hands warmly and took their positions opposite each other. It was evident this wasn't their first meeting. The second man was in his mid-fifties, with dark brown hair, lightly frosted at the sides, and his gaunt face resembled an axe blade.

The maître d' scuttled off inside the restaurant and the two men wasted little time on small talk before engaging in an animated conversation about the delicate matter in hand. Across the plaza, one floor up, above a small bar, a woman made her final checks before easing her body into position. No one in the square noticed the tip of her rifle appear through the gap of the open window frame. The elevated position gave her a clear line of sight to her victim, and seconds later the top of Santacruz's head was perfectly framed in the duplex crosshair of the scope. The straight black vertical and horizontal lines were thick on the perimeter and thin in the middle. The thick lines allowed the eye to quickly locate the centre of the target and the thin lines enhanced precision aiming. As she studied Santacruz's features through her scope, the assassin mused to herself that a hit worth five million dollars shouldn't be like this. It was almost too easy.

She watched the conversation play out and waited patiently until the drug baron stopped talking to listen to his companion, which meant his head would remain still. The rifle suppressor did its job perfectly as no one in the plaza heard the shot that virtually blew the top of Santacruz's head clean off. For a moment everything seemed to happen in slow motion as Santacruz's body jerked backwards in his chair. The enormous blood spray caused by the impact was over ten feet high and, as his lifeless body slumped forward onto the table like a rag doll, screams rang out from horrified diners who leapt from their tables desperately searching for cover.

Two thousand miles away in New York, a second co-ordinated assassination attempt was about to be carried out inside the city's most fêted nightclub.

About the Author

Before becoming a full-time novelist, Brian Klein worked as an award-winning television director for over thirty years. His work still regularly appears on Netflix, Amazon Prime, BBC and Sky. Among his directing credits are twenty-eight seasons of the iconic car show, *Top Gear*, which in its heyday was the most popular factual entertainment TV show in the world, with over three hundred million viewers watching in over one hundred countries.

As a student, Brian studied modern history and politics at Queen Mary College, University of London, majoring on the origins of the Second World War. He lives in London with his wife Charmaine and daughter Jessica and their family dog, George.

The Spider Covenant is his fourth publication. His previous three are *The Counterfeit Candidate, The Führer's Prophecy* and *The Last Reich.*